Praise For
Our Share of Morning

"*Our Share of Morning* is a poignant and beautifully crafted novel that delves into themes of love, loss, and forgiveness. At its heart are sisters Violet and Gloria Campo, who navigate the complexities of family relationships, the pain of losing those most precious to them, and the often-fraught journey of moving beyond those losses. What's most remarkable is how Bonazzoli captures both the fragility and resilience of the human spirit. Weaving images of splintering and breakage as a way of revealing the sisters' inner lives, the novel culminates in an astute observation about grief—like "an ocean wave, gathering and gathering until it reaches a peak, then breaks." With a rich cast of characters and a narrative that intertwines the sisters' voices across multiple timelines, *Our Share of Morning* is a touching exploration of the heartaches that tear us apart, but more importantly, the bonds that hold us together."

—Cynthia Reeves, award-winning author of *The Last Whaler* and *Falling Through the New World*

"As I read *Our Share of Morning*, I came to feel myself a sister to these two sisters, Violet and Glory, as if I had grown up with them in that three-story tenement outside Boston and had shared their dreams and heartbreaks and joys. Reading Bonazzoli's beautifully crafted novel is a deeply moving experience."

—Jonna Bragg, award-winning author of *The Broom of God*, *Exit 8*, and *Hemlock Flat*

"A tenderly written account of the perennial trials women face and the strength they muster to overcome hardship, *Our Share of Morning* tells the story of two sisters navigating girlhood into womanhood in the 1930s and 1940s in a New England town. Violet, a photographer creating portraits of war veterans, and Glory, a budding poet, grapple with heartbreaking events and family secrets with the support of kind neighbors and through the making of their art. Readers will both cheer on and weep for these sisters. But through the darkness, threads of light lace the narrative, offering comfort in what remains beautiful and true— the enduring bond of sisterhood, forgiveness, and the healing power of art."

—Jodi Paloni, author of *They Could Live With Themselves*, a 2017 finalist for the Maine Book Award in fiction

"Told through the eyes of two sisters coming of age amidst poverty, illness, and misogyny, *Our Share of Morning* is the story of a secret that threatens to tear their family and community apart. Poetic and heartbreaking, it is beautifully written with tension and tenderness. Long after you finish reading, the characters will haunt you."

—Isabel Tutaine, author of *Song of the Wooden Sparrow* and *When Mist and Brine Touch*

Our Share of Morning

a novel

LAURA BONAZZOLI

Sibylline Press

Copyright © 2025 by Laura Bonazzoli
All Rights Reserved.

Published in the United States by Sibylline Press,
an imprint of All Things Book LLC, California.

Sibylline Press is dedicated to publishing the
brilliant work of women authors ages 50 and older.
www.sibyllinepress.com

Sibylline Digital First Edition
eBook ISBN: 9798897409921
Print ISBN: 9798897409938
Library of Congress Control Number: 2025938480

Cover Design: Alicia Feltman
Book Production: Aaron Laughlin

This is a work of fiction. Names, characters, places, brands, media, and incidents are either the product of the author's imagination or are used fictitiously. Any resemblance to similarly named places or to persons living or deceased is unintentional.

HUMAN AUTHORED: Any use of this publication to train generative artificial intelligence (AI) technologies to generate text is expressly prohibited.

for my sisters—everywhere

Our share of the night to bear –
Our share of morning –
                    —Emily Dickinson

PART ONE

SEPTEMBER 1933–APRIL 1935

GLORY

Mama's gone.

Is she still gone?

That's Violet and Aunt Blanche talking in the kitchen. Softly. Like they don't want to wake me up.

I don't hear Mama.

And she's not lying down on the sofa because I'm lying down on the sofa. Maybe she's in her room lying down.

But her pocketbook isn't on the hook. Papa's hat is.

So Papa's home. It's not nighttime, though. It's light in the parlor. Papa shouldn't be home until after the man with the ripped-up face lights the streetlamps. Didn't he go to work at all today? Maybe he did and Mr. Laval got angry because he was late and sent him home. Or maybe he said there's a slowdown, no work today. Or maybe Papa just didn't feel like going to work because Mama's gone.

When I got up for school, they were both gone. Violet said Papa took Mama to get her cough fixed. But that doesn't make sense. Mama never goes to see Doctor Cohen before breakfast. She goes to see him in the middle of the morning, and till I started school this week, I'd always go with her and we'd stop at the library on the way home so I could borrow another Nancy Drew Mystery Story. I've read six so far. *The Mystery at Lilac Inn* is my favorite. I told Violet she should start reading them, but she says they're too long and not everybody has a sped-up brain like mine.

Even if Mama did go see Doctor Cohen, she wouldn't stay all day. So where is she?

All morning at school—every time Sister Genevieve wasn't talking or when I got bored printing *A* and *E* because I can already print the whole alphabet, and my name, and poems—I kept thinking about Mama not being home sewing, or hanging out the laundry with Mrs. Rasmussen, or lying down, and I kept feeling the scared feeling like broken glass pricking my insides. When we walked home for lunch, I asked Violet if Mama would be back by the time we got there. She said she didn't think they could fix Mama's cough that fast. When we opened the door, her pocketbook wasn't on the hook. Neither was Papa's hat. The parlor was empty and nothing made any noise, like everything had stopped happening and everybody except us had gone far, far away. Then I heard the man with the ripped-up face come down the stairs past our door and that scared me even more. I looked at Violet. She shook her head a little, then said, "Let's go into the kitchen and see what we can find."

There was nothing in the icebox except butter, but Violet said that would do, because there was some bread in the bread-box. The broken glass was pricking me so bad I didn't want bread and butter, but Violet said if I'd eat some, she'd let me have sugar on my bread. She looked in the sugar bowl and said there was just enough for her to sprinkle a little on my bread and Papa would still have some for his coffee in the morning. Then all of a sudden, she said, "I know!" and told me to run down and pick some blackberries from the bush in Mr. and Mrs. Sadowski's yard and we could sprinkle the sugar on our blackberries.

Mr. Sadowski helps people with their money, Mama says, so that's why they have their own house and their own yard and even a garden. Mrs. Sadowski doesn't mind us picking her blackberries because she can't eat them on account of her sickness. I don't know what her sickness is, but she's skinny like

Mama. Violet says it's not the same sickness, though, because she doesn't cough and she's had an operation. Violet says they took some of her insides out.

Mrs. Sadowski wasn't home while I was picking her blackberries. I know because her car wasn't there. But thinking about her gave me an idea, and while we were eating, I asked Violet if she thought Mama had gone to have an operation like Mrs. Sadowski.

She said that was silly and they don't cut out your insides just because you cough. She finished her bread and butter and put her last blackberry on my plate.

I don't think Violet's ever scared about anything. She isn't scared of Papa when he hits her with the yardstick. She just stands there with her arms folded and stares at the wall. I know because I open our bedroom door a tiny bit and peek. She's not even scared of the man with the ripped-up face. Maybe because she's nine. Maybe I'll stop being scared of things when I'm nine, too.

Violet said we had to try and be extra good while Mama was gone. That made it sound like she'd be gone a long time, past tomorrow and maybe even Sunday and Monday or maybe past a week or a year. So I asked her what did she mean, and she said we'll have to take care of ourselves.

I told her I don't know how.

"I know you don't," she said. "Neither do I. But Aunt Blanche is making us supper tonight and I'm going to ask her to teach me how to cook." She got up and said she'd do the dishes. She sounded a little like Mama when she said it, and even more like Mama when she told me to put on my shoes and tie the laces twice because she didn't want to have to stop on the way or we'd be late back to school.

I did tie the laces twice, and they didn't come undone, but when we got to the black gate in front of Saint Isabel's, Sister

Felicity was already in the schoolyard ringing her bell. She's Violet's teacher and I hope she's never mine because her face looks like a shriveled-up apple in the middle of a white table-cloth. I know it's a veil. All the sisters wear it to show they're married to God. But it's not soft like the veil Mama's wearing in her wedding picture. It's stiff like a tablecloth. On the first day of school, Sister Felicity told Violet's class her name means hap-piness, but she never seems happy to me. When we ran across the schoolyard to our lines, she said, "One more minute and I'd have been forced to report you to Sister Superior," and her face shriveled up even more.

When you get sent to Sister Superior, you have to kneel in front of her, say the Act of Contrition, and hold out your hands for the ruler. That's what Violet said Jimmy Conlan told her. Jimmy is in fourth grade like Violet and gets sent to Sister Superior a lot, usually for talking in class, but one time for wet-ting his pants. Violet was sent to Sister Superior once. It was last year, when Papa couldn't pay the money for school. Violet was going to have to leave, but Uncle Eddie gave us the money. When Violet brought it to school, Mrs. Jusseaume said it was late and made her bring it to Sister Superior. Violet said her office is all white inside, with a statue of the Blessed Mother in a blue dress holding Baby Jesus, and right in front of her desk there's a kneeler like the kind in church except it doesn't have the vel-vet where you kneel. Violet didn't have to kneel. Sister Superior took the money and gave her a piece of paper for Uncle Eddie that said, "Paid in full."

Violet said Sister Superior smiled at her when she gave her the paper, so she's not scared of her anymore. And she didn't sound scared when she got in the fourth-grade line and told Sister Felicity we were very sorry for being late and she'd make sure it didn't happen again. I was scared, though, because Sister

Felicity was looking right at me when she said, "See that it doesn't!"

After that, the lines started marching through the red door into Saint Isabel's. First the sixth-grade line, then the fifth, and then I watched Violet's line go. Violet was last in her line, and right when she got to the doorway, she turned and looked at me. She smiled a little, and then she was gone, and when I couldn't see her anymore, everything broke apart—the red door and the wall and the steps and everything—like it was all glass and the glass just broke. And I felt like somebody opened me up and poured all that broken glass inside me so I couldn't march or even breathe. When I fell down, everything around me was black and sparkly at the same time, like the sky at night all broken in pieces, but I knew they weren't really pieces of sky, because they were screaming and screaming that Mama was never coming back.

I don't remember anything after that until I woke up in the schoolyard and Sister Genevieve was feeling my ankle. Then Violet came and helped me walk home—I remember some of that—and Mrs. Rasmussen carried me upstairs. I guess after that I fell asleep and that's why Violet and Aunt Blanche are talking so softly in the kitchen.

Wait. I remember one other thing. While I was falling asleep, somebody picked up my hand. I think it was Papa, because his hands are rough from Mr. Laval's machines. Yes—it *was* Papa, because he kissed my hand, then squeezed it a little and whispered, "*Bambolina.*" I think I tried to answer, but I was too sleepy.

And then he let my hand go.

VIOLET

I'm glad Glory's asleep.

That means I did a good job today taking care of her. I wish I could fall asleep, too. And then I wouldn't have to hear the wind in the alley. Or think about Papa.

Why didn't he take Mama to Doctor Cohen? Or to the hospital on Union Street where Mrs. Sadowski had her operation? Why did he take her so far away?

Maybe it's 'cause he doesn't love her anymore. Maybe he hasn't loved her for a long time.

He doesn't know we hear them fighting. I get in Glory's bed and hold her so she won't have a spell. And Glory's bed is better 'cause it's right up against the wall and I can hear some of the words. Lots of times I can tell they're fighting about money, 'cause Mama says something about the rent or the gas bill and asking Uncle Eddie, and Papa hollers at her to keep Eddie the hell out of it. But sometimes when they fight Mama just cries and says a name that sounds like Ava or Ada. It's always worse then. Papa starts hollering Italian and the bedroom door slams and then the front door. Glory gets scared he's gone to Aunt Marcellina and Uncle Giacomo's in New York. I tell her that's silly 'cause he hasn't packed his suitcase. But I'm not sure either. So when I get up in the morning I go in the bathroom and open the medicine cabinet. If his shaving brush is wet, I know he's come home in the night and now he's gone to work. If it's dry, he's still not home or else he's sleeping late 'cause it's Sunday or

Mr. Laval's had a slowdown. If it's gone, that means he came back in the night and packed and took the train to New York.

He doesn't always go to New York all of a sudden like that. Sometimes he goes for things like a wedding or Aunt Marcellina's birthday and we help him pack, and even though Mama cries and says is he sure he has to go, he doesn't get mad. And he only stays a few days. When he goes all of a sudden, he stays a lot longer.

The last time he went all of a sudden was in the summer after our baby brother was born too soon. I woke up and they were fighting. Mama was crying so hard I couldn't make out much of what she was saying, but I'm sure I heard that name again. Ava. Or Ada. And "How could you?" She said that twice in a row. I don't know what she meant, but I guess Papa did 'cause he said how many times did he have to tell her it was a pack of lies and if he ever found out who said it, he'd kill them with his bare hands. Then I didn't hear anything until Papa talked again. He asked her something in a soft voice like he was trying to make her feel better. When she answered him, whatever she said must have made him mad again, 'cause he hollered that he couldn't take it anymore and then he started hollering Italian and banging stuff around. I heard him come out of the bedroom and go in and out of the bathroom and open the hall closet. Then I heard the front door slam. He went to New York that night. He was gone for a lot of days.

Since Mama's been sick, he's only gone for Aunt Marcellina's birthday. They still fight, though.

Last night, they only fought a little. And their voices were soft the whole time, like they were more sad than mad. I fell asleep. When I woke up, it was just starting to be light. I could smell coffee and hear them talking in the kitchen. It sounded like Mama was crying. "It's not right to just disappear!" she said. I heard her coughing. And then I saw Papa standing in the doorway of our room. He looked at Glory. She was fast asleep. He put his finger to his lips and waved for me to follow him. So I got up and went into the parlor.

That's when they told me they were going to a place that fixes people's coughs. "Don't worry," Mama said. "I'll be back soon." She smiled, but I could tell she was trying not to cry again. Then she said Aunt Blanche would be coming to make us breakfast and told me to be good and help Glory get to school on time.

Papa came out of their bedroom with a suitcase. I put my arms around Mama and hugged her. I smelled lavender.

Papa helped her into her coat and they went out. I watched them go down the stairs. At the bottom, Mama looked back at me and smiled. Then Papa opened the front door and they went out. I ran to the parlor windows. Uncle Eddie's car was parked in front of our building. Papa helped Mama get in, then put her suitcase in the trunk. And then he got back inside and drove away.

Up and down the street, all the windows were still dark. My throat felt tight, so I went and brushed my teeth and drank some water, then I tiptoed into our bedroom and got dressed. Seeing Glory sleeping helped me remember I wasn't really alone. When I came back out to the parlor, I heard Mr. Owen's door open and his footsteps come down the stairs past our apartment. Glory's scared of Mr. Owen, but I like him fine—as long as I don't look straight at his face—so I went back to the windows and watched him come down the front steps and start turning off the lamps. Then Aunt Blanche came out of her duplex and crossed the street. She had her pocketbook over her arm and was holding a paper bag. I heard her unlock the front door and come up the stairs and I let her in.

She looked surprised. "Violet!" she said. "You're already up!" She looked pretty in her green sweater with the bow in front and her green skirt and high-heeled shoes, but her eyes were all red. "Did you say goodbye to your mama and papa this morning?"

Seeing her looking like she'd been crying made my throat get tight again. So I just nodded.

She hugged me a little, then showed me inside the bag. There were two eggs and butter and a loaf of store-bought bread. She said she was going to fix Glory and me some breakfast. She walked really fast into the kitchen without asking if I wanted to help. So I looked out the windows again. I watched people coming out of their buildings and getting in their cars or walking into town, and then I saw Uncle Eddie come out and cross the street. Our buzzer rang and Aunt Blanche went downstairs and let him in. He was wearing his shop uniform with *Eddie LeGrand, Foreman* embroidered on the front pocket, and when he came over to me, he smelled like he'd had some of Sergeant McGowan's hooch with his breakfast. He put his big hand on my shoulder and asked me loud like he always does, "How's my Vi?"

I told him I was okay.

Aunt Blanche brought two plates of scrambled eggs and toast to the table. She said we girls would be fine getting off to school by ourselves, wouldn't we, as she and Uncle Eddie had to get to work. "Sure," I said. Then she said she'd be back after work and we'd make fish chowder together.

After they left, I went to the windows and watched them walk down the street. They'd only gone a little way when they stopped. Aunt Blanche opened her pocketbook and got out a handkerchief and wiped her eyes and blew her nose. Uncle Eddie put his arm around her shoulders and they started walking again. I watched until they were gone, then I got Glory up and made her eat breakfast and washed the dishes and helped her get dressed and we walked to school. The whole time, she kept on asking and asking where Mama was. I kept saying Papa had taken her to get her cough fixed and she'd be home soon. I didn't tell her about the suitcase and Aunt Blanche crying.

Why did Mama have to go away today? Today was the last day of the first week of school, and I wish I could have told her how, when we got there this morning, I heard Sister Genevieve talking to Sister Superior about moving Glory to second grade. I think they should move her to fourth. That way, I could look after her. Besides, she can read and write better than lots of kids in my class, and she remembers all the poems Mama recites. Every time the wind blows, she says, "Who has seen the wind? Neither you nor I . . ." I can't remember it all, but she can. And long poems by Shakespeare and that lady with the saint's name. She says she wants to be a poet someday. I don't know how she could know that, in first grade.

I don't know what I want to be. I don't even like to think about being grown up and having to get married and leave Mama and Papa and Glory. Maybe I'll be a nurse and take care of Mama.

Anyway, even though she just started school, Glory didn't seem afraid all week. She seemed to like school. Until this afternoon when Sister Felicity sent me back to the schoolyard and Sister Genevieve said she'd taken a fall. I knew right away Glory hadn't fallen. I knew she was having one of her spells like she does sometimes when Mama and Papa fight or like that time with Mr. Owen.

The reason Glory's scared of Mr. Owen is part of his face got blown off in the war. That's what Papa says. He has a pension. I don't know what that is, but Papa says it's not much for a man to live on. So he works for the town lighting the lamps around Mill Street, and he paints pictures. One time he was lighting the lamp right in front of our triple-decker when Glory and I were coming back from visiting Aunt Blanche. All he did was tip his hat and say good evening, but Glory screamed and ran up the steps. When she couldn't get in 'cause I had the key, she banged and banged on the door until I got it open, then fell down in the front hall like she was dead. Mrs. Rasmussen came out and carried her up the stairs. Mama had to throw cold water on her face to make her wake up. Then she told her she should be ashamed of herself for making poor Mr. Owen feel bad. That made Glory cry like she was a baby again, even though she'd just turned five. I remember 'cause it was the time Papa was gone to New York a little after our baby brother died.

I guess Glory didn't scream today, and that's why Sister Genevieve thought she just plain fell. When I got out there, she was trying to get Glory to talk. But she was staring like she was blind. So I told her, "It's me. Violet. You're okay now." A big shiver went through her. I helped her sit up, and Sister Genevieve told us to walk a little. She said she thought it was just a sprain. "Violet, you girls live close by, don't you?" When I nodded, she said, "Then help your sister home and, when you get there, tell your mother to wrap her ankle in cloth and pin it good and tight. Then have your sister put her ankle up on a footstool." She lifted Glory's chin. "Gloria!" she said. The sisters all call Glory by her baptized name. "No playing outside tonight. Or tomorrow for that matter. If you rest it, you should be fine by Monday."

I put my arm around Glory's waist like I was helping her walk. We pretended all the way, even when we got to Mill Street, and when we came into our building, Mrs. Rasmussen heard us and asked what happened and, just like that time before except Glory's bigger now, she carried her all the way up the stairs. I opened the door and she put Glory down on the sofa. She said she'd sit with Glory, but I told her Sister Genevieve had told me what to do. So she went home. I noticed she didn't ask where Mama was. I guess she knows.

Glory fell asleep. Then Papa came home. When he asked what happened, I told him Glory'd had a spell. He sat with her a minute, then kissed her hand and called her his little doll like he does sometimes. Then he made himself a cup of coffee and went in his room.

Gosh, it was quiet. Always before, Mama's been here when we get home from school. My throat got tight like it did this morning and I wanted to cry. But then I remembered Mama saying the best cures for sadness are work and prayer. So I sat in the chair in front of the parlor windows where I could watch Glory, and wrote my paragraph about Saint Isabel. It took a long time to remember how to spell all the words, but I didn't wake up Glory and ask her. After I finished, I got out my rosary beads and prayed a whole rosary for Mama. When I got to the end, I was still feeling sad, but then the door opened and Aunt Blanche came in. She put down her pocketbook and the bag of groceries she'd brought and gave me a hug and that made me feel like I wasn't so alone.

When she let me go, she put her finger to her lips and waved for me to follow her into the kitchen. She closed the door behind me and whispered why was Glory napping. I told her about the spell. "Dear oh dear," she said, then asked if I was ready to help her with the fish chowder.

While we were peeling the potatoes, I asked her where Mama'd really gone.

She stopped peeling and looked at me across the table like she was surprised. Aunt Blanche and Mama have green eyes like mine, except Aunt Blanche's are kinda sad looking, like Saint Isabel's in the painting over the door that goes into the convent. I don't think my eyes are sad. Not when I look in the mirror anyway.

"Didn't they tell you?" she asked.

I said all they'd told me was she was going to a place that fixes people's coughs.

She frowned a little. "Well, it's a special hospital for people with your mama's sickness. They take care of them all together so other people won't catch it. Anyway, it was all very sudden."

"But where is it?" I asked.

She said it was near Boston, so then I asked her where's Boston. I said, "I know it's where the radio comes from, but how far away?"

"Oh, less than an hour by car. Your papa can take the train most of the way, and then a bus goes right by. So he'll be able to visit her—weekends, anyway—and your Uncle Eddie and I will visit, too, so you'll know how she's doing."

She said "weekends." That means she thinks Mama will be gone a long time. I asked her how long. I thought if she said a month, I could put a mark on a paper under my pillow every night, and count to thirty-one.

But she said they weren't sure. I guess "they" means the doctors and nurses. "The most important thing is, she's getting the care she needs and as soon as she's better, she'll be home." She finished peeling the last potato and put all the peels in the can of scraps we keep for Mr. Zina's pigs. After that we cut up the potatoes and onions and celery. We cooked them in butter, then added some water and the fish, and then some milk.

Uncle Eddie came with two bottles of orange soda. His big voice woke Glory up. I called Papa from his bedroom and we all had supper together. The fish chowder was so good I had two bowls. I didn't tell Aunt Blanche we hadn't had any fish or meat in all the days since we went to their apartment for Sunday dinner.

Even though she must have been hungry, too, Glory didn't eat much. She didn't say much, either. But after the dishes were done, we sat in the parlor and Uncle Eddie drank from his flask of Sergeant McGowan's hooch and started making his bird whistles. They got sillier and sillier until he made her laugh. Then Papa said it had been a long day and Aunt Blanche and Uncle Eddie went home.

When we went to bed, I held Glory until she fell asleep. Now I'm back in my own bed. I wish the wind would stop. It sounds sad. Like me.

If I could visit Mama, I know I'd feel better. I'd sit on her bed and she'd put her arm around me and I'd tell her how I'm learning to cook so when she comes home I can make supper and she can rest. And I'd tell her how I'm taking care of Glory. How I helped her dress for school and made us lunch and brought her home after she had her spell. And how, before we went to bed, I made sure we said our prayers.

GLORY

Why does Papa have to go?

Or why won't he take us with him? And then on the train and the bus I could sit in his lap and he'd kiss me like he did this morning when I had a bad dream. "I love you, Papa! I love you!" He doesn't hear me. His footsteps keep going down the stairs. And the pieces of glass are pricking me worse than in the dream.

It was about the man with the ripped-up face. His name is Mr. Owen and I'm not to call him anything but Mr. Owen, Mama says, even when he can't hear me, but I can't help it if that's the name I think. I don't mean to. I just do. I even dream it. Like last night. It was dark and I was out in the street and he kept looking at me from his window. I tried to go inside but the door wouldn't open so I pushed the buzzer for Mrs. Rasmussen but she didn't answer. Then I saw Violet at our window and she asked me what I was screaming about and I said the man with the ripped-up face was staring at me. I didn't say Mr. Owen. Not even in my dream. If Mama knew, she'd say she was disappointed in me.

I wish Mama did know, because that would mean she was here.

I must have screamed in my sleep and that's why Papa came in and woke me up. Violet was awake too. After he kissed my forehead, he said it was just as well we were awake because we needed to get up early this morning. I asked him why, and he said we were expecting company. Then he said to wash and come to breakfast.

When we got to the kitchen, Papa looked so handsome in his white shirt and his red scarf, like he was dressed for Mass, except his sleeves were rolled up. He'd heated the chowder that was left from last night and made some coffee. We sat down for breakfast, and he poured a little coffee into two glasses of milk and gave them to Violet and me. I asked if I could have sugar in mine. He looked inside the sugar bowl and said there was only a little stuck to the bottom, but he scraped it off for me. After we finished breakfast, he said to go get dressed in the dresses we wear to Mass.

Violet asked him why we had to wear our Sunday dresses on Saturday. All he said was, *"Fa' presto!"*

I like wearing my Sunday dress, but Violet says they're stiff and silly and hers is too small. She buttoned me into mine, but I'd only buttoned half of hers when we heard the buzzer, then voices in the parlor, Papa's and a lady's. I didn't know all the words they said, so I asked Violet what they meant. She said she didn't know either and to button her top button and come on.

As soon as she saw us, the lady smiled. She had on a white dress and a black sweater and a white cap with a black stripe. I knew she was a nurse because Doctor Cohen's nurse wears the same clothes.

Papa gave her his chair and told us to sit on the sofa. Then he went and sat by the windows.

The nurse took a pencil and paper from her bag and started asking us questions, like how old we are and how often we cough and whether we ever wake up at night hot and sweaty. Then she took our temperature and felt our neck. That was to see if our glands were swollen, she said.

Violet started to ask the nurse about the words we'd heard her and Papa say. Except she couldn't remember them, so I said, "TB sanatorium."

The nurse looked at me funny. Then she said TB is a sickness spread by germs, and when people with TB cough, they can spread it to other people, so it's best for them to live in a sanatorium. She said it's like a big house where everybody with TB lives until they get better.

Violet asked the nurse how long it takes to get better, and she said everybody's different. "But once your mother's a little better, you can go visit her. And in the meantime, you can write to her, and she can write back."

She took something out of her bag. It was long and skinny like a pencil, and when she took off the cap, a needle stuck out. She said she had to prick our arm with the needle to find out whether or not we had TB. She wiped Violet's arm with a little cloth and, even though I looked away as fast as I could, I saw her push the needle into the place where she'd wiped.

I put my arm behind my back. "Now, Gloria," the nurse said, "you saw your sister take the test. Did it hurt, Violet?"

Violet said, "A little. But before you even feel it, it's over." She tried to take my arm, but I wouldn't let her. Then I remembered Sister Genevieve saying whenever we disobey, God tells the angels to put a black mark on our soul. So I held out my arm and closed my eyes. It hurt a lot.

The nurse put her things away and said she'd come back and visit again in a few days to be sure we didn't have TB. "Aren't you going to check Papa?" Violet asked. The nurse didn't answer, because Papa got up and said he'd fought the germs off a long time ago.

After the nurse left, Papa tried to give Violet some paper and a pencil. "Write to your mama," he said. "I'm visiting her today." But Violet just stood there, looking at him. He told her to take the paper and pulled on her arm. It was the one where the nurse had put the needle. "Write her a letter!" he said. His voice was loud. "And don't tell her anything about what happened at school yesterday." She still didn't move.

I was afraid he'd go get the yardstick, but then she said, "Why did you take Mama so far away? Why didn't you take her somewhere closer?"

Papa let go of her arm. He put the paper and pencil on the table and said, "The sanatorium she's gone to is the closest. Besides, I had no say in it." His voice wasn't loud anymore. He bent down and pulled us both right up next to him.

I leaned against his arm. It's thick like a tree. Mama says Papa's strong from working on the machines.

"*Va bene*," he said. "Write a pretty letter for your mama."

He waited while we wrote a whole page and I decorated it with flowers, and then he put it in his pocket and said he had to go. He said Aunt Blanche and Uncle Eddie would make supper with us tonight. He put his hands on our faces like he does sometimes, and then he went out. I heard him go down the stairs and the front door close, and then there wasn't any sound left at all. And now the broken glass is pricking me again, like the needle the nurse put in my arm, except the broken glass is pricking my heart.

VIOLET

I wish I could love Papa the way Glory does.

After he left and we were alone, her big black eyes got that look like Papa's when he's staring out the window but you know he's not seeing anything.

At first I didn't know how to make her feel better. Then I thought of Mrs. Rasmussen.

We changed into our regular dresses and went downstairs and rang her doorbell. As soon as she opened the door, she said, "I bet you girls have come to pet Sir Lancelot!" He's Mrs. Rasmussen's cat. She pointed to where he was sleeping on the little bed she made him on her front windowsill. He has a round face and lots of fluffy cream and grey fur, so he looks like a big cloud. I wish we could have a cat, 'cause maybe it would help Glory not be so scared. Once Mama and Mrs. Rasmussen found a litter of kittens in the back alley where they hang the washing. We knew Sir Lancelot must have been their father 'cause two of them were cream and grey like him. Glory and I begged Mama to let us have one, a male with folded-down ears, but she said didn't she have enough to worry about.

I feel sorry for Mrs. Rasmussen 'cause, except for Sir Lancelot, she lives alone. Mama says her husband died in the war, and both of her boys are in the Merchant Marine. That means they work on big ships that take things far away. She gets some money from the government on account of her husband, and her boys send her a little and she sews clothes. She can sew better than anybody, even Aunt Blanche. She made my first Communion dress out of the scraps she kept from the dresses she made for some other girls in my class. She wouldn't take a cent for it.

She gave us raisin cake and glasses of milk. While we were eating, she said she'd seen the nurse come, and asked if she'd answered all our questions about Mama.

I told her I guessed she'd told us the important parts.

"And what might those important parts be?" she asked.

I slowed down to make sure I got it right. "That Mama's in the TB sanatorium and we can write her letters, but we can't visit her yet."

Glory had been stroking Sir Lancelot, as if she wasn't even paying attention. But when I finished talking, she shot out of her chair and shouted, "But those aren't the important parts!"

"Why, Glory, what are the important parts, then?" Mrs. Rasmussen asked.

She clenched her hands into fists. "The important parts are, when is she coming home and do people ever go to the TB sanatorium and never come home? The nurse didn't tell us that!"

Mrs. Rasmussen reached over with both her hands and stroked Glory's fists like she was petting Sir Lancelot. "I don't suppose the nurse can say for sure when your mama's coming home, Glory dear." Her voice was so soft, it made me think of when the pigeons coo on the fire escape outside our bedroom window. "But lots of people who go to the sanatorium do get well. And come home to their children."

"But sometimes, even sometimes, do people never come home?"

Mrs. Rasmussen stopped stroking Glory's fists and just held them. "I don't myself know of anyone who went to the TB san-atorium and didn't come home," she said, "but I imagine some people who go are old and weak. Whereas your mother is young and strong." She sat back in her chair and said, "One thing I do know is that it's never helpful to give in to fear."

I saw her look at the side table. I thought maybe she was looking at the photograph of her boys waving in front of a big ship, so I asked her, "Mrs. Rasmussen, which of your boys is which? I always forget." It wasn't a lie. I do always forget 'cause they look almost like twins.

She brought the photograph to us and pointed to the man who was a little shorter. "This is Walter. I just had a letter from him a week ago. He's a good correspondent, much better than Leonard, maybe because he's older. There are three years between them, just like with you girls. Walter is sensible, like me. Whereas Leonard is always looking for excitement. He takes after his father."

I asked her what she meant.

"Well, for instance, my husband didn't have to go to the war. He could have asked for an exemption. Because we had the boys, you see. But he wanted adventure. When he shipped out, they were still in grade school."

Talking about her husband seemed to make Mrs. Rasmussen sad, so I asked her some more about her boys. "I don't remember Walter," I said, "but I think I remember Leonard."

Mrs. Rasmussen smiled. "Of course you remember him! Last time he visited, oh—it'll be two years this Christmas—he brought you girls sweets, remember that?"

"I remember!" Glory said. "Chuckles!"

"That's right! And Caramel Creams! He has a sweet tooth himself. He wrote me once that whenever they get shore leave, all his buddies stock up on cigarettes, but he heads straight to the nearest candy store!" Now she was laughing, and Glory started to laugh, too.

"Are Walter and Leonard always on the same ship?" I asked.

"No. I think the bosses like to keep family members separated. Even when this photo was taken, it was only Walter who was heading out. Leonard was still in training on shore."

"Mrs. Rasmussen?" Glory whispered. She looked like she was about to cry. "Why don't they visit you more?"

I thought her question might hurt Mrs. Rasmussen's feelings, but it didn't seem to. "They work so hard," she said, "and travel to such exotic places. When they have leave, they want to enjoy themselves—see the world." She put the photograph back on the side table. "I know they'd like to visit their mother for a day or two. But then they'd get restless. So I'd just as soon have their letters and know they're happy." She went to the windows and started stroking Sir Lancelot. The sun on her face lit up her grey eyes and made them look shiny, like silver. I've known Mrs. Rasmussen ever since I can remember, but today was the first time I ever noticed she's beautiful.

Aunt Blanche always looks beautiful. Tonight she was wearing her green dress that matches her eyes, and her hair was pinned up in gold waves so you could see her gold earrings. Uncle Eddie came while we were making supper and put his hands around her waist, but she pushed him away and said he smelled liked cigarettes and hooch and how much had he lost to Sergeant McGowan. He said he never loses to McGowan, that he's too much of a cop to know how to bluff and they both lost to Tiny Bly. Aunt Blanche said how much. He said only two bucks. She said that's two bags of groceries. After supper, though, he put on the radio and pushed aside the sofa and they danced.

The whole time Glory was watching them, she looked sad, so when "Dinah" came on, I pulled her up and spun her around until she started to laugh. Then they played "Wrap Your Troubles in Dreams" and Uncle Eddie put his arms around me and Aunt Blanche put her arms around Glory and we danced that way. I wished I was dancing with Aunt Blanche 'cause Uncle Eddie did smell like cigarettes and hooch, and besides, he was holding me too tight. So I was glad when Aunt Blanche stopped dancing with Glory before the song even ended. "Speaking of dreams," she said, "I think it's time for two young ladies to get to bed."

We said good night and washed and said our prayers. I tucked Glory in, then got in bed and we listened to the songs on the radio until Glory fell asleep.

A little while ago, I heard Papa come home. Aunt Blanche asked about Mama and he said she has to stay lying down flat and Doctor Murphy says rest is the cure. Aunt Blanche said there was a plate for Papa in the oven, and then she and Uncle Eddie went home. Everything's quiet now. Papa must be eating in the kitchen. I wish I could go sit with him. I'd tell him how I took care of Glory all day. Maybe then he'd look at me the way he always looks at her, like he loves her more than anybody else in the world.

VIOLET

Today sure didn't feel like Christmas.

It felt sad. Even sadder than an ordinary day. I wonder if Mr. and Mrs. Sadowski feel extra sad on Christmas, too. And why Mrs. Rasmussen said their daughter being gone is too sad a story for Christmas night.

Gosh, I never knew Mr. and Mrs. Sadowski even had a daughter. And I sure never knew her name.

We went to Aunt Blanche's for Christmas. We always go there, even before Mama went away, 'cause she has a separate dining room and a bigger parlor and she always buys a Christmas tree. Mama used to say she doesn't mind that Aunt Blanche has more than we do, that she deserves it 'cause after Grandpa and Grandma died, she had to manage everything. She was only sixteen, but she left Saint Isabel's and got herself a job typing for Mr. Drake, the boss at the shoe mill. Then she married the foreman, Uncle Eddie. Mama is five years younger than Aunt Blanche, and he treated her like a daughter. That's the way Mama always told it, and she always ended with how he walked her down the aisle on her wedding day. Uncle Eddie and Aunt Blanche can't have children. Mama said that's another reason not to begrudge them what they do have. So Aunt Blanche kept on working. Even when Mr. Drake had to let some people go, he couldn't do without his foreman and his secretary, so they have two paychecks, and that's how they can live in a duplex. There's an upstairs and a downstairs and the kitchen has a separate pantry with shelves and drawers, and Aunt Blanche has a sewing room. The outside is white with blue shutters and two blue doors. Our triple-decker is brown.

Maybe 'cause she doesn't have children, Aunt Blanche always gives Glory and me an extra-nice Christmas present, like a new coat or shoes or boots from the mill. But this year, when she asked me what I wanted for Christmas, I said I wanted to visit Mama. We were all having supper together, so right away she said to Papa, "How about it, Roberto?" The way Aunt Blanche says Papa's name is so funny, like it's three different words. "Couldn't we all visit Yvonne on Christmas Day?"

Papa told her he'd look into it, and went back to eating his supper.

So right up until Christmas morning I kept hoping our present would be visiting Mama. Instead, Papa came into the kitchen while we were eating breakfast and gave us each a wrapped present. Mine was a book of recipes called *Kitchen Fun*, and Glory's was a book of poems for children. After we got dressed, he took us to Aunt Blanche and Uncle Eddie's. He only stayed a little while, and then he drove Uncle Eddie's car to the sanatorium by himself. I tried to seem happy so Aunt Blanche and Uncle Eddie wouldn't know how disappointed I was. They'd plugged in the lights on the Christmas tree even though it was morning, and under the tree there were two boxes each for Glory and me. The bigger boxes had white dresses Aunt Blanche made us with fluffy underskirts and a satin sash, both the same except my sash is green and Glory's is red, and the smaller boxes had shiny black shoes. I wish Aunt Blanche had made me a checked shirt and a pair of overalls like the ones I saw at Woolworth. They were on a girl mannequin with pigtails and she was holding a fishing rod and looking at her made me want to go to the park and sit on the bridge over the river and catch fish to take home for supper. Of course I didn't say any of that. I just said thank you. At least now I have a Sunday dress that fits.

After we opened our presents, Mrs. Rasmussen came with a dish of scalloped potatoes and a box of candied chestnuts from Leonard, and we had Christmas dinner.

Later in the afternoon, Mr. and Mrs. Sadowski came over for apple pie. Mr. Sadowski always looks nice. Today he was wearing a blue sweater vest and a white shirt and a blue bow tie. Mrs. Sadowski tries to look nice, too. She had on a red dress and a dark green velvet hat with three red roses on the side. It was such an elegant hat, it would have made Aunt Blanche look like a lady from the picture shows, but it just made Mrs. Sadowski look like she was pretending not to be sick.

I think Mrs. Sadowski is sicker than Mama even. I asked Aunt Blanche once why they don't make her go to a sanatorium and she said it's 'cause you can't catch Mrs. Sadowski's sickness. I feel sorry for her 'cause she can't eat nice things like apple pie. She just poked at it with her fork and put it down. Then she asked Aunt Blanche about Mama. "She must feel so sad," she said, "away from her children on Christmas Day."

"And away from her sister!" Aunt Blanche said. That made me think about how she misses Mama, too, just like I'd miss Glory if she had to go away. "This is the first Christmas we've been apart," she said. "I went with Bert to see her last week, though, and she did seem better." "Bert" is what everybody calls Papa when he's not around. Uncle Eddie says "Roberto" is too much of a mouthful.

Up till now Mr. Sadowski had been quiet, but all of a sudden, he said, "I lost my sister to TB on Christmas Day."

I guess I knew that sometimes people die from TB, but I'd never heard of it happening to anybody in particular. So when Mr. Sadowski said that, I got real scared. I looked over at Glory. Her eyes were big like she was scared, too.

Uncle Eddie said, "I don't think you've ever mentioned that before, Stan. When did it happen?"

"We were thirteen," he said. "Twins. Her name was Ada."

Ada! I felt shivery. But then I wondered, why would Mama cry about Ada when Mr. Sadowski said she died a long time ago?

For a second, Mrs. Rasmussen looked confused, too. "Her name was Ada?" she said. Then her voice got louder. "Like your Ada."

"Yes," Mrs. Sadowski said. "Like our Ada."

I couldn't figure out what they meant, and Mr. Sadowski went right back to talking about his sister. Then he drank the rest of his coffee straight down and said, "At any rate, my folks never got over it."

Mrs. Sadowski made a big, fake smile. "We should stop being so morbid! It's Christmas!" She waved her coffee cup in the air. "Blanche, might I have some more coffee?"

After Mr. and Mrs. Sadowski left, I wanted to ask Aunt Blanche who they meant by "their Ada," but Mrs. Rasmussen said she'd take us home, so I decided to ask her instead. I waited until we were sitting at her parlor windows, watching for Papa and petting Sir Lancelot and eating candied chestnuts.

"She's Mr. and Mrs. Sadowski's daughter," she said. "But she left years ago. You couldn't have been more than—oh, two or three. Glory wasn't even born yet." She looked out into the street. "I hope your father's nearly home. It's starting to snow."

"But I've never met her," I said. "Doesn't she visit?"

Mrs. Rasmussen kept staring out at the snow. "It's too sad a story for Christmas night, darling." Then she got up and put a record on her phonograph. It sounded scratchy. That was 'cause she played it so much, she said. She told us the lady singing was Helen Morgan, and the song was called, "Why Was I Born?"

Before the record finished playing, Mrs. Rasmussen's doorbell rang. It was Papa. He said he'd stay in the hallway 'cause he was covered in snow.

Glory asked him how Mama was feeling.

"A little better, I think." He told us she'd read our cards over and over.

Glory went into the hallway and asked him, real quiet, "Are you sure she's better?"

"Yes, *bambolina*," he said. "I'm sure." He stroked her hair. "Now let's get upstairs."

I picked up our coats and the bag with our presents. Glory kept looking at Papa. "Promise," she said, "that Mama won't die like Mr. Sadowski's Ada."

Papa's eyes got real big, like Glory's before a spell. He was looking at Mrs. Rasmussen, but I'm not sure he could see her.

"His twin sister," she said in a rush. "Stan mentioned it this afternoon. Evidently, when they were children, she died of TB on Christmas Day. I'm sure it must have frightened the girls to hear it."

Papa closed his eyes. "Of course. It must have." When he opened his eyes again, he seemed all right. "And I'm sorry to hear that about Stan." He lifted Glory into his arms and promised her that Mama's getting better. Then he thanked Mrs. Rasmussen for sitting with us, and we went upstairs.

I can't sleep. If Mama knew I was worried about her, she'd say she was in God's care, and to pray to Saint Isabel. I've tried, but the words won't stay in my head. I keep wondering why God let Mr. Sadowski's sister Ada die on Christmas Day, and why Mama used to cry about somebody named Ada, and why Mr. and Mrs. Sadowski's daughter Ada went away and never comes home.

GLORY

Papa says I'm to stay in bed today.

That's because yesterday was Easter Sunday and we visited Mama and saw something bad. We weren't supposed to see something bad. We were only supposed to see Mama, and then we were going to have Easter Sunday dinner at Mrs. Rasmussen's. But after everything happened, we just went home. Or at least Papa and I went home. That's what Violet says, anyway. I don't remember.

We didn't know we were going to visit Mama until Saturday night. Violet and I were taking turns reading each other poems from Mama's book by Edna St. Vincent Millay when Uncle Eddie came. He said he'd called the sanatorium and Easter Sunday was family day and he and Aunt Blanche were going to visit Mama so why didn't we all go together? At first Papa said no, it wasn't safe, but Uncle Eddie said we'd just stay a few minutes. I grabbed Papa's hand and said, "Please, Papa, please!" and then he said all right.

After we went to bed, even though most of me was happy, my insides were prickly. I kept asking Violet what she thought the TB sanatorium would be like, and if she thought Mama would still look like Mama, and if she'd still cough, and what she'd say to us, and what we should say to her, but Violet kept answering she didn't know and I should just go to sleep so morning would come and we'd find out. When I finally did fall sleep, I dreamed I was in the sanatorium except it looked like Saint Isabel's. I was standing on the altar trying to recite "First Fig," but a lady in the back kept coughing. She looked like Edna St. Vincent Millay in a photograph Mama showed me in the newspaper once. Every time I said, "My candle burns at both ends; / It will not last the night," she coughed so much I had to stop and start all over again. Then I woke up and it was morning.

Violet fixed fried eggs and toast, but the smell made me feel so sick I threw up. Papa said since I was sick I couldn't go, but Violet told him it was because I was nervous and I'd be okay, and she brought me some water and told me to lie down. She got dressed in her white dress from Aunt Blanche. Then she gave me the book of poems by Edna St. Vincent Millay and plumped up my pillows and told me to memorize a new poem while they were at Mass so I could recite it for Mama when we saw her. I heard Aunt Blanche and Uncle Eddie come in, then Aunt Blanche telling everybody to go on to Mass and she'd stay with me. Uncle Eddie said that would be a mortal sin, but Aunt Blanche said she thought God told us to care for the sick. Then the front door closed and Aunt Blanche came into my room.

"Hello, darling," she said. "How are you feeling?" Aunt Blanche looks pretty even when she's cooking or sweeping the floor, but yesterday she looked especially nice. She had on the pink suit she sometimes wears in the spring, with a pink-and-green scarf and pink shoes.

"I'm okay," I told her. "Thank you for staying with me."

"My pleasure," she said, and she winked at me. "How about if I bring you a cup of tea and a piece of dry toast?"

I said yes. While she was in the kitchen, I opened the book. The poem I opened to has a big word in the name. It's "The Philosopher." Mama says it means somebody who likes to think. I don't know why it's called that, because it's really about how Edna St. Vincent Millay misses her boyfriend. The first two lines are, "And what are you that, wanting you, / I should be kept awake." Those were easy to remember because they reminded me of how I couldn't sleep the night before and all the nights since Mama went away. Then I memorized the next two lines, "As many nights as there are days / With weeping for your sake." It made me sad to think of Edna St. Vincent Millay weeping because her boyfriend left her, even though Mama says she got married to somebody else. Then I thought maybe it was good that I felt sad because it was better than the prickly feeling and besides, it gave me an idea.

I opened the drawer of our night table and took out one of the old envelopes we keep there. I turned it inside out so it was all clean. Then I took out a pencil and wrote my own poem.

To Mama

Today I will see you again.
Easter Day is here.
Why am I so sad?
Why do I shed a tear?
Because I will see you and then
We will part again, Mama dear.

I folded up my poem and put it in the pocket of my white dress. Then Aunt Blanche came back with the tea and toast. She asked me if I was scared to see Mama again.

Aunt Blanche has gone to see Mama lots of times. When Papa visits, he only says things like, "Mama was better today. She hopes you're doing your schoolwork and your chores and saying your prayers." But when Aunt Blanche gets back from her visits, she comes right across the street and tells us Mama's pink and plump and never stopped asking about us the whole time.

If Mama looked pink and plump, I wasn't sure if she'd still look like Mama or if I'd still love her the way I always used to love her or if she'd still love me the way she always used to love me. So I told Aunt Blanche I *was* scared. A little.

"After all these months," she said, "a lifetime to a child, of course you are." She stroked my cheek. "But you know what I think, Glory dear?"

I shook my head.

"I think, as soon as you lay eyes on her, everything will be just fine."

My insides stopped prickling when she said that, and I drank my tea and ate a whole piece of toast. While she did the dishes, I tried to memorize some more of Edna St. Vincent Millay's poem: "And what are you that, missing you / As many days as crawl . . ." That made me think of Mama again, and of how the days since she left had crawled. "I should be listening to the wind / And looking at the wall?" I listened for wind outside the window, but I couldn't hear any, so I looked at the wall. I looked and looked, and the cracks in the blue paint gave me a funny feeling, like they might open up to someplace big and dark and I might fall through and never find my way out again.

There was a sound at the door and I looked up and Papa was standing there frowning. He said it was too bad, but he couldn't take me to visit Mama looking like that. He'd have to leave me with Mrs. Rasmussen. But then Aunt Blanche came back into the bedroom and held out her hand and said, "You ready to go see your mama, Glory?" And she helped me get dressed, and Papa let me go with them.

Outside I felt good, but Uncle Eddie's car was hot inside, like the air was all used up. I sat on the back seat between Violet and Papa, and after we'd gone a little way, the sick feeling came back. I pulled Violet's sleeve. She turned from the window and looked at me, then she smoothed her coat across her lap and pointed, and I knew that meant it was all right for me to put my head there. When I did, she took off my hat and petted my hair.

I fell asleep. When I woke up, we were in a parking lot in front of a spread-out brick building with a white tower in the middle that had a clock on it. Uncle Eddie looked at us and said, "You ready, girls?"

Violet told him yes.

We went through the big doors at the top of the steps into an open place with a staircase and a lady sitting behind a counter. Papa went over and talked to the lady, and she pointed to a big door with glass at the top of the stairs. Papa took my hand and started tugging me toward the staircase. I was scared to go up, so I asked him to carry me, and he did—right up to the door with glass, but then he put me down. "*Vieni!* We don't want Mama to think I had to drag you."

I followed him a little way into the room. At the back there were more doors with glass and they were all open and the cold air made me feel better. There were people everywhere—nurses, and people in normal clothes, and people covered in blankets sitting at tables or in rocking chairs or chairs with long seats that let them stretch out their legs. They were all talking to each other or eating chocolates or playing cards or checkers, but I couldn't see Mama. She wasn't there.

Then Violet took my hand. "Come on, Glory," she said. "Let's go find Mama!" She brought me to the window-doors, and I saw a big porch with a long row of people on the stretching-out chairs. She pulled me through one of the doors and right up to Papa. He was talking to a lady in a stretching-out chair. She was wrapped in a blanket that went up past her waist, but I could see the top of her dress. It was the dress Mama always wore to Mass. Except Mama's dress wasn't loose on this lady. It fit her perfectly. Then I heard Violet whisper, "Hello, Mama," and the lady turned and threw out her arms and pulled Violet and me against her.

When she let us go, she reached into her dress for a handkerchief and dabbed her eyes, and when she took the handkerchief away, Mama's face was there, just like a puzzle picture when you put in the last piece.

"Violet! Glory! My goodness, how you've grown!"

Violet said, "Mama, you look pretty. I was scared you might look like you were even sicker, but you don't. You look like a rich lady."

Mama smiled. "As well I should! They only allow us to rest and eat, rest and eat, for months on end! We're even told not to laugh! Then in time they let us walk a bit. I'd say they're spoiling me, except that I miss everyone so much."

The whole time Mama was talking, I kept looking at her face—now that I could tell it was her face—and remembering how it used to smile just like it was smiling now.

"Nothing to say, Glory?" Mama asked.

I couldn't talk, even when Violet told Mama I'd memorized a poem to recite to her. I couldn't even think of the name. Then I remembered my own poem. I unbuttoned my coat and reached into the pocket of my dress and held it out to her.

"What's this, Glory? Is it a letter for me?" She unfolded the paper and read it. When she looked up, I could see tears in her eyes again. Her hand curled around my cheek. "I pray every day that God will heal me so I can come home, and when He does, we won't cry, either one of us, anymore, and we won't be parted again. Not until you're all grown up and a famous poet giving readings in New York!" Her hand felt so soft, I wanted her to hold it there forever. "Papa told me how the sisters almost moved you up to second grade," she said, "though I think they made the right decision to keep you with children your own age. Still, I'm proud of you." I wanted to say thank you, but my voice still wouldn't work. Mama looked at Violet. "And Violet, Papa and Aunt Blanche both tell me how much you do at home, cleaning and cooking."

"I don't mind, Mama," Violet said. "I want to help."

"I believe you. Still, for a girl who's only just turned ten years old! Which reminds me." She nodded to Papa. "Berto?"

Papa reached into his pocket. "Happy birthday!" he said, and held out a tiny box tied with a bow.

Violet just stared at it.

"Take it, darling," Mama said. "And tell me if you still like it."

It took her so long to untie the bow I wanted to shout at her to hurry up. Then she took the top off and lifted up a little square of cotton. Her eyes got really big, and she said, "Mama, you remembered!" as if she couldn't believe it.

Mama laughed, and it sounded just like it used to sound, like little bells. "Of course I remembered!" she said. "I went back to Woolworth the day after we saw it, and the clerk set it aside for me with a nickel down. The rest of the summer, whenever I could, I put another nickel down. After I came here, Papa made some payments, and your Uncle Eddie and Aunt Blanche pitched in, too."

Violet thanked them. Then she hugged Mama. "Every time I wear it, it'll be like we're together."

Words burst out of me. "What is it?"

"Well, that got you talking!" Mama said. She told Violet to show me.

She held out the box. I lifted the cotton. Underneath was a pin shaped like a bouquet of flowers painted dark purple, with tiny white centers, and green leaves behind them, and gathered stems that looked like a little bundle of gold. "Is it real gold?" I asked.

Uncle Eddie laughed at me. "Kid, you don't get real gold for a dollar and twenty cents!"

"Still," Aunt Blanche said, "it's a lovely design."

"Are they violets?" I asked her.

She nodded. "That's right. It's a little sprig of violets."

Mama took the box and gave it back to Violet. "Remember, Blanche, how the violets started to bloom up and down Mill Street a few days before Violet was born? Even the gaps in the sidewalks were sprouting violets." Then she told Violet, "And that's where you got your name."

"Where did I get my name?" I asked.

"Well," Mama said, "as I'd named your sister after the flowers in bloom when she was born, I thought—if you were a girl, of course—I'd do the same for you. And the flowers that start to bloom in July are the morning glories. Every spring, Magda—Mrs. Sadowski—plants them by her porch. And the very morning of the day you were born, I'd been out walking, trying to help you move down and—" She looked at Aunt Blanche. "You remember, Blanche, you were walking with me, you and Violet."

Aunt Blanche nodded. "We noticed them climbing the railings of Magda's porch. And you said, well then, if the baby's a girl, I'll name her Gloria, and we can call her Glory." She put her arms around me and said, "Of course, by the time you made your appearance, the sun had set, so the blossoms had died. They only last for a day. But in the morning, new ones bloom. That's why they're called morning glories."

Aunt Blanche talking about the morning glories dying gave me the feeling I got when I was looking at the cracks in the wall in my room. But then a pretty lady dressed in white said hello to us. "With all this talk of flower names, I just had to ask your mother to introduce me!"

Mama smiled. "Everyone, this is Rose. She's a patient here, too, and a friend."

"Your mother has been like a sister to me," Rose said. "But we're soon to be parted because I'm going home."

"We hope," Mama said. "Rose is having tests this week and if they're clear, she gets to go home. But forgive me, Rose, for not introducing my family." She told Rose each of our names, then Uncle Eddie gave Rose his chair and went to get another.

"Where is home, Rose?" Aunt Blanche asked her. "And who's waiting for you there?"

Rose laughed a little. "Home is four miles away! And I'll live with my mother again. I came here after my father died of TB. I'm nearly twenty, you know!"

Uncle Eddie came back. He said all the chairs were taken, and he didn't mind standing. But Aunt Blanche said he could have my chair and I could sit on her lap. That's why I was right next to Rose when she started coughing. She'd been telling us she was finally going to finish high school, and her eyes were twinkling like stars. But then they got big and afraid, and coughing burst up out of her and wouldn't stop, and blood spilled out of her mouth, and every cough pushed more of it all over her white dress.

Aunt Blanche tried to push our chair away, but before she could I felt Rose's blood on my face and saw it in front of me, hanging from my eyelashes. And behind the blood I saw Rose fall out of her chair onto the floor. Everyone around us was shouting and a nurse came and grabbed me away from Aunt Blanche and started wiping my face, and then screaming burst out of me, just like the coughing burst out of Rose, and it kept on screaming, even though I wanted it to stop. It kept on screaming even when a man carried me away from the porch and took me through the big room and into another room and put a needle in my arm. After that I don't remember anything until I woke up at home in my bed.

Today is Easter Monday. We don't have school. Papa said that's a good thing since he wants me to stay in bed. Violet brought me some bread and butter and milk, and I asked her what happened to Rose. She said she didn't know and she'd ask Papa when he came home for lunch.

He's home now. I can hear them talking in the parlor. I can hear her asking him, and him answering. I can hear him telling her Rose is dead.

VIOLET

Today was such a wonderful day I don't want it to end.

When I got up, I knew it would be a nice day, 'cause it's Glory's birthday. But I sure didn't know it would be a wonderful day until Mama came home. She's gone to bed now, but I know she's home for real. 'Cause I can still smell lavender.

In all the months and months since she went away, we only saw her once. It was Easter Sunday, and we didn't even stay an hour 'cause of what happened. After that, Papa wouldn't take us to visit her again, even though it wasn't our fault. Or Mama's. She didn't cough blood. She looked just like Aunt Blanche said she would. Pink and plump, like a lady in a big house who doesn't have to do any work and can just sit on one of those long chairs petting her cat all day. But after her friend Rose started coughing blood, and Glory started screaming, I never even had a chance to say goodbye. And ever since then, I've wondered if Mama ever coughed up blood like that. Or even if she didn't, if some day she would, and maybe she'd die the same way. But now I don't have to worry anymore. 'Cause she's home.

This morning, Aunt Blanche and I baked Glory a birthday cake and Uncle Eddie and Papa went out. When I asked Aunt Blanche where they'd gone, she said they must have gone to get a present for Glory, mustn't they? Papa only worked two days this week, so I thought maybe Uncle Eddie was helping him buy the present.

Aunt Blanche let Glory frost the cake, then we sat in the parlor and played Rummy. Then all of a sudden the door opened and Mama was there, in the same dress she was wearing on Easter, and a new summer hat. She put her pocketbook on the hook and opened up her arms. "Happy birthday, Glory," she said, and her eyes were so shiny I thought she might be about to cry.

Glory was sitting on the sofa next to me. She looked like a statue, not moving at all, just holding her cards and staring across the room. And then, so fast I almost didn't see it, she was gone. I wouldn't even have known where she went except I heard our bedroom door slam shut. I ran after her. When I opened the door, she wasn't there. Then I heard the tiniest noise, like a mouse scratching, under her bed. So I got down on the floor and looked under and sure enough, she was there, right up against the wall. She was barely making a sound, but I could tell she was crying 'cause her whole body was shaking.

I asked her what she was crying about. She wouldn't answer me. I told her she was making her dress all dusty and Mama was waiting, but she just kept shaking and crying. So I reached under the bed and slid her out. Then I pulled her head into my lap and stroked her hair the way she likes me to. There was a noise and I looked up and Mama and Papa were standing there. Papa came over and lifted Glory into his arms. I got up, but before I left, Mama reached out and squeezed my hand.

They were in there a long time. Uncle Eddie picked up the newspaper. Aunt Blanche asked me if I'd like to help her make sandwiches. When we got into the kitchen, she gave me a big hug and said how happy she was that Mama was home.

"To stay?" I asked.

"Doctor Murphy thinks so," she said. "Though he warned her she has to be careful not to overdo it."

I told her I'd help Mama. She said she knew I would, then she asked me what was wrong with Glory. I said I wasn't sure.

By the time we brought out the sandwiches, though, she was sitting between Mama and Papa on the sofa.

After everybody had eaten, we cut the cake and Glory opened her presents. Mama and Papa gave her a book about a girl named Dorothy who meets a wizard, and Aunt Blanche gave her a pair of cream-and-grey slippers she knitted. On the top part she embroidered faces that look like cats.

While I was washing the dishes, I could hear Aunt Blanche and Uncle Eddie saying goodbye to Mama over and over and Papa thanking Aunt Blanche for taking care of us. Then the door closed, and it got quiet. When I finished the dishes and went out to the parlor, Glory was on the sofa wiggling her feet in her new slippers, and Papa was in his chair watching her. For a second I got scared 'cause I didn't see Mama, but Papa said she was washing up for bed and when she finished we should do the same.

When Mama came out of the bathroom, she was dressed in her summer nightgown and robe, the same ones I remembered. She said that even though it was barely dark, she was tired and heading to bed. She held out her arms and we both hugged her. She smelled like lavender.

VIOLET

It's so dark out.

I can't see any moon. We left the window open 'cause it was hot and now there's a breeze, but it's making a noise in the alley like somebody's crying.

I hope it's not Mama.

She always cries when they fight. And it's my fault they did. Uncle Eddie paying the rent made it worse, but that's not what started it. It started when I asked her if our baby brother was baptized. It was like she got sad and mad at the same time. And then nothing anybody said or did mattered anymore.

When we got home from school, Mama was in the kitchen ironing. It was hot in there, even with the window open, and she looked tired. So I told her to sit down and I'd finish the ironing. She and Glory sat at the kitchen table, and Glory told her how Sister Colette had been teaching her class how to say the Our Father in French. I learned the Our Father in French in second grade, too. And the Hail Mary. You have to memorize them before your first Communion. Glory started reciting it, and right away Mama did, too. I looked up from the ironing, and she was leaning back in her chair with her eyes closed. They got to *Donne-nous aujourd'hui notre pain quotidien*—and then Mama started to cough. She got up and got herself a glass of water. She was looking out the window while she was drinking it, but then she threw the water into the sink and said, "Girls, let's go up to the roof! I'll bet there's a breeze up there."

We'd been on the roof before, but always with Papa. He takes us up sometimes to see the moon, and once we went up in the daytime to watch a wrecking ball smash a tenement on Lower Main. After Mr. Owen's apartment, you turn a corner and the stairs get skinnier and you go to a little blue door at the top. There are folding chairs stacked beside the door, and I took three onto the roof. I opened them near the door where there was a little shade. I guess it was hard for Mama to hurry up the stairs like that, 'cause after she closed the door tight behind us, she leaned against it and coughed and coughed.

When she stopped coughing, she walked to the edge of the roof—the side above Mill Street. She looked down for a second, then backed away and sat down and whispered to us to sit down, too, and keep still.

"Why, Mama?" I whispered. "What's wrong?"

"Mr. Tompkins is here to collect the rent," she whispered, "and I haven't got it yet." We heard the front door of the building slam. Mama put her finger to her lips.

Glory's eyes got big, and she tried to climb into Mama's lap, but Mama whispered it was too hot and to sit down. Then we heard knocking and Mr. Tompkins hollering. "Mrs. Campo? It's no use hiding! I have my key and I'm comin' in!" Another door slammed. I guess it was the door to our apartment. We waited. I almost didn't dare to breathe.

A door opened and slammed again, and then I heard footsteps pounding on the stairs. But almost as soon as they started, I heard Mr. Owen's voice. It sounded as if he was right on the other side of the door to the roof. He talks kinda funny 'cause of what happened to his face, but you can still understand what he says. "Afternoon, Mr. Tompkins. You're looking for Mrs. Campo?"

"Certainly am, Will. You seen her, or that lazy guinea husband of hers?"

"Saw Mr. Campo go off to work this morning as I was putting out the lamps. Now Mrs. Campo? Happened to be by the window painting just now, and I saw her walking down toward Saint Isabel's. Probably thought she'd walk the girls home."

"Saint Isabel's! They got money to pay the pope but not to pay their rent. Listen, you tell them if they don't get the rent to me by tomorrow afternoon, I'm slapping on a five-dollar late fee!"

"Will do, Mr. Tompkins. Will do."

There was pounding on the stairs again, but this time it got softer. Then the front door slammed. Glory almost talked, but Mama shushed her. We waited a long time, then Mama whispered to me to peek over the edge of the roof toward Lower Main and see if I could see Mr. Tompkins. I was just in time to see him turn the corner. I told Mama he was gone.

Glory stood up and put her hands on her hips. She looked so fierce she reminded me of Papa when he's mad at Uncle Eddie. "We don't pay the pope!" she fumed. "We pay the sisters!"

"He doesn't understand," Mama said. "He sent his sons to the public school. That's free. But they don't teach prayers there, or the sacraments, or take you on Fridays to make your Confession." She looked at me. "Violet, did you go to Confession today?"

I said I did. "The fifth and sixth grades went together, right after lunch."

"I'm scared to go to Confession," Glory said.

Mama's eyebrows went up. "And what are you afraid to confess? That you're too busy reading to help with the chores?"

Glory dropped her head. I wanted to tell Mama I can do all the chores. I like cooking and setting the table and drying the dishes and putting them away. I don't need Glory to help. I'm not sure I even want her to.

"After you make your first Communion," Mama said, "you'll have to confess such things. Because doing whatever you fancy—" Her voice got sharp. "Well, Glory, that's a sin."

Glory kept looking down. I felt like it was me who'd hurt her, even though I hadn't said anything at all. And then Mama grabbed her hand and pulled her toward her chair. "Glory? What do you say to that?"

"I don't know what to say, Mama." Her voice was almost like a baby's. "And I don't know what to do! I can't make my Confession until next spring. If I die before I get a chance, will I go to Hell forever and ever?"

"Of course not!" Mama said. "You're too young to commit a mortal sin. A child who's been baptized—"

All of a sudden, Mama stopped talking.

I got a feeling—I don't know why—that maybe she was thinking about our baby brother. So I asked her if he'd been baptized. I'd never thought about it before, and I wish I hadn't thought about it then, 'cause as soon as I asked her, she got up out of her chair and, real slow, walked away from us to a corner of the roof and stood there staring at the sky.

"Mama," I said, "are you all right?"

She didn't move.

Glory looked scared. I told her to go get a glass of water.

She ran downstairs. Then I heard Papa's voice. Hollering. "On the roof? What do you mean, they're on the roof?" I heard footsteps running up the stairs, then the blue door banged open and he started hollering again. "How many times have I told you not to come up to the roof without me?"

Glory ran over to me. I put my arm around her.

When Mama turned away from the sky, she didn't look like Mama anymore. Her eyes seemed smaller and her lips were kinda twisted, like she had a bad taste in her mouth. She looked at Papa that way a long time, and he looked at her. Then she said, real slow, that we'd come up to get away from Mr. Tompkins. "We're a week late with the rent, and he—"

"I don't care if we're a month late," Papa snapped. "He shouldn't be coming after you for it, and you shouldn't be coming up here to the roof to hide. I've told you again and again—"

The blue door swung open. Mr. Owen came out. His shirt was loose over his pants and covered with splotches of paint. "Evening, Mr. Campo. Mrs. Campo. Violet. Glory." As he went past us, Glory ducked behind me. When he got to the edge of the roof, he lit a cigarette. He had to kinda tug his mouth around it so he could inhale, but then he lifted his head and blew a long puff of smoke out into the sky. "Beautiful evening. Especially up here."

Papa frowned. "A little warm for my liking."

"I thought you were born in Sicily."

"I was. But we left when I was a boy." Papa's frown relaxed a little. "What about you, Will? Where—"

"Right here. Born and raised."

"What kept you here?"

Mr. Owen took a long time before he said, really quiet, "My heart, Mr. Campo. My heart." He turned away and another stream of smoke went up to the sky.

Mama crossed over to the blue door and told him good night. Without turning to look at her, he said good night, too. Papa picked up the chairs, then he and Glory left. I was going, too, but then I had an idea. "Mr. Owen?" I asked.

"Yes, Violet?"

"Thank you for what you told Mr. Tompkins," I said.

He turned around this time, and half of his face kinda smiled. "You're welcome," he said.

When I got back to our apartment, Mama and Glory were watching Papa open a big box. There was a metal fan inside. Papa said Mama could put it in the kitchen or the parlor or wherever she was working to keep her comfortable.

Mama didn't even smile. She said she didn't see how we could afford it when the rent was due.

"Never mind the rent," Papa said. "You come first. And besides, it was on sale. End of the season." He put it on the table next to the sofa and plugged it in and turned it on. It made a little whirring noise and the blades started going around faster and faster until they disappeared. When Glory and I stood in front of it, it was like we were standing in a breeze.

Mama watched it for a while, then she said, not to anybody in particular, "Well, it's done now." She went into the kitchen.

I followed her and told her I'd finish the ironing. She said it was too hot to iron anymore, and too hot to cook, and to open a can of sardines and put them on a plate. She washed and sliced a tomato and cucumber. She didn't talk. I could tell she didn't want to. I didn't mind, though, 'cause I liked listening to our new fan making a breeze in the parlor. Then I heard Glory recite for Papa the Our Father in French. He told her it sounded very beautiful.

"I'll learn it in Italian, too," she said, "if you'll teach me."

"I'm not sure I can remember it. You go into the kitchen now and help with supper."

Mama told Glory to set the table. Papa moved the fan away a little while we ate. Afterwards, he listened to opera on the radio and Mama let out the hem of my white dress and Glory and I did our homework. But then Mama got up and said she'd run out of white thread and was going across the street to see if Aunt Blanche had some. While she was gone, the opera ended and Papa told us to get to bed.

We'd just turned our light off when we heard Mama come home, and that's when, almost right away, they started to fight again. Papa said something about Uncle Eddie, and Mama said why not, he was happy to do it, and then Papa started hollering,

"Give it to me! Give it to me or take it back yourself, but that money's not staying in my house!"

"I don't have it," Mama said. She sounded kinda flat, like she didn't want to fight. "He said it was just the night for a walk, and he took it down to Mr. Tompkins while I was talking to Blanche."

That seemed to make Papa even angrier, 'cause he hollered even louder. "How dare you! I'd have had the full amount next week—"

"But will it be enough to pay the gas and electric, too?" Mama asked. "And the girls' school fees, and our account at the market? Will it be enough for all that?"

Papa seemed to explode. "No, it won't be enough! Nothing I ever do is enough! I work every hour I can, Yvonne, and for what? The first chance you get, you sneak down to your brother-in-law and betray me!"

"Betray you?" Mama's voice sounded almost like she couldn't get her breath. "Betray *you*?"

I didn't have a chance to think what she meant, 'cause right after she said it, I heard the front door slam. And then Mama must have turned off the new fan 'cause everything was quiet. Except Glory. She was turned against the wall, crying. I went over and got into her bed and stroked her hair. After a while, she fell asleep and I went back to my own bed.

I wonder if nights without a moon are unlucky. Mama says there's no such thing as luck. That everything is God's will. But does that mean that Mama and Papa fighting is God's will? Or Glory not doing chores? Or Mr. Owen trying to pull his mouth around his cigarette and blow smoke up into the sky? Maybe it's just big things that God wills. Like fires and floods and people dying. Like our baby brother. Or that lady Rose. I wonder why God didn't let her go home to her mama like she planned.

At least He let Mama come home to us. Even though she still coughs. And she and Papa still fight.

I wonder if Papa's just gone for a walk. He can't have gone to New York, 'cause he left so fast, he doesn't have his suitcase.

Is that the wind, or Mama crying?

I wonder if she'll cry all night.

I wish I could fall asleep, 'cause then it would be morning. I'd bring Mama a cup of tea and tell her to stay in bed all day if she wants, 'cause it's Saturday and I'll take care of everything.

GLORY

Is Papa still gone?

I remember them fighting. Then Papa walked out. Maybe he's come back and that's what woke me up.

No. I guess it's the wind. I can hear it in the alley. But something else too. Mama crying. Maybe Papa's out walking in the wind and that's why Mama's crying. She's missing him, like Edna St. Vincent Millay when she's listening to the wind and looking at the wall.

Maybe if I visit her, she won't be sad anymore.

The floor is cool. Wind blows on my legs. Oh! Mama left the parlor windows open. The chairs and the sofa look like big animals. Mama's door is open. Her lamp is on. She's lying in bed holding her rosary, but she's not saying her rosary. She's saying the Act of Contrition. Why is she saying that?

"Mama?" I stay at the door.

She looks up. "Glory! What are you doing out of bed?"

I come closer. I ask her why she wants God to forgive her.

She doesn't answer.

I pet her hair like Violet does to me. I ask her why she's crying.

She takes my hand away. "I'm just being silly."

I ask her where Papa's gone.

She shrugs. "Oh, he's out for a walk." Her voice sounds like when we were little and she read us stories.

"But it's so windy outside!" I say.

"Just what he needs to cool his temper!" She tries to smile, but the smile falls back down.

I ask her if he's going to New York.

She shakes her head, then starts to cough. She turns toward the wall.

I ask, "Want me to get you some water?" I wait, but she doesn't answer.

I tell her I'll go back to bed now.

She stays turned toward the wall.

I tiptoe back to bed. The wind is still blowing. The door downstairs bangs. My heart thumps. Footsteps. It's not the man with the ripped-up face. His footsteps are slow. These are faster, and big. Papa's footsteps. The door opens and closes. Papa throws his keys on the hall table like he always does. A light goes on in the parlor. But now something else is happening—our bedroom door is opening. It happens so fast I don't have a chance to close my eyes.

"*Bambolina!*" he whispers. "What are you doing awake?" He comes and stands next to my bed.

I ask him why he was walking in the wind.

He sits on the edge of my bed. He puts his hand on my cheek. It's cool. "I like the wind," he says. "And the night. And walking by myself. Now you try to get to sleep."

I tell him I will.

He stands up. The light coming in from the door makes his black hair shine. Why does he have to go so soon? "Papa?" I whisper.

"Yes?"

I don't know what else to say. And then I think of the most wonderful thing in the world. "Promise me you and Mama won't fight anymore."

He turns a little so I can't see his face. "I'll try," he says. "I promise to try." Then he's gone.

I hear him in the bathroom. I hear water running. He goes into his room. The door closes. I listen. I don't hear anything else. Just the wind.

GLORY

Mama was sad tonight.

She's better now, I think, because she's sitting with Papa on the sofa and they're listening to the radio. Maybe he has his arm around her.

Today was the Feast of the Immaculate Conception, and we all went to church together—even Aunt Blanche came. We don't usually go to church on Saturday nights, but it's a holy day of obligation. Father Bouchard lit all the candles around the statue of the Blessed Mother and Jimmy Conlan brought him the big golden cup with the incense in it and he swung it up and down until it looked like the Blessed Mother was floating on a cloud.

I love the smell of incense—it makes me feel like I'm in heaven—but it made Mama cough and she went outside. She came back just in time for Holy Communion. I usually have to sit all alone in the pew while everybody else goes to Holy Communion because I haven't made my first Communion yet. But tonight Aunt Blanche kept me company. I liked not having to sit by myself, but when Mama came back and saw Aunt Blanche with her arm around me, she stopped in the middle of the aisle and just looked at us. Aunt Blanche got up right away and moved back to her pew, so I almost wouldn't have remembered it except for what Mama said later.

After Mass, we all went to the Twelve O'Clock Diner. That's because it was Mrs. Sadowski's birthday, and Mr. Sadowski invited us. I've read about restaurants. Nancy Drew goes to restaurants all the time. But I'd never been inside one before. I always wondered what it would be like to pick whatever I want from a menu, and have a lady serve it, and not have to clear the table or do the dishes. And tonight I found out.

The Twelve O'Clock Diner is beautiful inside. It has a long counter covered in black and white tiles, with stools in front with shiny red seats, and lots of red tables with red chairs. Mr. Sadowski took us to a long table at the back. "They don't usually reserve tables here," he said, "but Ernie and Molly are friends of ours."

Violet and I sat together between Mama and Papa, and a lady in a black dress with a red apron came to our table and gave us each a menu. There were lots of words on it I'd never seen before, but then I read "American cheese sandwich," so when the lady came back to ask us what we wanted, I told her I wanted that. Papa said it wasn't enough and I should order something to go with it. I didn't know what else to ask for, but then Violet said she was having a frankfurter and a dish of bananas and cream, so I said I'd like a dish of bananas and cream, too.

When we'd all said what we wanted, the lady walked through swinging doors behind the cash register. Almost right away she came back out carrying a tray with two tall pink drinks. She brought them to a table where Dorothy Pope—she's in my grade—was sitting with her mother and father and her sister, Louise. She put the drinks on their table and started talking to Dorothy and Louise. I wonder if they eat at the Twelve O'Clock Diner all the time.

While we were waiting for our food, Aunt Blanche said wasn't it warm in the diner, and Uncle Eddie helped her off with her coat. She was wearing a dress I'd never seen before, with shiny fabric like watery grass, and a necklace with green beads.

Mrs. Rasmussen said the dress was gorgeous and told her, "If you made it, I'll have to insist on borrowing the pattern!"

Aunt Blanche laughed and said she'd be happy to let Mrs. Rasmussen borrow it.

"You both put me to shame," Mrs. Sadowski said. "I can't even make an apron!"

Mr. Sadowski told her she makes lots of other nice things, like plum wine. He said it got him through Prohibition. I don't know what that means, but after he said it, Uncle Eddie raised his glass of beer and said, "Here's to the end of Prohibition, and to Magda! Happy birthday!"

Everybody raised their glass and said, "Happy birthday," even Violet and me. Except Mama just lifted her water glass and took a sip and put it down again.

When the lady brought us our food, I made myself eat all my sandwich before I took even one bite of my bananas and cream. But then Mrs. Sadowski smiled at me and said, "I used to love bananas and cream!" I didn't want to offer her the rest of mine, but it was her birthday, so I did. Even though I shouldn't have been, I was happy when she said no thank you, she couldn't eat such things anymore. Then she said to Mama, "Yvonne, you've barely touched your meal. Are you feeling all right?"

It seemed like Mama didn't hear her at first. Then she said she was fine and just wanted to save room for the birthday cake she'd heard was coming.

But when a lady—Mr. Sadowski said it was Ernie's wife, Molly—served us the cake, Mama only took one bite even though it was so good, chocolate with frosting that tasted like the inside of a Caramel Cream. Even Mrs. Sadowski ate her piece.

When we came out of the Twelve O'Clock Diner, it was snowing big, fluffy flakes spread way far apart in the sky. Mr. Sadowski offered us a ride home. "In fact," he said, "why don't you come back to our place? I'll put on some records and we can dance."

"What a wonderful idea!" Aunt Blanche said. "I haven't danced in ages! What do you say, Eddie?"

He put his arm around her and pulled her next to him like he was going to dance right there on the sidewalk. "Only if you'll promise me the first dance," he said.

She slapped him with her pocketbook and said, "If I must." But the whole time she was smiling.

Mr. Sadowski asked Mrs. Rasmussen if she'd like to come.

"Well, I haven't a partner," she said, "but I'd love to listen to the music."

"Stan will be your partner," Mrs. Sadowski said. "Won't you, Stan? I've never been much for dancing."

Mr. Sadowski must have been in a silly mood, because he took his hat off and bowed to Mrs. Rasmussen and said, "I'd be honored."

After that, everybody got quiet. Then Mama said, "I wish we could join you, but I'm a bit tired. I hope you all have a lovely time. And Magda, happy birthday again." She took Violet's hand and started to walk away. Papa said good night to everyone.

"But wouldn't Yvonne like a lift?" Mr. Sadowski asked him.

Papa said no. "The fresh air does her good. Thanks anyway." Then he took my hand and even after we'd caught up with Mama and Violet, he kept holding it all the way home.

When we got upstairs, he threw his keys on the hall table and said, "*Una bella serata*. It was good of Stan to include us."

"Yes," Mama said. We took off our coats and then, right away, she told us to get ready for bed. I washed and put on my nightgown, but while I was waiting for Violet, I stood in the door of our bedroom. I don't think they knew I was there.

Mama had put on her bedroom slippers and was sitting in the chair by the windows, leaning back with her eyes closed. "It must have cost Stan a small fortune," she said. "Meals for all of us, and that cake!"

Papa was standing near the windows, looking at her. "Stan's his own boss," he said. "No production cuts. No lay-offs. I bet he even has savings. And what else does he have to spend it on? He—" All of a sudden, he stopped talking.

Mama's eyes opened, and she stared at him.

I felt my skin prickle.

But he leaned over Mama and took her hand. "It was a long evening for you, *cara*," he said. "Maybe too much, too soon."

I didn't know what he meant, and I didn't understand what Mama said back either. "Doctor Cohen said it's over, and he's right. No bleeding at all today. It's over." She closed her eyes again. "Did you notice Blanche didn't take Communion?"

Papa didn't answer.

"Then again, she hardly ever goes to Mass anymore. Let alone Confession. And what a glamorous dress. You'd think we were dining at the Ritz. I can't say I approve of the cut, but the fabric! She didn't buy that at Woolworth."

Papa stroked her hand. Her eyes were closed, so she couldn't see that his face was sad. "You may not have glamorous clothes," he said, "but you're even lovelier than Blanche. I wouldn't trade you for anyone else in the world."

Mama opened her eyes and looked at him, and even though she didn't say anything, it was like she was talking to him with her eyes, and what her eyes said made him let go of her hand.

He went over to the radio and turned it on. "Let's sit and listen," he said. "The New York Philharmonic comes on at nine." He helped her up and they went to the sofa. That's when he saw me and said it was time to say good night.

After Violet and I were in bed, I asked her if she knew why Mama'd gone to see Doctor Cohen. She said no.

For a while, we listened to the radio. Sometimes we heard their voices, but mostly just the music. Then Violet fell asleep. I could tell because when I whispered to her, she didn't answer.

Mama's coughing again. I can hear Papa's footsteps, and water running in the sink. He's bringing her a glass. He's calling her *cara*. I hope someday a man as handsome as Papa tells me I'm beautiful and calls me *cara*.

A lady is singing. The Blessed Mother is floating on a cloud of smoke. She's smiling at me.

VIOLET

Papa's gone to New York.

He says he's looking for work. Whenever Sister Superior prays to Saint Isabel, she starts, "Blessed Saint Isabel, princess and patroness of the poor." I never really thought about that meaning us. Until yesterday.

It was Saint Isabel's feast day. That's always a special day at school, so I thought it would be a good day. At first it was.

Papa met us in the assembly hall after school. He'd gone to work, so I thought he'd left early to come. I wish I'd told him how happy I was he did. He sat between Glory and me and put one arm around each of us while Sister Superior gave a speech about our patron saint. Then two eighth-graders brought a basket around for donations. We were sitting next to Jimmy Conlan's parents and I saw Mr. Conlan take out his wallet and drop a bill into the basket. He handed it to me to give to Papa, and the whole basket was full of dollar bills. I held it out for Papa. He looked into it, then at me, and then he took out his wallet and he dropped in a dollar bill, too. After that we sang a hymn and had madeleines and tea in paper cups, and Glory and I took Papa to our classrooms to see our work.

We went to Glory's classroom first. Sister Colette was talking with Dorothy Pope's parents. We've never met them, even though Dorothy and Glory are friends, but we know what they look like 'cause Dorothy's father brings her and her sister, Louise—she's in fourth grade—to school every morning in his big red car and Dorothy's mother picks them up every afternoon in her little blue car. Dorothy's mother had her arm around Dorothy. It made me feel sad that Mama wasn't there. She wanted to come, but at breakfast she said she didn't feel well enough to walk to the school on such a cold day.

After she'd talked to Dorothy's parents, Sister Colette walked over to us and put her hand on Glory's shoulder. "Mr. Campo," she said, "the first time I saw Gloria, I thought of how much she takes after you."

Papa smiled a little when she said that. "In her coloring, yes," he said.

"And I'm sure in her intelligence. It must reflect your own."

"Well . . ." Papa looked down. "I'm a machinist, Sister Colette."

"As was my father," she answered.

Papa looked up again. "Is that right?" he said.

Sister Colette told Glory to show us the book of poems she's writing. It has a cardboard cover and string tied through holes on the side to hold the pages together. The cover says *Poems* in black crayon, and beneath that, *by Gloria Campo*. "It's not finished," she said. "It only has seven poems. A real book of poems has lots more. Edna St. Vincent Millay's has twenty-three."

"I like to let Gloria work independently," Sister Colette said. "As soon as she's finished her classwork, I allow her to read or write. I believe this collection is intended as a Mother's Day gift, isn't that right, Gloria?"

Glory nodded and put the book back in her desk.

"I'm sure your mother will be pleased to have it," Papa said. "And now we should say goodbye and let Sister Colette visit with the other parents."

Sister Colette reached out her hand. "You will give my regards to Mrs. Campo, won't you?"

"Of course," Papa said. "Of course." And then he and Glory followed me upstairs to the fifth-grade classroom. I thought Sister Bernadette would show Papa my paper about Eleanor Roosevelt, but instead she brought us to her desk and showed him my notebook of science drawings. "I bring objects into the classroom," she said. "Leaves, feathers, shells. And I challenge my students to observe. These are Violet's drawings, and I think they're exquisite." That's the word she used. I'll never forget it 'cause until then I'd never heard anybody say it about anything I'd ever done.

Papa took a long time looking at them, then he asked me, "You did all these?"

That's when I thought for sure it was a good day. I thought so all the way home, too, 'cause Papa walked between us holding our hands, and when we got to the top of our steps, he said, "I'm proud of you both."

But when we got inside, the look on his face changed, and when he put his keys on the hall table, they made a snapping noise.

I could smell meat cooking. We all hung up our coats, and Papa went into the kitchen. I heard him talking to Mama, and she came out to the parlor and told us to go into the kitchen and keep stirring the boiled dinner so it didn't stick to the bottom of the pot. We went into the kitchen and washed, but I told Glory to stir while I set the table.

I thought Mama might scold me for not staying in the kitchen, but she and Papa didn't seem to notice me. She was sitting on the sofa, and Papa in his chair, and he was telling her how nobody at Laval's had any more work until the State came through with the money. Mama asked him when Mr. Laval thought that might be.

"March 15th," he said. "They'd promised it by the first, but it got held up."

"How will we manage?" Mama whispered. She sounded scared. "The rent is due Friday." I put the silverware on the table quiet as I could.

Papa sounded like he does when he's trying to keep Glory from having a spell. "We'll manage. I'll give Tompkins half the rent and promise him an extra five dollars when I give him the rest."

"But by the time you get paid again—"

"I know, Yvonne!" Papa's voice got louder. "Do you think I haven't thought it all through myself? But we've lived here for twelve years! He's not going to throw us out!" He got out of his chair and sat beside Mama and put his arm around her. "I wish you wouldn't make everything a disaster, *cara*. We have a nice home, two talented girls—"

Mama pushed him away and walked past me into the kitchen. I heard her scold Glory for letting the potatoes stick to the bottom of the pot. Then I heard her coughing. Papa stared at the floor. I went back into the kitchen and filled four glasses with water and took them to the table.

Mama brought out the boiled dinner. There were carrots and onions and potatoes and big pieces of meat. As soon as Papa looked in his bowl, he asked Mama where she got the meat.

"Blanche dropped it by," she said.

I saw Papa clench his fist beside his plate, but he didn't say a word.

I was glad Aunt Blanche had given us the meat, especially since Mama's so skinny again. I asked if we could say grace, and then we started to eat. Except Glory just sat there staring at the middle of the table. Mama said, "Glory, I worked all afternoon to make this meal. I expect you to eat it."

She didn't move. So Mama said, "All right, then, go to your room."

But Papa reached across the table and tilted her chin up. "*Bambolina*—"

Before he could say anything else, Mama snapped at him. "Stop spoiling her! If she won't eat, she'll go without. Glory," she said, "go to your room right now."

I didn't want Glory to have to go without supper. "Try some," I told her. "It's good!"

But Mama got mad at me, too. "Be quiet, Violet! It's time you both stopped treating her like a baby!"

Papa got up. "Stop it, Yvonne!" he said. "This has nothing to do with her!"

And then they both started hollering, but at each other.

I didn't know I was going to, but I pulled Glory out of her chair and into our room and closed the door. They didn't follow us. They just hollered at each other for a long time. I told Glory not to listen, and we got into my bed and took turns reading *The Secret Garden* until they stopped. Then we put on our nightgowns and went to bed without washing or saying our prayers. For a while, I kept listening, but I didn't hear anything else. Glory fell asleep. I almost did, too, but then they started up again. This time they sounded like they were sad. Then I heard their bedroom door open and footsteps in the parlor and the bathroom and the hall. The front door opened and closed and everything got quiet. After that I guess I fell asleep.

When I woke up this morning, Glory was still sleeping. I went into the bathroom and opened the medicine cabinet. Papa's shaving brush and soap and cup were gone.

I dressed for school as quietly as I could and went out to the parlor. Nobody was there or in the kitchen. The door to Mama and Papa's bedroom was open. I went in. Mama was lying in bed. I went closer. She was holding the photograph of her and Papa on their wedding day. She wasn't looking at it, though, or at anything really. I went even closer. Her face and eyes were puffy. "Violet," she said, "you're up early."

I asked her if I could bring her some tea, and she said yes. Before I'd even left the room, she started to cough and cough, and when she stopped, she said I should go phone Aunt Blanche and ask her to come. When I went into the parlor to phone, Glory was sitting on the sofa. She heard me talking to Aunt Blanche, but she didn't say anything. She just watched me with her big black eyes. And when Aunt Blanche came in and took off her coat and boots and said good morning, she didn't answer.

Aunt Blanche went into Mama's room. I made two cups of tea and put them on a tray with sugar and milk and brought it in. Aunt Blanche set it down and said, "Your mama and I need to talk for a little while, dear. Help Glory get ready for school, and I'll ask your Uncle Eddie to drive you. Do you mind closing the door on your way out?"

Before I left, I asked them, "Has Papa gone to New York?"

Aunt Blanche looked at Mama, but she looked away. So Aunt Blanche nodded.

I went in the kitchen and made some scrambled eggs and toast. Glory only ate a little of hers, then said she had to get dressed. While I was doing the dishes, I heard Aunt Blanche let Uncle Eddie in. By the time I went out to the parlor, they were all in Mama's room again.

I went and stood near the door. Mama's voice was soft and hard to hear, but Uncle Eddie's was louder. "Looking for work. Right. As if New York's got jobs for the taking. We all know why he's—"

Aunt Blanche interrupted. "Eddie!" Her voice was like when you bang a spoon against metal.

Nobody said anything after that, at least not that I could hear, so Glory and I put on our coats and sat on the sofa.

The door opened and Uncle Eddie came into the parlor. "You two ready for school?"

While we put on our boots, I asked him why Papa had gone to New York.

Uncle Eddie is a lot taller than Papa, and when he throws out his arms like he did just then, it's like he fills the whole room. "You ever hear of kids running away from home?"

"Sure," I said.

"Well, when your father's angry, he gets this crazy idea in his hot Sicilian head to run away from home." He motioned for us to follow him downstairs. "You understand?"

I said I guessed so. He looked back at Glory and asked her if she understood, too. She shrugged. On the way to school, he whistled like the siren on a fire truck, and that made her smile a little.

When we went home at lunch, Mama heated up some boiled dinner. Glory said she was sorry she hadn't eaten last night, and finished her bowl. After school, we did our homework, then Glory read Mama a story she'd written about Sir Lancelot and his son with the folded ears, Sir Galahad.

When Aunt Blanche and Uncle Eddie came to make supper, Uncle Eddie said they'd met the Western Union man outside our building. He held the telegram out to Mama, but she told him to read it to her. "Arrived. Looking for work. Hope to send money soon." He looked up.

"Is that all?" Mama whispered.

"Afraid so," he said.

"And where was it sent from?" Aunt Blanche asked.

"East Harlem. See for yourself." He offered her the telegram, but she told him to give it to Mama and took the bag of groceries she'd brought into the kitchen.

"Imagine," she said when I followed her in.

"Imagine what?" I asked her.

She shook her head.

I still don't know what she wanted me to imagine.

VIOLET

Mama went back to the sanatorium today.

So now they're both gone.

Papa's been gone nine days. Every night before I go to bed, I make a mark on a paper I'm keeping under my pillow. Tonight there are nine marks.

Until today, Mama and Aunt Blanche and Uncle Eddie were all here. After work, Aunt Blanche would bring a bag of groceries and we'd make supper together. Uncle Eddie would come in his after-work clothes and bring beer and orange soda. When supper was ready, Mama'd come out from lying down. After supper, they'd all listen to the radio. Most nights when we fell asleep, they were still here.

Tonight we went to bed by ourselves. I'm not sure if Glory's awake or asleep 'cause she hasn't said anything since we came home for lunch.

When we walked in, Aunt Blanche and Uncle Eddie were here with Mama. They all had their coats on. Aunt Blanche told us Doctor Cohen said they had to take Mama back to the sanatorium. I don't think I felt surprised, and part of me was even a little glad 'cause Mama's been sick for a long time and at the sanatorium she'll get pink and plump like she was before.

Aunt Blanche said they should have left already, but Mama had insisted on waiting for us to get home for lunch first.

"I'm not supposed to," she said, "but—" She held out her arms. I hugged her, then kissed her cheek. It was hot and damp. I tugged at Glory, and she went up to Mama and kissed her cheek like I had. Then she pulled away, and she and Mama looked at each other for a long time, until Mama pulled her right into her coat. She looked at me over Glory's head. She blinked her eyes and I could tell she was trying real hard not to cry. "Violet," she whispered, but it was a loud whisper, like she was mad at me, even though I knew she wasn't. "You take good care of your sister." She looked straight into my eyes. "Promise me?"

I looked straight into her eyes, too, right into the middle where the gold spreads into the green. I told her I promised.

As soon as I said it, her eyes clenched shut and she pushed Glory away and started to cough, over and over, into the sleeve of her coat.

When the coughing stopped, Aunt Blanche and Uncle Eddie helped her up and through the door. I heard their footsteps stop partway down the stairs and Mama coughing again, and then I heard the front door bang shut. I tugged Glory to the windows. We watched them help Mama into the back seat of Uncle Eddie's car. They got in the front, and Uncle Eddie drove away.

We ate some bread and butter, and then we walked back to school. I thought Glory would ask me how long Mama would be gone or when we could go see her, but she didn't say anything at all. In the schoolyard, she got in her line and I got in mine and we went inside.

A long time after we got home from school, we saw Uncle Eddie's car park outside our building. He and Aunt Blanche came upstairs. Right away Aunt Blanche started fixing supper. While we ate, Uncle Eddie said that lots of people at the sanatorium had welcomed Mama back, and that she was going to get strong again. He drank two bottles of beer. But Aunt Blanche was quiet, and didn't put much on her plate, and as soon as she'd eaten, she picked up her dishes and went into the kitchen. When I went in with my dishes, she was standing over the sink crying. She wiped her face with her apron, then asked me how school was today. As soon as we'd finished the dishes, she and Uncle Eddie went home.

When I locked the door behind them, I felt like I couldn't move or even think, like there was nothing inside me. Then I saw Glory's eyes all big and black, just staring. So I asked her if she had any homework she needed to do.

She shook her head.

"Well, maybe you should do some anyway," I said, "and then Sister Colette might ask Sister Superior to move you up a grade."

I thought she might say that she likes Sister Colette and doesn't want to move. But she just went into our room and put on her nightgown and washed and went to bed.

I sat up and did my sentences in French, then my long division. Then somebody knocked. It was Uncle Eddie. When I opened the door, he bowed as if he was a servant and I was a queen, and gave me a tin lined with waxed paper. "May I request the pleasure of your company?" he asked. His voice was loud and he smelled like something stronger than beer.

I put the tin on the dining table.

"Raisin cookies," he said. "Freshly baked. Your aunt asked me to bring them." He took off his coat and boots and looked around. "Glory already in bed?"

"Yes," I said.

"What about you? Too tired for cookies?"

"I guess not," I said.

"Me neither," he said. "The night is young!" He pulled out a chair.

I went into the kitchen and got some milk, two glasses, and two plates. But after I poured the first glass, he covered the top of the other and winked. "Brought my own." He pulled out his flask and took a drink. I watched his Adam's apple go up and down. Then he put the flask back into his pocket and held out the tin of cookies. "My lady?"

I took one. I didn't feel much like eating, but I didn't want to talk, either. So I took a bite. It was still warm. I said it was good and to thank Aunt Blanche.

"Will do," he said. Then he asked me, "Your birthday's coming up, isn't it? How old will you be?"

"Eleven," I said.

His eyes got big like he was amazed. "I thought you were eleven already! Maybe even twelve!" Then, almost like it made him sad, he said, "You know, you look like your mother did right around the time I first knew her." Then he smirked. "Except for your nose." He reached out and almost swiped it, but I backed away. He went on talking. "In those days, she was the prettiest girl in town. Could have married any guy she wanted. Everybody loved her." He leaned right over me. "Everybody."

He was leaning so close I could see squiggly red lines in the white part of his eyes. They looked kinda like spider legs.

"When you grow up, my Vi, you think long and hard before you give your heart to some two-bit Romeo. Lots more important things than a handsome face. There's decency. There's character."

I picked at the crumbs on my plate 'cause I didn't want to have to keep looking at him.

He lifted my chin with his finger. "You understand?"

I said I guess so.

"Course you do. You're a smart girl." He settled back in his chair. "Your aunt and I would've given anything to have a girl like you."

He stared at me a long time across the table. Then he got out his flask again. His hands were shaky. He took a drink, then pushed himself up and went to the door. "You need anything tonight, or tomorrow morning before school, just give us a call." He pulled on his coat and boots. "Promise?"

"Promise," I said.

He bowed again. "See you tomorrow night, my lady." Then he was gone.

I locked the door and wrapped up the cookies and washed the dishes and went to bed.

I wish Aunt Blanche had come tonight instead of Uncle Eddie. 'Cause even though I told him I understood the stuff he said, I don't. And even though I don't, it still makes me feel bad inside. Everything about today makes me feel bad inside. Maybe like Mrs. Sadowski feels. Like somebody took my insides out.

GLORY

Papa is home and I have a doll.

I never had a doll before, except a cloth doll Mama sewed for me and stuffed with rags. This is a real doll, a baby doll like they sell in Woolworth, with painted-on brown hair and blue eyes that open and close and a blue dress with puffy sleeves and three underskirts and panties. I'm holding her tight because, when I fall asleep, I don't want her to get mixed up in the covers and not be able to breathe or fall on the floor and hurt her head. And I don't want her dress to get wrinkled or dusty. I want her to always stay as beautiful as she is right now.

I didn't know Papa was home or that I had a doll until I woke up in the night. The moon was shining in our bedroom window and Sir Lancelot was yowling out back, and all of a sudden I noticed I was holding something. I sat up, and I saw it was a doll. At first I thought Mama had come home and brought her, except Mama wouldn't come home in the middle of the night. So then I thought she was a present from Aunt Blanche.

Last night, she and Uncle Eddie stayed for a long time after we'd gone to bed. We could hear them talking in the parlor. Violet kept whispering to me to tell her what they were saying, because my bed is closer to the door than hers. One thing I heard was Uncle Eddie saying he wished Bert would answer the goddamn wire. I don't like it when Uncle Eddie swears or when he calls Papa "Bert," so I left those parts out. Violet said maybe Uncle Eddie had wired Papa about Mama going back to the sanatorium. A while after that, I heard Aunt Blanche say she was going to check on us and make sure we'd gone to sleep, so I whispered to Violet to close her eyes, and I closed my eyes, and we heard the door open, then Aunt Blanche told Uncle Eddie we were asleep, and they went home.

When I whispered to Violet that they were gone, she didn't answer, so I knew she'd gone to sleep for real. Until then, I'd been brave the whole day, ever since Sister Colette asked me to read aloud the morning prayer. When I read the part about God bringing us safely through the night and protecting us throughout the day, I felt all the sunshine in the room fill me up and I knew, I just knew, that God had kept Mama safely through the night and would watch over her all day, like the sunlight, and that He was protecting Papa and Violet and me, too. Sister Colette said I read so beautifully that I'd earned a star, and she drew a star on the card with my name on it at the front of the classroom. That's how I stayed brave all day.

But after Violet fell asleep, I started to think about Rose, the lady who coughed up blood and died. I thought about the blood spilling out of her mouth and onto the front of her dress. God must have been angry with Rose or He wouldn't have let her cough like that and die. Or maybe God was angry with Rose's mother, or maybe Rose's dead father had been a bad man and was in Hell and God wanted to punish him by making him watch Rose die. Then I wondered if God is angry with Papa because he skips Mass sometimes and doesn't go to Confession. Or maybe God is angry with Mama. I don't think so, though, because except when she's too sick, she goes to Mass every Sunday and makes her Confession every Friday and says her rosary every night before bed. Then I thought about how Violet is always so good, making supper and washing the clothes and all sorts of things, and lots of times I don't help because I'm reading or thinking up words that rhyme for my poetry book. So I thought, maybe it's me God's angry with, and that's why He's taken Mama away. After that I couldn't sleep for a long time, until finally I closed my eyes and told God I was sorry and that I'd help Violet get breakfast in the morning, and clean the kitchen and dust the parlor, and be kind and considerate, too, if that would help Him change His mind and let Mama come home.

And then I must have fallen asleep, and maybe God heard me and changed His mind a little bit, because the next thing I remember I was awake in the dark and holding my doll.

I heard water running in the bathroom and the gurgling Papa makes after he brushes his teeth, and then I knew he'd come home, and he must be the one who gave me my doll. He must have brought her home with him from New York. I looked at her in the moonlight, and I could see she was a baby girl and I could see her eyes open and close when I rocked her. I wondered if Papa had brought Violet a doll, too. But I didn't get out of bed to see. The only thing I wanted to do was hold my doll, and that's what I did, and I was still holding her when I woke up again and it was morning.

Violet was already up. I kept holding my doll while I put on my robe, and we went to the kitchen together. Violet was stirring something in a bowl, but as soon as she saw me, she stopped and her eyes got really big. "Glory!" she said. "Papa gave you a doll!" She put down the bowl and asked to see. But I couldn't bear to let anyone else hold her, even Violet, even for a second, so I just turned her so she could look.

"She's beautiful," Violet said. "What's her name?"

I told her Daisy, even though last night I didn't even think about her name. But that's because I didn't see until this morning she has five white daisies embroidered on the front of her dress.

Violet smiled at me and said that was a pretty name. So then I asked her if Papa had brought her a doll, too.

"I'm not real keen on dolls," she said. "Especially baby dolls. Besides, dolls are for kids like you. I'm almost eleven!"

I asked her hadn't Papa gotten her anything?

"I told Violet I've brought her something from New York, but she'll have to wait until her birthday. I can't afford to be giving her two presents." I didn't know Papa'd come into the kitchen until he said that. His hair was slicked back and shiny, and he was wearing a blue shirt I'd never seen before with his red scarf filling the space between the buttons at the top. Whenever I read the Nancy Drew Mystery Stories, I pretend Carson Drew looks just like Papa.

Even though I was still holding Daisy, I put my arms around him. "Thank you for my new doll, Papa," I said. "I missed you."

Papa said he missed me, too, and hugged me back.

Then I remembered about being helpful, so I asked him if he'd like me to pour him some coffee.

"No, thank you, Glory," he answered. "I've had breakfast. Now I'm going out to visit your mama. But Mrs. Rasmussen says to come downstairs for lunch." He let me go. "I'll be back before supper," he said. I followed him out to the parlor and watched from the windows until he turned at the corner of Mill Street and disappeared.

Violet cooked scrambled eggs, and I pretended to give some to Daisy. "Don't you think your grandpa is handsome?" I asked her. Violet was watching me, so I tilted Daisy backward and forward to make her blink.

"I wonder where Papa got the money to buy that doll," she said. "Or the present he says he has for my birthday. Or his new shirt."

A silly thought came into my head, and before I knew it was silly, I told Violet maybe he'd robbed a bank in New York.

Of course she said it was silly, because Papa didn't have a gun and wouldn't break the law to buy a new shirt and a doll.

"Probably Aunt Marcellina gave him one of Uncle Giacomo's shirts and got the presents for us."

I told Violet she was wrong. Maybe Papa'd found work like he'd planned, I said, or maybe Aunt Marcellina had given him the money, but I knew he'd chosen Daisy for me.

"How do you know that?" she asked me.

"I just do," I said. Then I told her Daisy and I would do the breakfast dishes.

She asked me if I was feeling okay.

I said I was feeling fine and was just trying to be helpful. Then I remembered the part about being kind, too. "Like you," I said.

Daisy kept me company the rest of the day. I introduced her to Mrs. Rasmussen, and to Aunt Blanche and Uncle Eddie. When Papa got home, Aunt Blanche told him Daisy was a lovely doll and asked him where he'd found her.

"I'd gone into Woolworth to get a cup of coffee," he said, "and I noticed it in a group of toys left over from Christmas. The price was right, and I decided Glory should have a doll."

That's how I know Papa chose Daisy for me. I held her up and told him that she wanted to know when she could meet her grandma. He said we'd have to wait for Mama's doctor to decide.

I don't think it's up to Mama's doctor. I think it's up to God.

Tomorrow I'll be kind and helpful all day. Then maybe God will change His mind the rest of the way and let Mama come home.

VIOLET

I don't care it's my birthday.

I don't want it to be.

Birthdays are supposed to be good days. Today started out good 'cause Papa gave me the present he brought from New York and we went to the sanatorium to see Mama. But then we didn't see her. Except from far away.

Why did Papa take us to see her at all? When he told us about it, I asked him if he was sure, 'cause Mama only left a few weeks ago, and last time she was there for months and months before she got better enough for us to see her.

"Of course I'm sure," he said. "And you'd better hurry, because you've got a birthday present to open before we go."

I gulped the rest of my breakfast and brought my dishes to the sink. Then Glory surprised me, too. "You get dressed, Violet," she said, "and Daisy and I will wash the dishes because it's your birthday."

So I made my bed and washed and put on my Sunday dress and my violets pin. When I came back to the parlor, Papa was already there. He called Glory, and she came out from the kitchen holding her doll. "Come watch your sister open her birthday gift." He gave me the box. "You'll have to send a letter to thank Aunt Marcellina and Uncle Giacomo, because it belonged to your cousin Enzo. They bought him a new one last Christmas, and gave me this one for you."

Enzo is a lot older than I am, and he's a boy, so I was excited to see the present. But when I opened the box, there was only another box inside. It was black, with three round holes and a strap at the top. I'd never seen a little box like that before, but it didn't look like much. I tried not to sound disappointed when I asked Papa what it was.

He said it's called a Brownie, and that it's a camera.

A camera! A happy feeling shot all through me.

I wondered if Glory would mind that I got a camera and she only got a doll, but she didn't seem to. She said she and Daisy were going to get dressed, and she went into our bedroom and closed the door.

Papa reached into his pocket. "This is a present from me," he said, and took out something small wrapped in yellow paper with writing on it. He said it was a roll of film, and that film is like a canvas that a painter paints on, but instead of the picture being made with paint, it's made with light. He said I had to be very careful to keep the paper cover on the film until I was ready to put it in the camera, 'cause if light got at it, it would be like spilling a whole can of paint on a canvas. I watched him take the key out of the side of the box, open it, and put the film inside. He showed me how to line up the film and start it and close the box and wind the key until I see the hand in the red window.

When the film was ready, he called Glory. Our bedroom door opened and she took one step into the hall. But when Papa told her I was going to take her picture, she said she didn't want her picture taken. He asked her why not. For a second, she didn't answer, and then she asked him real softly, "Does it hurt?"

"Don't be silly, *bambolina*!" he said, but not in a mean way. "Of course it doesn't hurt to have your picture taken. All you need to do is sit still!"

But she shook her head. "Somebody else go first!"

I said, "I know! I'll take a picture of you and Papa both!"

He brought Glory to the sofa and put his arm around her. One at a time, he told me all the steps for taking a picture, then he told Glory to hold still when I said "Ready" until I'd counted to four.

As soon as I said "Four!" Glory squirmed out of Papa's arms and ran over to the camera.

"Where's the picture?" she asked.

Papa laughed. I guess I forgot how nice it sounds when he laughs—it made me think that nothing could be bad today. He told Glory we have to send the film away to be developed after I use it all up. He said I could take five more pictures, and that I should bring the camera this morning and take a picture of Mama.

The doorbell rang, and Aunt Blanche came in carrying a basket. She smiled at me and tapped the sides. "Your birthday cake! And this afternoon, we'll go into town and you can choose some fabric and a pattern for a pair of those overalls you keep asking for."

I had a camera, we were going to visit Mama, and Aunt Blanche was going to make me a pair of overalls. I felt so happy that I jumped up and threw my arms around her and she would have toppled over if Uncle Eddie hadn't caught her.

"Happy birthday, my Vi!" he said. "What's that, a Brownie?" He picked up my camera.

When Papa answered, his voice didn't sound as happy as it had when we were alone. "It belonged to Violet's cousin," he said. "My sister gave it to me for her birthday."

"Lucky girl!" Uncle Eddie said. "Have you taken a picture yet?"

"One," I told him. "Of Papa and Glory on the sofa. But Papa says I can bring the camera today and take a picture of Mama."

When I said that, Aunt Blanche got a funny look on her face. But then Papa told us to put on our coats and boots and we went downstairs. We got in Uncle Eddie's car and everything felt just the same as last year except it was my birthday instead of Easter, and Glory had her doll and I had my camera.

When we got to the sanatorium, Uncle Eddie parked and we all went up the front steps and through the tall doors just like before. Papa went to the counter and spoke to the lady. She picked up her phone. While she was talking, she held up her hand to Papa like she was telling him to wait. Then she put down the phone and told him something that made him look at the long staircase. For a long time, nobody came up or down. But then the doors at the top opened and a short, round man in a white coat came down the stairs and waved his hand at Papa like he wanted him to follow him through the door behind the counter. So Papa did, and we all stayed where we were.

Glory asked where Papa had gone. I looked at Aunt Blanche. Her lips were pressed tight together and I thought at first she wasn't going to answer. Then she said, "He's talking with Doctor Murphy, your mama's doctor." She looked at Uncle Eddie, and he looked at her, and they didn't say anything else.

The door opened again, and Doctor Murphy went right back up the stairs. Papa looked at us a second like he didn't know who we were. Then he kinda shook himself and said, "Blanche."

Aunt Blanche walked over to him. They started talking, but so quietly I couldn't hear. She kept nodding, and then I saw her do something I never saw her do before. She put her hand on Papa's arm. He turned and went up the stairs, not fast like Doctor Murphy, but like he had to keep telling his legs how to go.

Aunt Blanche came back. At first, she just stood there. Then she said, "Girls." That was all she said. Then Uncle Eddie squeezed her shoulder, and she started again. "Girls, Doctor Murphy says your mama's not up to a visit today. But your papa has gone up to see her, and he's going to have her sit by the window so we can all wave to her from the grounds. And Violet." She looked at me. "You can take a picture if you like, of the building and of your mama in the window."

"That sounds like a fine idea!" Uncle Eddie said. His voice was even louder than usual.

I turned to Glory. I thought she might want me to hold her hand. But she was holding her doll. I whispered, "You okay, Glory?"

She kept looking down at her doll.

Then Uncle Eddie said, "Let's go, girls. Let's find your mother's window." He put his hand on my shoulder and we went out.

He led us around to the back of the building where there was open space with grass and a long path and a row of trees with bare branches. Aunt Blanche said they were apple trees and any day now they'd be thick with pink and white blossoms.

I wondered if Mama would be able to see the blossoms from her window. Or maybe she'd come for a walk and see them, if she was better than she was today.

Aunt Blanche stopped walking and shouted Mama's name.

I looked up. There were three rows of windows, and Aunt Blanche seemed to be waving at one in the top row. I could see shapes in front of the window—somebody's head and another person standing behind. So I waved and shouted, "Hello, Mama!" but I didn't know if she could hear me or if it was really Mama.

I looked at Glory. She was looking up, not at the window, but into the branches of the apple trees. "Glory," I asked her, "why don't you wave to Mama?" But she just stood there holding her doll and staring at the trees.

My hands were cold, but I turned the key in the side of my camera and wound the film and looked down. All I could see were the windows right in front of me. So I ran farther away and looked again. This time I could see right up to Mama's window above the apple trees. It was small and dark, but I held my breath and took the picture. Then I ran back closer. Something moved behind the window, maybe Mama's handkerchief or her sleeve, or maybe it was Papa's arm above her, waving to us. I couldn't see Mama's face. I shouted up real loud, "Mama! Mama!"

Why couldn't Papa bring her closer to the window, just for a minute? Instead he got smaller, and the moving behind the window stopped. I shouted even louder, "Mama! I miss you!" But then my voice stopped working, so I couldn't shout anything anymore, and even if I could have, there was nobody in the window to hear me.

GLORY

I have to go home now.

I can't start crying. If I start crying, God might think I wish I hadn't done it. And that's not what I wish. What I wish is that all the days until Mama comes home could be over, that it could be my birthday and she could come home all better and bring me a big box and I'd open it and inside would be a brand-new Daisy.

I thought of it at Mass. Uncle Eddie took us because Papa's gone back to the sanatorium. Father Bouchard's sermon was about the Ten Commandments, and how the first one was the most important of all. He said that not having any strange gods before the real God means we can't love money, or liquor, or our possessions more than God. He said we can't even love our country more than God, or our family. That made me think of Mama, and how I love Mama more than God.

I know I do.

Then I thought of how I love Papa and Violet more than God, and Aunt Blanche and Uncle Eddie, too, and Mrs. Rasmussen, and maybe even Mr. and Mrs. Sadowski. Then I thought about Daisy. After that, I couldn't look at Father Bouchard anymore. I couldn't, because I knew I even loved Daisy more than God.

I thought about her out in Uncle Eddie's car, waiting for me to come back. I'd wrapped her up in my old crib blanket so she'd be warm while we were gone. And then I thought of Mama sleeping at the sanatorium. She was probably all wrapped up in a blanket, too, out on the porch like when we visited her last Easter. Papa was probably there by now, and maybe God was angry at him for missing Mass again. I couldn't stop Papa from making a mortal sin, but maybe I could show God I was trying to love Him more than Daisy. I thought about it a long time, and just when Father Bouchard made the sign of the cross over the gold cup, I thought of what to do.

I couldn't let myself keep thinking about it, though, because I knew I had to do it and it made me feel like my heart had broken glass inside.

Violet and Uncle Eddie went to Communion. If Aunt Blanche had come to church, maybe she'd have put her arm around me and I wouldn't have started to cry. But I was alone, and I did cry—a little. Then I wiped my eyes with my handkerchief and prayed the Our Father in French. And when Violet and Uncle Eddie came back, I thought of how happy they'd be if what I did made God change His mind. How happy everybody would be. And that helped me feel like I could be brave enough to do it.

When we got back to Uncle Eddie's car, I held Daisy in her blanket right against my coat. That made tears prick my eyes again, so I looked out the window and tried to read all the words that went by without missing even one.

We had Sunday dinner with Uncle Eddie and Aunt Blanche. She was kind of quiet, and when Uncle Eddie said grace, she just stared at her plate. And even though she'd fixed a big roast and I only ate a little, she didn't seem to mind.

After we did the dishes, Uncle Eddie read the paper and Aunt Blanche helped us write a letter to Mama. When we finished, she told Violet to go back to our apartment and get the rest of her birthday cake and she'd make some tea. I said I'd go with her. I brought Daisy. And when we got here, I told Violet

I was tired and wanted to take a nap. So she left me alone with Daisy.

I went to the parlor windows and watched her go back inside Aunt Blanche and Uncle Eddie's. Then right away, before I could change my mind, I took Daisy out into the hallway and up the stairs past Mr. Owen's apartment and all the way to the top.

When I opened the door to the roof, the wind was blowing so hard it almost pushed me down, and the sky looked big and dark, like God was angry with me. So I stopped and closed my eyes and said the Act of Contrition. I tried to see God while I prayed, but He wouldn't let me. Even so, I knew He was watching and listening, so I told Him I was sorry I'd loved Daisy more than Him. I told Him I didn't know that until today. "Please forgive me," I said, "and forgive Papa for missing Mass today."

After that, I opened my eyes. I went up to the edge of the roof, the part over the alley so if there was anybody on Mill Street they wouldn't see. I got so close to the edge that the toes of my shoes touched the little ridge and I saw way down to the clothesline. That made me dizzy, so dizzy my legs felt jiggly and I had to step back. And then I looked at Daisy. I didn't mean to, and seeing her face made the broken glass prick my heart so hard I thought I might fall down, but I knew if I fell down I'd never do it. So I asked God to help me. And then I pushed my feet up to the edge again.

The wind blew around my legs, but I held Daisy out, past the edge of the roof, and squinted my eyes so I almost couldn't see her anymore. I took my left hand away so I was just holding her with my right hand around her waist. Then I lifted my fingers up one at a time until only my pointer finger and thumb were holding her. But even with God helping me, I couldn't get my mind to make my finger and thumb let go. Then a big gust of rainy wind blew all over me. It made me cough, and I thought of Mama coughing like Rose coughed with blood spilling out of her mouth, and all of a sudden my whole body shook all over, all the way up my arm and up to my hand and my pointer finger and my thumb.

And I let Daisy go.

VIOLET

I saw Mr. Owen's apartment today.

I wonder if Papa's ever seen it. I don't think so. I wish I could go out to the kitchen and tell him what it's like. But then he'd ask me what I'd been doing in Mr. Owen's apartment and I'd have to tell him about Glory's doll. And that would make him sad. And he'd want to know how it happened, and I'd have to say I don't know.

Even though maybe I do. My idea is, Glory thought she'd be kinda like Abraham when he almost sacrificed Isaac. Except Daisy is just a doll, so God didn't bother sending an angel to stop her.

When I got back from Aunt Blanche and Uncle Eddie's last night, Glory was already in bed. She looked like she'd been crying. I figured she was sad 'cause of Mama. Then I noticed she didn't have her doll. I thought holding her doll would help her feel better, so I asked her where it was. When she didn't answer, I told her I'd go find it. I looked in the parlor and the kitchen and the bathroom and Mama and Papa's room. I even went back to Aunt Blanche and Uncle Eddie's in case she'd left it there. But I couldn't find it.

By the time I got home, she was fast asleep.

When we got up for school, I asked her where she thought she'd lost her doll, but she still wouldn't talk. Not even at lunch or on the way home from school. And now she's in our room with the door closed.

I did my homework by the parlor windows so I could watch for Aunt Blanche to get home from work. Then I decided to go outside and wait. She was just turning down Mill Street. Mrs. Sadowski was getting her mail, and they started talking. Then Mr. Owen came out to the sidewalk and lit the lamp in front of our building. I said hello and sat on the steps and watched.

After he climbed down his ladder, he came over to me and said, "Violet, I noticed a funny thing this morning. May I tell you about it?"

I nodded.

"Well," he said, "I was having a cigarette out on the fire escape. I always look before I throw down my cigarette butt, just in case Mrs. Rasmussen's hanging out her wash or Sir Lancelot's down in the alley. Wouldn't want to catch his fur on fire!"

When I look at Mr. Owen, I try to just look at his forehead and eyes, so I don't have to see the missing part of his face. But even so, I could tell he was smiling.

"Well, I looked down," he said, "and that's when I saw something strange. Something that looked—not to frighten you, since it wasn't that at all—but it looked like a baby. I go out to the alley, and there's a doll with her head all smashed in. As if she fell there from out of the sky. And then I thought maybe I recognized that doll, thought maybe I'd seen your sister carrying her around." His eyes got sadder. "Did your sister lose her doll?"

I told him I hadn't seen it since yesterday. "I asked Glory if she lost it, but she won't say. Is it still in the alley?"

"No. Didn't seem right leaving her there, where a dog might find her, so I brought her back to my place and cleaned her up a bit. Would you like me to bring her to you?"

I nodded.

Mr. Owen walks funny, and when he climbs stairs, he has to take each one by itself. I thought about all the stairs he'd have to climb just to bring me Glory's doll, so I raced to the top step and told him I could get the doll if his door was unlocked and he told me where to find it.

"My door's not locked," he said, and fished his cigarettes out of his pocket. "You'll find the doll on my kitchen table, on the towel I dried her with."

I ran up the stairs. I'd always wondered what Mr. Owen's apartment looked like. But when I reached the top landing, even though I know he lives alone, I was scared to open his door. When I turned the knob and felt the door unlatch, I pushed it open just enough so I could peek through the crack. I couldn't see anything. I opened it a little more, then a little more.

It was exactly like our apartment, with a coat closet and the parlor windows looking out on the street and the kitchen off to the side. But it was completely different. Our parlor has a crucifix on the wall, and a mirror, and a painting of the Blessed Mother holding Baby Jesus. But Mr. Owen's walls are covered with so many things I couldn't count them all. One wall has bookcases all the way to the ceiling almost, every shelf full of books. Another has lots of masks. One looks like a hippopotamus and another like a crocodile, and one is a man with ears so big they hang down way past his chin. And everywhere else you look there's paintings—all kinds of paintings—of people and streets and boats in the water and fruits on plates—paintings on the walls and standing up in corners and even stacked on chairs, except for the two rocking chairs in front of Mr. Owen's parlor windows. And the wall in between.

There's only one painting there.

It's big—maybe bigger than I am—and it's of a lady. She has reddish-brown hair coming down past her shoulders, and creamy skin and blue eyes and lips that remind me of the inside part of a peach. She's dressed in a white dress, and she's sitting under a tree and her arms make a circle and the fingertips of her hands are just touching in her lap and the skirt of her dress is spread out all around her.

She's so beautiful, I wanted to look at her forever.

But then I remembered Mr. Owen was waiting.

I went into the kitchen. On the table, I saw a bright blue towel. On the towel was Glory's doll.

Mr. Owen was right. The head was all smashed in. One eye was open and the other was shut, and a crack ran down from where the hair was painted on all the way across the forehead to the open eye. While I was looking at the doll, the whole room got darker, almost like night, so I grabbed it and ran as fast as I could down the stairs and back outside.

Mr. Owen was sitting on the bottom step, stubbing out his cigarette.

"I found it!" I said.

He looked up at me. "And is that Glory's doll?"

"Yes," I answered. "Daisy. I don't know how it got this way, though."

"You have a doll, Violet?"

I told him I was too old for dolls.

His eyes looked like he was smiling again. Then he got up and lifted his ladder. "Good night!" He started to walk away, but then he turned and put his ladder back down. "You ever play with anything at all?"

"Papa gave me a camera for my birthday Saturday," I said.

His eyebrows went up. "Well, you be sure to use it. And happy birthday!" He picked up his ladder again.

This time I stopped him. "Mr. Owen?" I asked. It was hard to find the right words. "That picture in your parlor. The big one, between the windows. She looks like a princess—or an angel. Who is she?"

For a second, I didn't think he'd answer, 'cause his eyes looked like he'd gone someplace far away. Then he said, "You're exactly right about that. Some folks used to call her the Princess of Mill Street. But to me she was an angel. And still is. An angel named Ada."

I felt all shivery. But before I could think of what to say, he touched his hat and crossed the street and it was too dark to see him anymore.

"Violet!" Aunt Blanche came up behind me. "You've found Glory's doll!"

I gave it to her.

"However did this happen?" she asked.

I said I didn't know, but I thought we should hide it.

She nodded, and tucked it under her arm. "You go back inside before you catch cold. I'll be over in a few minutes and we'll have a nice supper." She turned to cross the street.

"Aunt Blanche?"

She looked back at me.

I wanted to ask if she'd ever been in Mr. Owen's apartment and seen the painting of Ada. And if she had, if it was Mr. and Mrs. Sadowski's Ada and if she was the same Ada Mama meant when she'd cry. Instead, I just thanked her for taking care of Glory and me. Then I ran inside.

A few minutes later, she and Uncle Eddie came over with two cans of carrots, a meat pie, and Uncle Eddie's beer. Aunt Blanche said she'd made the pie last night. "It's one of your uncle's favorites, and I know Glory likes it, too." We cooked the carrots while it warmed in the oven. It made the kitchen smell so good.

But Glory had only a couple bites of her supper before she asked to be excused. Aunt Blanche stroked her hand. "Don't you feel well, darling?" she asked.

Glory shook her head.

"You worried about your mama?"

"I guess so," she whispered.

Uncle Eddie told her Mama was getting the best care there is. "Tip-top! Doctors and nurses looking after her day and night." He drank the rest of his beer and opened another bottle. "More important, she's in God's hands."

Aunt Blanche looked at Uncle Eddie like she wanted to say something sharp to him, but instead, she just told Glory that Mama would want her to eat. That made Glory start eating again. When she finished, she thanked Aunt Blanche and asked to be excused.

"Of course," Aunt Blanche said. "Why don't you get ready for bed? Violet and I can manage the dishes." The word "dishes" seemed to make her come alive. She stood up and said, "I'll do the dishes!"

"Well, the rest of us haven't quite finished yet," Aunt Blanche said, "so why don't you just wash your own things?"

The way Glory answered, "Yes, ma'am," it almost sounded like she was disappointed.

After we'd eaten, Aunt Blanche made a plate for Papa and put it in the oven. While we did the dishes, she told me she didn't see how Glory's doll could be repaired. She said she'd go to Woolworth on Saturday and look for another. "I can't imagine," she said to me, "how the doll could have ended up in that condition." She finished rinsing the sink and looked at me. "You're sure you don't know how it happened?"

I told her I was sure. And that wasn't a lie, 'cause when she asked me, I hadn't thought yet about Glory and Daisy being like Abraham and Isaac. And anyway, I don't know if I'm right, and even if I am, did God tell Glory to sacrifice Daisy, or did she think it up on her own?

I wonder why God told Abraham to sacrifice Isaac. And why did Abraham almost do it? Maybe he thought it wouldn't be a mortal sin 'cause he was following God's orders. But what if the angel hadn't stopped him in time?

Sister Bernadette says if we knew everything God knows, we'd understand why He does the things He does. Still, if I could ask Him some questions, I would. Like why Mama had to get so sick I couldn't take her picture, or what Mr. Owen meant when he said Ada was an angel, and still is.

GLORY

Why did Papa ask God to forgive him?

I wish I hadn't woken up. Or that Violet was awake, too, so I could ask her what Papa meant. And she could hold me like she did this morning.

We've barely seen Papa for days and days. When we get up for school, he's already gone to work, and then he visits Mama and doesn't come home until after we're in bed. He did that today, too, even though it's Saturday, because of the job for the State and having to take a train and a bus to visit Mama. When I got up and went into the kitchen and Papa was gone even though it was Saturday, I told Violet I couldn't eat any breakfast. She put her arms around me and held me tight like Aunt Blanche does sometimes. Then she made me toast with butter and cinnamon and sugar, and after we did our chores, we went down to visit Mrs. Rasmussen.

She said she'd been expecting us and showed us a bureau scarf she's embroidering and said she'd teach us how to embroider. She took us to Woolworth and bought us each a handkerchief and two colors of embroidery thread.

While we were in line waiting to pay, we saw Aunt Blanche. She invited Mrs. Rasmussen to join us for supper.

We stayed at Mrs. Rasmussen's the rest of the afternoon working on our embroidery while she cooked tapioca pudding. Violet and I both made lots of mistakes at first and Mrs. Rasmussen had to help us take the stitches out. But we got our first corner done by the time we saw Aunt Blanche and Uncle

Eddie crossing the street. Aunt Blanche was carrying a big bag. On their way in, Uncle Eddie knocked on Mrs. Rasmussen's door and bowed and said would she do us the honor of joining us for supper? She laughed and told him she'd been making tapioca pudding for dessert.

Before we ate, Uncle Eddie said a prayer thanking God for our food and asking Him to take care of Mama and keep Mrs. Rasmussen's boys safe on the high seas. I didn't say it out loud, but I reminded God that I'd stopped loving Daisy and I'd helped Violet with our chores, and I promised to do the dishes after supper, too.

But when after supper came and I said I'd do the dishes, Aunt Blanche said it's a big job for one little girl and that everyone would help. Except for Uncle Eddie, everybody did, and I only got to dry the silverware. Afterwards, Mrs. Rasmussen said it was time for dessert, but Aunt Blanche said, "Wait, Esther! I have a little surprise for the girls."

Then Violet took my hand like she knew all about it and led me to the sofa and we sat down. Aunt Blanche came from the front hall with the big bag. She took out a flat box and held it out for Violet. It was wrapped in paper like a birthday present, even though it wasn't Violet's birthday anymore. She told Violet, "Since we never got to town last week to buy fabric for your overalls, I went ahead and chose some ready-made for you. I hope you like them."

Violet unwrapped the box and took out a pair of light green overalls and two shirts to wear underneath. They don't have any flowers or anything, so I don't think I'd want to wear them. But I guess Violet likes them, because she jumped up and ran over to Aunt Blanche and hugged her.

While she was still holding Violet, Aunt Blanche looked at me. Her eyes were sparkly, like she might be going to cry.

"And now it's time for your present, Glory." Violet sat beside me again, and Aunt Blanche pulled another box out of the bag. It was wrapped in paper, too.

Looking at the box gave me the prickly feeling. "But Aunt Blanche," I said, "my birthday isn't till July."

"That's all right," she said. "This is a hard time with your mama away, and when I saw this at Woolworth, especially since your baby doll seems to have disappeared, I thought you might like it."

Her saying that made the prickly feeling get even stronger, and when I lifted the tissue paper inside the box, everything inside me started breaking apart. That's because I saw the most beautiful doll in the whole world. She has real hair, not painted on like Daisy's, in golden curls all over her head. Her eyes open and close and have real eyelashes, and her dress is pink with little blue flowers and white lace around her collar and sleeves, and socks made of lace, and real shoes. On the front of her dress there's a pin with a photograph. It says her name is Shirley Temple. I looked at Aunt Blanche. "She looks like a real little girl," I said. "She even has her own name. It's Shirley Temple."

"That's right!" Aunt Blanche looked from me to Violet. "Don't you girls know who Shirley Temple is?"

And then I remembered Dorothy Pope at school saying she and her sister had gone to a picture show starring a little girl called Shirley Temple. So I asked Aunt Blanche if Shirley Temple is in pictures, and she said she is and that she'd take us to a Shirley Temple picture next time one's playing in town. But I almost didn't hear her, because I was thinking so hard about what to do. I knew I couldn't keep Shirley Temple, because I knew I already loved her more than I love God. And I couldn't drop her off the roof. Even if God wanted me to. I knew I couldn't. She was too beautiful. So I put her back in her box and covered her with the tissue and the lid and gave her back to Aunt Blanche. "Thank you for buying her for me," I said, "but I can't keep her." And then I went to my room and closed the door.

After that, they all started talking. I didn't want to listen, and I didn't want them to hear me crying, so I pressed my face in my pillow. In a little while, somebody turned on the radio. The music reminded me of angels playing their harps. That helped me stop crying and talk to God. I asked Him if He'd made Aunt Blanche buy Shirley Temple to test me. He didn't answer. Even so I told Him I hoped He was pleased with me and would let Mama come home soon. Then I put on my nightgown and got under my covers and I guess I fell asleep.

And then I was awake again and the front door was opening. I heard Papa's keys on the hall table, and the closet door open and close. There were footsteps outside our bedroom, and the door creaked. I closed my eyes tight. The footsteps came into our room and stopped. I'm not sure how, but I knew Papa was standing near my bed. Then I heard a sound like something heavy on the floor. I let my eyes open the tiniest bit, and I saw Papa there. He was sort of kneeling, but it didn't look like he was praying. It was more like a crumpled-up kneeling, with one hand touching my bed and the other touching Violet's, and his eyes staring at the wall. And then he squeezed his eyes shut and I heard him whisper, "God, forgive me. Forgive me. Have mercy upon me." But it wasn't a praying whisper. It was a begging whisper, like he needed God and hated Him all at the same time. After that, he whispered something long in Italian. Then he got up and went out. The light in the parlor went off and I heard the door to his room close.

Why do Mama and Papa both need God to forgive them? And why did Papa ask God for mercy? Because Mama's still sick?

He doesn't know I gave Daisy to God. If he knew, maybe he wouldn't be so sad.

I wish I could tell him. But I don't want him to think I didn't love Daisy.

I know. I'll tell him as soon as God sends Mama home.

VIOLET

I'm awake.

It's dark in our room, but not nighttime, 'cause I can see the edge of the window shade. The phone is ringing. Papa answers. I can't hear the words. I hear him put the phone down, then pick it up again and dial. The only word I hear is "Blanche."

My heart beats hard. I hear Papa moving. He goes out.

It's quiet.

Mr. Owen comes down the stairs.

The light at the edge of the window shade is spreading onto the wall.

I hear voices on the stairs. Aunt Blanche and Mr. Owen. Our front door opens and closes. I get up. I put on my robe. Glory is sleeping.

I go out. I see Aunt Blanche in the chair by the parlor windows. She's staring at the street. Tears are running down her face. She hears me and looks up. When she reaches out her arms, I don't move. She says, "Darling." She stops. She says, "Your uncle's taken your papa back to the sanatorium." She sounds like she's choking. "Violet. Darling. Your mama died in the night."

What does she mean?

Mama didn't die.

Mama is sleeping under her blankets on the sanatorium porch, or sitting by the window in her room looking at the blossoms on the apple trees.

Somebody died in the night, but not Mama. I'd know if it were Mama.

I'd know.

Aunt Blanche isn't in the chair anymore. She's pulling me into her arms. She's rocking me back and forth and crying and saying she's so sorry, darling, so sorry. She smells like Aunt Blanche always smells, like gardenias.

Not like lavender.

Not like Mama.

Because Mama died in the night.

Our bedroom door opens. I see Glory.

GLORY

I see Violet.

Why is Aunt Blanche holding her?

Why are they staring at me?

Aunt Blanche's face is all wet. It looks like Mama's after she and Papa fight, but it's not Mama's face because Mama is dead.

They're not saying it. They're not saying anything.

But Mama is dead.

I hear screaming.

The floor breaks open. I fall down down down.

My face stings.

Gardenias.

Mama is dead.

Aunt Blanche slaps Glory.

She goes limp like a doll. Aunt Blanche carries her into the bedroom. She puts her in bed and strokes her hair and tells her to close her eyes and sleep. But she just stares. Aunt Blanche tells me to watch her while she makes some tea.

I get dressed and sit on Glory's bed and hold her hand. I tell her I'm here, and that everything will be all right.

I try not to think about Mama. About whether she coughed up blood like Rose or just went to sleep and didn't wake up, or if a doctor or a nurse was there, or if she knew a few minutes or an hour or a day before it happened that she was dying and had a chance to say goodbye to Glory and me in her mind.

Aunt Blanche brings a tray of tea and toast. She touches Glory's cheek. "Glory," she says. "Do you understand what's happened?"

Glory blinks.

"Your Mama died last night."

Glory's eyes fill with tears. They spill out onto her face. She doesn't say anything. She doesn't make any sound at all.

Aunt Blanche gets out her handkerchief and dries Glory's face. "I'm sorry I slapped you, darling," she says. "I hope you know how much I love you." She looks at me. "How much I love you both."

Glory does something strange. She sits up and touches Aunt Blanche's face. She says, "I love you, too." It's just a whisper, almost like she's scared to say it. She turns to me. She talks a little louder. "And I love you, Violet." Then she stares straight ahead. "With all my heart," she says, like she's talking to the air. It makes me think of Uncle Eddie playing poker, when he puts down lots of chips and dares Sergeant McGowan and Tiny Bly to bet against him. Then she takes the cup of tea Aunt Blanche gives her and says that, if Aunt Blanche hasn't already promised Shirley Temple to somebody else, she'd like to have her after all. Aunt Blanche brings the box from the parlor. Glory holds Shirley Temple with one arm and has her toast and tea.

I ask Aunt Blanche when Papa and Uncle Eddie will be home. She says she isn't sure, since they have a lot of arrangements to make. We finish eating. We're putting the dishes back onto the tray when the doorbell rings. It's Mrs. Rasmussen and Mr. and Mrs. Sadowski.

Mrs. Rasmussen's carrying a basket covered with a cloth. She looks at us and starts to cry. She and Aunt Blanche hug. Then she shakes her head like she's trying to shake the tears away. "Coffee cake," she says, and takes the basket into the kitchen.

Mr. and Mrs. Sadowski have an Easter lily. They give it to Aunt Blanche. "Stan and I hope this will be comforting," Mrs. Sadowski says. "A reminder of the resurrection."

"How thoughtful," Aunt Blanche says. "Please sit down." She looks for a place to put the lily.

"I'll take it," Glory says. She pushes Shirley Temple into my arms and carries the lily into the kitchen just as Mrs. Rasmussen comes out.

They all sit down in the parlor. I don't sit anywhere. I don't want to sit. I want to go into Mama and Papa's bedroom to see if maybe looking at Mama's face in her wedding picture will help me believe she's gone. Because everything feels the same as it always does. Everything—even Glory having a spell, and Mrs.

Rasmussen bringing coffee cake—everything feels ordinary. Like Mama's still alive.

I don't even feel sad. I don't feel anything at all.

No one says anything. Then Mrs. Sadowski looks at me and tells me Glory and I are being very brave.

Glory comes out of the kitchen. She takes Shirley Temple back and holds her right up against her cheek.

Mrs. Sadowski tells us our mother's in heaven now. "You know that, don't you?"

I don't answer. I can't picture Mama anywhere but in her room at the sanatorium, looking out over the apple trees.

Glory doesn't answer either.

Mr. Sadowski stands. "Well, Magda and I just wanted to give you our condolences. We'll come by again later on. In the meantime, anything you need, you let us know."

Aunt Blanche goes with them to the door. When she sits down again, she looks at Mrs. Rasmussen. "I'd just as soon you stay a while, Esther," she says. "Until the men get back. If you don't mind."

"Of course I don't mind," Mrs. Rasmussen says. Everybody's quiet again.

There's a car in the street. Glory crosses to the parlor windows and holds up her doll. "Look, Shirley," she says. "That's Uncle Eddie's car. And that's Uncle Eddie and Papa getting out. Wave to Papa, Shirley!" She lifts her doll's arm. "I'm sure they'll be happy to meet you. Mama would have been happy to meet you, too. But she never will, because God killed her."

Mrs. Rasmussen gasps. She says, "Now, Glory, God didn't kill your mother!"

Glory spins around. "Yes, He did!" she shouts. "And Shirley and I know it!" She runs into our bedroom and slams the door.

I follow her. She's sitting on her bed with her arms around her doll. She shouts at me to go away and leave her and Shirley alone. I don't. She picks up our book of Edna St. Vincent Millay's poems and throws it at me.

It hits my arm. I pick it up and put it at the bottom of her bed. She doesn't say she's sorry. She just looks at me. I hear Papa's and Uncle Eddie's voices in the parlor. I walk out.

Papa is sitting with his hands almost covering his face. Uncle Eddie is telling him he'll go see Father Bouchard after Mass gets out. "I'll take care of the plot," he says. "There's space next to their parents."

Papa looks up. His face moves like he wants to talk, but he doesn't.

"Father Bouchard will ask about it," Uncle Eddie says.

Papa leans his face on his hands again.

Mrs. Rasmussen gets up and says, "Why don't I make everyone some coffee? Violet, would you show me where things are?"

I go into the kitchen ahead of her. There's dirt on the floor. It isn't much, a little clump near the can of scraps for Mr. Zina's pigs. I open the can. Inside are white Easter lily petals and twisted threads and pieces of stems and leaves.

I hear Mrs. Rasmussen behind me. "Never mind," she says. She takes the lid out of my hand and puts it back on. "Never mind." She squeezes my shoulder. "Now—where's the coffee pot?"

I don't think about the lily. I don't think about Mama. I show Mrs. Rasmussen the coffee pot and coffee and sugar bowl.

I take plates out to the parlor.

Papa is on the phone. He's talking in Italian. "*Grazie*," he says. Thank you. "*Certo*." Sure. Then he says some words I don't know. He says them again, then, "*A presto!*" Goodbye. He hangs up.

Uncle Eddie is walking behind him, frowning. "What was that all about?"

Aunt Blanche gets up and pulls on his arm.

Papa stares at the phone. "Marcellina and Giacomo are coming to the funeral. Enzo, too."

"What else?" Uncle Eddie shakes his arm free. "What's so *certo*?"

Aunt Blanche says, "Eddie—"

"She's invited me and the girls to come live with them." His voice is soft and he's looking at Aunt Blanche. "There's more work in New York. Better pay. When I was there last month—"

"You son of a bitch!" Uncle Eddie's voice is so loud I shake inside. "Why don't you go right now! Pack your bags and get on the next train!" He pushes Aunt Blanche away and shouts in Papa's face. "But you're going alone! The girls are staying with Blanche and me, and you and your girlfriend can go to hell!"

Why is Uncle Eddie calling Aunt Marcellina Papa's girlfriend when everybody knows she's his sister?

Now Mrs. Rasmussen is in the parlor and she and Aunt Blanche are shouting at Uncle Eddie to stop.

He doesn't stop. He says Papa sent money to his girlfriend instead of providing for his family. He says he broke Mama's heart and she should have left him years ago. He says, "All those visits to your sister in New York! Who did you think you were fooling? We all knew you went to see Ada!"

"Mr. and Mrs. Sadowski's Ada?" It's Glory's voice. Everybody looks at her.

Nobody answers.

Aunt Blanche sinks onto the sofa like she can't stand up anymore. "How could you?" she whispers. I guess she means Uncle Eddie, 'cause she's looking at him. "With the girls here and their mother barely cold. How could you?"

He doesn't answer.

"Eddie." Mrs. Rasmussen sounds like Sister Superior. "You owe Roberto an apology."

He just stares at Papa.

Aunt Blanche talks instead. "Roberto," she says, "my husband won't apologize, but I will. You're the girls' father, and you can do as you like. Still . . ." She looks at me, and then at Glory. "I think it would be cruel to take them away from everything they've always known. At least—at least for a while."

When Papa answers, his voice is soft. "I only said I'd think about it." He walks over to Glory, picks her up, and holds her.

She puts her arms around his neck and talks into his ear, but I hear her. "Isn't Mama ever coming back?"

He nuzzles her face. "No," he says. "No, *bambolina*, she—" His voice stops. He puts her down and goes into his room.

Uncle Eddie watches until the door closes, then looks at Glory. His face is still angry, but he says, "Your Mama is in heaven now. With God. And happy."

Glory frowns. "How could she be happy with God when He took her away from us? Why doesn't she hate Him? I do!" she shouts. "I hate Him!" She runs back to our bedroom. Aunt Blanche follows her, then me. She's on her bed, holding her doll and crying. Aunt Blanche sits next to her and tells her it's okay to be angry about Mama dying. She says she's angry, too. But at her sickness. "I don't believe God had anything to do with it," she says.

I wonder if Glory knows what she means. I don't.

I go out to the parlor. Uncle Eddie is pouring something from his flask into his coffee. Mrs. Rasmussen gives me a cup. "Take this to your father," she says.

I knock on Papa's door and ask him if I can come in.

He makes a noise. I turn the knob and go in. He's sitting in front of the bedroom window, but the shade is down. "Papa?" I say. "I brought you some coffee."

He doesn't answer.

I put the coffee on Mama's dressing table. "Papa?"

"Yes?"

"May I borrow your wedding picture?"

He nods.

I take it and go out.

I go back to my room. Aunt Blanche is pulling down the window shade. She puts her finger to her lips and points to Glory. She's asleep, holding her doll. I take the picture to the window and lift the shade a little. I hold the photo so Aunt Blanche can see. The sunlight makes everything that's white in the picture glow—not Papa 'cause he's standing in the shadows behind Mama's chair and he's wearing a dark suit with a dark tie. But Mama is sitting in the light. Her whole face glows, and the veil over her hair, and her white dress and gloves, and white roses.

I look at her a long time. I see her pretty eyes, and her mouth smiling a little, and how one gloved hand is holding the roses, and the other is next to her shoulder, holding Papa's hand.

I guess I must be crying because her face and her dress and her hands all come apart till they're just shapes of light, moving and sparkling, and I can't see Mama anymore.

GLORY

Mama isn't in the box.

That's what Aunt Blanche said on the way to the cemetery. She said to remember when they put the box in the ground that the only thing inside it is Mama's body, left behind like a worn-out coat.

I asked her, if Mama's not in the box, where is she?

She said nobody really knows.

Uncle Eddie was driving us—Papa was in the long black car with the box—and he snapped at Aunt Blanche. "What do you mean, nobody knows? Of course we know. Yvonne was good and kind—and nobody could question her faith. She's in heaven. No doubt about it."

"That's what you believe," Aunt Blanche said quietly.

"It's not what I believe!" he shouted. "It's what I know!"

Aunt Blanche didn't say anything else.

When we got to the cemetery, Father Bouchard read some prayers, then they started putting the box in the hole. I tried to imagine the only thing inside it was Mama's old winter coat. I tried, but I kept seeing Mama inside the box and worrying she couldn't breathe. Then I saw some sparrows flying above the box on their way in and out of some bushes, and I got afraid that a sparrow might have flown inside the box and couldn't breathe, and then I couldn't breathe either, and I started falling into the hole. Violet pulled me against her and told me not to look. So I closed my eyes and in my mind I made a picture of Mama wearing a new coat. It was a coat of brown and white feathers, and I made her a matching cap and gloves and shoes. And then I turned her into a sparrow, and I made her fly away with all the other sparrows, away from the hole and Father Bouchard and the men with the ropes and shovels, up and up into the sky.

After we got home, I wanted to go to my room and write about the sparrows, but Papa said Violet and I had to stay in the parlor because everybody wanted to see that we were all right.

After a while, Father Bouchard drove Aunt Marcellina and Uncle Giacomo and Enzo to the train station, and Mr. and Mrs. Laval went home, and Doctor Cohen, and the man with the ripped-up face. Then Mrs. Sadowski said it was time for them to leave, too, but before they did, she had a present for us. She reached into her pocketbook and took out two little boxes and gave one to Violet and one to me. They were exactly the same. A little gold cross on a chain to wear like a necklace. "You can wear yours when you make your first Communion," she said to me. "I gave my Ada one just like it on her first Communion day."

Violet said thank you, but I didn't, because I don't want the cross and I don't care about first Communion. Instead, I told her I'd like to meet Ada someday if she visits from New York.

She stopped moving, as if she'd frozen. It was just for a second, and when she unfroze again, she didn't seem angry with me. She just asked me, softly, "Now Glory, what makes you think Ada is in New York?"

I didn't have a chance to tell her that's what Uncle Eddie said the day Mama died, because she kept on talking, but louder, like she was talking to everybody in the parlor, not just to me. "Ada's not in New York," she said. "How marvelous it would be if she were. But Ada died seven years ago. Eight this November."

Mrs. Rasmussen crossed herself and said, "God rest her soul."

But I don't think Mrs. Sadowski heard her, because she kept on talking. "And I miss her as much as the day she died. Sometimes I think even more." Then she took Mr. Sadowski's hand and they left. I went over to the parlor windows and watched them walk down the street to their house. It looked lonely, like nobody was waiting for them there.

Will I miss Mama more in eight years than I do right now?

I hope not.

Or maybe I hope I do. What if I stop missing her? Will that mean I don't love her anymore?

I hope I'll miss her forever. More, even, than Mrs. Sadowski misses Ada. Every time I see a sparrow, I'll think of her. Tonight, I'll write a poem about a sparrow, and put it in the book I made her for Mother's Day. It will be the very last poem.

PART TWO

APRIL 1946–AUGUST 1948

VIOLET

Glory's missing.

The telephone rang while I was drying the supper dishes. Papa answered in the parlor. I heard him say, "No, she's away at college." Then he shouted to me that it was the housemistress from Norcross and to pick up the extension. When I got on, I heard her explaining that Glory has been missing since Sunday. It was all a bit complicated, she said, because on Thursday night, her suitemates had come home and found that Glory had taken all her things and left a note for them saying she'd moved out. The housing office confirmed that she'd applied for a new placement, but they'd told her it might take several days. She spent that night through Sunday afternoon with her friend Beatrice, who's in another dorm. On Sunday, she dressed up to go out and told Beatrice not to wait up. Beatrice hasn't seen her since. She said that Glory had hinted at some sort of trouble between her and one of her suitemates, Jean, but when the housemistress asked Jean about it, she claimed the two were the best of friends. And neither of her other suitemates knew why Glory'd moved out either. All anyone knew was that Glory hadn't been seen anywhere on campus for the last two days. But before she informed the campus police, the housemistress said, she needed to ask if Glory had other relatives, or close friends, or—here, she hesitated—a boyfriend she might be staying with.

Papa protested. "Glory's not that kind of girl!"

The housemistress paused, then asked if I knew of anyone she might be with. I said no, that she didn't share much of her campus life with me.

"That's all right," the housemistress said. Her voice was kind—and calm. "Listen, I doubt there's anything seriously wrong. My guess is she did have a quarrel with her suitemate and now she's cooling off somewhere, not realizing that people are worried about her. These things happen more often than you'd think. I'll get back in touch just as soon as I find out anything more. Try not to worry."

We said goodbye and I got back to the dishes.

I'm not afraid for Glory. Just annoyed. Of course she's with her boyfriend. Though I have no idea of his name. I overheard a conversation between her and her friend Dorothy when she was home on spring break. I admit I'm still hurt that she talked about him with Dorothy and not with me. Still, if she hasn't shown up by tomorrow, I guess I could swallow my pride and call Dorothy and ask if she knows who Glory's boyfriend is— and where.

Then again, even if she's staying with him overnight, why would she miss two days of classes—jeopardizing her scholarship at Norcross? How many people like us even get into a place like that, let alone on scholarship? I'll never forget Papa waving the letter in the air. "On the strength of your academic achievements and impressive manuscript . . ." After everything she'd put us through—her late nights, her refusal to go to Mass or Confession—after all those horrible quarrels when Papa seemed close to despair, she'd pulled it off, a full scholarship to Norcross, a ticket to a life of culture and refinement. Just what she'd always dreamed of.

And me? My ambition had been so much simpler. A nursing program at our local hospital. And I hadn't managed even that. It wasn't the academics. I've always been able to apply myself when I put my mind to it—bones, muscles, diseases, drugs. And even though I wasn't wild about drawing blood or changing catheters, I loved working with patients. I just couldn't stand the doctors! Especially Pixton. One morning I promised myself that if he called me "Girl" again, I'd ignore him. An hour later, I was giving an elderly patient a sponge bath when he shouted at me from beside another patient's bed. "Girl!" I didn't respond. "You! Girl! Come clear away Mr. Lindemann's tray." I finished the sponge bath, settled the patient back in his bed, gathered my basin and towels, and walked out. That afternoon, my supervisor called me into her office and put me on probation.

On my way home, I stopped off at Mr. Crane's camera shop to pick up some film. He had an advertisement in his window for a clerk. I've been there three years now. A shop clerk and, when Mr. Crane delegates, an assistant photographer.

While Glory is skipping classes at Norcross.

I hung the dishtowel to dry and went back to the parlor. Papa was standing at the windows staring into the street. He looked almost afraid.

"Don't worry, Papa," I said. "I'm sure she's perfectly fine. And you should know—she does have a boyfriend. I overheard her saying something about him to Dorothy Pope last month. So most likely—"

He spun toward me. "What are you saying? That she's sleeping with him?"

"I'm not saying anything!" I tried to stay calm. "Because I don't know. But if she's still missing tomorrow, I'll call Dorothy and ask her if she knows who this boyfriend is and how to reach him."

"I swear, if she's—"

"Papa," I pleaded, "let's not jump to conclusions. Is there anything I can do tonight to help? Phone Aunt Blanche and Uncle Eddie, let them know?"

He shook his head. "Nothing they can do. Besides, if she *is* sleeping around . . ." He looked out into the street again. "That stays in our family."

Eventually, I got him to sit down and put the radio on. We both pretended to listen. At eleven, we said good night and went to bed. It must be past one now. I wonder if Papa's asleep.

If Glory's asleep.

Again, I'm not worried.

But if only she'd call. Just call.

GLORY

Overwrought, platitudinous nonsense!

Break free of your romantic tendencies! You are far too enchanting for such tricks!

Dear Professor Turner, go to hell. To hell.

Honeycomb and oil . . . her steps take hold on hell.

Thou shalt not kill. In Mission Hill.

A growth. A few cells. That's all. A pea.

Your pea. Ruler to subject. *Sorry, kid, not my problem. How do I even know it's mine?*

Not his problem, kid. Your womb, your problem.

Here, take it. Do it right.

In Mission Hill, thou shalt kill.

Fuck you, Jeremy. Boston Brahmin Jeremy. Blue blood pure-bred thoroughbred snake.

That's all. Some cells. Don't talk. Don't tell. A little purple pea. Girls like you need me.

Need you. Don't talk. Won't talk. Won't tell.

Don't tell Papa. Can't tell Papa. Papa—Papa—

Jean. Don't tell Jean.

Jean, Jean, rich as a queen.

Rich and mean. I should have foreseen. Jealous Jean.

Mama, I'm sorry, sorry . . . *et pardonne-nous nos offenses . . .*

Very much in need of further discipline!

Vi, where are you?

Mama's disappointed in me, Vi.
Vi, Vi, better than I!
Where are you, Vi?

VIOLET

I found Glory.

Or rather, a nurse phoned and told me where she was. And now she's here, asleep in her bed. It's funny. Last September, I missed her so much. But now, all I want is for her to be back at Norcross again.

When I woke this morning, my first thought was that no one had phoned during the night. I couldn't just go off to work with Glory missing, so I made a plan. I'd call Mr. Crane, drop Papa off at work, then go see Dorothy. If she couldn't help, I'd drive to Boston and talk to Glory's friends. I got up and put on a pot of coffee.

The phone rang.

I expected the housemistress, but the caller identified herself as Irma Bond, a nurse at Boston Community Hospital. She asked for me by name. She said that Glory had shown up in the emergency room on Monday night, incoherent. That she had no purse, no identification, and had only now come to her senses enough to tell them who she was and ask them to phone me.

"Will she be all right?" I asked.

"Yes. She's still somewhat confused, but she's recovering. The surgeon was able to stop the bleeding."

"Surgeon? What bleeding? Why?"

She paused, then asked gently, "How old are you, Miss Campo?"

"Twenty-two. Why?"

"It was uterine bleeding. Not menstruation. Hemorrhage. Her dress and even her coat were soaked."

"Uterine?"

"Yes." She paused. "In these situations, it's not uncommon. And sometimes worse."

Her words made no sense to me. Or maybe they did, and I couldn't accept it.

She went on. "Sometimes the woman dies."

I felt a flood of panic. "But Glory's all right?"

"Yes. She got lucky."

Lucky?

"The surgeon even thinks she'll still be able to have children."

Finally, I understood.

I asked if I could speak with her, but she told me Glory needed to rest. "Will you be coming today?"

"Yes. This morning."

"You know where you're going?"

"I have a map," I said. "I'll find it."

Papa came into the kitchen. I told him Glory was in a hospital in Boston.

"What's happened? Was there an accident?"

"Yes," I said. I didn't hesitate. If he found out the truth, he might forbid Glory from ever coming home. "She tripped getting off the subway." I turned my back and poured his coffee. "She fell down the steps onto the platform. She didn't break any bones, but she was unconscious when they brought her in. They didn't know how to reach us until this morning."

"But she'll be all right?"

"The nurse says she'll be fine." I handed him his coffee.

"What was she doing on the subway? Why wasn't she in class?"

"I'm sure she'll tell us once she's feeling better."

I said I'd drop him off at work and drive in to see her. He wanted to come with me, but I dissuaded him. I told him I hoped I'd be bringing her home with me.

I reached the hospital by mid-morning. At the front desk, I asked the receptionist to phone a nurse named Irma Bond.

As I waited, the double doors to an interior hallway opened. An orderly entered, pushing a wheelchair in which a young woman sat holding a newborn. He wheeled the chair outside. Through the windows, I saw a car pull up to the curb. A young man, beaming, jumped out and opened the passenger door. He tucked the woman and newborn into the car, and then they were gone. The orderly returned to the lobby, wheelchair empty, and disappeared through the doors.

A moment later, the doors swung open again. A nurse approached the desk. She was young and slender, with straight brown hair pinned up beneath her cap, and it occurred to me that that's what I would have looked like if I had finished my nursing program. "Miss Campo?" She crossed toward me and extended her hand. It was firm and warm. "I'm Nurse Bond. Let's go upstairs."

I followed her onto an elevator. On the third floor, she gestured to a waiting room off the lobby. It was empty. She hesitated, then said quietly, "Miss Campo. I'm sorry. I know this must be difficult for you."

Perhaps it was the warmth in her voice, but I wanted, inexplicably, to hug her. "Yes," I managed. "Thank you for understanding."

She nodded and turned toward the door. "Have a seat. I'll get Doctor Doherty."

I sat down. On a side table was a stack of magazines: *Good Housekeeping. Woman's Home Companion.* An issue of *Life Magazine*: Spring Fashions.

The door opened again. Nurse Bond introduced Doctor Doherty, a middle-aged man with ruddy skin and thin red hair. "He's been caring for your sister since she came out of surgery."

I offered my hand. "Violet Campo."

The man's lips twitched upward as he touched, then released, my hand. He took a chair, placed it opposite mine, and sat.

Nurse Bond seemed to hesitate, and I had the sense she was reluctant to leave.

"Nurse!" Doctor Doherty barked.

"I'll get back to my patients," she said.

After she left, the room felt cold. I pulled my coat around me. "Miss Campo." His tone was cool. "I believe Nurse Bond told you that your sister appeared in our emergency room two nights ago, hemorrhaging, yes?"

I nodded.

"And she explained why, yes?"

"Yes, Doctor."

He peered at me. "Campo—that makes you Italian, doesn't it?"

"Yes," I answered. "Sicilian. French on my mother's side."

"That would make you girls Catholic, wouldn't it?"

I felt myself tremble. "Yes. We were raised Catholic."

"Which makes your sister not only a criminal, but a sinner."

I tried to keep my voice light. "I'm afraid I don't understand."

"Then allow me to enlighten you." He leaned in closer and smiled. "The Commonwealth of Massachusetts has laws prohibiting crimes against chastity, morality, and decency. One of those laws prohibits women from 'procuring a miscarriage.' Quaint phrasing, isn't it?" The smile vanished. "And so, Miss Campo, if your sister ever returns to this hospital in a similar condition, you may be assured I won't hesitate to notify the authorities. You might wish to tell her so, and that she should consider herself fortunate that I'm discharging her today into your care." He drew himself back in his chair. "Finally, Miss Campo, allow me to remind you that, worse than a crime against the Commonwealth, abortion is a sin against God. A mortal sin. However, I'll leave the salvation of your sister's soul to her priest."

I held his gaze. "Please do," I said, then stood. "And now, if you'll show me to my sister's room."

He led me down a wide hallway and stopped at a door midway. "Check with Nurse Bond before you leave. And remember." The smile returned. "I don't give second chances." He strode to the end of the hallway and disappeared. I waited to stop shaking. Then I tapped on the door and went in.

The room had two beds. The first was empty. In the second I saw a head turned to the wall. I crossed quietly and touched my sister's black curls. "Glory?" I murmured. "It's me."

She turned. "Vi," she whispered. Then again, "Vi."

She looked pale and fragile, like a porcelain doll. My instinct was to take her in my arms. But my anger—and my shame—were stronger. I told her to get up. I helped her dress. I stuffed her bloodstained coat into a bag Nurse Bond gave me, and insisted she wear mine.

On the way home, I told her to lean back and close her eyes. I wanted her to sleep because I didn't want to talk. When we got home, I washed her, changed the dressings, and settled her in bed. I brought her lunch on a tray, took her temperature, and changed the dressings again. I told her the explanation I'd given Papa, that she'd fallen getting off the subway. I didn't say a word about my conversation with Doctor Doherty—or my feelings. Perhaps someday when she's stronger, I will.

For now, I'll keep focusing on that—helping her get stronger. And maybe in time I'll forget all the ugliness and she'll be my Glory again.

GLORY

Lament

Every night he comes to me,
my little sin, my carnal pea,
accusing me, accusing me.
Murderess Mother. Hear my plea!
You stopped me, Mother.
You stopped me.
I wanted to run. I wanted to see
fire and snow and sing off-key
and write you lovesick poetry
and you stopped me.
You stopped me.
And now, for all eternity,
unbaptized, a soul unfleshed,
I dwell in Limbo. Think of me.
Remember me. Pray for me.
For me. For me. For me.

What garbage. A nightmare that gushed onto paper—without my permission.

Right. Face the truth. It's yours. Your overwrought nonsense. Tear it up. If anyone saw it, they'd think you were a lunatic.

Maybe they'd be right. The Norcross dropout. Half catatonic, sitting in her daddy's parlor in a nowhere town, pen in hand, notebook open, crazy pea poem on one page, nothing on the other.

Here's looking at you, kid.

All I need is the drink.

Yesterday was better. When I woke up, I could see sunlight marbling the bedroom walls and Sir Lancelot dozing on the fire escape. I could hear Mrs. Rasmussen's voice in the alley, singing. Smell the coffee Violet had left me on the stove. No shroud—or at least, it had lifted for a while, long enough for me to light a cigarette and pull out my notebook and write. And somehow, astonishingly, everything I wrote seemed new. As if Sappho's heart were breaking in a twentieth-century tenement parlor. As if stale coffee and cigarette smoke were wine and myrrh and my own faithless lover were Phaon. As if 2,000 years from now someone would read my words and feel understood.

But most days aren't like yesterday. Most days the shroud is there when I wake and never lifts. Impenetrable, but invisible. A shroud window. A devil's window, blocking all colors, all sound and taste and scent and touch. Even pain. What's shrouded becomes nothing—a blank—a gap.

And everything is shrouded.

Until something—some externality—intervenes. Maybe a key clicks in a lock and Violet coos, "Glory, darling, will you have lunch with me?" And there's a table again. A chair. A plate. A path is laid. From there to a bit of bread, some soup. The path leads to an armchair by windows overlooking a street, to a notebook and pen and cigarettes and—before the externality vanishes again—a steaming cup of tea. Then she—Violet—the externality—looks up from the sidewalk, waves, and heads back into the world. And she and the street and the world and the nothing that's me—all shrouded again.

I count both of those—the days I fool myself that I can write, and the days I don't exist—as good days.

Bad days are like today. When I don't fool myself, and I feel everything. Fear, hatred, shame. The useless questions, useless rage. They hound me.

The fear is for my future. That it's been destroyed. That I'll always be nothing.

The hatred is for men. All men, even the men who say they're victims, too, they're the ones who die in the wars and the mines and the fires and toil all their lives building our cities and growing our food and curing our diseases, and it's the men in power, the takers, the selfish men I should hate. But I don't. I can't. I hate them all. Because they all show—even as they teach me or doctor me or serve my drink or dance with me or make love to me—especially when they make love to me—they show their utter disdain.

Why not? Aristotle did. Philosophy 101. "The relation of male to female is that of superior to inferior. Ruler to subject."

Player to plaything. Jeremy—Boston Brahmin Jeremy—to Glory. As if he'd marry me. A mill town guinea. Marry me and accept our baby. His blue blood mixed with mine. How naïve.

But my beauty! My brilliance! My poetry! Our wild nights in his royal bed!

"Sorry, kid, but it's not my problem." His languid shrug. "Put yourself in my place. I mean, how do I even know it's mine?" The flare of his nostrils when I threatened to wait three months, then show up at his parents' brownstone sticking my swollen belly—and his pitiful love notes—in their faces. His sneer as he opened his wallet, drew out a fifty-dollar bill, folded it into a triangle, and tossed it at my feet. "Keep the change."

When I bent to pick it up, the knock at the downstairs door. His airy voice. "Oh, that must be Jean. Mind letting her in on your way out?"

Jean. My suitemate Jean. I nearly fell to my knees.

"Spare me the melodrama, kid. Get over it. Move on."

Maybe I could move on, Jeremy, if I could hurt you like you've hurt me.

Maybe I can.

Pen. Notebook. Here's looking at you.

VIOLET

Tonight Papa went after Glory again.

It was like when she was in high school, when she'd miss her curfew or come home smelling like cigarettes and booze or refuse to go with us to Mass. And just like then, I couldn't stop him. Something else takes over. It's like he's desperate to change her. Maybe because he loves her so much.

Aunt Blanche and Uncle Eddie had come for supper. I felt relieved when Glory agreed to join us—she often doesn't. During the meal, she kept quiet, but still, it was a start. Until Uncle Eddie spoiled things. I'm sure I'm wrong, but the way he said it—so casually, as if he'd rehearsed it—made me think he was goading her. "We're hiring at the shoe mill, Glory. If you want, you could start Monday."

She looked startled, as if she'd gone somewhere else in her mind and didn't even know what he'd said. Before she could answer, Papa banged his coffee cup down on the saucer and said what the hell was he talking about, Glory was a college student, not a factory girl.

Instead of answering him, Uncle Eddie kept looking straight at Glory. "So you're going back to Norcross in the fall?"

I held my breath. Last month, she'd asked me to send a letter to Norcross saying she was too ill to finish the term. But she hadn't shared her plans for the fall.

She got up and gathered her dishes piece by piece. She was almost to the kitchen before she answered him. "No. Not this fall." She sounded as if she was saying no to a second piece of pie.

Papa stared at the kitchen door. His whole body was tense. But then he settled back against his chair and looked at Uncle Eddie. "Not this fall," he repeated, as if confirming something he'd known all along. "She needs more time to recover. But next year, she'll be back in school. And meantime, I don't want her working in the mills. She can look for something better when she's up to it."

Uncle Eddie frowned. "How is it you've got no problem with Violet being a shop clerk, but Glory—"

Aunt Blanche interrupted. "Violet's more than a shop clerk. You know that. Mr. Crane told me just the other day she's a talented photographer. He's teaching her the business." She stacked Uncle Eddie's dishes on top of hers. "At any rate, the girls have grown up. They're making their own decisions now. I'm sure if Glory wants a job at the mill, she'll let you know." She started to gather the rest of the dishes, but I told her Glory and I would clean up.

When they left a few minutes later, Glory didn't come out of the kitchen. I brought the dishes in. The air was warm with the steam from the basin of hot water, and the pots and pans were already stacked in the dishrack, gleaming. When Glory helps with the dishes, that typically means drying them. I can't remember the last time she scrubbed the pots and pans.

Before I could thank her, Papa burst in behind me. "What do you mean you're not going back to Norcross? Did they kick you out?"

Glory didn't turn from the sink. "No, Papa," she said quietly. "I wasn't expelled. But I'm not going back."

"Why not?"

She didn't answer.

He took a step toward her. "Look at me when I'm speaking to you! Why aren't you going back?"

She turned and glanced at us. Her eyes were dull. "I don't care to." She turned back to the sink again.

"I told you to look at me! And that's no answer!" He crossed to the sink and wrenched her around. "What happened at Norcross?"

"It's none of your business!" Now her voice was defiant.

"None of my business? I'm your father! I paid to get you there! Eighteen years—food, clothes, tuition at Saint Isabel's—"

"Except when Uncle Eddie paid."

It was too far. He grabbed her and shook. "How dare you? How dare you?"

I shouted at him to stop, but he shouted louder. "Tell me the truth! They kicked you out, didn't they? They found out you were sleeping around, and they kicked you out! *Puttana! Puttana!*"

I'd never heard Papa say that word before. I don't know what it means, though of course I can guess. But maybe saying it shocked him a little, because he went still for a moment, then dropped his hands.

"You're mistaken, Papa," she said. She sounded exhausted. "I left because I wanted to. And that's why I'm not going back. It's my own choice." She turned back to the sink.

Without saying another word, Papa strode out. The front door slammed.

I told Glory I was sorry it had happened.

"What are you sorry for?" she answered. "It was my fault."

"At least let me finish the dishes."

She shook her head. "Would you bring the rest in?"

Later, we sat up for a while reading. Around ten, we got ready for bed. I'd just turned the light out when I heard the front door open, then Papa's keys on the hall table. He went into the bathroom and closed the door.

"Glory?" I whispered. "You studied Italian at Norcross. Do you know what *puttana* means?"

I've been lying here for a long time, but she hasn't answered.

GLORY

*P*uttana.

Yes. I know what it means.

Oh, esteemed Professor, whom should I be reading?

I was so naïve. And cocky. I thought I'd charm him with my smile, with my oh-so-demure blouses and fake pearls and poor-girl-gets-scholarship story.

But he was ready. "T.S. Eliot said there are only half a dozen men of letters—and no women—worth reading. Start with my work."

Of course, Professor Turner. Anything to win the favor of Your Worship.

But it wasn't just worship he wanted. And he was the one in control—always—of everything. At least, everything that was mine.

We were in his office. Snow was falling outside his window. He opened a desk drawer, took out a flask and a small glass, and poured a shot of something—whiskey, I assume—while delivering his judgment. "Your poems, my dear, are overwrought, platitudinous nonsense. They have craft, certainly, but they lack rationality and vigor." He downed the shot.

So what if my heart shattered? The snow was still peacefully falling. Watching it calmed me. I told him I'd been admitted to Norcross on the strength of my chapbook.

He laughed. "Since when are members of an admissions committee poets?"

"But it won an award," I said. "And publication!" What a fool. I was like one of those birds Sir Lancelot traps beneath his paw, chirping frantically just before he snatches it into his mouth.

"Which just goes to show how desperate these small presses can be." His tongue swiped his chapped lips. Pale, thin—almost no top lip at all. "Tell me, how many copies has it sold?"

I said I didn't know, that I was to receive my first royalty statement in June. Foiled again. I might as well have given him a knife.

"I guarantee that statement will reveal that fewer than—" his eyes narrowed—"eighty human beings, fifty of whom are personal acquaintances, have purchased said chapbook. And believe me, this will represent the height of its sales."

I kept watching the snow. The way it muffled everything.

"I don't make such a prediction, lovely Miss Campo, to discourage you. No, no!"

I heard him open his drawer and pour another shot into his glass. I kept on watching the snow.

"I say this with precisely the opposite intent—to encourage you to break free of your emotions, free of your personal, subjective concerns, and to engage your brain, Miss Campo! Your brain!" He stood and took a slender book from a shelf. "Here." He tossed it onto my lap. "Take this home and read it. My fifth book. A real book. And winner, as you'll see, of several real prizes. And a week from tomorrow I'll expect on my desk a new—no—two new poems—breakthrough poems in your new voice. Forbidden topics: romantic love, death, and birds of all kinds."

His fifth book. I read it that night, straight through. But it was just like his others. I couldn't understand it. Or only a few lines here and there. No poem in its entirety. Not a single one. I read the whole book again. Drowning.

Six days passed. I wrote nothing.

On the seventh day, after classes, I walked to Kenmore Square, to a café, and ordered tea. I told myself I couldn't leave until I'd written two poems. Some men were sitting at the next table, talking. I recorded their conversation. When they rose to leave, I ended the poem. For the second, I described, in minute detail, as if for a fine arts catalogue, their table and empty chairs, the cups, saucers, spoons, paper napkins, plates with remnants of cake. I didn't describe the pigeon that swooped down for the crumbs. I put the poems beneath the front cover of Professor Turner's volume and left both at his office the next day.

"Meet me in my office after class."

He called the new work a failure. "Certainly an effort at breaking free of your romantic tendencies, but a failure nonetheless. Gimmicky." He downed a shot straight from his flask. "And you are far too enchanting for such tricks."

No snow fell that day. Instead, the snow on the ground was hard and studded with dirt.

The department secretary knocked and reminded him of a faculty meeting.

"Ahh!" He gathered some papers and I rose to leave. He touched my sleeve. "Two more poems next week. And we'll meet somewhere quieter, where we won't be interrupted."

Somewhere quieter was a small French restaurant off Newbury Street. I brought two poems I'd written the previous semester and revised to remove every last hint of sentiment. He called them "promising, but very much in need of further discipline." Then, over dessert, he reached across the table. His finger swept back and forth over my wrist. An insect. I pulled my hand away and picked up my fork. As we left, he invited me to his place for a nightcap.

"Sorry," I said. "I have a thousand lines of *Beowulf* waiting." All the way home, the sidewalks churned.

At the next class, he passed back our work with comments—and a grade. Mine was a "D."

I'd lose my scholarship.

Beneath the grade, he'd written a note: *Only a few weeks to pull up this grade, Miss Campo. Let's talk about it over dinner Thursday night. Same place, 8 p.m.*

I didn't go. That was the day I told Jeremy I was pregnant and discovered he'd dumped me for my suitemate Jean. I moved out. But then, the next day, the housing office said I'd have to pay a ten-dollar transfer fee, and when I phoned to schedule the abortion, she wanted sixty-five dollars, not fifty.

I phoned him.

Sunday night, I said.

We met at the restaurant. Afterwards I went to his apartment. And drank three whiskeys straight.

In the morning, while he showered, I dressed, opened his wallet, and took two twenties. I walked out. I caught the subway to Mission Hill. I remember the darkness inside the tunnels, and then, when we surfaced, grass, trees, blinding sunlight. I thought of Millay. *To what purpose, April . . .* And Eliot. *April is the cruellest month . . .*

But that's not when I decided to leave Norcross.

I decided later, in that filthy room in Mission Hill. She said it was best not to watch, so I stared at the narrow gap of window beneath the broken slats in the blind. I kept telling myself that in just a few minutes, just a few minutes, I'd be gone from here. Gone. But then I saw in the alley a man—the eyes of a man—and the eyes stopped and stared at me.

That's when I gave up.

I think. It doesn't matter. It happened somehow.

Anyway, yes. I know what *puttana* means.

VIOLET

Glory went missing again tonight.

It was only for a few hours this time. I don't know what happened, and I doubt she'll ever tell me. But I don't care. I don't really want to know.

I worked late developing the photos Mr. Crane had taken of Saint Isabel's graduation ceremony. I was glad he hadn't asked me to go—it would have been too painful, thinking of Glory's graduation a year ago, and how she's ruined everything.

On the way home, it began to rain. I was waiting to cross the street when a police car pulled up. My heart pounded. I know it's stupid, but ever since I brought Glory home from the hospital, I've been afraid of the police. That they might find out, somehow. And charge Glory with a crime. Sergeant McGowan was driving. When he saw me, he lowered his window and asked if I needed a lift home. I told him no, thank you. He nodded. Then the light changed and he drove on.

When I got home, Papa was standing at the windows. "You didn't see Glory in town, did you?"

"No," I said. "Did she say she was meeting me?"

"She didn't even say she was going out. But when I got home an hour ago, she was gone." He seemed agitated.

"Why is that a problem?" I asked. "She sits at home all day, day after day, while we're at work. On a Saturday night, why shouldn't she go out?"

"Because she's Glory," he snapped. "And I don't trust her."

I hung up my jacket. "Did she get any calls today?" I told him I'd run into Dorothy Pope a few days ago and she'd asked after Glory. I'd said she'd been ill and was home and suggested she give her a call.

But Papa said no one had called. "Not while I was here."

"How long were you out?" I asked.

"A few hours. I went down to Stan's to listen to the baseball game. I asked Glory if she wanted to come. She said no, so I went alone. The Sox won. Fifteen runs. We had a beer to celebrate, and Stan started talking about how he still misses Magda. He asked me how long it was after your mother died before I got over it. I said I don't think I ever have. We talked for a while longer, then he said he needed to get some bills out. So I walked home, and she was gone."

"I'm sorry, Papa."

"Why should you be sorry? It's your sister who's—"

"No, I mean about Mama."

"Never mind that. Let's focus on Glory." He crossed to the side table and picked up the newspaper. "Did you see this?" He pointed to an article. "From now on, TB patients at the sanatorium where your mother died are going to be confined to the west wing. The rest of the facility is being converted into a hospital for the insane." He flung the paper down and went back to the windows.

"Papa." I hadn't intended it, but my voice was sharp. "Glory will get through this just fine. Let's have supper. I'm starving."

During the meal, I got him to tell me about the game. Afterwards, we sat and listened to the radio. There was an interview with Joe Dobson, who'd pitched today. It ended. I heard footsteps coming up the stairs. They were too heavy and slow for Glory. Mr. Owen. But instead of continuing up the stairs, they stopped on the landing. I was walking to the door when it opened. Mr. Owen and Glory were standing side by side. She was leaning on his arm, but she didn't look unsteady. In fact, she looked radiant—that was the word that came to me—with her hair damp and curling beneath her hat, a hint of eye makeup, bright red lips, and her blue-and-white scarf knotted at her throat at the top of her raincoat. With his free hand, Mr. Owen dropped her key into her purse. "Good evening," he said. "I happened upon Glory in town and thought I'd walk her home."

"Thank you," I said. I leaned forward and he shifted Glory toward me. I could smell liquor. "But where—"

"I'll be heading upstairs now."

Glory turned to him. "Good night, Will," she said slowly. "And thank you."

I helped her get ready for bed. As I was turning out the light, she said, "I used to be afraid of Mr. Owen. Do you remember that?"

"Yes," I said. "I remember."

She closed her eyes.

In the parlor, Papa was standing by the windows, the newspaper in his hand. "What the hell was that all about?"

I said I had no idea, and what did it matter, as long as Glory was back.

"But what's wrong with her?" He looked at me as if he were sure I knew the answer.

I said she was probably still disappointed about Norcross.

"Disappointed?" He flung the newspaper onto the sofa. "She's more than disappointed. She's—"

"Look, Papa, I'll try to keep a closer eye on her."

"Don't try. Just do it!" He went into his bedroom and closed the door.

The rain is falling steadily now. The street is gorgeous— pools of light on the wet pavement. I wish I could capture it in a photograph. Escape, I guess. From Papa and Glory and their endless pain.

GLORY

Mr. Owen—Will—rescued me tonight.

He would say it was nothing. But it was everything.

When Papa left, I hadn't written a word all day. I went out to the parlor. I thought maybe having the place to myself would help, but it didn't. Instead of the back alley, I stared at the street. Mr. Owen passed our door and went out. I watched him shuffle toward town. I wanted to be out, too. Out of my cage.

And then I saw it. On the hall table. The mail. An envelope addressed to me. I picked it up. The "desperate small press" that had published my chapbook. My hands shook. I tore it open. One page. A few lines of type. A number: 78.

Believe me, this will represent the height of its sales. I heard him laughing. Felt his tongue in my mouth, his hands on my thighs.

I pushed the statement back into the envelope. Hid it between the pages of my notebook.

My platitudinous nonsense.

If I could have, in that moment, I would have chosen the shroud.

I went into the kitchen and opened the cupboard where Papa keeps his chianti. I drank what was left. One glass. I searched for a new bottle. There wasn't one.

My purse was empty. I took the change Papa had left on the hall table. Bourbon. The smallest bottle. If I could get someone to buy it for me.

I fixed my makeup and hair and put on my most respectable clothes. Then I walked into town and stood outside the liquor store. I asked a man going in. "Sorry, Miss," he said, and tipped his hat. I got scared he might tell the clerk inside about me, so I left.

I went into Gallagher's. The lighting was dim, but I wasn't taking chances. I sat at the table farthest from the bar. *What are you having?* Bourbon, I said. He brought it to my table. I put down my coins, told him to keep the change. I drank, eyes down. I guess that's why I didn't see Mr. Owen.

The pain backed off. If I could have one more. But I'd spent Papa's change. I picked up my purse to leave. A man slid into the seat across from me. *Like another, miss?* Sure. He told me his name and that he was new in town. *What about you?* I said I was here visiting a friend. I didn't want any more questions, so I asked him things, kept him talking until my glass was empty again. He offered another. I smiled. Everything dark and heavy was gone. I said no thanks, that I had to meet my friend. *What a shame. Whoever this guy is he can't be much of a friend since he isn't taking proper care of you.* I told him I didn't need anyone to take care of me. *Looks to me like you do.* He leaned in close.

And then I heard a voice I knew. Mr. Owen's voice.

"Evening, Miss. Steve sent me to walk you home." He lifted my purse off the table and handed it to me.

"Hey, wait a minute! What do you think you're—"

But the bartender was already at our table, clearing my glass. "I believe Will's helping this young lady get home."

"You going with *him*?" The way he said it, as if he couldn't believe it, must have hurt Mr. Owen's feelings. But he offered his arm as gallantly as a seventeenth-century suitor, and I walked out as steadily as I could.

When I say Mr. Owen rescued me, I don't mean from the bar. I mean what happened afterwards, after I asked him who Steve was and he said it was the first name that had come into his head, and we both laughed.

I don't remember much of what we talked about, or exactly how long it took us to get back to Mill Street, but I remember rain was falling, and he said he liked the rain, and that he'd never understood what made folks run away from it as if they'd melt. And I remember suddenly realizing that I could feel something that wasn't pain. I could feel the rain—the drops sprinkling my forehead and cheeks and the bit of my wrists between my sleeves and my gloves, and springing up from the pavement to tap my ankles. I knew then that I was going to be all right, because I could feel the rain.

And then we turned into Mill Street, and above us was a streetlight. I pulled back on his arm. He stopped. I asked if I could look at his face.

"Of course," he said.

He took off his hat.

And for the first time in my life, I looked at his face without turning away. For the first time, I saw the line of his thick hair along his brow, his heavy lids, his blue eyes, the hollow of his left cheek above his jaw. And then I looked at the right side of his face.

His scar glistened with rain. I focused on that before I let myself look at his mouth. But there, something caught the light. A raindrop had landed like a tiny diamond on the left side of his lower lip. The right side was gone—that I had always, somehow, known. But now I saw it as it really is—a wound long healed. And as I gazed at that wound, his whole face beneath the street-light changed, and I felt as if I were studying the face of a valiant warrior king, a king worthy of an ode I might someday learn to write.

"Thank you, Mr. Owen," I said.

He said I was welcome, and to call him Will. He put his hat back on, lifted his arm, and we started toward home again.

He must have wondered when I stopped him one more time as we reached our steps and said, "Will, I don't hate all men." Because at first, he looked puzzled. But then I saw him smile, and that was for the first time, too.

GLORY

Why are some people so good, so noble, so unselfish? So unlike me.

Yesterday, I saw Mrs. Rasmussen in town and we walked home together. On the way, she told me that while Father Bouchard was on vacation, a young priest was filling in. He'd graduated from the seminary only a few months after Pearl Harbor and had spent the war working as a chaplain in a military hospital. "I wish you'd come and hear his sermon tomorrow," she said. "You'd have loved the stories he told last week."

I asked her what they'd been about.

"Oh, talking with the soldiers and . . . and giving them the last rites." Her eyes filled with tears.

I remembered her kissing Walter so tenderly the last time he'd visited before he died. I told her I'd go to church with her.

The morning was hot and already humid, so Papa insisted on driving. When we entered Saint Isabel's, Mr. Sadowski was sitting alone. We joined him. Just as the organ sounded, Uncle Eddie slid into the pew in front of us. We stood and began to sing. "Come, Holy Ghost." The altar boys entered, then the priest, singing with us. He was slender, even slight, with thick, dark hair and tanned skin, and he smiled as he sang—as if he were basking in the sound of all the voices surrounding him. It was the same as he chanted the liturgy—he seemed almost blissful. Before he began his sermon, he introduced himself: Father Francisco Garcia.

I can't remember all of his sermon. I'm not sure I could even say the theme. But I remember the way he smiled as he spoke, the way he lifted his arms toward us sometimes, as if he wanted to embrace us. And I know he talked about his work as a chaplain during the war, of suffering so stark and vast that he lay in his bed night after night unable to sleep, begging God for an understanding that never came. One morning he woke before dawn to the sound of a woman singing. He sought the voice, and found a nurse singing a lullaby to a soldier who was dying. And in that moment, he said, he realized that God isn't some mighty power ruling the world from the heavens, but the love that's within us all.

When he said that, I thought of Mrs. Rasmussen kissing Walter, of Will walking me home from Gallagher's in the rain, and of Violet, forever trying to shoo my demons away.

After the service, Father Garcia stood outside the church shaking people's hands. As he took mine, I noticed his brown eyes glistening, exactly as if he were holding back tears. Perhaps that's why, although I'd only meant to say good morning, I found myself thanking him for his sermon, and telling him my name.

"Gloria," he said. "One of my favorite names. Thank you for the gift of your presence here this morning."

If anyone else had said something like that, I would have thought it sentimental, or even pretentious. But I knew he was sincere. I asked him if he'd be saying Mass next week as well.

"Unfortunately, no. Father Bouchard will be back, and I'll be filling in elsewhere."

"You don't have a permanent parish?"

"No, I prefer to serve the area hospitals."

"They're fortunate to have you, Father," I said.

As I joined the others, Uncle Eddie passed without speaking. Once we'd reached the parking lot, though, he frowned at us and snapped, "What kind of sermon was that?"

"What do you mean?" Papa asked.

"Claiming God isn't omnipotent!"

"I found the sermon comforting," Mrs. Rasmussen said quietly. "I'd hate to think that God could have stopped the war, but didn't."

"Or that He could stop sickness," Mr. Sadowski added. "I mean, if He could, why wouldn't He?"

Uncle Eddie shot back another frown. "It's not for us to question God's will."

"I think Father Garcia would agree with you," I said quietly, "though perhaps for a different reason."

He wheeled around. "And what would that be?"

I felt myself flush, but I answered him. "I think Father Garcia would say it's pointless to question God's will because God is love. The love that moves us to sacrifice for another, like our soldiers did, or to comfort, as that nurse did, or to grieve, like Father Garcia grieved."

"Are you saying you don't believe in God?"

The heat rising from the asphalt was dizzying. Papa took my arm. "Let it go, Eddie. We all need to figure it out for ourselves."

Mrs. Rasmussen invited everyone to her place for a glass of iced tea.

"Great idea," Violet said. "Why don't we bring some sandwiches—all right with you, Papa?"

"Of course," he answered.

Uncle Eddie unlocked his car. "Blanche was fixing something for dinner when I left, so don't wait for us. Maybe we'll stop by later." He got in his car and pulled away.

"Stan?" Papa asked.

"I'd be happy to come for a short time," he answered. "But I've got work to do this afternoon. I'm behind in my filing, my billing, my scheduling." He shook his head. "Magda used to take care of all that for me, and now, well, I keep thinking I should hire a girl, but I never seem to find the time to sit down and write the ad."

"I'll do your billing, Mr. Sadowski," I said. "And the other things."

His blue eyes widened. "Are you sure? It's not—well, it's no work for a scholar like you."

I laughed, and suddenly, it seemed as if the laughter itself made me happy. "That's all right," I said. "I'd really like to do it. And I hope I can do it well."

"You're hired!" he said. "This afternoon, I'll introduce you to the office. I'm afraid there's a lot to catch up on."

After lunch, we walked the half-block to his house. I'd been in his kitchen and parlor before, but had never realized the house had an office. It's upstairs and has windows looking onto Mill Street. There's another room on the other side of the stairs, but the door was closed. I wondered if it had been his daughter's bedroom. Perhaps because of the photograph. It was on a small table at the top of the stairs, and when I first saw it, for a moment I had the oddest impression that it was a photograph of my suitemate Jean. Mr. Sadowski saw me looking at it and said it was his daughter Ada's senior-year photo. She had large eyes, high cheekbones, and a wide, fearless smile. "I'm sorry," I whispered. "She was beautiful."

"Thank you," he answered simply. "It's all I have left of her."

As soon as he said that, I realized I'd never heard him mention visiting Ada's grave. "Mr. Sadowski," I said, "I hope you don't mind my asking this, but—Ada's not buried beside her mother?"

"No." He turned away from the photograph and went into his office.

With a large window fan, the room stayed relatively pleasant, and we worked together the rest of the afternoon. By the time I left, I'd organized everything into billing, deposits, filing, and scheduling. Mr. Sadowski gave me a key so that I could work while he was at his office in town.

When I got home, Violet was at the kitchen sink, washing some lettuce. I asked what I could help with.

"You've been working all afternoon," she answered. "You don't have to do anything."

"But I want to," I said. "What are we having?"

"Just some bread and cheese and a salad. It's too hot for anything else."

"Then let me help with the salad."

As I was peeling the cucumber, she came and sat beside me. She didn't say anything, just watched me. "Yes, Violet?" I asked.

"It's nothing." She started to gather the peels into a little pile. "You know, Uncle Eddie stopped by after you'd gone. I overheard him talking to Papa. He was saying he thought you should see someone. A psychiatrist." She tossed her head. "So I butted in! I told him you were fine. That we'd been cooking and cleaning together these past few days, and that you'd just started working for Mr. Sadowski. But . . ." She hesitated. "Maybe you could . . ."

I shook my head. "No. You were right."

She leaned toward me. "Glory, what happened? I mean— you published a book of poems, for Pete's sake—"

"It was just a chapbook."

"All the same, it won a contest, and helped you get into Norcross!" She put her hand over mine, I guess to make me stop peeling. "What went wrong? Why aren't you going back, and why have you been so—I don't know—sad?"

I thought about the pain I must have caused her. Papa, too. But I couldn't answer. I can't share what happened with anyone.

So I shared something else. "It's the way the world is," I said. "The way we are. Human beings. The cruelty. The greed. My mind gets—stopped, I guess. With questions."

"What do you mean? What kinds of questions?"

"About everything. Everything that matters. To me, anyway. Why we live. Why we cause each other pain."

She was watching me intently.

"Do you ever have questions like that?"

"Maybe." She nodded a little. "Sometimes. But I try to offer them up."

I guess I'd expected an answer like that. I guess that's why we'd never talked about it before.

"Anyway," I said, "sometimes the questions get so loud, I feel as if I'd do almost anything to stop them."

"Like?"

I thought of Jeremy. Of my discovery that a lover's embrace could silence the questions. Something else I couldn't explain.

"Like have a few drinks," I said instead.

"And that's what happened a couple of weeks ago. When Mr. Owen brought you home."

I nodded.

"Do you ever get any answers to your questions?" She sounded doubtful.

"Not from drinking," I admitted. "Though it makes them go quiet for a while." Then I thought of Mr. Owen—Will. "But sometimes, I get close to answers when I look into the eyes of someone kind," I said. "Or when I'm writing a poem. If it doesn't get stupid. Trite."

She said she thought she understood. And yet, as we finished making supper—all evening, really—even when we said good night—a distance was there. On both our sides.

It's hot tonight. Even with the bedroom window open, the air is heavy and still. I was lying awake, thinking about Ada Sadowski, when I heard Violet's voice, tentative, in the dark.

"Glory? That night you came home with Mr. Owen. When we didn't know where you'd gone. I was wishing then that I'd told you something."

"What is it?" I sat up.

She sat up, too. "It happened in April. When I came to get you at the hospital."

Despite the heat, I felt a chill up my spine. "What happened? I don't remember much."

"It was before I came into your room. Your doctor—Doctor Doherty—he threatened me. Threatened you, I mean." She pulled her pillow into her lap and punched it down.

I waited.

"He said he could have called the police. And that if you ever showed up there again—like that—he would."

Like that. Lying in a pool of blood on the hospital floor.

She punched the pillow again. "I hated him, Glory. I'm sure I've never in my life hated anyone as much as I hated him."

I managed to say I was sorry she'd had to go through that, and thanked her for telling me. We wished each other good night and lay down again.

It's past midnight now. Violet's been asleep at least an hour. She's dreaming. I can tell because the moonlight is touching her face and it's twitching. Doctor Doherty?

For three months, she's carried that secret, that hatred, alone. And I'm the one who caused it.

I wonder if Violet ever guesses how I envy her. Her prudence, her purity. The fierce generosity of her life.

VIOLET

I'm angry with myself.

Today is Armistice Day and there's so much to be grateful for—peace, of course, and the sacrifices of people all over the world. So why do I feel so rotten?

I was fine while I was photographing the parade. I think I got a good shot of Mr. Owen marching—sort of—with the other World War I vets. The parade ended at the bandstand. Everyone took a seat, and the chaplain of the VFW read a prayer. Then he introduced the next speaker, Corporal James Conlan. Jimmy Conlan—my classmate. I'd heard he'd come home wounded. It was only when he stepped to the podium, though, that I realized he'd lost his left arm. His voice boomed as he read President Truman's Armistice Day Proclamation. *Whereas the Armistice of November 11, 1918, silenced the guns of World War I and brought to humanity hope and promise that the wars of nation against nation were at an end . . .*

I took some photographs, then went and stood next to Mrs. Rasmussen. Glory was just in front of us. Maybe it was the message of the Proclamation, or the way Jimmy read it, but she looked rapturous as she listened. The skies had been overcast before the start of the parade, but now the clouds broke, and sunlight streamed onto her upturned face. I took her photograph. She must have heard the click of the shutter, because she turned to me. I lowered my camera and she smiled her dazzling, bright-red-lipstick smile.

After Jimmy, another veteran stepped forward. He read the names of our soldiers killed in the Second World War. Mrs. Rasmussen folded her arms across her chest and stared at the ground. Walter had served in the Merchant Marine, so his name wasn't mentioned, even though his ship had been torpedoed by the Germans and he and his shipmates were lost at sea. Three years ago, she buried an empty casket beside her husband's grave.

As we were walking home, she asked softly if anyone might be available to drive her to the cemetery. "I'd like to honor my son today."

Mr. Sadowski told her he'd be pleased to take her. "I was heading there myself this afternoon to pull up the mums at Magda's grave."

"Thank you, Stan. And by the way," she continued, louder, and to no one in particular, "I've heard from Leonard. He'll be visiting this Christmas!"

"Oh," Glory exclaimed, "what wonderful news!"

I didn't say anything. We haven't seen Leonard since his brother's funeral, and though I'm glad for Mrs. Rasmussen's sake that he'll be coming, we barely know him.

"It'll only be a brief visit. They're keeping him busy even with the war over." She smiled. "But I'm certainly looking forward to having him home."

Everyone came to our apartment for lunch. Glory and I had made minestrone soup, and while we were reheating it, the doorbell rang. I heard Papa say Mr. Owen's name, then he came into the kitchen. "Glory," he said, "Will has a favor to ask you."

She looked surprised. "Me?"

"He's bought your book of poems and would like you to sign it. He's waiting in the hall."

For a second, she just stood there holding the bowls she'd taken from the cupboard. Then she nodded. "Yes, Papa. Of course."

When she came back to the kitchen, she didn't say anything, but as I was carrying out the pot of soup, I saw her standing at the window with her apron to her cheek. She was wiping away a tear.

Now she's gone with Papa and the others to a charity supper for the Knights of Columbus. She's wearing a knock-out red dress—one Aunt Blanche made her last year—and a choker of fake pearls—good ones, though, that she bought at the jeweler's. She looks as if she's a princess, or a film star. Or a soon-to-be-famous poet.

I could have gone, of course, but I didn't want to. Maybe if I could have worn comfortable clothes, so no one would think I was trying to compete with my glamorous sister.

A few minutes ago, I heard Mr. Owen coming up the stairs. Nothing I do today makes sense, but I went and opened our door as he reached our landing. I said good evening, then my mind went blank. What in the world was I doing? Then I remembered the photograph. "I took your picture at the parade today," I said. "If it comes out well, I'll make you a copy."

He smiled. "Thank you. That's very kind." His words were a little more slurred than usual and I could smell liquor on his breath. He started up the stairs. "Good night."

I said good night and went back inside and closed the door. I felt like a fool.

Good thing Papa and Glory will be gone at least another hour. I guess I'll fix myself some dessert and read the paper. Maybe by the time they get home, I'll be myself again, whatever that means.

GLORY

Leonard Rasmussen loves me!

He's going to apply for discharge and we're going to marry and live in Boston and attend lectures and concerts and films, and I'm going back to college. As the wife of Leonard Rasmussen, who lost his father like I lost my mother, who grew up poor and fights every day for respect. A man as unlike Jeremy as anyone could be. So yes, I'm going to marry him. And no one will use me again.

I admit it's a whirlwind romance. But not for him. He told me he's loved me for three years—ever since Walter's funeral! I was only a kid—I had no idea he'd even noticed me. But he's thought of me ever since. Every port city. All through the war. Every day at sea, he's been thinking of me.

When the war ended, he wanted to head straight home to see me, but he couldn't get leave. The Merchant Marine had to bring the troops and supplies back home, and everything was delayed while the sea was cleared of mines. When they finally gave him leave for Christmas, he worried he might be too late. Had someone else found me? That's why his mother threw the welcome-home party. He told her to. Told her to make sure to invite Papa and Vi and me.

Vi phoned and said she was running late photographing a Christmas play, so Papa and I arrived without her. I'll never forget the moment when Mrs. Rasmussen opened the door. He was standing by the Christmas tree, smoking a pipe and wearing a silk shirt and a gorgeous blue cravat that matched his eyes. And he was staring straight at me. He put down his pipe and crossed the room and lifted up my hand and kissed it. He kissed my hand! "Miss Campo," he said, like he'd just stepped out of a Jane Austen novel. "It's good to see you again. Merry Christmas! Or to be precise, a merry winter solstice."

"The same to you," was all I could think to say. I guess all this time at home I've forgotten how to flirt, but just the same I felt him squeeze my hand a little before he let it go.

The doorbell rang and Aunt Blanche and Uncle Eddie came in. Mrs. Rasmussen asked if they'd like to set up a game of cards. "Whist or Hearts," she said to Uncle Eddie. "No poker—and no betting!"

Leonard touched my shoulder and asked me what I'd like to drink. After months of Papa's chianti, the thought of a real drink made me almost giddy. "I don't suppose your mother has a bottle of bourbon hiding in the cupboard, does she?" I asked.

He winked at me. "I think she might have acquired such a bottle this very afternoon. How would you like it—with soda?"

"Neat."

He didn't look surprised, just went to the cabinet, took out the bottle, poured two glasses, and handed one to me. Then he made a toast. "To the brightest star on the darkest night of the year!" The line seemed fake—rehearsed. I thought of Jeremy. How he'd deceived me. But then we touched glasses, and I looked into his eyes. His desire was unmistakably real.

He brought a box of chocolates from the cabinet and gestured to the sofa. "Why don't you tell me what you've been up to since high school?"

Of course I didn't. I just said I'd gone to college for a year but it hadn't worked out, and now I was Mr. Sadowski's office girl and working on my second book of poems. Leonard said he loved poetry. "Especially the old Romantics. 'Come live with me and be my Love' and all that." I knew what he meant, of course—the poem is terribly romantic, even if Marlowe was an Elizabethan. He said he'd like to read my first book of poems and did his mother have a copy? I said I'd given her one, and then I got him to talk about himself—all sorts of things—the war, and all the places he's traveled, and what it's like to live on a ship, and how he plans to apply for discharge soon because there are plenty of civilian jobs for men with his experience and he's tired of life at sea. By the time Violet walked in, we were on our second drinks and third chocolates and sitting so close I could see the flecks of gold in his blue eyes. I couldn't help noticing that, when he greeted Violet, he shook—didn't kiss—her hand.

Mr. Sadowski had joined the card game by then, and Aunt Blanche called over to Violet to see if she wanted to make a sixth. She said no and took a chair by the sofa. Leonard sat beside me again, but farther away than before. I didn't want to share Leonard with Violet, but all the same I was relieved to have her there, keeping us from getting too close for an evening in his mother's parlor.

We made polite conversation: Leonard asked Violet about her photography, and said he enjoyed taking pictures himself, in the cities he visited.

"Did you bring any of your photographs?" Violet asked. "I'd love to see them!"

Leonard paused for a moment, then said no, he liked to travel light. Then he asked if Boston was still "as staid as ever," and talked about the blues and jazz clubs he'd visited in Rome.

"Jazz in Italy?" I asked, not sure if he was joking.

"That's right," he said. "Don't tell me you've never heard of Luigi Braccioforte?"

Violet raised an eyebrow. "No, word of his fame hasn't yet reached staid New England."

Leonard smirked. "He's quite good, actually. Sounds just like Louis Armstrong." He lifted his arm and made a fist. "Get it?"

We both laughed.

The card game ended and Papa announced that it was time for us to go home. Of course I didn't want to, but I said good night and followed him and Violet upstairs. As we were getting ready for bed, Violet asked if I'd enjoyed the evening. "I guess," I answered, not wanting to share.

"Leonard was certainly putting on the charm," she said. "I don't recall him ever paying much attention to us before. Of course, the last time we saw him was at Walter's funeral. And I can't even remember the time before that."

"It was in 1940," I said. "At Christmas. I remember them both predicting, because of the shipments they'd been making to England, that it was only a matter of time before we entered the war. That was Walter's last visit home."

"You're right," she said softly. "I'd forgotten all about that."

I went to bed but lay awake for hours. Sometime after dawn, I dreamed I was on a ship with Leonard. German warplanes were dropping bombs all around us. He shouted to me that he knew of an escape route and to follow him. I ran behind him through a long corridor below deck, but as I rounded a corner, he vanished.

That afternoon, he phoned. Was I busy that evening? He had me put Papa on and asked to borrow his Buick. When he came to the door, he was wearing a cream-colored suit with a white shirt and black bow tie. I felt awkward in the bright red dress Aunt Blanche had made me for the Christmas Charity Ball at Norcross, but he said I looked "stunning." He took me to a place he'd heard about in Boston, and after dinner, to a club playing Cuban music. We danced until I thought my legs would give out. Then we sank into our chairs and just listened. He put his arm around me. When we pulled up to our building, the lights were out in Mrs. Rasmussen's windows and ours, and Leonard said he'd walk me upstairs. I told him not to be silly, but he insisted. As soon as I'd unlocked the door, he kissed me, and it felt as if he knew something none of the men I'd kissed before had known, some secret way to make my mind stop asking anything but to be in his arms. And then he opened the door and pushed me in and closed it after me and I was all alone in the dark, and shaking.

I didn't see him at all the next day. I was working for Mr. Sadowski, so it wasn't as if I worried about it, but when he didn't call that night, or the next day—Christmas Eve—when I was home all day, I was sure he'd gotten tired of me. I started thinking about Jeremy again, how crazy I'd been for him right up until he'd tossed me that fifty-dollar bill.

Late afternoon, I went down to pick up the mail. There was a card for me from Jean, a large card with a photograph of her parents' house covered in snow and *Greetings from Chestnut Hill!* printed on the front. How strange, I thought. We'd exchanged cards last year, but—now? Her message said all our friends at Norcross missed me and wanted to know if I'd be returning in the new year. "Of course we're sophomores now," she wrote, "but maybe you could double up on classes for a while and catch up. You're the only person I know smart enough to do it! Write soon! I'd love to visit, but we'll be at our house in Palm Beach. Merry Christmas!" Clearly, she was no longer dating Jeremy. If she were, she'd have made sure to mention him.

Christmas in Palm Beach. I looked out the windows onto Mill Street. It was nearly dark. Papa was still at work. Violet was photographing a holiday party. Aunt Blanche was home, though. I could see lights in her windows. She was probably making her famous bouillabaisse for supper after midnight Mass. The only movement in the street was Will, making his slow way home. I wondered if he'd be alone on Christmas Eve.

The phone rang. It was Leonard. I was so relieved my voice nearly broke with tears.

"What's the matter, doll?" he asked.

"Nothing," I lied. "Nothing. I was napping."

"Good idea. We'll all be up late tonight." He paused. "Look, Glory, I can't stop thinking about you. Could I see you tonight? Just us, I mean?"

I sank into Papa's armchair. Slowly, keeping my voice steady, I said it was such late notice, and that I had plans, and why hadn't he called before now.

He said he'd been visiting a friend. "We've been buddies since grade school. He's moved to Springfield, teaches math at the new junior college in Holyoke. We always try to spend time together when I'm on leave—if his wife and kids don't keep him trapped at home."

"I suppose we could meet for a little while," I said, "but I can't stay out long. I promised Papa I'd come to midnight Mass, and he always wants to get there early."

"What's early?"

"Around eleven. Even then, nearly half the pews are filled. Your mother usually comes with us. Will you be going, too?"

"No," he answered. "And neither will you."

A wave of heat swept through me. "What do you mean?"

"Tell your father you have a headache. I'll wait until everyone leaves, then I'll come upstairs." He paused. "You'll let me in."

And I did.

He brought chocolates and bourbon and a gift wrapped in gold paper with a red bow. It was a book by the German poet Rilke. I'd read some of his sonnets at Norcross, but this wasn't a book of poems. It was letters: *Letters to a Young Poet*. I told Leonard I'd never heard of it.

"You'll love it," he said. "Almost as much as I love your poems."

"My poems?" *Overwrought, platitudinous nonsense!* I backed away. "You've read my chapbook?"

"On the train to Springfield. And again on the way back." He pulled me into his arms. "I mean it, Glory. They're . . ."

I looked into his eyes. I don't think it was my imagination. I think they were shining with tears.

"I don't have the words. That's why you're the poet, I guess, but . . . At first, they made me sad. I felt as if I were grieving— for Walt, our childhood, everything we lost when our father died. But then, as I read the final poems, I began to feel grateful, just to be alive." He'd been looking away, but now he met my eyes again. "And to know you."

He kissed me.

I knew what would happen. I wanted it to happen. Before the clock struck midnight, we'd moved from the sofa to my bed.

I told him I couldn't risk getting pregnant, and he said of course not, and put a little packet on the night table. He told me what it was and said you could get them at drug stores all over Europe. I told him I'd only read of such things, and he laughed and said that's because Massachusetts was founded by Puritans. "Someday, Glory," he said, pulling me back into his arms, "we'll travel the world together and I'll show you lots of things you've never dreamed."

Later, when he arrived with his mother at Aunt Blanche and Uncle Eddie's, we both pretended we thought the other had been at Mass. When I said no, I'd been home with a headache, and he asked if I was feeling better, it was as if we were still making love, right in front of them all, but they couldn't see.

When he and his mother visited on Christmas afternoon, we kept on pretending nothing had happened, but for the next few days, I'd come home from work early and he'd come upstairs.

Tonight—New Year's Eve—he took me to a dinner dance in Worcester, at the Bancroft Hotel. As we ate, he told me he was determined to leave the Merchant Marine in the coming year. "You know," he said, "my father and Walt both died younger than I am now. I've decided not to tempt fate."

We were the last couple on the dance floor. The band played "Prisoner of Love," and he sang the lyrics in my ear. The music stopped, but he didn't let me go. He told me he was going to buy me a ring in New York before his ship left port. "I don't want to take the chance of losing you," he said. "I want everyone to know you're mine." And then the clock struck twelve, and the band played "Auld Lang Syne."

When I got home, I tried not to wake Vi, but she sat up as soon as I opened the bedroom door. "I wasn't asleep," she said. "Papa went to bed, but Mrs. Rasmussen and I stayed up till midnight. We listened to the New Year's Eve concert and had a glass of champagne."

I felt sorry for her spending New Year's Eve with Mrs. Rasmussen, but I didn't want to share the details of my night with Leonard. So I undressed quickly, slipped on my robe, and went out to the bathroom to wash. When I came back, she was still sitting up, her arms around her knees.

"Glory?"

"Mmm-hmm?" I slid into bed. I just wanted to close my eyes and imagine that Leonard was holding me again.

"Mrs. Rasmussen's invited us to a send-off for Leonard Friday night. She told me his train leaves Saturday at dawn."

"Yes," I said. "That's right."

"You okay about it?"

"Of course I'm okay about it!" I said. And snapped off the light.

I heard her lie down again. In a few minutes her breathing changed and I knew she'd fallen asleep.

I haven't told her, so how could I expect her to understand? She will soon, though. Because I'll be wearing his ring. And then she'll know—everyone will know—that he's going to marry me. Protect me. Forever love me.

VIOLET

Last night I slapped Glory.

I'd never done anything like that before, and I never thought I would. Of course I didn't plan to. But she was acting so crazy! Because I told her about the photograph. And now she's disappeared again.

I didn't ask to find it. It was Leonard's fault, leaving it sticking out of the pocket of his jacket. Why shouldn't I look at it? "I didn't bring any photographs with me," he'd said. "I like to travel light." So how was I supposed to know? *Leonardo, amore mio, torna presto! — Cecilia* And a date. She'd given it to him a month ago.

All right, maybe I'd suspected it. Something about him, something slick, something phony, from that first night when I walked in and saw them sitting together on the sofa. I knew in an instant he'd done this before, lots of times. The handsome American comes into port, seduces a beautiful girl, then sails away again.

How many girls like Cecilia were waiting for him to *torna presto*? And within hours Glory would be one of them. If I could figure it out, with zero experience, why couldn't she? I felt so frustrated I left the party, went upstairs, and went to bed. But of course I lay awake, my stomach in knots.

I heard Papa come in around eleven, Glory not until after midnight. She opened our door and stumbled toward the closet. She seemed to be having trouble unfastening her dress.

I turned on the bedside lamp and offered to help.

"Oh, Vi, I thought you were asleep!" She swayed toward my bed, then sat heavily with her back to me. I unfastened the hooks and eyes, unzipped the zipper. She turned. I smelled bourbon and perfume and cigarettes. And then she told me that Leonard had asked her to marry him, and she'd said yes.

"Marry him? After two weeks?" I couldn't take it in. "You don't know the first thing about him!"

She laughed. "What's there to know? He loves me!" She threw her arms around me. "He's been in love with me ever since he saw me at Walter's funeral! And he's never stopped thinking about me since!" She whirled away and collapsed on her bed. "So you see, Vi? It's not really two weeks! Not for him! He's been courting me in his mind for years!"

"Courting you in his mind?" I threw off the bedclothes. "In his fantasies, maybe! What does he know about the real you? Have you told him anything—anything at all?"

She sat up and squared her shoulders. "What do you mean? What's to tell?"

I pulled on my robe. "Does he know about the hospital last spring? Or how you fell apart when you got home?"

Her eyes were defiant. "I'm sure his mother must have told him some of it."

"Did she tell him he's marrying a girl who ruined her chance of a Norcross degree because she couldn't stay home at night? Who's had an abortion? Though for all I know, maybe that wasn't the first one!" I'm not proud of saying those things, and if I could take them back, I would. She had every right to be angry. And she was.

She rose, slowly, and faced me. "How dare you? My poor, long-suffering sister. Saint Violet! Virgin and martyr." She grabbed my shoulders and shoved me toward the dressing table. "Take a look in the mirror, Vi. You're shriveling up. Ever since my book was published, you've envied me, and now I've got

Leonard. Your secret love!" She sauntered to the closet and slid out of her dress.

Her words sickened me, though not as much as the thought of her giving herself to a cad like Leonard. "You're wrong," I said. "I couldn't care less about Leonard Rasmussen. But I do care about you. And tomorrow, he'll board that train and head back to his ship and disappear, and when you fall apart again, I'll be the one left to pick up the pieces." I spoke quietly, but even to myself, I sounded cruel.

She just smiled—a carefree, boozy smile. "You should shut up, Vi, when you don't know what you're talking about. He's buying me a ring when he gets to New York." In the lamplight, her white slip—the silk slip I'd bought her for Christmas— rippled over the curves of her breasts and hips like water in moonlight. "He's going to apply for discharge and look for a job in Boston. That's right—I'll be living in Boston again. Leonard thinks I should go back to college. Evelina Stern teaches at Brighton. After we've settled, I'm going to send her my chap- book and ask her if she'll meet me for lunch."

Evelina Stern. Last week I read a glowing review of her latest book of poems. "You don't have to wait," I said. "You could send her your book tomorrow! Maybe you could take her class this spring!"

She put on her robe, laughing again. "Didn't you hear me? I've got a wedding to plan!"

I stood and pulled her around to face me. "Please, Glory!" I begged. "Don't waste the next few months waiting for someone who won't be waiting for you!"

She stiffened. "Why do you keep saying that? Of course he'll be waiting for me!" She stared into my eyes, and suddenly her voice rose. "What do you mean, anyway?" I tried to turn away, but now she was the one gripping me. "Vi! What do you mean?"

"Nothing," I lied. "It's late. I want to go to bed."

Her hands released me but her eyes—black and cold—held me there. "You're right," she sneered. "There's nothing to tell. You're just like Jean. A jealous bitch who only wants to hurt me!"

Drunk or not, how could she say such a thing? "I don't want to hurt you," I said. "I love you."

"Then prove it!" she hissed. "Tell me what makes you so goddamn sure Leonard's been lying to me."

And so I told her. "It was a photograph," I said. "That's all. I saw a photograph. I went straight to the party after work, so I hung up my coat and camera in Mrs. Rasmussen's closet. There was a photograph sticking out of a pocket of Leonard's jacket."

I stopped. Her eyes were blank. And then, two words. "A girl."

"Yes," I said. "I know I shouldn't have looked at it. I don't know why I did, except—I guess I thought maybe it was a photo of you. But it wasn't you. It was a girl named Cecilia. She'd written on it—just a few weeks ago—calling him *amore mio* and telling him to come back soon."

There was no movement in her face. Nothing. I touched her arm. "I'm sure it doesn't mean anything," I said. "I'm sure it doesn't."

For a moment longer, she stayed like that, as lifeless as a doll. Then she pulled away and began to laugh. Not softly, like before, or like her usual throaty laugh. This was shrill, raucous, and as she laughed, she started to spin in circles in the pool of lamplight between our beds.

"Glory, stop it," I begged. "Please! Stop! You'll wake Papa!"

But she kept on laughing and spinning until I caught her shoulders and slapped her.

She lurched away from me.

"What's going on?" Papa was standing in the doorway. "Why aren't you two in bed?"

"I'm sorry, Papa," I said. "I'm sorry we woke you."

But he wasn't looking at me. "What's the matter, Glory?" he asked. His voice was soft, gentle.

She didn't answer. I pulled her robe back onto her shoulders and tightened the belt at her waist. Unresisting, she watched me. Then she turned and walked steadily past him. I heard the bathroom door close.

"Is this because Leonard's shipping out tomorrow?"

"I suppose," I said.

"We've known all along he was only here on leave."

"Yes." I sank down onto my bed.

"Well, you'd better watch her for a while. Make sure she's okay."

I heard him go into the kitchen. He came back with a glass of ginger ale and some soda crackers. He put them on the night table. "See if you can get her to have this before she goes to sleep," he said.

I told him I'd try.

When Glory came back from the bathroom, I gestured toward the night table and told her Papa wanted her to eat something before she went to sleep. She got into bed and sat up against the wall. She reached for the glass and sipped.

I lay down and turned toward the window. After a while, I heard her put down the glass. The light went out and her bed creaked.

I reached out and lifted the window shade. Wet snow was falling—fat flakes that melted into rain. I watched it for a long time before I fell asleep.

And now it's morning, and she's gone.

GLORY

He's gone.

All the doors are closed, and all the window shades are drawn or else the people behind the windows aren't Leonard. The train pulls away.

People shout. A man counts money. A door stands open to the rain.

Pellets of rain. A hand holds an umbrella. A gloveless hand spattered with rain. Soaked shoes. A puddle, slick with oil. A voice calling. "Hey, miss, you all right?"

A storefront. Glass. A dark-eyed woman holds an umbrella. She moves on.

Cracks in the sidewalk. Little canyons. She steps to the side. Forward. To the side.

At last her hand unlocks a door. Then another. She puts a wet umbrella in a stand, removes two wet shoes, hangs a wet coat.

The woman enters a room and sits at a window.

The clock ticks. The second hand jerks down. Stop. Down. Stop. Down. Stop. Up again.

Rain spatters the windowpane. Rain. Pane. Pain.

Words.

A blank page becomes words.

And the woman becomes someone again. Gloria Campo. Poet.

January 4, 1947

DISSOLUTION

After we say goodbye, no one holds an umbrella.
A hill is climbed but no one climbs it.
No footstep sounds on stairs.
No one's soaked shoes sit by a door.
The rooms no bare feet reach are vacant.
Silent.
As if this were a house abandoned.

Out beyond this window, dawn
emerges from the clouds
to light a spider's web
still holding the storm

while here at this desk, words
emerge from this phantom pain
to hold our lost bodies
and these strands of rain.

VIOLET

Glory wasn't lost, and didn't need me to find her.

Though I went after her, driving like a lunatic toward the train station in the freezing rain. The car skidded, and I nearly hit a pedestrian before managing to pull over. That broke the spell. I don't know what I thought I was doing, rushing after a grown woman, trying to—what? Rescue her? From what? Why do I keep interfering? Why can't I let her live her own life? And find a way to live mine?

I looked at myself in the rear-view mirror. *Shriveled up.* Nice thing to say to your own sister. I put the car in gear again and turned on the radio. The announcer was reporting on the trial of Nazi doctors in Nuremberg. I thought of Evelina Stern, the poet. The review of her new book said she'd lost her parents and her brother at Auschwitz. And here I was, me and my petty problems.

Slowly, I pulled back into the street. Within a few minutes, the rain stopped. I didn't pass Glory. When I let myself into our apartment, I saw her wet shoes by the door.

Before lunch, she left again, and was gone until supper. After thanking me for the meal, she did the dishes. Since then, she hasn't said a thing. So who knows what happened this morning at the train station? I'll probably never know.

If Leonard surprises me and comes back and marries her, then someday, maybe at their wedding reception, we'll all have a good laugh about last night, how I doubted him, and frightened her.

But what if he doesn't come back?

VIOLET

Tonight I wrote to Leonard.

With Glory's permission. Not in response to a letter from him, or even a postcard, let alone a ring.

I got up later than usual this morning because I didn't have to work until almost noon, taking photographs at a bridal shower. When the bride's mother had booked the session, I'd thought a shower on a Friday was unusual, but when I wrote it down in our calendar, I realized it was Valentine's Day.

While I was in the bathroom brushing my teeth, Glory rushed past me. She vomited again. I told her to go back to bed, that I'd bring her some tea and soda crackers.

Waiting for the tea to steep, I phoned Mr. Sadowski and told him Glory wasn't feeling well. Then I called Doctor Cohen's office and made an appointment for that afternoon. When I told Glory, she shook her head and said she didn't need to see him. "It's nothing. It'll pass."

"You've been saying that for the last few days and it hasn't passed."

"But it will, Vi!" She looked straight into my eyes. "It's not what you think."

"All right," I said, "I believe you." And I did.

But she went on, still holding my gaze. "That's not what I meant. We were lovers. But he took care of it."

Lovers. After two weeks. Maybe—how did I know?—after two days. I tried to focus. "He took care of it?"

"So I wouldn't get pregnant."

"Okay," I said. "Still. Maybe there was an accident."

"There was, once. But he said it was all right. That he'd—managed it."

Who was I—*Saint Violet, virgin and martyr*—to question my worldly sister? I told her that was all the more reason to see Doctor Cohen and get to the bottom of it.

I took a cab to the client's address: Mayflower Estates, a new residential development. It's only a few miles away, but so different from Mill Street it could be another country. No duplexes or triple-deckers, just single-family homes, two or three stories with wide front porches and long driveways leading to a two-car garage. Each house has a few acres of land, and despite the snow, I could make out ornamental trees, statues, stone benches, a gazebo. The house where the shower was being held even had a swimming pool covered in snow.

I rang the doorbell. It was answered by a slender woman in grey. "Ah. The photographer." She nodded. "This way."

She led me into an enormous kitchen. Mrs. Hopkins, our client and the mother of the bride, was taking from a woman in an apron—presumably her cook—a tray of heart-shaped sandwiches. As soon as she saw us, she handed the sandwiches to the woman in grey. "Take these out to the table, Irene." I began to say hello, but she interrupted me. "Thank you for being on time, Violet." She started from the room. "Come." I followed her red pleated skirt back out to the front hallway. "Hang up your coat here, and then get set up as quickly as possible. Some of Pauline's friends have already arrived!"

I asked where I would be working. "Dining room and parlor. Follow the hallway past the kitchen. Luncheon first, then gifts, then cake." In the distance, a phone rang. "Photograph everything!" She swept away.

I'd just finished adjusting the lighting in the parlor when several young women entered with gifts and placed them on a large side table. I took their photographs beneath a cluster of paper hearts suspended from the ceiling. Someone entered with a box wrapped in pink and gold, so large it completely obscured her face. "Champagne flutes," the bearer announced from behind the box. "Three dozen!" She slid the box onto the table, and I snapped her picture. Auburn curls, blue eyes, curves like Glory's in a close-fitting turquoise dress with gold bangles at her wrist and a gold choker at her throat.

"Jean?" I took the camera from my eyes.

"Yes?" For a moment, her face was blank. Then she gasped. "Glory's sister! Violet!" She shrieked. "Oh, good heavens, I wondered if I might see Glory today—not here, I mean, but out and about on the street or—Violet! What are you doing here?" Before I could answer, she continued on. "Of course! Taking pictures! Glory told me you're a photographer! I'd completely forgotten! How marvelous!" She whirled past the others and shouted toward the stairs. "Pauline! You must meet our photographer! It's Glory's sister, Violet!"

A petite blonde leaned over the banister. "Glory's sister? Who's Glory?"

"Pauline!" Jean cried. "I've told you about Glory! One of my suitemates last year! Most of last year anyway!"

The girl's eyes widened. "Glory's here?" She hurried down the stairs and into the parlor.

"No, you silly! Pay attention! This is Glory's sister, Violet! Our photographer today!" She turned to me. "And this is my cousin Pauline—the bride-to-be."

"Pleased to meet you," I said. "Congratulations!"

"Thank you!" She beamed. "I've never met your sister, but Jean has told me how talented she is!"

"A poet!" Jean announced, then turned back to me. "And how is Glory?"

"Well!" I answered firmly. "She's working and writing. A new book of poems, I think."

"Is she?" Her arched brows rose even higher. "She never answered my Christmas card, the naughty thing. Is she planning to come back to Norcross?"

"I'm not sure." I lifted my camera. "Let me get a photo of you and Pauline."

They put their heads together, cheek against cheek, beneath the dangling hearts. Pauline's arm encircled her cousin's shoulder. I noticed her ring—a row of three enormous diamonds. And nothing, I thought—not even a piece of cut glass—from Leonard. I'd opened our mailbox every day hoping to see a tiny package. And hoping not to.

After everyone had lunch, Pauline opened gifts, then Irene served cake and coffee and Pauline opened more gifts. The last wasn't unwrapped until nearly three. I quickly snapped a picture, then went into the kitchen and phoned a cab. I'd packed my things and was waiting by the door when Jean appeared again.

"You're leaving already?"

"Yes," I said. "I'm afraid I have other work to get to this afternoon."

"Do you need a lift home?" She was already opening the closet door. "I'll drive you!"

"No need!" Did she want to see where we live? To see Glory? "A cab is on the way."

"I'll tell Irene to call and cancel it." She turned toward the kitchen.

"Thanks, but—"

She stopped. Her blue eyes held mine.

"It's very kind of you, but the cab's already here." I opened the front door. "It was nice to see you again, Jean. I'll tell Glory you said hello."

"Yes, do!" She held the door as I walked out. Thank goodness the cab was just turning into the driveway.

When I got home, I didn't tell Glory about seeing Jean. And I still haven't told her. Too much has happened.

When the nurse called her into Doctor Cohen's examining room, she asked me to come with her. During the exam, I didn't say a word. Then Doctor Cohen helped her sit up and told her she was pregnant.

She didn't respond. She didn't even look as if she'd heard him.

And so I spoke. I asked him if he was sure. "Couldn't it be a stomach flu?"

He went to the sink and started washing his hands. "No, Violet. Your sister is pregnant. Several weeks along." He reached for a towel. "I gather the news isn't entirely welcome." He looked at Glory and waited.

She pulled the sheet tighter across her thighs.

"It's just—a bit of a shock," I explained.

He leaned against the sink and glanced from Glory to me. "You girls are Catholic. There are places Catholic girls can go, convents where you can stay until—"

"No!" Glory said quietly. She was staring at her knees.

"Well, it's your decision, of course. If you stay in town, I can recommend an excellent obstetrician. In the meantime, when you get queasy, try ginger ale with ice. If you find you can't even keep fluids down, call me. And Glory?"

Her eyes rose slightly.

"In a few weeks, the nausea will pass." He turned to me. "You look as if you want to ask me something."

My heart was racing. I did want to ask him something. But how could I? We've known Doctor Cohen since we were children. What would he think of us? Besides, the specter of Doctor Doherty was there in the exam room, sneering at me. So I said no. Nothing.

We picked up a bottle of ginger ale at the market on our way home. Neither of us spoke until we got to our building. At the foot of the steps, Glory stopped. She looked at me and said, with no expression I could name, "Maybe I just made it all up."

I had no idea what she was talking about. "Made what up?"

She shook her head. Then she went upstairs. I followed her into our bedroom. She opened her purse, took out a packet of cigarettes, and threw them away.

I started a question. "Have you thought about . . . ?"

She understood. "No. You remember what you told me about Doctor Doherty. Besides, I'll never put myself through that again."

Over supper, Papa told us that Mr. Sadowski had invited Mrs. Rasmussen on a date. "He told me he hasn't felt so nervous since he was courting Magda."

"Did she accept?" I asked.

"She did. They've gone to Worcester, to the Bancroft. Apparently they have a Valentine's dinner dance."

Glory rose. "Thank you for cooking, Vi," she said quietly. "The fish was perfect. I'll do the dishes. You must be tired." She picked up her silverware and plate.

"I'll help you," I said.

She paused at the kitchen door. "Keep Papa company."

I looked at Papa's black eyes, his Roman nose, his unlined face and shiny black hair. *What about you?* I wanted to ask him. *Why aren't you dancing at the Bancroft?* But I'd asked him similar questions over the years and gotten no answer.

After supper, he put on his hat and coat. "I'm going to a film." His voice was flat. "Gregory Peck. A Western. You girls wouldn't like it."

After Glory finished the dishes, I asked her if we could talk.

"Of course," she murmured. She sat in Papa's armchair, leaned back, and closed her eyes.

"What will you do?" I asked.

She shrugged. "Either I'll lose the baby or I'll have it."

I thought of Pauline's diamond ring. "Leonard," I said. She opened her eyes. "You've got to write to him. Tell him."

She shook her head.

"Yes!" I insisted. "It's his baby, too!" A rage I hadn't known I was feeling surged through me. "His responsibility as much as yours—more than yours!" I threw open the front door and ran downstairs, intending to ask Mrs. Rasmussen for Leonard's address. But then I remembered. She was at the Bancroft, dancing with Mr. Sadowski. I stopped on the bottom stair.

Glory came out to the landing. "Vi." Her voice was quiet. "I have Leonard's address."

Still seething, I went back in and closed the door. Glory came out of the bedroom and handed me a small card. I took a sheet of writing paper from the desk and placed it on the dining table. "Here," I said. "I'll sit with you."

"No," she said again, as firmly as before. "You write it. You'll know what to say." Then she turned toward the bedroom. "Vi." Her back was to me.

"Yes?"

"Don't ask for anything. Just tell him."

The letter is in my purse. I'll post it tomorrow. I know he won't answer it, and I hate myself for knowing and being glad.

GLORY

I don't hate him.

That doesn't make me noble. Or even good. After all, I still hate Jeremy. At least I think I do. And Professor Turner. Others.

But Leonard? He never pretended he was better than I. Or threatened me. He simply saw me, wanted me, and did what he thought he needed to do to have me.

Lied to me.

And I believed him. Why should I be ashamed of believing he loved me? I still do. A little. There were times when he'd look at me . . . Even with everything that's happened, when I remember that look . . . But then, at the farewell party, when we said good night, the look had changed. It wasn't love. I sometimes think it was regret.

And then he disappeared. As if he'd never been here at all. As if last Christmas never happened, or happened in a story I read about somebody else.

Except for one thing. The cells growing inside me. Cells of what someday will be a child. My child. It's nothing I ever wanted for myself—a secretary, an unwed mother, scribbling poems at night while my baby sleeps. But why not?

Already, for reasons I can't understand, can only feel, each morning when I wake, and all day long—booking an appointment for Mr. Sadowski or chopping potatoes or writing a poem or even now, listening to the rain—I'm overcome with love.

How could I hate the man who abandoned me to love?

VIOLET

L eonard says he's not the baby's father.

He told Mrs. Rasmussen in a letter, though he's never answered mine.

It's tax season, so even though it's Saturday, Glory worked all morning for Mr. Sadowski. After lunch, she said she was tired and wanted to nap. Papa announced he was going into town on some errands—I suspect to buy me a birthday gift. I decided to walk to the park. I brought my camera. The afternoon was perfect—bright sun casting long, curved shadows from the arched bridge over the river. Children were playing on the river bank. Someday, Glory's child will be one of them.

I took pictures until I ran out of film, then sat and watched the mothers chatting together. They all looked younger than I am.

I can't believe I'll be twenty-three tomorrow, and I've never even had a date. I know I'm not beautiful like Glory. I'm too thin, and I don't like my Roman nose. It makes Papa look distinguished, but it's all wrong for me. Still, my eyes are nice. Like Mama's and Aunt Blanche's. Sometimes I think I'm as pretty as they were at my age. Or almost. But they'd been married for years by twenty-three, whereas no one's ever shown the slightest interest in me.

Maybe because I'm not interested in them.

Am I? I'm interested in most people. But men? Why do I even have to ask myself something everybody else takes for granted?

I thought about it the whole way home, until Mrs. Rasmussen met me coming in. Ever since Valentine's Day, I've noticed a lightness in her. "I was hoping to catch you," she said. "Can you stop in for a moment? I have a little something for your birthday."

I said she was kind to always remember.

"Well, it's nothing much." She closed the door behind me. "I thought these would make a nice gift you could share with your father and Glory."

It was a large tin of cookies, tied with a bow. "Sugar cookies! Wherever did you find them?"

"They were on special at Woolworth this morning. There were only a few left when I got there."

"I hope you bought one for yourself!"

She blushed. "I did. I thought I'd share it with Stan."

"I was just going upstairs to make some tea," I said, thinking I'd invite her to join us. But then it occurred to me that she and Glory hadn't spent any time together since Leonard left, and given everything, it wasn't up to me to break the ice. So instead I simply said Glory and I would enjoy them.

I started to go, but she clasped my arm. "Violet?"

I waited.

"There's something I should let you know, and you can tell Glory as you think best." She paused, then seemed to push herself on. "I know Glory's expecting."

"How did you find out?" I asked.

"Leonard told me. I got a letter from him this week."

"Of course. I should have realized he'd write to you." And yet he hadn't written to Glory. Not a word.

Mrs. Rasmussen tucked a strand of hair behind my ear. "You know I'd do anything not to hurt you, but I think it's best you know something else. Leonard told me that you and Glory say the child is his, but . . . he says it's not."

I love Mrs. Rasmussen, and I think she loves us. But this, I thought, could tear us apart. I pulled a chair out from the table and sank down.

In a moment, she'd taken the chair across from mine. "Violet." Her voice was steady. "I believe you."

"You believe us?"

Her grey eyes, usually so soft, looked almost cold. "I know my sons. Walter was quiet. He liked to tinker with machines and—well, he kept to himself. But Leonard—" She shook her head. "I have no reason to doubt he's the father of Glory's child."

I thanked her for her honesty. "And though I'm not excusing Glory," I said, "there's something else you should know. While he was here, he asked her to marry him."

As soon as I said that, I wished I hadn't. A spasm crossed Mrs. Rasmussen's face, and she turned away.

And then I found myself saying something I'd never even considered before. "Maybe he really meant to. And then, after he left, changed his mind."

She turned back to me. "Perhaps." The lightness with which she'd greeted me was gone. "Still, I'm so sorry."

"I know you are." I rose. "I think I'll go make that tea now."

"Wait. Does your father know?"

I shook my head.

"When will you tell him? Better to find out from you before he suspects it himself."

"Yes," I said. "I'm sure Glory will tell him soon."

"I won't say a word to Stan until you tell me your father knows."

I thanked her and went upstairs.

When I came in, Glory was on the sofa, reading. "Are you all right?" she asked. "You look terrible!"

"Thanks." I tried to smile. "How about I make us some tea?" I put the tin of cookies on the table. "These are from Mrs. Rasmussen."

"How thoughtful she is!" Glory said. "But I'll make the tea. You go lie down."

I told her I didn't need to lie down, but she insisted, and in truth, it was a relief to lean back against the pillows and close my eyes. How would I tell her?

She brought in the tea and pushed a plate of cookies toward me. "Take more than one! I am!"

"You're eating for two," I said. "Which reminds me." I took a gulp of tea. "I've just had some rotten news."

"Really rotten?" she asked softly. Her expression was almost childlike.

"Really rotten."

"Oh, Violet, what is it? Tell me!"

"It's just . . . After Mrs. Rasmussen gave me the cookies, she told me she'd had a letter this week."

"From Leonard." She tossed her head a little. "So! What did he have to say?"

"He told his mother what I'd written. Then he told her that . . ."

"That the baby isn't his."

"Yes!" I said. "How did you guess?"

"Oh, Vi." She shook her head. "It's what they all say."

"But she doesn't believe him! She believes he *is* the father."

"Dear Mrs. Rasmussen." She poured the rest of the tea into our cups, then looked at me straight on. "It's over, Vi. Sometimes I think I knew even then it was over. Suspected anyway. Something in his voice, his eyes—the night we said goodbye." She offered the plate of cookies again. "Try the one with the chocolate icing."

I took it and tried to smile.

"I hope she hasn't told Mr. Sadowski yet! I'm a little afraid he'll fire me!"

"Why would he do that? He depends on you. And he's too soft-hearted to fire anyone, let alone someone he cares for."

"I know. He's a sweetheart." She grinned. "And besides, it's not as if his customers ever see me. I'm just a voice on the phone and a bill in the mail!"

"Mrs. Rasmussen promised she wouldn't tell him until we've told Papa. Which we have to do. Before he suspects. And then Aunt Blanche and Uncle Eddie."

Worry flickered across her face. "I'd like to wait a little longer."

"It won't get any easier."

"I know, but I've been reading. They say if you're going to lose the baby, it usually happens in the first three months. I must be about there, but I'd like to wait another week. Till Easter. Just to be sure." She rose. "I'll do the dishes. This is your birthday weekend. You just rest."

"Thanks." She was nearly at the door before I called her back. "Glory?"

"Mm-hmm?"

"You sound as if you want the baby."

"I do," she said softly. "I do."

GLORY

Today I told Papa I'm pregnant.

I dreamed last night that I told him and he threw me out on the street. I stood there crying, and Will opened his window and called down that he would take me in. I woke drenched in sweat and queasy. I got up and poured myself a glass of ginger ale and took it back to bed.

I must have woken Violet, because as soon as I'd settled back against the pillows, she sat up and asked me if I was okay. I said I'd dreamed that Papa threw me out. She came over and sat on the edge of my bed. "It'll be okay," she said. "If he threatens it, I'll tell him I'll leave, too, and then he'll have no one to cook his meals for him!" We both laughed. Then her face got serious again, and she asked me when I wanted to tell him.

"Let's wait until after Mass," I said. "I'll come. Maybe the Easter service will put him in a mood to forgive."

As we walked home from church together, the queasiness came back. I tried to reassure myself that, no matter what Papa said, I'd still have the baby, and Violet. And my poetry. And perhaps, someday, I'd make him proud of me again.

As soon as we'd hung up our coats, Violet looked at me. I nodded. She told Papa that before we got to work in the kitchen, we had something we needed to talk to him about. He was just sitting down with the paper, but set it aside and looked back and forth from Violet to me. "What's all the fuss?" he asked. "Go ahead."

Violet sat on the sofa.

I looked at Papa's face—unsuspecting, trusting. How could I tell him? He would be overcome with shame. My shame. The words—I couldn't let them come. But then a different feeling—that strange, pure love—washed over me. And I heard myself say it. Declare it. For my child. "I'm pregnant, Papa."

His face went completely still.

I went on. "The baby's due in September. I'm sorry. I know it must be a shock."

Still nothing.

"I promise I won't be a burden to you and Vi. As soon as I've recovered, I'll go back to work for Mr. Sadowski. I'm sure Mrs. Rasmussen will agree to look after the baby while I work—"

The look on his face stopped me. "The father," he said, and seemed almost to be choking. "Leonard Rasmussen."

I nodded.

He lunged at me.

I didn't move, even though I knew he would hit me. Behind him, I saw Violet leap up. But she was too late. The force of his hand struck my face to the side. "*Puttana!*" He grabbed my shoulders. "Twice you drag this family's name through the mud! "*Vergogna!* Shame on you!"

He threw me aside. I heard our front door hit the wall, footsteps heavy on the stairs, then pounding on Mrs. Rasmussen's door and Papa's voice shouting her name.

"Are you all right?" Violet whispered.

I nodded. My face burned, but I was more concerned about Papa throwing me out. Would Mrs. Rasmussen take me in?

"Roberto, whatever is it?" Her voice from downstairs.

"You send that son of yours a message from me! He'd better get himself home and marry my daughter, or the next time he shows his face around here, I'll kill him!"

I followed Violet out to the landing. "Papa!" she cried. "This has nothing to do with Mrs. Rasmussen. It's between Leonard and Glory. We've written to Leonard, but he hasn't answered. And Glory—" She turned to me.

"I don't want anyone in my life who doesn't want me," I said.

He looked up at me and shouted even louder. "You'll have him whether you want him or not!" He spun around to Mrs. Rasmussen again. "And if he doesn't marry her—"

He stopped. Stopped shouting, stopped moving. I couldn't see his face, but Mrs. Rasmussen's eyes widened. "Roberto," she asked, "are you all right?"

His arms dropped to his sides. Then he turned and rushed up the stairs past Violet and me. I heard the closet door slam, the scrape of his keys. Then he was back on the stairs again, his jacket in his hand.

Violet shouted after him. "Where are you going?"

The downstairs door slammed shut.

I went back inside, into the kitchen, ran some cold water on a dishcloth, and pressed it to my face.

Violet followed me, but before she could speak, Mrs. Rasmussen shouted our names.

"In here," Violet called.

She came into the kitchen. Her voice shook. "I'm so sorry—"

"It's all right," I began, but she went on.

"No, I've been thinking day and night about this, and I want to say my piece. Glory, I'm ashamed of my son. Of course he's your baby's father!" She paused as if struggling to go on. Then her voice strengthened. "But since he won't admit it, and help you, it's up to me as the baby's grandmother to do all I can. First thing is, from now on, I'll be giving you the money he sends me. It's never much, but it'll help."

Our sweet Mrs. Rasmussen. "You don't have to do that," I said. "Mr. Sadowski pays me a good wage, and I've managed to save quite a bit."

She held my gaze. "I insist on it. I got a little pension when my husband died, and a little more when I lost Walter. So let me do this. It'll help me feel better about it all."

I couldn't think what to say. Then Violet squeezed my arm. "Thank you," she said to Mrs. Rasmussen. "It's more than anyone could expect, and we're grateful."

She let out a sigh. "Now, where do you think your father went?"

"I have no idea," Violet answered. "But I hope he'll cool down in time to join us for dinner."

"Are you coming?" I asked. "To Aunt Blanche and Uncle Eddie's?"

She smiled. "Not this year. Stan's taking me out for dinner! It's the first time in my life I've ever eaten out on an Easter Sunday, and I'm looking forward to a nice meal and no dishes afterwards!" It was only then that I noticed she was wearing a new silvery grey dress that exactly matched the color of her eyes.

"Mrs. Rasmussen?" I asked. "Would you tell Mr. Sadowski about the baby for me? And that I asked you to?"

"Of course," she said. And then she seemed to hesitate, as if she'd suddenly thought of something distressing.

I asked her what was wrong. She shook her head sharply. "Nothing at all. I'll tell him."

At four o'clock, Violet and I brought a pot of baked beans and Violet's pound cake to Aunt Blanche and Uncle Eddie's. As we walked in, Aunt Blanche was setting the table. "Where's your father?" she asked.

"He left in the car a few hours ago," Violet answered. We brought the food into the kitchen, then hung up our coats. "We assume he's gone to cool off."

"Cool off?" Uncle Eddie's eyebrows lifted.

"Yes," I said. I was determined to tell them at once. "After we got home from Mass, I told Papa I'm pregnant."

The silverware in Aunt Blanche's hands clattered onto the table. The sound faded to silence before she spoke. "Leonard Rasmussen. I knew he was up to no good."

Uncle Eddie took a step toward me. "You're pregnant with Leonard Rasmussen's child? After you were together—what? Three weeks?"

"Two," I said.

"Gloria Campo." His lip lifted in disgust. "Never in my life did I imagine a niece of mine—" His voice rose. "Your poor mother would be ashamed of you! She tried to raise you girls in a good, Catholic family, but with a—"

"Eddie," Aunt Blanche said sharply. "Spare us the family history."

He glared at her. "It's not my family history, Blanche, or yours. But—"

"Stop it!" I don't remember ever hearing Aunt Blanche raise her voice to him that way. He scowled and strode into the kitchen. I heard the refrigerator open and slam shut.

"Glory?" Aunt Blanche crossed to me. "Leonard Rasmussen is the father of your child?"

"Yes," I said. "But he denies it."

"I see. Well." She looked shaken. "I wish that weren't the case. But there are worse things. Such as having to marry someone who doesn't want to marry you. Still, it won't be easy—for you, not having a husband, or the child, not having a father." She managed a smile. "Though I'm sure you'll marry one day. And in the meantime, once he gets used to the idea, your uncle will enjoy having a grand-niece or grand-nephew to spoil. As will I!"

Uncle Eddie appeared in the kitchen doorway with a bottle of beer.

"I'm sorry I've disappointed you," I said to him.

"I can't condone sin. Even if my wife can."

"Judge not, that ye be not judged," Aunt Blanche said quietly.

"Fair enough," he answered. "But while you're being so enlightened, Blanche, you do realize this means that Glory's ambitions—finishing her degree, for starters—they're over."

I didn't wait for Aunt Blanche. "Not necessarily," I said. "Some women go to college when their children start school. I could do that."

"Right. I won't be taking any bets on that one." He crossed to the window and gazed into the street. "It's a cruel world out there, Glory. For a single mother and a bastard kid."

Aunt Blanche raised one eyebrow. "Jesus of Nazareth was—"

"For cryin' out loud, Blanche! It's Easter Sunday! Can you give it a rest?"

No one spoke for a moment, then Violet asked brightly if dinner was ready.

"It was ready when you girls walked in," Aunt Blanche answered quietly. "I'll just finish setting the table."

"Shouldn't we wait for Papa?" I asked.

Violet shrugged. "After what he did to you, I'd just as soon go ahead without him."

"What did he do?" Uncle Eddie demanded.

Softly, I told Violet that it didn't matter, but she answered him anyway. "He slapped Glory across the face. Hard."

Sneering, he muttered something I couldn't make out. Then he said, louder, "We can't start without him." He gestured toward the window. "He's here."

I felt sad, suddenly, for Papa, so sad that tears pricked my eyes. He was so proud of me, so loving, when I was a girl, but lately all I've caused him is disappointment and shame.

He rang the doorbell. Violet began to rise, but I touched her shoulder and went out to the front hall. I opened the door. He stood on the steps in the slanting sunlight, his hat in one hand and in the other a bunch of daffodils, tied in twine. "Here," he said, and pushed them toward me. "I drove—I don't know where. A farm had a roadside stand. I got them for you."

GLORY

This love is like the light of an ever-expanding star.

Five months now, and with each day that passes it seems to radiate further and further beyond us. I find myself loving indiscriminately. The stray cats, the birds, the strangers who smile, the neighbors who whisper. Even my failures. And questions. I embrace them. It's like what Rilke says in his *Letters to a Young Poet*. I hadn't been able to open that book for a long time after Leonard left, but in the last few weeks, I've read it over and over. Rilke and my child. I've long stopped wishing for Leonard to give me a diamond. These are the jewels he left me.

This morning we went to the Decoration Day parade. Violet took pictures. As we were sitting with Papa this evening, she told us about an idea she'd had while she was photographing Will. Portraits of wounded veterans. Each with a story, in the veteran's own words, of how he'd been wounded, and what the injury meant to him.

Papa didn't seem to understand. "What *can* an injury like Will's mean to him," he asked, "except the ruin of any chance of a normal life?"

"We might assume that," Violet said quietly, "but has anyone ever asked Mr. Owen? I'd like to do that, and share his answer with the people who see his photo."

I told Violet I thought it was a beautiful idea. "Maybe you could put together a gallery show."

She looked up from her knitting—a blanket for the baby. "Maybe. But first I need to find other veterans like Mr. Owen who'd be willing to let me take their picture and share their story."

"So he's agreed?" Papa asked.

"Yes. I'm photographing him tomorrow."

"Where? Here?"

"No, I thought—if the sun is out—I'll photograph him in the park."

"I don't know." Papa rustled his newspaper. "The whole thing sounds morbid to me. Why don't you photograph children?"

"I do photograph children, Papa—as you know. Just today, Dorothy Pope's sister, Louise, asked me to photograph her baby. And I'm looking forward to photographing my niece or nephew one day soon."

"I can see it now," I laughed. "Baby Campo—the most photographed baby in history!"

Papa lowered his newspaper. "Campo?"

"Yes," I said quietly. "As the baby grows up, it'll be easier—at school and so on—if we have the same name."

"And tell Papa what you've decided for a first name," Violet said quickly.

"If it's a girl, she'll be Roberta, and if a boy, Robert."

I admit I expected Papa to be pleased. Instead, a look of uneasiness passed over his face. "It's your decision," he said, and lifted the paper again.

Violet turned to me and shrugged.

I picked up her hand. She gave me a puzzled look. I put my finger to my lips and placed her hand on my middle. The baby was moving, and I wanted her to feel it. Her eyes widened for a moment, then her whole face broke into a smile. She'll be a dream auntie. And one day—I know it—Papa will fall in love with his grandchild. And forgive me.

I made a discovery today.

About Mr. Owen. Will, I mean. And maybe, too, about myself.

We'd planned to shoot at the park. But when Mr. Owen rang our doorbell, it was raining heavily. I opened the door. He was wearing his uniform, the jacket and breeches pressed, the black boots shining. He carried his cap in his hands. "I see it's not a day for taking pictures—not by the river anyway."

I nodded, but seeing him there in the soft grey light on the landing, I was determined to begin. I told him I might want to photograph him more than once, against different backgrounds, in different lighting, until I discovered what's best. "So I'd like to get started indoors today. But if you'd feel more comfortable outdoors, we could wait until tomorrow afternoon."

"Well, Sundays I take the train to Porter Square. There's a group of us that meets, sort of the way you might go to church. And I bring some of my art. A friend of mine has a little store. Nobody'd buy from me. But Pilar, well . . . It's not easy saying no to Pilar." There was a hint of mischief in his eyes. "Anyway, if you'd like to start today, we could use my place."

Mr. Owen's place. I vaguely remembered books and masks and paintings. Of course! It would be perfect.

As I set my equipment down in his parlor, he offered me a root beer. I accepted, and he disappeared into his kitchen. I could feel my heart pounding. There's an intimacy in taking someone's portrait, and I wasn't sure I was ready.

I forced myself to breathe deeply and study the room. It's mostly as I'd remembered it—all the walls and shelves filled with paintings and other objects. Though the painting of Ada Sadowski is gone from between the front windows. Instead, there's a painting of a couple—their faces obscured—locked in an embrace.

As I scanned the bookcases, I noticed, sitting on top of a row of poetry volumes, Glory's chapbook. I opened it. *To Will Owen, artist, neighbor, and friend, with love—Gloria Campo*

"One of my favorites." He handed me my root beer, then carried his own to a rocking chair. "Would you read me the title poem?"

"Of course." I took a gulp of my soda before turning to it. I looked up. Mr. Owen was leaning back in his chair, rocking. His eyes were closed. I began to read.

THIS BRIGHT LIMIT

(in memory of my mother)

this fleeting fire—crest of dusk
ruddied branch—bird hushed

shimmer of scarlet clouds in this window
gossamer scrim of this denouement

remnants of morning's ripest gleanings
memories of meetings—memories of leavings

anyone's eyes—anyone's tears

anyone's hands—wounds—scars

poems unfinished—questions unanswered
journeys under invisible stars

blossoming night—abscission of memory
breath—this ecstasy

this bright limit

I looked at Mr. Owen. His eyes were still closed, and I wondered if he'd fallen asleep. The side of his face toward me was handsome, even noble: a broad, high cheekbone, full lips, a strong jaw. What kind of injury could so destroy one half of a man's face, and leave the other half untouched? As quietly as I could, I replaced the book on the shelf and crossed to my camera. The room was dim, but I didn't set up my light. I inserted a flashbulb, focused, and pressed.

He opened his eyes and looked across at me. "The first time I read that poem," he said, "it astonished me. That a young girl—a Catholic girl—had written it. And then I started to think about how you'd lost your mother."

I didn't know what to say. I've never understood the poem, or why Glory dedicated it to Mama. So I changed the subject. "What's your religion, Mr. Owen?"

"Uncertainty." He shrugged. "Art. Love." His gaze drifted to a photograph centered on a little table, a votive candle to one side. It was of a woman, young and beautiful, with large eyes and a mouth that looked soft as velvet.

"'She cannot fade, though thou hast not thy bliss, / For ever wilt thou love, and she be fair.'" He looked up. "Keats," he said. "Drink your soda before the ice melts. And if you don't mind, call me Will."

As I drank, he told me the story of his service. He was eighteen when his number came up in the final summer of the war. After training, he was shipped out to France. He was wounded in the Battle of the Argonne Forest, a week before the armistice. "Thousands and thousands wounded," he said. "And we were the lucky ones."

"How did it happen?"

"We were advancing toward a railroad line when the sky erupted. I don't remember more than that. Shrapnel dug a trench up my right side from my hip to my face. The surgeon told me later, my arm should have been blown clean off. I guess the sheer irrationality of war spared it."

I wanted to ask him more, but he rose abruptly. "Let me help you set up that light you brought. Where do you want to start?"

I asked if I could see his studio. A faint smell of paints and solvents grew stronger as I followed him into the room above Papa's bedroom. Unlike his parlor, it was nearly bare, with white walls adorned only by the window and three portraits. The one facing me as I entered was of a smiling woman in a blue dress with a small dog at her feet and, like portraits I've seen of Saint Francis, her hand extended to a bird. "Your mother?" I guessed.

"Very good."

I turned to the portrait on the left wall. "And this one?" A woman in a low-cut dress draped in a long strand of pearls, her dark eyes dreamy.

"You don't recognize Helen Morgan? Guess I'll have to have another go at her."

"No, it's my ignorance, not your painting!" I protested. "I've never known what she looked like, though I've heard her records—Mrs. Rasmussen plays them."

He nodded. "The way she sang—you just knew she'd lived that grief. Not surprising she died so young."

I turned to the last portrait, on the right, of a young woman with blue eyes and long auburn hair, dressed in white, and sitting beneath a magnolia tree. I gasped. "Ada Sadowski! I remember from when I was here before. When I was little. I've never forgotten it."

He gazed at the portrait without answering.

"You moved her in here. Why?"

He shrugged. "I decided I like to have her by me while I'm painting."

There was an awful sadness in the way he said it. And then I remembered the photograph.

When I asked him, he told me it was her graduation photo and that she'd given him a copy. He shuffled closer to the painting and gazed up at Ada's face. "When I was in the trenches, I'd dream of her. She was only fourteen then, but I figured, when she got older, the few years between us wouldn't matter." He turned to me. "Then I got home—like this. I think she always knew I had feelings for her, though of course I never said a word." His eyes went back to the portrait.

I asked if she'd sat for it.

He smiled. "Wouldn't that have been something? But no. It's from memory. Of watching her blossom. Before everything happened."

"But what did happen?"

"You've never heard?"

I shook my head, and then he told me what he knew, how Ada had been popular with the boys in high school, then, after graduation, had gotten a secretarial job at Laval's and started dating older men. "Her parents were strict. Especially Magda. She chafed at it. I sometimes think her beauty was her undoing. She expected it to lift her out of all this." He gestured toward the windows.

"Mill Street?"

"Mill Street. She wanted—even more than romance, I think—power. To know her own power. Like it was a game, I thought. A game she'd grow out of. And in time, find happiness. But then, one spring, she disappeared."

A gust of wind flung a thick band of rain against the window. He shuffled toward it and pushed it tightly closed. Then he stayed there, looking at the rain. "Everybody wondered about it. Not just me. Though there wasn't anything we could do. We knew it wasn't foul play."

"How?"

"Because Stan and Magda never called the police, never even spoke about it unless you asked. I did once, after I hadn't seen her for a couple of weeks. They said she'd gone to New York. Turns out it was a dodge. I never knew the truth until just before Magda died."

He told me how he had come upon Mrs. Sadowski one afternoon, sitting on her front steps, waiting for her husband to come home. "She said she was fine, but her face was shiny with sweat, and every now and then, as she talked, I saw her wince a little. I didn't think of it then, but afterwards I figured she knew she was dying, because all of a sudden, she started talking about Ada, about seeing her again. 'If the Lord has forgiven her,' she said." He leaned against the window frame, not looking at me. "I asked her what Ada could possibly need forgiveness for, and that's when she told me about the baby. Ada wouldn't tell them who the father was. They sent her to a Catholic place somewhere north of Boston."

"You mean—she died in childbirth?"

"Afterwards," he said. "Some sort of fever."

"And the baby?"

"A girl. Lived. The nuns said there was a couple in Chestnut Hill, wealthy, could give her all the advantages. So Stan and Magda let her go." He straightened, then gestured toward the door. "Maybe we should set up in the parlor. Too many ghosts in here."

I followed him out.

I sat him in front of his books. At first I photographed him in profile—left, then right—but after a few shots I realized I couldn't favor one face. I had to show both in the same moment, both gazing into the light.

With those next few shots, I began to relax, and to look at him as a professional, without concern for rudeness. And as I did, I realized that I'd been wrong to look away so quickly all my life. To study his face—all of it—was respectful, and right.

I asked him to stand, and arranged my light so it shone down from above. But he looked awkward in his stiff jacket. I asked him to take it off. We would photograph him in his shirt, I said, though it was plain. "Where are your I.D. tags?" I asked. "Do you still have them?"

"Of course." He began to unbutton his collar. "Only one, though. The scout thought I was dead, so he took the other. Never did get it back." He pulled the tag out from beneath his shirt.

Light glanced off the tag like a spark. "Mr. Owen," I said.

"Will."

"Will. I'm asking you this as a professional—"

"As an artist."

"Yes. As an artist." I searched for the words.

"Violet." Looking straight at me, he began to unbutton his shirt. "I'd like to show you the scar in my side." He paused. "If you'd like to photograph it."

"Thank you," I said. "If I may."

He removed his shirt, and then, in one sweep, his undershirt. He turned his right side to me. I asked him to touch his dog tag with his right hand. I picked up my camera and looked through the lens. First, at his eyes—soft, distant, as if watching faraway children play. Then at his body. The scar is a river of rust dividing his torso in two halves, chest and back, as if a saber had sliced from his hip through half his ribs and the blood that had flowed was forever dried there. The scar is beautiful. Mr. Owen—Will—is beautiful.

VIOLET

Why don't I like being kissed?

Everybody else does. But it didn't make me feel the way it seems to make everybody else feel. Crazy happy. Taking Will's photograph made me feel that way. Taking any photographs. Including of Jimmy. Though I never thought about it until tonight.

After I finished photographing Will, he suggested I ask Corporal James Conlan. I told him Jimmy and I had been classmates, but I felt uncomfortable asking him. He said he'd be seeing him at the VFW the following Tuesday night and would have him phone me. Jimmy called that same night.

I photographed him last Saturday on the bridge where the river runs through the park. The weather was perfect—sunny and warm, but not hot. He wore his full uniform, the left sleeve of his jacket sewn together at the elbow, but my camera focused on his face—his high forehead, thick brows, and slender jaw. I asked him, "Has anyone ever said you look like Bing Crosby?" It felt natural to tease him—we're old schoolmates. But maybe he didn't see it that way. Maybe he thought I was flirting with him.

"A couple of times, yeah," he answered, "but nobody's ever said I sound like him!"

"I remember!" I laughed. "All those Christmas concerts when the sisters would ask you not to sing!"

"That's why I took up the trumpet," he said.

Remembering how well he'd played trumpet made me feel rotten. I put down my camera. "You were great," I said. "I'm so sorry."

"It's okay," he shrugged. "Some of my buddies had to give up a lot more than that."

I asked him if he'd like to sit for a while in the park and tell me his story. "I'll do one better," he said. "I'll tell it over a chocolate shake at Woolworth."

"Deal," I said, "but make mine strawberry."

I enjoyed walking back into town with him. I guess it made me feel important to have a handsome veteran at my side. For a while, we reminisced about Saint Isabel's and his trips to Sister Superior's office. "You were always in trouble," I teased him.

"And you were always teacher's pet! What got you into photography?"

"My father gave me a camera for my eleventh birthday," I answered. "From the first day, I was hooked. Do you remember, during high school, I took photos for the yearbook—of the football games, and the marching band?"

"Sure I do! I'd forgotten all about that!"

"Anyway, after I graduated, I tried nursing school, but—" I shrugged.

"Wasn't a good fit?" he asked kindly.

"Wasn't a good fit," I repeated. "And then I started to work for Mr. Crane, and he took me on as an apprentice."

"And this veterans project. That's your own idea?"

I said it was.

"What are you planning to do with the photos?"

"I don't know. You're only the second vet I've photographed. I'll just have to see how it goes."

He gave me the names of two friends he felt I should meet. One of them, he said, had been badly burned. "You sure you're up for this?"

I said I wasn't sure, but I was going to try.

At Woolworth, we had our pick of tables. "I guess everyone's outdoors today," he said.

I assured him the interview wouldn't take long.

"Oh, I'm in no hurry," he said. "I still take pleasure in the things I used to miss during the war, like a chocolate shake, and talking to a girl."

I was glad the waitress came just then to take our orders. It made me uneasy to hear him say he took pleasure in talking to a girl, knowing that girl—at least today—was me.

I got out my notebook. "How did it happen?" I asked.

He told me he was wounded in the Battle of the Bulge. It was January, bitterly cold, and snowed day after day. "It seemed as if God was on Hitler's side." He described defending a fuel depot when a shell exploded "from out of nowhere. I dodged it—or thought I did. Until I looked down and saw blood all over the snow, and a bloody stump where my arm had been. Next thing I knew I was laid out flat on a stretcher, looking at the sky. I don't remember much else until I woke up after the surgery. And then I was on my way home."

"And now?" I asked. "How has it changed you? Your life, day to day?"

He shrugged. "Not much. Had to relearn some things. Like how to dress, cut my food, drive. But—"

I looked up from my scribbling. His face was still. "But?"

"Lying in the field hospital, I felt guilty for leaving my buddies behind. But I was damned grateful to be alive. And that feeling?" His eyes held mine. "It stays with me."

The waitress brought our shakes and two paper-wrapped straws. He held his straw upright, pushed the paper down, lifted the straw out, and stuck it into his shake. Then he looked at me and smiled. "Thanks for not offering to help."

"You're welcome," I said.

After that, he asked me about Glory—he'd heard she'd been accepted to Norcross. "How's she making out?"

I didn't want to lie, but couldn't tell him the truth. Not the details. "She did well until nearly the end of her first year," I said. "Then she got sick. She was hospitalized briefly. And spent the next couple of months recovering."

"I'm sorry to hear that. And now?"

"Oh, she's fine now. She's working and writing and—" I took a quick sip of my shake, then leaned back and looked directly into his eyes. "She's expecting a baby in September."

His brows lifted a little, but he didn't look away. "I got you. How do you feel about that?"

"I'm looking forward to being an aunt," I said.

He smirked. "Good for you."

As we were heading back out to the street, he asked me to a film—*My Favorite Brunette*. "It opens next Saturday. A comedy. Bob Hope playing a baby photographer! Should be right up your alley, with a niece or nephew on the way!"

I laughed, but I didn't know how to answer. We'd met for professional reasons. But going to a film together . . . That would be a date, and I didn't know if I wanted to date Jimmy Conlan. He was waiting for an answer. "Sure," I said. "That sounds like fun."

I spent most of the week trying not to think about seeing him again. That worked until this afternoon, when Glory said she was heading down to Mrs. Rasmussen's to work on clothes for the baby's layette, and I realized I'd be alone with nothing to do except imagine the night ahead. I admitted to Glory I felt sick with nerves.

She said I was nuts. "Close your eyes," she commanded. "Now, can you imagine yourself kissing him?"

My eyes flew open. "Glory!"

She laughed, then asked what I was planning to wear.

"I don't know! I haven't even thought about it yet!"

"Your pink dress!" She hugged me and started down the stairs. "It brings out your green eyes!"

She seemed so happy for me. I thought, maybe there really was something wonderful about being with a man, about holding his hand, kissing him. How would I know, when I'd never done any of those things? Glory knew, and if she was happy for me, there must be a reason.

That's what I kept telling myself. But then, after the film, in the back of the cab he'd called, Jimmy took my chin in his hand and reached down and kissed me. His lips were cool and moist, almost clammy, and seemed to be trying to pry mine apart. A chill went down my neck. The cab turned into Mill Street. He leaned away again. "This is you," he said. The cab pulled up to the curb. "You're a special girl, Violet. I'll give you a call next week."

I made myself smile and slid out of the cab and said good night. Then I ran up the steps. Already my eyes were swimming with tears. I fished in my purse but couldn't find my key. Mrs. Rasmussen opened the door. "Stan and I saw you come up the steps—have you lost your key?"

I forced myself to sound happy. "Oh, I'm sure it's just hiding at the bottom of my purse. Thanks for letting me in!" I rushed past her.

"Of course!"

"She okay, Esther?" Mr. Sadowski asked.

"I'm fine!" I called. "Good night!"

When I got upstairs, I heard *Traviata*—Violetta and Alfredo's final duet. I hung up my coat, wiped my eyes, and went into the parlor. Papa turned off the radio. "So how did it go, this date with Jimmy Conlan?"

"It wasn't a date, Papa," I protested. "We just saw a movie together. Bob Hope and—"

"Since when is seeing a movie together not a date? By the way, Glory made macaroni for supper. If you're hungry, there's some left over."

"No thanks. We ate before the movie." I headed toward the bathroom.

"You went to dinner and a movie, but it wasn't a date? I don't understand young people these days." He stood and stretched. "So how is Jimmy Conlan? Still getting into trouble?"

"No, Papa. He's just earned his real estate license."

"Real estate! Good for him! And do you like him?"

I didn't want to talk. I just wanted to go to bed. "He's a very nice person," I said. "Good night!" I went into the bathroom and scrubbed my teeth and face.

Glory was sitting up in bed, writing. She set aside her notebook. "Tell me all about it!"

As I undressed, I recounted some of our conversation, about Jimmy going into real estate, hoping to capitalize on what he called the postwar housing boom. Then I described the movie. "It was all right. Pretty silly, actually." I got into bed.

"What about after the movie?" she asked. "Did he kiss you?"

"Yes," I said. "In the cab. But—"

"But?"

"I don't know." I tried to explain, but I felt so childish. Finally, I turned and faced her. "Glory, what do you feel when a man kisses you?"

"Well, some men are good kissers and some not so good. With the good ones, I feel over the moon. Why?"

I didn't answer.

"Jimmy's not such a good kisser?"

I shrugged. "How would I know?"

"You'd know, Vi. You just would."

I imagined Glory kissing Leonard. Making love with Leonard. What does it feel like, to want a man that way? "I know it's early," I said, "but do you mind if we turn out the light?"

"Not at all. I'm tired, too."

In the darkness, I could hear her turning . . . And then she fell asleep.

I wish I didn't feel so empty inside. I want to be in love. Like Glory was with Leonard. But I'm not.

GLORY

Today was the most beautiful day I can remember.

The light! Everything, for a few moments, was only light. And everything made sense. Or I no longer needed it to.

Maybe that's why Millay writes so often of the sea. Maybe it makes lots of people feel this way. Back in high school, even with the gasoline rationing, Dorothy Pope and her family would spend weekends at the beach all summer. We never did. Papa didn't even have a car until my senior year. It had been Mrs. Sadowski's car, and Mr. Sadowski sold it to him for "next to nothing," Papa said. That's when they really became friends.

Today they went to Fenway Park to watch the Red Sox game. Papa had told Violet she could use the car, so when Jimmy phoned during breakfast and asked if she'd like to go to the lake, she said why don't we all go to Hampton Beach instead.

When we arrived, we found a parking space right on the boardwalk and set up our blanket and umbrella close to the water. We'd assumed the beach would be crowded, since yesterday was Independence Day, but Jimmy said he thought people were scared off because the weather forecast said a fifty-fifty chance of thunderstorms in the afternoon. "Fifty-fifty means it's just as likely they won't happen," he said. As it turned out, the skies were still clear after lunch, so we strolled down to the water again.

While I waded in to my knees, Violet and Jimmy bobbed back and forth in the waves. Even with one arm, Jimmy's a good swimmer. He went farther out than Violet, then let the waves send him crashing back. Violet was standing in water about hip-high, and he reached out and grabbed her by the waist and pulled her down into the waves. She came up laughing.

I thought I should leave the two of them alone, so I went back and settled myself under the umbrella with a book of poetry, *North and South*, a first book by a poet named Elizabeth Bishop. I was reading a strange poem about a creature who tries to reach the moon when, all of a sudden, I heard my name. I looked up. Dorothy Pope was crossing the sand, waving. I didn't think about the fact that I'm six months pregnant, and that we hadn't seen each other since before I'd met Leonard. I got up and waved back.

"Glory!" Her face broke into a smile as she reached our umbrella. "It's so good to see you!"

In my loose sundress, I don't think she noticed at first. But then she threw her arms around me. As she drew away, her eyes were wide. "Glory! You're expecting!"

Before I could answer, Violet and Jimmy came running up from the water. Violet said hello to Dorothy and threw herself onto the blanket. Jimmy grabbed his towel. "Dorothy," I said, this is Jimmy Conlan—he was in Violet's class at Saint Isabel's." I turned to him. "Jimmy, do you remember Dorothy? She was in my class."

He threw his towel over his shoulder and extended his hand. "I think I do remember you. Your father used to drop you and your sister off at school every morning in his red Cadillac!"

Dorothy laughed. "That's right! He went by the school on the way to his office!" She turned and called out across the sand. "Louise! It's Glory and Violet!" Then she turned back and looked from Jimmy to me. "Congratulations to you both!"

"Oh," I said, "Jimmy and I aren't—"

"For heaven's sake! I'm sorry!"

"Not at all." Jimmy's voice was kind. "It's a natural enough mistake. No, I'm just . . ." He glanced at Violet. "A friend of the family."

Dorothy's sister, Louise, had crossed the sand. She was holding a chubby toddler with golden curls and a bright pink mouth that, just then, was curled into a pout. "This is Billy," she said, "but I'm afraid he's not at his best." She held him out to Dorothy. "Auntie's turn? He needs a nap."

"I'll take him," I said. "I need the practice!"

She put him in my arms. He seemed content, or perhaps he was too tired to protest, because his little curly head drooped onto my shoulder. Violet smiled at me. A gentle breeze rippled the umbrella, and a cloud drifted over the sun. "May I walk with him a bit?" I asked Louise.

"Be my guest!" she laughed.

It might seem silly, but as I walked toward the water, I whispered to him that soon I'd be holding a baby of my own. "Maybe a little boy just like you."

A hazy yellow tinged the sky. Seagulls cried. Two boys sprinted into the sea. Billy's body went limp with sleep.

I looked out at the glistening waves. And that's when it happened. Suddenly, there was no ocean anymore, or horizon or sky. There was only light. Oh, it's so hard to explain, but for that moment, nothing else existed. Not even I myself, or little Billy in my arms. Everything—everything—had dissolved into light.

Then I heard Violet's voice. "Glory? We're packing to go. Dorothy and Louise, too."

I turned.

Her face was as radiant as an angel's.

She touched my arm. "Glory?"

The world returned—but far more beautiful than I'd known it before.

"He's asleep," I said. "I wish I could hold him forever."

She slid her arm around us both. "We'll come back next summer, and you'll have your own baby to hold."

We walked up the sand together. Jimmy and Dorothy and Louise were talking about the war. "You were so brave," I heard Dorothy say. "So much braver than I could ever be."

Louise turned to me. "He's just dropped off," I said, and lifted Billy into her arms. He fussed for a moment, then settled again. We said goodbye and they headed back across the sand.

I helped Violet pack up our things while Jimmy took down the umbrella. Just as we reached the car, we felt the first drops of rain.

Except for the sound of the rain and the wipers, it was quiet for most of the ride home. As we pulled up in front of Jimmy's house, he thanked Violet for driving. "I had a great time," he said in that boisterous way some young men have. I saw him place his hand over Violet's on the steering wheel. "Can I see you tomorrow? There's a matinée showing of *Blue Skies*."

From the back seat, I saw the tension in her face as she glanced out the window into the street. "Don't forget, Violet," I said softly, "Aunt Blanche and Uncle Eddie are having us to Sunday dinner, and they'd asked us to stay to watch that program they like on their new television set."

Jimmy's hand dropped away. "Sounds like you've got a full day. But I'll see you at the VFW picnic next weekend!"

Now Violet looked at him and smiled. "Right. See you there."

I waited until we were in bed tonight before I asked Violet if I'd done the right thing. "Should I have said that about dinner with Uncle Eddie and Aunt Blanche? Or did you want to go to the matinée?"

She didn't answer. I could hear the rain slapping against our bedroom window. Finally she got out of bed and came and sat beside me. "I was glad you said it. I had fun with you and Jimmy today. I really did. But . . ."

"But what?"

"I wish Jimmy and I—" She crossed her arms in front of her chest and stomped her foot on the ground. "Oh, why can't we just be friends?"

"Have you asked him that?"

"No. I don't know how!' She jumped up, crossed to the window, lifted the shade, and looked out at the rain.

"Tell him exactly what you just told me—that you like him as a friend."

"You make it sound so easy."

"And—why isn't it?"

She let the shade fall, then flung herself back into bed. "I don't know," she said, and pulled up the covers and stared at the ceiling.

I noticed my copy of Rilke on the bedside table. I pushed it over to her side. "In the morning, if you're in the mood, why don't you borrow this?"

She glanced at the book.

"Rilke," I explained, "was a German poet. He said we should be patient with everything we're uncertain about. That we shouldn't keep trying to answer our questions. Instead, we should try to love them—and live them. Isn't that beautiful?"

She nodded. Then, suddenly, she sat bolt upright and asked me about the title poem in my chapbook. "Why did you dedicate it to Mama?"

I said it was hard to explain, but that one night, at dusk, I'd been thinking of Mama and had the sense of something beautiful—even ecstatic—hovering there, at the boundaries of our lives. She looked puzzled, so I asked her what had made her think of it.

She shrugged. "I just wondered."

We said good night and I turned off the light.

I know there'll be hard days when I have my baby. Teething and fussing and all that. But there'll be days like today, too. I wish Mama could be with me then—on the beautiful days—not so much to help me, but . . . just to hold her grandchild, the way I held Billy.

Maybe I'll dream about her tonight, that we're together at the ocean on a summer day, and I place her grandchild in her arms, and all three of us, and the sand and the waves and the sky, dissolve into light.

VIOLET

I shouldn't have left the house today.

Not that I could have changed what happened. I'm not claiming that. I would have been just as helpless as Papa. But at least I could have been there from the start.

Instead, I was at a picnic.

When Jimmy asked me to go, I agreed because I knew we wouldn't be alone—even Will was going. And though I still wish I'd stayed home, one good thing came of it—something I'm glad to have over with. While we walked to the park together, Will convinced me to tell Jimmy the truth.

At first we talked about the other veterans I've photographed—their stories, and how the sessions have gone. But as we turned down Park Street, he stopped and looked straight at me and asked me if I had feelings for Jimmy.

It was so unexpected, I guess I stalled for time. "Romantic feelings, you mean?"

"Those usually are the kind of feelings young people have for each other."

His eyes, soft and untroubled, made me feel he deserved a full and honest answer. "No," I said. "I don't have romantic feelings for Jimmy."

"So the way you see it, you're friends." He started walking again.

"Yes. Is that wrong?"

"Of course not. As long as he sees it the same way. Which he doesn't."

I said nothing.

"Have you told him?" he asked.

"Not exactly."

"Why not? You're not lacking in courage. Or kindness."

"What do you mean—kindness?"

"Everybody has a right to look for that special someone. The longer you string Jimmy along, the longer you keep him from finding her."

I wondered, was that what I was doing—stringing him along? "I keep thinking," I said, "if I just give it a little more time . . ."

"It's true that the flame can grow, but . . . There's no spark at all?"

"No," I murmured. "No spark at all." And then I understood. I was never going to fall in love with Jimmy. I didn't even want to.

We turned into the wrought-iron gates at the entrance to the park. Up on the bandstand, musicians in uniform were setting out their chairs and instruments and music stands, and on the lawn, parents were unpacking baskets onto picnic tables while their children played tag or took turns on the swings.

"And how's Glory doing?" Will asked. "Can't be easy, carrying a baby in July."

I told Will she'd been complaining of backache and nausea. "She was lying down when I left. I don't plan to stay long."

"I'm sorry to hear that. But you try to have a good time while you're here, okay?" He headed for a set of chairs beside the bandstand.

Jimmy and I had arranged to meet on the bridge. He was standing mid-span, talking with a much taller man with dark blond hair and a trim mustache. When he saw me, he smiled his boyish smile and waved, then as I approached, grabbed me around the waist and pulled me close. The gesture caught me off guard, but I pretended to take it playfully as I pushed him away.

The other man looked surprised. "Who's this?"

"This is Violet Campo, a former classmate. Violet, meet Lieutenant Harold Morgan, United States Navy. He fought in the Pacific."

"Thank you for your service, Lieutenant," I said.

He nodded. "Afternoon, Violet. And you can call me Hal."

"Are you from around here?" I asked.

"Nope. Newburyport. But my wife is. I work for her father's insurance firm. Speaking of work, has Jimmy told you one of his clients just made an offer on a house?"

I turned to Jimmy. "Congratulations! When was all this?"

"Yesterday." He seemed to blush a little. "Looks like it'll be my first sale. I showed them six houses, and they made an offer on one in that new development—Mayflower Estates. Have you been there?"

"Yes," I said. "I had a client there."

"Are you in real estate?" Hal asked.

"Violet's a photographer," Jimmy explained. "She works for George Crane, downtown. But in her spare time, she's photographing veterans."

"And taking down their stories," I added. "I'm not sure where it will lead."

He looked out over the river. "Sounds like quite a project." His voice was stiff, and in a moment, he gestured to the riverbank. "Will you excuse me? My twins are a little too close to the water." He strode to the end of the bridge and down the bank.

I watched him tug two young boys up from the edge of the river. "Hal seems nice," I said to Jimmy. "How long have you known him?"

"Just a few months. Since I got into real estate. He handles the homeowner's insurance. Does a bang-up business. You'd like his wife, Suzie. She couldn't come today because the baby's got a cold."

"They have three children?"

He nodded. "All boys. Hal says next time they're hoping for a girl." He leaned over the side of the bridge and looked down at the children playing. "That's what I'd like, Violet," he said. "Children. A home of my own. Prosperity and peace."

My stomach lurched. "Does a wife fit in somewhere?"

He looked up. "Yes." His tone was quiet, simple. "I don't mind admitting I'm looking for a wife."

"In that case," I said, "I hope you and she find each other soon."

He seemed almost to wince.

"I can't stay," I continued. "Glory's not feeling well." I touched his shoulder and said goodbye.

I felt like a heel for disappointing him, but I knew I'd done the right thing. And anyway, as soon as I started walking home, I found myself worrying about Glory—so much so that, as I turned down Mill Street, I could barely keep from running. And then, as I got near our building, I saw Mrs. Rasmussen at the top of the steps. "Violet!" she cried. "Thank heavens you're home. Your father's taking Glory to the hospital!"

In the hall, Papa shouted at me to get in the car as he carried Glory, sobbing, down the stairs. She was still in the loose shift she'd been wearing when I left her, but her hips and legs were wrapped in a bedsheet. It looked soaked. As they reached the landing, she screamed. I'd heard screams like that—crazy-with-pain screams—on my maternity rotation in nursing school. Then the sobbing again, this time with words: "No! Please, baby, wait!"

Mrs. Rasmussen held open the hall door.

"Call the hospital!" I said. "Tell them we're coming!"

I ran out to the sidewalk and helped Papa get Glory into the car. As he drove across town, I tried to hold her while her pleas—"Baby, wait! Wait!"—turned into screams again as the contractions came. Too strong, I knew. Too fast.

The car jerked to a stop at the emergency room entrance, and Papa jumped out. He opened the door, gathered Glory up, and carried her inside. I parked in the visitors' lot and dashed back. As soon as the doors parted, I heard Glory's pleas, "No, baby, wait!" She was on a gurney. Papa was talking loudly to a nurse, his hands gesticulating wildly. Two orderlies began to wheel Glory down the hall. I ran to follow them. "It's all right, Glory!" I shouted. "I'm here! I'm here!"

The orderlies stopped at an elevator. "There's a waiting room across the hall," one of them said.

"But I can't leave her—"

"If you care about your sister, that's exactly what you'll do!" The nurse who'd been speaking with Papa strode into the elevator ahead of the gurney. "Wait in the room across the hall. I'll update you as soon as I can."

The doors closed. Glory was gone. I looked at Papa and burst into tears.

He put his arm around me, and we went into the waiting room and sat down. Only one other person—a young man— was in the room. He was reading a magazine.

I made myself calm down and, drying my eyes, asked Papa when it had started.

"A few minutes before you got home. I think she'd been sleeping, and the pain must have woken her up. I heard her call for you, so I went in. She was dazed. Like she was still asleep. The bedclothes were soaked. I knew that meant her water broke. And then she screamed, just like your mother screamed with the two of you, and more water came out. All over the bed. She seemed to realize then what was happening, and—" He struggled to speak. "The look on her face. So help me God, I'll never forget it." He rose and crossed to the windows. For a long time, neither of us spoke.

When he sat beside me again, he asked why I'd come home so soon. I couldn't tell him about Jimmy. Not then. So I said I'd had a bad feeling.

He nodded. "You've always been close like that."

A few minutes later, a nurse came in and told the man across from us that his wife had given birth to a beautiful baby girl. His face lit up, but clearly he had overheard Papa and me, so he tried to suppress his elation.

"Congratulations," I said, and managed a smile. He nodded, then left with the nurse, and Papa and I were alone.

Hours passed before the nurse who'd spoken to us in the hallway returned. Her earlier brusqueness was gone. "Gloria is recovering," she said softly, and took a seat across from us. "We expect she'll be fine. But the baby was stillborn." I felt Papa's hand clench mine. "It was a boy. I'm so sorry."

Six months along. Of course he'd died. And yet he'd been alive just this morning. Hadn't he been alive this morning?

She went on. "A nurse is bathing and dressing him. Sometimes it's helpful for the parents to see the child. It can help them accept the loss. Is the baby's father—"

"He's overseas," I said quickly.

"Ah. Well, then." The nurse sighed. "We'll bring the baby to Gloria if she decides she'd like to see him. You can go to her now."

"Wait," Papa said.

"Yes, Mr. Campo?"

"Did someone baptize my grandson?"

"We're trained to perform emergency baptism for Catholic patients, Mr. Campo, but no—I'm sorry—I couldn't. Baptism is for the living. Your grandson died before he was born."

He stared at her blankly, as if he hadn't heard.

"Papa." I clasped his arm. "Let's go see Glory."

"You go," he whispered. "Tell her . . ." He shook his head.

The nurse motioned to me to follow her. We took the elevator to the third floor. "We've put your sister on the general ward. That way she doesn't have to see or hear the other mothers and babies. And it's a single room."

"That's very thoughtful," I managed. "Thank you."

She led me down a hallway and stopped in front of a door. "She's groggy, and may not remember much. It's the medication. We've told her about the baby, but she may need to be told again." She opened the door.

I went in. Above the pink hospital gown, Glory's face was ashen, her curls matted to her head. I stepped softly to the edge of the bed. "Glory?" I whispered.

She opened her eyes. "Vi?" she asked, as if she couldn't comprehend how I could be standing there.

"Of course, darling." I stroked her curls.

She looked at the window, then the blank wall. "Vi, where am I?"

My throat burned. "In the hospital," I whispered.

She frowned. "Why?"

"You don't remember?"

She shook her head. "I thought I was home. When I went to sleep, I was home."

"You don't remember waking up?" My voice broke.

Her eyes were frightened and trusting at the same time, and—somehow, as she gazed at me, her face became the face in the first photograph I ever took of her, as a child.

"Why are you crying?" she asked.

"It's the baby. That's why you're here."

She looked at me uncomprehendingly.

"You went into labor and—" I made myself go on. "The baby was stillborn."

She frowned. "What do you mean, Vi? My baby's still inside me."

"No," I said gently. "You gave birth a little while ago. It wasn't your fault. Not yours or anybody's. It was just too soon. And the baby died."

"My baby died?"

"Yes," I whispered. "He died."

Her eyes slid off my face. "A boy?"

"Yes. A boy."

She turned away.

There was a gentle knock on the door. A nurse crossed to the bed. "Mrs. Campo?"

I stepped aside. Glory didn't move.

The nurse touched her shoulder. "Mrs. Campo, I'm so sorry for your loss. One of the nurses has bathed and dressed your son. Would you like to hold him before—Would you like to hold him a while?"

Glory didn't answer.

"Some parents don't want to see their baby," the nurse continued. "They prefer to remember him as they imagined him. Other parents want to see the baby, but not touch him. And some parents ask to hold their baby for as long as they're allowed." She smiled at Glory's back. "No way is right or wrong. It's whatever you wish."

Still, she didn't respond.

"Glory," I whispered. "What if I hold the baby for a little while, and then you can decide if you want to hold him, too?"

Almost imperceptibly, she nodded.

I glanced at the nurse. "I'll be right back," she said.

As I held Glory's hand, I stared out at the road beyond the parking lot. The sun was just beginning to set. They'd be packing up at the picnic now. Hal would be taking his boys home.

The nurse returned holding something—not in her arms, but in her hand. A packet of blue blanket. "I'll leave you alone for a while. If you need me, there's a call button right here."

I parted the blanket and looked at Glory's son.

Splotches of deep red, purple, and dusky grey stained his skull like wounds, old and new. His eyes were closed, the lids swollen, a line of red where they met as if a seamstress had sewn them shut with bloody thread. But his ears, nose, and mouth were perfect. I traced my finger down the rippled skin of his arm to lift one of his hands. It was a flower, his fingers tiny petals. I touched his chest and silently begged God to make his heart beat. But there was no miracle—only silence.

Should Glory see him? It wasn't my question to answer. I whispered her name.

Slowly, she sat upright and turned to me. She reached out. I placed the bundle in her hands. At first, she held it without moving, not even looking.

"It's all right," I whispered. "He's bruised, but he's beautiful."

And then she looked. She parted his blankets and explored his chest, his arms, his tiny hands and feet, his face. She kissed his closed eyes. Then she brought him to her breast. She dropped back against the pillows and held him. Her lips barely moved, and I just barely heard her voice. "Bobbie, darling. My son. My son."

I couldn't bear it.

I turned away, the sobs I couldn't let myself release heaving inside me as her words repeated again and again, like a prayer. "Bobbie, I love you. I'll always love you. Always. Always."

I didn't turn around—couldn't—until the nurse came back. Glory was cradling the baby's tiny face to her cheek.

"I'll give you a bit more time together," the nurse said softly, then motioned to me. Inaudibly, she mouthed, "It's best."

I asked her if I might stay the night with Glory. She nodded.

"Could you let my father know?"

She said she would, and went out.

I looked back at Glory. She still held the baby's face against her cheek. After a while, her breathing changed, and I knew she'd fallen asleep. I pressed the call button, and the nurse returned and gently lifted the baby from Glory's hands. On her way out, she nodded to an extra blanket at the bottom of the bed. I wrapped myself in it and settled in the chair by the window.

Someone crossed the parking lot below. Papa, looking for the car. As I watched, he spotted it and strode toward it, but then paused. His head lifted. He looked up at the hospital, as if he were searching the windows for Glory's room. Then something in his stance changed, and I realized he wasn't looking at the building anymore. He was looking at the sky. A minute passed. Maybe two. Then abruptly he got in the car and drove away. I watched until his headlights disappeared along the road home.

Soon he'll be giving Mrs. Rasmussen the news about her grandson. She'll weep. Then he'll phone Aunt Blanche and Uncle Eddie. Maybe they'll all have a drink together. And from now on, July 12th will be the anniversary of the death of a child, and for each of us, in our own way, of a dream.

GLORY

*M**ea culpa.*
Through my fault.

My face in this splintered mirror. My body, seated at this dressing table. My blood, warm and sticky, seeping from between my legs, staining my blue dress crimson. It's Sunday, mid-morning, and this is my culpable face, body, blood. My reckless brain. *Mea.* Mine.

I know. I see. And all the while, there, in the parlor, they chatter on, unaware of what my body and I have done.

Killed Bobbie.

Not intentionally, of course. No deliberation. No malice aforethought. Just carelessness. Disregard. Every moment of my life, every thoughtless, selfish choice I've made, led to yesterday. A string of antecedents resulting in a consequence: my body opening too soon.

This morning, when I woke, I didn't know this. I saw the blank walls around me and the plain, heavy door and Violet asleep in the chair, and I remembered I was in the hospital and Bobbie had died. I felt my waist. Yesterday, it was round, tight. Now, it was soft. Bobbie was gone.

I knew he was gone.

But that—then—was all I knew.

I got up. Washed. Put on my dress. It was stiff. A musty smell. Dried amniotic fluid. A small package on the sink held a toothbrush, toothpaste, comb. I brushed my teeth and combed my hair. Then I woke Violet and told her I wanted to go home.

Before she could answer, a nurse came in. She checked my blood pressure. Normal. Nothing is normal, I thought. I told her I was going home. She said she'd check with the doctor.

As the door closed behind her, I asked Violet to call a cab.

The door swept open again. A middle-aged man walked in and introduced himself. Doctor Riley. "I understand you'd like to go home."

"Yes," I said. "I'm fine. There's no need for me to be here any longer."

He peered at me over his spectacles. "I understand you had quite an ordeal last night." He crossed to the foot of my bed and lifted my chart from its hook. He read silently, then looked up. "I'm sorry."

"Thank you," I said.

"I'll need to do an exam before I can approve your discharge. To make sure everything's healing properly, that you're not at risk for hemorrhage."

"I've already washed this morning," I said. "There wasn't much blood on the dressing."

"Nevertheless, Mrs. Campo, I—"

Violet rose. "I'll be with my sister," she said. "And I've had nursing training. I'll make sure to check blood loss, temperature . . . anything else?"

"No." He flipped the chart closed. "Nothing else." He replaced the chart and crossed to the door. "And now if you'll excuse me. I have patients this morning who need my services."

When we got home, Papa opened our door before we'd even reached the landing. "I saw the cab pull up. Why didn't you call me?"

"We didn't want to wake you," Violet said.

Papa and I stood there looking at each other. Then he pulled me to his chest and told me he was sorry.

I told him I was sorry, too, that he wasn't to have a grandson.

I felt his kiss on my head. Then he released me. "Have you girls had breakfast?"

Violet told him we hadn't, so he said he'd put the coffee on. "Violet, you make some scrambled eggs and toast." He nudged me toward the bedroom. "Glory, you go lie down!"

I didn't want to lie down. I wanted to crack eggs, slice bread, set out plates. I wanted normal. I didn't know then that I'd never have normal again.

I followed them into the kitchen. While we made breakfast, Violet said she'd ended things with Jimmy. Papa asked her why. "It wasn't his arm, was it?"

"Of course not, Papa," she said. "I just thought he deserved somebody who was crazy about him, and I knew that wasn't me."

We were washing the breakfast dishes when the phone rang. It was Aunt Blanche. She asked if she could see me.

"You should rest," Violet said.

I told her I wasn't tired, that I wanted to see Aunt Blanche and just needed time to change.

I showered, then put on a dress Mrs. Rasmussen had made me, loose-fitting and cool. I sat at the dressing table and began to brush my hair. But then I saw, in the mirror, the little stack of baby clothes on the bottom shelf of the night table. The clothes I'd been making with Mrs. Rasmussen. Bobbie's clothes. The clothes he would never wear. The hairbrush flew from my hand to the mirror. It cracked into a web, but stayed whole. My face splintered.

I went into the parlor and sat on the sofa. Papa was in his room, Violet in the bathroom. I heard Will's footsteps come down the stairs and stop on our landing. There was a knock. I opened the door.

"Glory?" His eyes widened. "I thought you were in the hospital! I was on my way to the train but wanted to offer my condolences to your father—well, I mean, to you." He passed his hat from one hand to the other. "Esther told me last night. I was so sad to hear it."

I thanked him and invited him inside.

He stayed on the landing. From the open parlor windows, a mourning dove cooed.

"As if for you," he said. Then, awkwardly, he offered his hand. I gave him mine.

"Thank you," I said again.

Papa came out of his room as I was closing the door. "Was that Will?" he asked.

"Yes. He offered his condolences." I sat down again. "Papa," I said, "don't let me keep you from Mass."

"I'm not going to Mass today." He sat in his chair and picked up his newspaper. "Violet, are you?"

She'd just come out of the bathroom. She said no.

Aunt Blanche arrived. As she pulled me into her arms, I saw that her eyes were rimmed in red. She'd been crying. For me. For her grand-nephew. And—of course. My baby's death must have brought back her own childlessness—or perhaps the death of Mama's child. Strange I'd only just thought of him. My baby brother born too soon.

Papa rose. "Blanche, sit here." He gestured to his chair. "I'll go put on a fresh pot of coffee."

She thanked him and took his chair, but kept her gaze on me. "Can you talk about it, Glory? About what happened?"

I said all I remembered was waking in the hospital room and Violet telling me my baby was dead.

Violet sat down beside me. "They gave Glory medication and it made her forget."

"But I remember holding him," I said. "His head was bruised. But he was beautiful."

Aunt Blanche's eyes filled with tears. "I'm so sorry. I wish I could have been there with you." She wiped her face with her handkerchief. "It was my one consolation when your brother was born—that I'd been there with your mother."

I don't remember anything about my brother's death. I asked her how it had happened.

"One morning, your mother asked me to stay home from work and watch you girls because she didn't feel well. She lay down, and I thought she must have fallen asleep. Not more than an hour later, she called out to me. The contractions had started. The baby was only five months along."

"Blanche." Papa was standing in the kitchen doorway. "I don't think this is the time."

Aunt Blanche began to apologize, but I interrupted. "No, Papa. It's all right. I want to know." He went back into the kitchen and closed the door. "Go on," I said.

"Well, I called Doctor Cohen. They said he'd be there as soon as he could, but it was all happening so fast, and I didn't know what to do, so I ran downstairs to get Esther. Thank goodness she was in. She came upstairs with me and, well, she was the one who helped your mother give birth. Though there was little enough to do. We barely had clean towels down before the baby came. And—" She looked at me.

"Yes?" I asked.

"Well, he was dead. But not like your baby. Not beautiful. Your brother was—he was damaged. He—"

There was a noise. We all looked up. Papa was standing in the doorway again. But Aunt Blanche went on. Her words were slow and distinct. "He had no brain. It was missing. The skull just—well—it was caved in. Your mother . . . It was a terrible shock. As you can imagine."

Violet's voice was a whisper. "We never knew."

"No. I'd told you girls to stay in your room. I think you must have been frightened out of your wits."

"Did they know why it happened?" I asked.

"No. Your mother—" She looked across the room at Papa, still standing in the kitchen doorway, and when she went on, and I looked from her face to his, she seemed to be weighing each word. "For several weeks she'd been—well—upset about certain things—never mind what, even then it was over and done with—and afterwards she always blamed that—her distress at the time—for causing it. But Doctor Cohen—he got there a few minutes after the birth—he said no one could ever say why it happened, and that it wasn't as rare as people might think, and that your mother going into labor so early was nature's way of ending a life that couldn't be lived."

She turned to me. "But you said your baby was beautiful. So do they know why your labor started too soon?"

Until then, the question hadn't occurred to me. But the moment I heard it, I knew the answer, as surely as if I'd read it in my chart. The abortion. Whatever had caused the hemorrhage had damaged me inside. And killed Bobbie.

Papa came with coffee cups on a tray.

I stood. I said I needed to lie down. I kept my voice strong. I walked steadily into our bedroom. Violet called out that she'd come and check on me in a minute. I told her it wasn't necessary, that she needn't worry, that really, I was fine.

I was lying. I'll never be fine again. Because I'll never be worthy of mercy.

Mea culpa. Through my fault.

VIOLET

I rode the swings today.

It was fun. But I don't know why I did it, how I could have, when Glory's in so much pain.

After she lost Bobbie, for a while I thought she'd be all right. I mean, she managed things. Hard things. Like the burial. We couldn't bury his body in the Catholic cemetery near Mama because he wasn't baptized, so we bought a plot in the town cemetery and had a service there. And she went back to work for Mr. Sadowski. There are so many new businesses in town, he needs her full-time. The first week in August, he moved to a larger office space with two rooms, hers in front, so that she could be his receptionist. Every morning she'd leave for work in a simple dress with her hair and make-up perfect, and when she'd come home at night, even if she didn't say much at supper, she'd eat a little, and help with the dishes afterwards, and sometimes she'd sit with Papa and me by the radio, or I'd go into our room and she'd be writing.

But then, as soon as the calendar turned to September, she changed. She'd come home from work, eat next to nothing, insist on doing the dishes by herself, then go to bed. No matter how I asked, or when, I couldn't get her to tell me what was wrong. One night—it was September 22nd, the date they'd said was her due date—she came home from work and didn't eat at all, just washed and went to bed. When I came in to check on her, she was turned toward the wall. I asked if she was all right. There was no answer. "Can you talk about it?" I asked. "Is it the baby?"

"I'd just like to be alone," she said. She wasn't crying. There wasn't any emotion in her voice at all.

I thought that, if we could just get through September, she might begin to feel better. But it's late October now, and I think she's worse. Last Saturday, after working for Mr. Sadowski until three, she walked all the way to the town cemetery and sat on a bench near Bobbie's grave. I know because Papa and I were so worried about her, he decided to go out in the car to look for her. He said he didn't know what gave him the idea to go to Bobbie's grave.

When they got home, he took her by the hand and led her to the table and insisted she eat with us. And she did, a little. But she seemed exhausted, and was coughing. I think she got a chill walking all that way, or sitting so long by the grave. Anyway, I told her I'd do the dishes and to get to bed.

Papa asked if I thought she was still sad about losing the baby. I nodded. "Maybe if she'd gone back to school this fall . . ."

He sighed. "We should have encouraged her."

"She could apply to one of the state colleges for January."

"You tell her that. And tell her I'll pay." He got up and said if I didn't mind, he was going to a film. After he'd put on his coat, though, he stood in front of the parlor windows, just looking down into the street. Then he seemed to realize I was watching him, and went out.

Our bedroom was dark but Glory was still awake. I sat on the side of her bed. "Papa and I were talking," I said. "It's not too late to apply to a state college for January. Papa says he'd pay." She said she'd think about it.

Today—Saturday—I finished a shoot early and, on my way home, stopped by Mr. Sadowski's office. I thought if Glory was finished working, too, we could walk home together. As I came in, she was taking a payment from a client. When she saw me, she seemed surprised, so I said I'd just been wondering when she was getting out of work. She said not for another hour or two, so I left again.

At first I went to the Armory. Papa and Mr. Sadowski were there helping to set up for the Knights of Columbus dinner dance tomorrow. I'll be taking photographs, so I scouted some spots for photographing the couples. Then I went to Woolworth to get Glory some cough syrup.

As I passed the lunch counter on my way out, I saw Jimmy. He was sitting in a booth, the same booth where we'd sat together in June. Across the table was Dorothy Pope. She looked up just as I passed. Her face was radiant. "Violet!" She waved. "Come say hello!"

I forced a bright smile. "Dorothy, Jimmy, how nice to see you both!" I crossed to the booth. They were drinking chocolate shakes.

Jimmy stood up. "Can you join us?" He gestured to the seat beside Dorothy.

"No, I'm afraid I'm in a rush," I lied. "I just popped in to pick up some cough syrup for Glory."

"Dorothy told me she lost the baby. I'm very sorry."

Dorothy seemed anxious to explain. "I ran into her a few weeks ago. She was so brave. We talked about getting together for lunch one of these days."

"I'm sure she'd enjoy that," I said, then, wanting to change the subject, asked Jimmy if he'd ever closed his deal on the house in Mayflower Estates.

"That and four more!" He smiled. "Business is booming! I keep telling Dorothy, next house comes up I like, I'll be the one making the offer!"

"I'm so happy for you, Jimmy!" I said, and realized I truly was—happy for him and Dorothy, too.

I stopped at the market, then started for home. As I passed the park, I noticed Will sitting on the bench by the entrance. He looked up from his newspaper and called hello.

I sat down next to him. It wasn't out of politeness. Or just to get away from my thoughts. I wanted to visit with him a while.

He pocketed his newspaper as I sat down. "Warm for October, isn't it?"

"Yes," I said. "It's lovely."

"And where's Glory on such a pleasant Saturday afternoon? Not home sick, I hope."

"Sick? Why do you—"

"I heard her coughing last night."

"You did? All the way from our apartment?"

"From the stairs. I was heading to bed—must have been past one—when I heard it. I opened my door. She was nearly at the top, right outside the door to the roof."

"The roof?"

"I said hello to her. Then I told her if she wanted to sit out on the roof, get some fresh air, I'd sit a while with her. She shook her head, but she thanked me. Didn't say anything else, just turned and went back down to your place. I thought you'd want to know."

"Yes," I said. "Thank you." I picked up the bag of groceries, then put it down again. "Will?"

He waited.

"My mother used to like to sit out on the roof," I said. "Those last few months. She said they'd taught her at the sanatorium that fresh air was healing. We'd go up with her after school, even though it was winter, and even though we knew Papa would be furious if he found out. You saw us head up there once or twice. Do you remember?"

"Yes," he answered softly. "I remember." Then he turned to face me. "How's all this for you?"

"I don't know," I answered. "I guess I don't think about things that way."

He nodded. Then, suddenly, he was on his feet. "How about we swing?"

I looked up. "I beg your pardon?"

"Swing. On the swings. Over there." He gestured to the children's play area: a seesaw, a roundabout, a slide, and a set of three swings.

"I don't know," I said. "I haven't been on swings since . . ."

"Since before your mother got sick, most likely." He motioned for me to follow him.

I did. No one else was there, but still, I felt foolish. "This is for children," I said.

He sat on the middle swing. "Put your things down and take a seat!" It wasn't an order. More an invitation.

I sat in the swing to his left.

"Push off like this," he said, and showed me how to walk the swing backward and then let go. "As you go forward, lean way back and pull the chain. Going backward, just go." I watched him rise higher and higher. "I get a little lopsided," he called out. "Once you catch on, you'll go higher than I can."

I followed his instructions. Or I thought I did, but somehow, I didn't seem to get much height.

"Keep at it!" he called, but then he dragged his feet on the ground and slowed to a stop. He disappeared behind me. "When I push you forward," he called, "you lean back and pull! Pull against the chains! When you go back, just relax!"

With each push, I rose higher. He came around to watch me. "Lean back lower and pull harder," he shouted. I leaned back and pulled as hard as I could. The toes of my shoes touched the outermost leaves of the trees. I swooped backwards, as if I were flying.

It's nearly midnight now. I just woke from a dream. I was back in the park, swinging, Will standing there, watching me and—his face perfect—smiling. Glory was there, too, just behind him, walking away from us across the bridge. I called out to her and tried to stop, but instead I kept rising.

GLORY

I can go on as long as I pretend you're here.

My mind moves. I make images of you. I dress you in a long coat of brown and white feathers, with a matching cap and white gloves and elegant white shoes. I don't know why, but it's how I imagine you might look if there really were a heaven, and you were there.

And I smell lavender. I know it's strange and I couldn't tell anyone or they'd think I was hallucinating. I suppose I am hallucinating. But I smell lavender.

And I make you talk to me. If you didn't, the shroud would come down and I wouldn't be able to see or hear or breathe. As long as you tell me things, you keep it away. I make you tell me to iron my blouse or drink my coffee or say good morning to Mr. Sadowski. One day when I'd gone to visit Bobbie, the shroud was suffocating me. But then Papa came and I pretended you'd sent him, and I could breathe again.

Before this, I never knew the shroud used to cover you, too, especially when Papa didn't have enough work, or left us and went to New York, or after you lost the baby, or when you were sick and had to watch Aunt Blanche hugging us.

Sometimes I imagine us talking about Bobbie. But I wish you wouldn't tell me I'll see him again someday. I like it better when you say, "He was too little when he died, so he's just a bit of stardust. Like your brother. A lovely bit of stardust."

Remember how we used to go up to the roof sometimes after school, the winter before you died? How we'd bundle up in our hats and coats and mittens, and sometimes we'd bring story books, or the Bible, and you'd read to us or we'd read to you until it got too dark to see, and before we went back downstairs, we'd look for the evening star? You used to say, no matter how cold it was, you always felt better on the roof. "It's easier to breathe up here," you'd say. "Everything feels less heavy. Even our problems. They seem to rise right up to the sky and drift away." And then you'd laugh your laugh that sounds like little bells. Like you did last night, when you said let's go up to the roof and look at the stars. And we would have. I wanted to. But then Will opened his door and said hello and I had to stop pretending you were there.

They're taking Glory away.

Tomorrow she'll be gone. I'll be alone here, and she'll be alone in some strange place with no one who knows her or cares about her.

If only she'd agreed to come with us to the Knights of Columbus dance. Papa tried to persuade her to. He said that, since I'd be taking photographs, she could be his date. Mr. Sadowski had invited Mrs. Rasmussen, and Uncle Eddie and Aunt Blanche were going, too. But she said no, she preferred to stay home.

When I said goodbye, she seemed better than yesterday. She'd had lunch with us this afternoon, and then Mrs. Rasmussen stopped by with a new dress pattern and offered to help Glory make a new dress for work. She said she'd like that. It was the first time in weeks she'd shown any interest in anything, so even though I didn't want to leave her alone, it never occurred to me anything bad would happen. We'd only be gone a few hours. I told her I'd leave as soon as I'd photographed the speeches and the first few dances, and Papa could go home with the others.

But she told me, "Stay and have fun. And make sure to dance with Papa. He'll like that." And then she did something I still don't understand. She got up and put her arms around me, but with her head turned to the side.

I held her. She felt so thin. I got her to promise me she'd fix herself some supper—later, she said, after she'd worked on one of her poems. On my way out of the bedroom, I saw her take her notebook and pencil from the night table. She looked back at me and smiled.

At the Armory, I photographed the couples arriving. Dorothy and Jimmy looked so happy together—I took several photographs of them. Then came the dinner and speeches. The whole time, whenever I thought of Glory, I imagined her greeting me with a finished poem—perhaps the title poem for her new collection. So when the band started playing and Papa asked me to dance with him, I did.

What if I'd gone home then? Instead, we all had dessert together, and Papa led me to the dance floor again. During that second dance, an attendant touched my shoulder and told me there was a phone call for me in the lobby. I thought it must be Mr. Crane. Then I heard Will's voice.

"I'm phoning from your parlor," he said. "There's nothing to worry about. Glory's in the bedroom lying down. I just thought I should let you know I'm here, so I don't surprise you when you get home."

I felt a rush of panic. "Why?" I asked him. "What's happened?"

"Time enough to explain when I see you. Meantime, you enjoy yourself."

His voice was calm, even reassuring, but I couldn't think of staying another moment. "I'm coming!" I said, and dashed back to the ballroom and told Papa I needed the car keys. He asked me why. When I told him about Will's phone call, he insisted on coming too. As I was gathering my equipment, he told Aunt Blanche that Glory wasn't feeling well and we were going home.

When we got to Mill Street, Papa let me off in front of our building, then went to park. I ran upstairs. The door to our apartment was ajar. The parlor was empty, our bedroom door open. I went in. Except for the light from the hallway, the room was dark. Will was sitting at the foot of Glory's bed. Glory was lying on the edge nearly touching the wall. Her eyes were closed.

"I'll be leaving now," Will said softly, and stood.

"Wait!" I said. "Please tell me what happened."

He shrugged. "Doesn't much matter, now you're home." He turned to go, but then he paused. "You'll keep an eye on her tonight, won't you?"

"Please, Will!" I said. "I need to know what happened."

His eyes rested on her. "Glory, you stop me if you want to tell it your way, okay?"

She didn't respond.

I threw my coat onto my bed. "Please go on."

He nodded. "You remember how I told you yesterday I'd seen your sister by the door to the roof?"

"Yes," I answered.

"Well, something about that didn't sit right." He shook his head. "So tonight I decided no records, no radio. After I got home from Porter Square, I sat down with the newspaper. Finished that and was looking for Mr. Chandler when I heard the sound I'd been listening for. Your door opened, then footsteps coming up past my door. I went out to the landing and saw Glory closing the door to the roof behind her. I went fast as I could up after her, but by the time I got out on the roof, she was near the edge. She was talking—at first I thought to me—but as I got close I heard her say, 'Yes, Mama,' natural as can be, like her mother was standing right beside her.

"I didn't know what to do." He looked at Glory. "If I said anything, there was the risk I'd startle you and you'd fall. But if I tried to grab you, I could miss and you might fall anyway." His gaze shifted back to me. "Well, I grabbed for her. Pulled her back hard as I could. And we both fell down, right down onto the roof. My guess is it caught us both by surprise. Glory got up before I did, and reached down to help me. Then I followed her back here and she lay down without saying a word. That's when I called you."

A shadow fell across the bed. Papa stood in the doorway. "What's going on?"

His back was to the light, and I couldn't see his face. "Will found Glory up on the roof," I said.

"On the roof? What do you mean, on the roof?"

Will answered. "No more than that, Mr. Campo. She was standing a little too near the edge, so I—well, we helped each other back down."

Before I even knew what was happening, Papa was leaning across the bed and pulling Glory up into his arms. *Bambolina,* he cried. "No! No!" It was the first time I'd heard him call her that in years. She lifted her arms around his neck and he rocked her.

Will shuffled toward the bedroom door. "I'll say good night."

I went out with him. "Thank you," I said. "We may owe you Glory's life."

His voice was gentle. "Maybe. Or maybe she was just talking to her mother and looking at the stars."

I followed him out to the landing. If I'd kept him talking just a minute longer, he'd still have been there when Aunt Blanche and Uncle Eddie arrived, and maybe he could have explained it that way to them, and things wouldn't have gone so wrong. But the same moment they threw open the front door, his door closed, and Uncle Eddie came shouting up the stairs. "What's going on?"

We went inside. Papa had come into the parlor. He gestured to the bedroom. "You stay with her."

From the bedroom, I heard Papa's voice, then Uncle Eddie's, louder, insisting that Papa call Doctor Cohen. "Call him right now before she wanders off again!"

I went back to the parlor and told them there was no need for Doctor Cohen, that I would look after Glory.

"No, Violet." Uncle Eddie's voice was cold. "Glory needs professional help. You have your own life to live."

How dare he? What did he know about Glory and me? "This *is* my life," I answered. "It's the only life I care to live."

I saw Papa hesitate. "What do you think, Blanche?"

Aunt Blanche looked from Papa to Uncle Eddie to me. "I'm not sure," she said quietly. "She's been getting herself to work every day—"

"Blanche!" Uncle Eddie shouted. "She's not eating, barely speaking, then the minute we leave her alone she wanders up to the roof. The edge of the roof! How much longer can this go on?" He strode to the phone. "I'm calling Doctor Cohen."

Papa sank to the sofa. His face was anguished, but he said nothing.

I couldn't bear to listen. Maybe Aunt Blanche felt the same, because when I went back to the bedroom, she followed me.

The light from the hallway shone across the foot of Glory's empty bed and onto the dressing table. She was sitting on the bench, her right palm flat against the splintered mirror, pushing against the glass. She looked at us uncertainly, then said, "There are stars inside."

Aunt Blanche crossed to the dressing table while I turned on the bedside lamp. I think we both saw the blood at the same time, trickling from Glory's right hand down her wrist and arm.

Aunt Blanche cried out. And then there was shouting—Uncle Eddie telling Papa he should have sent Glory to a psychiatrist a long time ago and Papa saying how dare he tell him how to raise his own daughters—while Aunt Blanche and I picked glass out of Glory's hand, washed and wrapped it, and got her to bed.

Doctor Cohen arrived wearing a sports coat and a casual shirt and slacks. "Good thing you called when you did," he announced. "I was just about to pour myself a nightcap." He asked Glory if she knew who he was.

"Doctor Cohen," she answered.

"And how are you feeling?"

"My hand hurts."

"Do you know why?"

She shook her head. "I don't remember."

"That's all right," he assured her in the same voice he'd used with us as children. Then he had her swallow something to help her sleep.

He turned to me and said I looked as if I could use something, too. I said no, I was just sad for my sister.

"Well, if I had a remedy for sadness, I'd be a millionaire."

He unwrapped Glory's hand, cleaned it again, and applied a new dressing. As he worked, he spoke to Papa. "I'll call the sanatorium tomorrow to have Glory evaluated. See what they think. Take it one step at a time."

"You mean the state hospital?" Aunt Blanche asked. "The one that used to be for TB patients?"

"Oh, it's still used for TB. The west wing anyway. They're only using the east wing for the mentally ill."

Aunt Blanche looked at Papa. "Do you think that's wise? I mean . . ."

Doctor Cohen looked puzzled.

"Yvonne died there," Papa explained.

"Oh, yes, of course," he said. "Well, unless you have the means to pay for private care, the state hospital is the only option. They've got a new young doctor there. Eaton. He's up on all the latest techniques. Psychoanalysis, medications, insulin, all that. I hear he's getting excellent results." He finished taping the bandage and tucked Glory's hand by her side.

She was sound asleep.

He gave me a packet with another pill. "Have her take this tomorrow morning. Just to keep her calm until you get her to the hospital."

He went out. Papa and Uncle Eddie followed. I heard him say good night. "I'll have my nurse phone you in the morning with an appointment time. And by the way, after she wakes, don't leave her alone."

I felt numb. Aunt Blanche sat beside me and took my hand. "It's just an evaluation. She'll probably be home in a day or two."

"Yes," I whispered. "I know."

But the truth is, I don't know. How could any doctor help Glory? No one can bring her baby back to life.

I'm sleeping beside her tonight in case the sedative wears off and she tries to get up. It's strange. It reminds me of when we were children and Mama was gone.

I wonder if she really was talking to Mama. Was she just imagining her? Or is she really there, somewhere?

But how could there be a heaven for Mama, and just a box in the ground for Glory's son?

GLORY

I can think again.

It's evening. The brief period of sanity between the lunch-time booster of Benzedrine and the Veronal for sleep. So my mind is clear. I can try to write a poem.

No writing during the day. They have their schedule, and poetry isn't on it. Breakfast is a struggle. They say I have to eat more. I have no appetite. The exercise is easier. Rain or shine, they take us for a morning walk. I look up to the third floor of the west wing and try to find the window of the room where Mama died. But I can't imagine her with me anymore. My mind's too jumpy. It keeps getting stuck on crazy phrases—"Breakfast with Benzedrine!"—or bits of nursery rhymes or songs. Sometimes just syllables stutter on and on.

The shroud is gone, though. Sometimes I even feel happy. This morning as we were walking, the first snow of the year began to fall, and as I watched it float down from the feathered sky, I was almost in ecstasy.

Afternoons begin with my analyst, Doctor Mader. Through a cloud of cigarette smoke, his eyes gleam and bulge. I wonder if he knows that his glasses make him look like a frog. A frog in smoke. That would be interesting to talk about. But we don't talk about anything interesting. He doesn't ask me about Bobbie. He asks me about Papa. What I felt for him as a child. Or about Violet. Does Papa favor her, or me? I don't care to answer, so I say whatever comes into my head—whatever I hope will make the questions stop, I guess.

Sometimes I think he suspects I'm making it all up. He'll change the subject and ask me about my dreams. I've told him on the Veronal I don't dream. So he'll ask me to describe an old dream, one from before I came here. So I invent one, and it doesn't matter if my mind is shooting in a thousand different directions because dreams are crazy anyway. I think he believes me, because he'll ask me what the broken doll or the flock of sparrows means to me. Or maybe he knows I'm lying and it doesn't matter, because even the things I invent can reveal something true. I don't know. It's like we're playing a game and only he knows the rules.

At the end of fifty minutes, a buzzer sounds and an orderly walks me back to the ward. On the way I look at the floor so I don't have to see Mrs. Keane unbuttoning her dress again, or Sonya twisting and twisting her hair. There's an hour until group. If I could, I'd write. But my mind is spinning. And after Doctor Mader's smoke, my lungs burn. I lie down and close my eyes and try not to cough but I do cough, and then it's Mama coughing and coughing until she coughs up blood all over her dress and a sparrow flies onto her breast and the sparrow looks like my son.

By early evening, when Ward Three returns from the dining room, my thoughts have finally slowed. I can write again. In crayon. Pencils aren't allowed. No matter. Tonight I'll write about the feathered sky and the floating snow.

VIOLET

Leonard is coming home for Christmas.

As I left to visit Glory this morning, Mrs. Rasmussen was waiting in the front hall. Her voice was soft, apologetic. "He arrives next week. I wanted you to know." I thanked her, then asked how much she'd told him. "As little as possible. That Glory took the baby's death hard and is in the hospital. I'm sure he's figured out the rest." Tears filled her eyes and she shook her head. "Violet," she whispered, "for the first time in my life, I don't want to see my son."

I wonder what Leonard would have said if he'd come with me this morning. We're only allowed to visit on Saturdays. I have to stop at the nurse's station, and they search my bag. Any sharp objects, even pens and pencils, have to be left behind. They're potential weapons, I'm told. When I approach Glory's ward, I don't know what I'll find. When I arrived today, she was wearing the blue dress Aunt Blanche had sent, and sitting in the chair beside her bed, the seventh bed and chair in a row of twelve, identical to the row on the other side of the room. She was staring at her open notebook, holding a crayon. Her hand was shaking, but I've come to expect that. Sometimes her voice shakes, too. And she coughs more. She says it's the medication.

I asked her what she was doing.

"Trying to write, I guess."

"How were the chocolates?" I bring her a present each visit. Slippers. The dress from Aunt Blanche. A new box of crayons. Last Saturday I brought her chocolates.

"The nurses took them. They said I wasn't allowed to have them."

A nurse at the next bed was buttoning the front of an elderly patient's dress. "We've explained to Gloria that she's not allowed sweets unless she finishes her dinner," she said. "Every night she fails to do that, we give one of her chocolates to a patient who does. Mrs. Keane has had one of them, haven't you dear?"

The woman stared uncomprehendingly.

The nurse continued buttoning. "I believe there are still a few left should Gloria decide to finish her dinner tonight."

I was so angry, I couldn't speak. Glory clutched my hand.

"It doesn't matter," she murmured. "I don't have much appetite."

We walked to the windows. They overlook a parking lot. Rain was falling steadily on the cars below. I drew a small package from my coat pocket. "I thought you might like this. And the nurses can't take it from you."

Her hands shook terribly as she unwrapped it.

"It's a pocket diary," I explained. "For 1948. You can use it to write down appointments and plans."

She turned the pages.

"Maybe it seems silly, given that you're here. But I wanted you to have something to look forward to. I saw Doctor Eaton downstairs as I was coming in. I'm meeting with him at noon. I plan to ask him when he thinks you can come home. I hope by Christmas. And then you can start making plans for next year."

She kept turning the pages, then abruptly stopped. "Your birthday," she said, pointing to the 30th of March. "When I get home, I'll write down your birthday. In pen." She smiled a little as she slipped the diary into her pocket.

Sometimes we go for a walk outside, but since it was raining, we went to the dining hall and I fixed us two cups of tea.

She waited until I'd sat down, then asked the same question she asks every visit. "How is Papa?"

She never asks why he doesn't visit. So even though she was on some kind of sedative the day we brought her to the hospital, perhaps she remembers.

None of us had been to the sanatorium since Mama died, but I remembered the parking lot, the stone steps, and the double doors opening onto the big hall. I wondered how Papa felt, coming back after all these years to bring his daughter to a psychiatric ward. At least we were in the east wing, whereas Mama died in the west wing.

Doctor Cohen was right—Doctor Eaton is young, even boyish-looking, tall and slender, with light blond hair. As he introduced himself, he gestured to a group of chairs while settling himself on the corner of his massive desk. His words were clipped, his tone almost flippant. He addressed Papa. "Now, what questions do you have, Mr. Campo?"

"How long will my daughter need to be here?"

He grinned. "That's almost always the first question. And the answer is almost always the same. We don't know. It depends entirely on the patient. We'll do an evaluation. That will give us a sense of what's going on, and how to approach treatment. We have a variety of excellent options. Your daughter is young and healthy, so I have every expectation she'll respond promptly. Next question?"

Though he hadn't glanced at Glory or me, I said I had a question.

"Of course, Miss Campo."

"Will we be consulted?"

His cheerful expression changed to a puzzled frown. "Consulted for what reason?"

"My father and I know Glory better than anyone else in the world. I should think we must have information—insights—that would be important to your evaluation and treatment."

"Oh!" His head snapped back. "You misunderstand the nature of our work, Miss Campo. As we establish the therapeutic relationship between patient and analyst, trust is essential. And confidentiality is key to building that trust. Besides, we're interested in the patient's view of his experience." He reached backward and pressed a buzzer on his desk. "From a therapeutic perspective, the family's view is irrelevant. And now let's bring Gloria up to the women's ward." An orderly entered. "Ward Three."

The orderly helped Glory into a wheelchair and led us to an elevator. I entered after them. Papa hesitated. The doors began to close. "I'll wait for you in the lobby," he said.

The following Friday, when I said I planned to visit Glory the next day and asked if he was coming, he told me I could take the car, since he'd be leaving the visiting to me.

And so now, whenever Glory asks me about Papa, I tell her he's missing her. I don't say anything more.

The windows of the dining hall look out over the front lawn. We sipped our tea and watched the rain fall. Then, quite suddenly, Glory asked me about my project—had I photographed anyone recently?

"Not in the last few weeks," I said, "but this afternoon I'll be meeting with a World War I vet in Arlington—someone who served with Will. He lost his sight, but Will tells me he's one of the most cheerful men I'll ever meet."

"Next time you see Will," she said, "please tell him I've been thinking of him. He's been so kind." And then she started to cough. It was light at first, and dry. She took a handkerchief from her pocket and held it to her mouth. The cough got deeper. She almost seemed to be choking. I went to the kitchen and asked an orderly for water. When I brought it out to her, the spell was over, and as she reached for the water, she again blamed the Benzedrine.

As noon approached, I told Glory I had to meet Doctor Eaton. She said, "Tell him I want to go home."

But when I did tell him, he dismissed it. "If she wants to go home, she should cooperate with her analyst. Doctor Mader tells me she's not doing that. She can't go home safely until we understand the root of her depression."

"Doctor Eaton," I said, "the root of Glory's depression is the death of her son. Not to mention his father's abandonment—"

"Ah, yes. The father. How long since she's seen him?"

"Since last Christmas, when he was on leave from the Merchant Marine."

"Ah! A sailor!"

There was a knock on his office door and a nurse entered. "Your wife's here."

"Tell her I'll be right with her." He smiled at me. "Christmas shopping in Boston. List a mile long."

I rose. "Perhaps you and I could talk again next week."

He reached across his desk for my hand. "Let's do that, Miss Campo."

I went back upstairs and told Glory I hadn't been able to get an exact date from Doctor Eaton. "He says he's worried about sending you home before they understand what caused your depression."

She looked puzzled. "But Doctor Mader never asks me about Bobbie."

I clasped her hand. "I know, and I don't intend to let Doctor Eaton keep you here while his staff figure out how to do their job. We'll be talking about it again next Saturday, and I promise to insist that you be home by Christmas!" I thought of Leonard. What if Glory did come home by Christmas? But what if she didn't? I couldn't bear to think of her spending Christmas alone in such a place. My eyes started to burn. I kissed Glory's hair and told her I needed to go. "But when I come back next week, you'll be one week closer to coming home!"

By the time I'd made my way out of the hospital, my eyes were swimming with tears. Maybe that's why I was nearly to my car before I realized that Doctor Eaton was walking in front of me. Sharing his wide umbrella was a woman in a fur coat. Suddenly the woman turned, as if she'd sensed me there behind her. She stopped short. "Violet Campo! The photographer!"

"Pauline!" I gasped. It was Jean's cousin, the bride-to-be I'd photographed on Valentine's Day. "But wait—is Doctor Eaton your husband?"

"That's right!" she giggled. "Mr. Crane took the wedding photos, so you've never met Alan. Or—wait!" She looked confused. "You *have* met!"

"Miss Campo was just visiting one of our patients," he explained.

"Yes. But if you'll excuse me, I'm afraid I'm running late for an appointment!"

"Of course!" Pauline said. They began to walk on, then she turned and called back. "Nice seeing you again, Violet!"

In the car, I blotted my eyes with my handkerchief, turned on the radio, and drove to the address Will had given me. I photographed his friend, then headed home.

Over supper that night, Papa asked me if I thought Glory would be home for Christmas. I told him what Doctor Eaton had said, that she shouldn't be released until they understood the source of her depression.

"Well, are they making progress? She's been there over a month!"

"Six weeks on Monday. But perhaps it would be better if she stayed until January. For other reasons."

He looked up from his plate. "Such as?"

I met his eyes. "Leonard will be home for Christmas."

For a long moment he sat unmoving, staring into my eyes. Then he threw his napkin onto the table and leaned away. "There are nights," he said quietly, "I dream of strangling him with my bare hands."

"So what will you do when he comes?"

"Nothing!" he snarled. "I'll do nothing! I wouldn't allow him to marry her now if he were the last man on earth. Besides—" He picked up his napkin again. "He's Esther's son."

After I visit Glory, I always lie awake for hours. Tonight I kept thinking of her shaking and coughing and Leonard coming back to Mrs. Rasmussen's with a new photograph of Cecilia or some other girl in his pocket. I thought back to the photographs I'd taken of him and Glory a year ago—at Christmas, or leaving for the Bancroft on New Year's Eve. I was glad I'd never given him a copy.

A little after midnight I gave up trying to sleep. I turned on our bedside lamp and took Glory's photograph album from the bottom shelf of the night table between our beds. I knew every photograph on the first several pages, as I'd taken them all. The very first was of Glory and Papa, sitting on the sofa the morning of my eleventh birthday, the first photograph I'd ever taken, with my Brownie. Glory looked so small, her eyes wide and frightened, but Papa's thick arm was around her waist, and he was smiling. I'd forgotten that. How he'd smiled that morning, presenting me with the camera, and then in the photograph. A few days later Mama died. Had he smiled in any photograph since? I turned the pages, thinking of Glory's high school graduation. Yes, he had his arm around her shoulders, and again, though more reservedly, he was smiling.

I turned the page. Glory's first day at Norcross, meeting her suitemates. I'd taken a photograph of them all standing side by side, awkwardly, Jean and the others in their cashmere twin sets and pearls, and Glory wearing a plain cotton blouse, no jewelry. I wondered what Jean's life had been like since I'd seen her on Valentine's Day. She'd be coming to the end of the fall term at Norcross, her junior year.

On the facing page was a color photograph of Glory and her suitemates at the Norcross Christmas Ball. Glory was wearing the bright red dress that Aunt Blanche had made for her, and Jean was in gold. They were sitting opposite each other at a circular table, everyone holding glasses aloft. Jean's face was in profile, and I noticed something I'd never noticed before, not even when I was taking photographs at the bridal shower. Jean's nose is Roman, like mine. And like me, she must have inherited that nose from her father, since her mother has small, fragile features. As I thought more about her mother—petite, with light blonde hair—I realized Jean must strongly resemble her father. He must be handsome, like Papa. But with auburn hair.

Again I turned the page. Last Christmas. Had I taken no photographs of Glory all those months before Leonard came? Then I remembered—I had photographed her. Once. On Armistice Day, listening to Jimmy Conlan's speech. But I'd kept that photograph with my own. And so a year had gone by, and a single turn of one page brought me to the photographs I'd remembered: Christmas. Glory and Leonard standing in front of Mrs. Rasmussen's tree. Leonard had been home on leave for—what?—four days, and they were already gazing into each other's eyes as if they were reading each other's souls. And then, the last photograph, New Year's Eve, just before they'd left for the Bancroft. Glory looked like a movie star, and so happy. And he looked handsome, worldly wise, the older gentleman who would always protect her.

I was about to close the album when I noticed some paper sticking out at the back. A small, handmade book I'd long forgotten: *Poems by Gloria Campo*. From second grade. She'd intended to give it to Mama that Mother's Day. There were ten poems. One was about Sir Lancelot. Another the scent of lavender. The last one was different from the rest. The printing more careful. The language, the thoughts, as if written by a much older child. It was about a sparrow. She'd called it "I Soar on the Wings of Morning."

GLORY

Nothing comes tonight.

What kind of poem can you write with a Burnt Sienna crayon anyway? Or Rose Pink. Or Violet. Violet.

Violet for my sister's name.

Lavender when my mother came.

Black like my father's eyes.

Then again, why not *Blue like my lover's eyes?* Or *Black like my lover's lies?*

Here's one. *Red Violet for our son's corpse.* But nothing rhymes with corpse. Nothing rhymes with nothing. Bobbie is nothing. Not even stardust. Mama was wrong. I was wrong. Bobbie is earthdust.

White like my son's bones decaying in his tomb.

And finally—Red. Oh yes. We'll end with . . .

Red for his mother's lethal womb.

Oh, esteemed Professor Turner, would you like to try some crayon poetry? But perhaps it's too much to ask, since you've never given birth to a corpse and have, in fact, no womb and no children, living or dead. So on second thought, I'll leave the rational, vigorous poetry to you, and you can leave the overwrought nonsense to me.

VIOLET

Today I had lunch with Jean.

It was her idea. She'd sent a Christmas card addressed to me, not Glory, so I knew even before I opened it that Pauline must have told her. Told her something, anyway. *Greetings from Chestnut Hill!* A note inside.

She included her phone number, but I wrote back. My first letter said I was sorry, but Glory and I had other commitments that day. When I read it over, I realized how desperate it would seem if she knew it was a lie. And she would. Just as I knew she was lying about suddenly buying Glory a Christmas present or asking to visit her here. So I tore the letter up and began again, this time offering to meet her for a late lunch at the Twelve O'Clock Diner. I would visit Glory first, then stop there on my way home.

I posted the letter last Saturday, on my way to the hospital.

Doctor Eaton met me when I arrived. He insisted, as he had the week before, that discharge would be premature and that they were still trying to get Glory's medications right. "There's a middle ground between a therapeutic response and an increased risk of side effects."

I asked him what kind of side effects. He rattled them off: "Rapid heartbeat, tremors, loss of appetite, things like that. And of course anxiety."

"Glory's hands shake so badly sometimes that she can't write," I said.

"Precisely my point, Miss Campo. We're still, as I said, adjusting her medications."

I suggested that Glory's anxiety might be due not only to the Benzedrine, but also to her surroundings. "I'm sure you and your staff do your best, but for a sensitive person like Glory, it must be quite frightening. If she were home—"

"Miss Campo." His voice was stern. "Doctor Mader believes your sister wishes to go home to die. Could you and your father prevent that?"

"Can you?" I asked. "Every time I see Glory, she's lost more weight. And she has a nagging cough—"

"As I've just said, her appetite will improve once we get her medications right. As for the cough, I wasn't aware of it, but I'll have someone look into it."

His tone was dismissive, but I wasn't ready to be dismissed just yet. As I stood, I told him I'd let my father know what we'd discussed. "I'm confident he'll agree that we'll be bringing Glory home after the first of the year."

"I certainly hope that's possible," he answered. "But a hospital is not a railway station, and a human mind is not a train."

When I went upstairs, I found Glory sitting as usual in the chair by her bed, the box of crayons I'd given her by her side. Her notebook was open on her lap, and there were dozens of words in various colors scrawled on the pages. When she saw me, she shrugged. "Crayon poetry."

I sat on the edge of her bed. A strange expression flickered over her face. "They named one after you." She pulled a purple crayon from the box. Her hand trembled as she held it out to me. *Violet.*

I didn't know what to say.

She put it back in the box. "Did you see Doctor Eaton?"

I told her I had. I didn't mention his condescension, just that he'd given me the same useless answer as last week. "So I told him that, whether or not he felt you were ready, Papa and I would be bringing you home after the first of the year."

"Really? You can do that?"

"Yes," I assured her. "We can do that."

I spent the next couple of hours with her, reading to her from a volume of Keats I'd borrowed from Will, then sharing some shortbread I'd brought from home. A light snow began to fall. I rose and kissed her goodbye. "What shall I bring you next week?"

"Nothing, Vi." She smiled. "I'll be home soon."

I stopped at the market to pick up some things for supper. By the time I pulled into Mill Street, the snow had thickened. I was heading up the steps with my purse and shopping bag when the front door swung open. "Looks like you could use some help."

The cold air clutched my throat. Leonard stepped back into the front hall to hold the door wide. I passed him without a word and started up the stairs. "Violet!"

I paused but didn't turn around.

"How is Glory?" His voice sounded sad, even tender.

I told him to ask his mother.

"I already have. I'm asking you."

"Why?" I looked down at him. "Does it give you pleasure to hear the results of your despicable—"

But he had already leapt past me up the stairs, stopping on the one above me and blocking my way. "You're wrong, Violet."

My eyes were level with his chest. I could smell his cologne. "Let me pass," I said.

"As soon as you hear me out. I'm sorry about what's happened to Glory. But it had nothing to do with me."

I couldn't speak.

"When you wrote me that she was expecting—" He grimaced. "Well, to tell you the truth, I felt conned. How else could I feel—to find out she'd been sleeping with someone else the same time she was with me. Or as soon as I left, anyway. It hurt. And not just my pride. I was angry." He looked desperate to convince me. "She shouldn't have laid the blame on me, Violet. That wasn't right. I don't know who the father was, but—"

"Take this," I said, and pushed the bag of groceries into his arms. Quickly, not allowing myself to think, I ripped the glove off my right hand, looked squarely into his face, and slapped it as hard as I could. Without pausing, I reached for the bag.

But his grip tightened. His eyes were furious. "How dare you?"

"Let my daughter pass!" Papa's voice was thunderous.

In an instant, Leonard had shoved the bag back and fled down the stairs. I heard Mrs. Rasmussen's door slam. Papa stood above me. Shaking, I lifted the groceries into his arms.

At supper that night, I told him about my conversation with Doctor Eaton. We agreed that, if he hasn't discharged Glory by the time Leonard leaves, we'll insist on bringing her home.

All week, I've been trying to avoid running into Leonard. This morning, when I heard Will's steps on the stairs, I threw on my coat and left the building with him. "Are you off to visit Glory?" he asked.

I said I was.

"Please tell her I've been thinking about her and wishing her well."

I promised him I would.

She seemed about the same as last week—thin, trembling, coughing, but happy to see me. I told her Papa had agreed that, no matter what Doctor Eaton said, we'd be signing her out of the hospital the first week in January. We talked about how she'd need to rest when she got home, and to see Doctor Cohen about her weight loss and cough. She asked me if Mr. Sadowski had found a new receptionist. I explained that he'd decided not to advertise for a replacement yet, and that Mrs. Rasmussen had been helping out. She seemed pleased to hear that he was holding the position open for her. After that she asked me about my own job. I told her I had the usual Christmas assignments, and lots of customers in the shop.

"And your project? Are you photographing anyone this afternoon?"

"No," I said. "It's too close to Christmas."

She seemed concerned. "You'll start again in January, though?"

"I suppose so," I said.

After that we walked to the dining hall and leafed through the pages of a magazine I'd brought. When an orderly announced lunch, I said I needed to go, and reminded her I'd be visiting on Christmas Day.

"When is that?" she asked.

"On Thursday. Just five more days."

"Christmas." She clutched my hand. "I'll see you on Christmas."

When I walked into the Twelve O'Clock Diner, Jean was already seated in a booth, waving to me. She was wearing a cornflower blue sweater set that matched the color of her eyes, a pearl choker, and a fur cap above her auburn curls. In the corner of her seat, a matching fur coat was slung against the wall. Beside her placemat was a package wrapped in gold paper with a silver bow.

"Hello, Jean," I said, and sat down. "I hope I haven't kept you waiting."

"Not at all. I just sat down myself." She linked her hands beneath her chin and looked at me without blinking. "Glory won't be joining us?"

I suddenly felt unsafe, off balance. Late last night, when I couldn't sleep, I'd decided to say as little as possible about Glory, but not to lie. So I told her no, and that I was sorry. "But I'm sure she'll be touched that you came all this way to bring her a gift."

"Well, as I said in my note, I'll be visiting my Aunt Margaret when I leave here. My cousin Pauline and her husband will be there as well. We're having an early Christmas dinner because my parents are leaving Tuesday to spend the holidays in Palm Beach."

"That sounds lovely," I said. "You won't be going?"

Her full red lips formed a pout. "Unfortunately not! Someone's got to run the business while Daddy's gone!"

As she was speaking, the waitress came to our table. Jean ordered a sandwich and a shake. I asked for tea and a cup of chowder. Jean's brows lifted. "That's all you're having for lunch?"

"I'm not very hungry," I said.

"Lucky you," she smiled. "I'm always hungry. Daddy's forever warning me to watch my waistline! Did I say I've started working for him?" She smiled brightly, but her fingers began to tug at the ribbon on Glory's gift.

"You mean, not just over the holidays?"

"Oh, no, it's a permanent position. I'm learning the business!"

"What does your father do?"

"He's in shipping." She winked and lowered her voice. "He made out like a bandit during the war, and things haven't let up since. Norcross was becoming a bore, quite honestly, so we sat down together and decided it was time for me to start doing something useful!"

"I see. Well—congratulations." The waitress brought my tea. "It must be quite a responsibility."

"Oh, it is. And I'm learning so much more than I ever did in college!" She held the package out to me. "Here," she said. "Why don't you tuck this into your purse before the food comes?"

It felt like a slender book. "Poetry?" I asked.

"Of course! *Braving the Rain* by Evelina Stern. I bought it after I heard an interview on the radio. She lost everyone, you know!"

"Yes," I said. "I'd read something like that."

"On the program, she read the title poem aloud. It's beautiful. Sad, though." Her eyes widened. "But not too sad! I mean—" She paused abruptly. When she spoke again, she sounded hesitant and, I think, sincere. "What I mean is, I thought Glory would like it and . . . and I wanted her to know I haven't forgotten her."

"Thank you," I said. "And I'm sure she hasn't forgotten you."

The food arrived and we moved on to other topics: finding a hairdresser, her new Chevy coupe parked just outside our window, her favorite television program, *Truth or Consequences.* I was happy to let her talk—in fact, I kept asking questions to keep her from asking me anything else about Glory.

When we finished lunch, she insisted on paying the bill. We were standing at the register when Leonard walked in.

Despite the cold, he was wearing only a trench coat, open, with a long blue scarf. He strode past me and took a seat at the counter. I watched him from the corner of my eye. The waitress tried to hand him a menu, but he waved it away. "Coffee and a piece of lemon meringue pie," he said, and scanned the room. His gaze found us—or rather, Jean—and lingered. And then he was standing beside me. "Good afternoon, Violet."

I felt my spine stiffen. "Good afternoon, Leonard."

He turned to Jean, who was just closing her purse. His blue eyes sparkled.

"Jean," I said, "this is Leonard Rasmussen, my neighbor's son. Leonard's home on leave from the Merchant Marine. Leonard, this is Jean Fields. She and Glory were suitemates at Norcross."

"Ah, yes!" Leonard said. "I believe I recall Glory mentioning a particularly charming friend named Jean." He bowed slightly and reached for her outstretched hand. "Miss Fields, you are a ray of light on one of the darkest days of the year."

Jean's cheeks flushed. "Let me guess," she said, her voice husky. "You must be the sailor who broke Glory's heart."

I was stunned. Suddenly it seemed as if everyone—Jean and Leonard, the waitresses, customers, the whole world—was mocking Glory and me, as if we were the poor, pathetic relations in a comic play. A customer pushed past me and I stumbled. "I must be going," I said.

Jean smiled. A dazzling smile. Like Glory's. "Goodbye, Violet! Wish Glory a merry Christmas for me!"

A merry Christmas. In an insane asylum.

I made my way out to the car and got inside. For a long time, I just sat there watching people walk by. The sun had begun to sink toward the horizon before I saw Leonard and Jean leave the diner together and walk toward her car. He opened the door for her, then shook his head. She'd offered him a lift home, I guessed. No. He wouldn't allow Jean to see where his mother lived. She started the car, then rolled down the window. They chatted a moment longer, than he stepped back and her car pulled away. He stood on the curb, watching, then crossed the street and disappeared.

Someone knocked at my window. "Violet, are you all right?"

It was Will. I realized I was shaking with cold. I rolled down my window. "Yes, Will," I said. "Would you let me give you a lift home?"

He got in. Before I started the car, he touched my sleeve. "You saw Leonard Rasmussen leaving the diner," he said. "And the girl who was with him."

I nodded.

"You were watching them."

"Yes," I said.

"You know that girl?"

"Jean Fields. She was one of Glory's suitemates at Norcross."

"I'll be." He sat back.

"Why do you ask?"

He gazed into the distance. "No reason except . . . as she came down the steps, I thought I was seeing a ghost. Ada Sadowski's ghost."

"Perhaps it's her hair," I said. "I remember—from your painting—Ada's beautiful auburn hair."

He nodded slowly. "Maybe that's it."

I drove the half mile home. As I pulled the car into an empty space, he turned to me. "And how was Glory today?"

Maybe it was a delayed reaction to seeing Leonard with Jean, or her casual admission that she knew of Glory's heartbreak. Or maybe just the tenderness in Will's voice. But I couldn't speak. I shook my head quickly, not wanting to cry. He said nothing, just sat patiently, waiting. I pulled my handkerchief from my purse and pressed it to my eyes. "I don't know what's gotten into me," I whispered. "I'm sorry."

"You've got nothing to be sorry for. Remember that."

He turned and opened his door. I got out, locked the car, and joined him. We walked in silence toward our building. When we reached the steps, he touched his hat. "Good night, Violet," he said, then shuffled away in the direction we'd come.

GLORY

Today I coughed blood.

No one saw. No one knows.

Maybe Mama knows.

No. That's ridiculous. How could Mama know?

I want her to know. That's it. I'm twenty years old, and I still want my mama.

Papa would do, though.

I'd take you, Papa, if you'd only take me. My heart belongs to Daddy. And to Bobbie. Now just a memory. Soon, maybe, my own heart will be just a memory. Two memories laid to rest side by side.

Though maybe it's not TB. Or maybe it is, but I'll survive. Plenty of people do. Even heartless people. And people with broken hearts.

But not half-starved lunatics. So I have to eat. If I want to live.

And I do. How strange. I want to live. I want to write. Even if I never publish another poem. Write like Emily Dickinson, stuffing notebooks full of shells and birds and letters to the world.

And I want to teach. I want to teach young women without asking anything in return except their best attempt at voicing their souls.

Since I'll never have another child, I want to teach.

I will eat. In ten days, Violet will take me home. I'll do everything Doctor Cohen tells me. I'll get off the Bennies and Veronal, and if I can't sleep, I'll rest. I'll get better. I know I can. Once I'm home.

VIOLET

Glory has TB.

Last night I dreamed it, and today I found out it's true.

I couldn't visit her on Christmas. There was a blizzard and the public was asked to stay off the roads. I phoned the nurse's station. When I asked to speak with Glory, the nurse hesitated, then spoke quickly, brusquely, telling me they were short-staffed because of the holiday and the storm and couldn't spare anyone to accompany patients to the phone. When I asked her to at least have someone tell Glory I couldn't come because of the storm, she said she was sorry but she needed to ring off.

Papa and I had Christmas dinner at Aunt Blanche and Uncle Eddie's, though the snow was falling so thickly we went home before dark. All day yesterday, it kept on falling. I was restless. Midmorning, I phoned the hospital again. The nurse who answered said there was only "a skeleton crew" and she had to get back to her patients.

I baked, cooked, cleaned, mended. After supper, Papa and I listened to news reports on the radio about the storm, and then I went to bed.

I tossed and turned for hours before I fell asleep. Sometime toward morning, I dreamed about Glory. She was sitting in the chair by her bed. As I approached, she looked up, smiling. But then she began to cough. She didn't stop. I screamed for Doctor Eaton, but Doctor Murphy—Mama's doctor—came instead. I woke up, my heart pounding, and thought: Glory has TB.

I looked out the window. The snow had stopped.

After breakfast, Mrs. Rasmussen, Will, Papa, and I all went out and cleared the front steps and sidewalk. Aunt Blanche and Uncle Eddie and other neighbors were out doing the same. Papa asked Mrs. Rasmussen why Leonard hadn't joined us. She looked flustered. "Oh, he's not home," she answered, then went right back to clearing the snow. No one pressed her, but her answer didn't make sense. No trains had been running. Everyone had been stuck at home. So where was Leonard?

Papa shoveled out our car. The roads had been plowed overnight, and with the sun shining strongly on the asphalt, they'd begun to clear. When he finished, I headed out.

When I entered Ward Three, there was no one at the nurse's station to check my bag. I didn't wait—just strode into the room with Glory's bed. Even with the dream to warn me, I was shocked. The chair next to her bed was empty, and in the bed was a middle-aged woman, raving.

I whirled around. A nurse I didn't recognize was leading a small group of patients through the double doors out to the nurse's station. "Excuse me," I said, catching up with them. "Where is Gloria Campo?"

The nurse stopped and frowned. "I'm just covering for the holidays. Who is Gloria Campo?"

I went back to the nurse's station. Now there was a nurse behind the counter. Her face was familiar to me from previous visits. When she saw me, her eyes widened. "Good morning, Miss Campo. You must be looking for Gloria. She's been moved to the medical unit. The west wing. Go back down to the lobby, then—"

"Miss Campo!" Doctor Eaton hurried toward me. "Good morning. Why don't we talk in my office?" He gestured toward the stairs.

"Why has Glory been moved to the west wing?" I asked, not moving.

"My office, Miss Campo." He turned and headed toward the stairs.

I had no choice but to follow him. As soon as he'd closed the door behind me, I repeated my question.

"Your sister has been diagnosed with tuberculosis," he said.

I felt as if I'd fallen through ice.

"I realize . . . it's unfortunate news."

I asked him when.

"Christmas Eve. The nurse on Ward Three was filling in. She usually works in the TB wing, and noticed what she felt were characteristic signs, so we sent your sister over for testing. When the results came back, she was transferred immediately."

"Why did no one inform her father or me?"

"I'm sorry, Miss Campo. I've been away the last three days, and it seems that, in my absence, and with the storm affecting staffing, no one got to it."

"How bad is she?"

"You'll have to ask Doctor Murphy," he said. "He's the pulmonologist in charge."

"I know who Doctor Murphy is," I said. "Twelve years ago, he cared for my mother."

He looked puzzled.

"She died here."

"Ah." He grimaced. "I see."

I found my way to the west wing. I thought I might recognize some feature of the place, but nothing looked familiar—not the cheerful paintings in the lobby or the large windows overlooking a lawn. And then I remembered. We'd visited Mama on a porch that opened from a large room upstairs from the central lobby. We'd never entered the west wing.

I approached the front desk and told the receptionist I was there to visit Glory. She placed a call, then told me to take the elevator to the third floor. "Doctor Murphy will meet you at the nurse's station."

I stepped out of the elevator. "Miss Campo?" Though I had seen him only once, twelve years ago, he was exactly the same as the man in my dream. I introduced myself and told him he had cared for my mother. "So your sister tells me," he said. "And that—sadly—she died here."

"But I understand that many of your patients recover," I said.

"Oh, indeed. I'm sorry that wasn't the case with your mother, but yes, we have considerable success when the disease is caught early."

"And is that the case with Glory?"

He gestured to me to follow him into his office and closed the door behind us. "Not as early as I'd have liked." He gestured to a chair in front of his desk. "Please sit down." He remained standing. "Miss Campo—"

"Call me Violet."

"Violet. A lovely name. So." He paused as if reluctant to continue. Then he began again. "Your sister's disease is in both lungs, and is quite serious. However, TB treatment options have expanded in the years since your mother died, and we may be on the cusp of further innovations. So there is hope. Let me explain."

As he was speaking, he searched among the stacks of papers on his desk until he'd located beneath them a notepad and a pen. He then sat down and made three quick strokes on the notepad, which he turned toward me. "In our fight against TB, we have three lines of attack." He pointed to the top line. Above it he wrote, *Bed Rest*. "Resting the lungs, by avoiding exertion, even talking, for most hours every day, harms the bacteria because, among other things, it deprives them of the oxygen they need to survive."

"That's what you did for my mother, I think."

"Quite likely. If strict and prolonged, bed rest has been known to prompt even large cavities to close. However, as in your mother's case, it can be inadequate." He lifted his pen again. Above the middle line he wrote, *Procedures*. "The second option is a variety of collapse therapies. These can be more effective in resting the lung and suffocating the bacteria. But they aren't ideal for your sister, because she has lesions in both lungs. That leaves our third option."

Above the bottom line he wrote, *Medication*. "Our newest option is a drug called streptomycin. Other drugs are being tested as we speak, but for now, it's the only one available. And unfortunately, it's problematic. In some patients it achieves a complete cure. But in patients with established disease, the bacteria often outwit the drug and return stronger than ever. And the side effects can be severe."

He paused, then asked me when I'd last seen Glory. I told him the week before. "I'd planned to visit her on Christmas Day, but the storm wouldn't allow it."

"No indeed. But as you've seen her recently, you must realize she's quite debilitated."

I thought of Glory clutching my hand as I said goodbye to her last Saturday. I'd recognized how ill she was, hadn't I? No. I couldn't have, or I'd never have promised her she'd be home in a few days. So why hadn't I seen it? Why had it taken last night's dream to show me what should have been obvious? Doctor Murphy was saying Glory might die.

I looked at him. He'd removed his glasses and, as he wiped them with his handkerchief, gazed back at me. His eyes are green, like mine, and kind. "I was worried," I said. "I felt she was getting worse—physically—with each visit."

He nodded. "Her inability to eat may well have been exacerbated by the medication she was given. Which, by the way, we've reduced, and will discontinue as soon as possible." He put his glasses back on. "I have every confidence in Doctor Eaton's talents; however, the options in psychiatric treatment, as in tuberculosis, are limited."

I told him I understood.

"But to return to our third option. When a patient arrives debilitated, I start them on ample food and strict bed rest until they're strong enough to withstand the side effects of streptomycin. And that is what I have ordered for Glory."

"When do you think you might be able to try the drug?"

"Once we've entirely weaned her off the amphetamine, we should see her weight increase. That's critical, because streptomycin can trigger nausea and vomiting."

"I see." My throat tightened, but I had to ask him one more question. "Why did Glory get TB, and not me?"

He shook his head slowly. "No one can answer that. However, among my female patients, I've seen many cases like your sister's. The infection may lie dormant for years. Perhaps—given your mother's tuberculosis—since childhood. In most people, it remains dormant. But Glory became pregnant. Pregnancy weakens the body's defenses, you see. They back off a bit, to avoid rejecting the baby. And that can enable the TB bacteria to multiply. Glory's emotional response to losing the baby made matters worse, particularly because she became malnourished."

I told him I understood.

"And now, I assume you'd like to see your sister?"

I rose.

As we walked, he told me that Glory was already eating more. "We tell our patients that food is medicine, and we administer it six times a day." We entered a long, narrow room with a single row of beds, cupboards alongside, facing tall, open windows that flooded the room with winter sunlight and cold, fresh air. In each bed rested a woman covered in thick blankets, some flat on their back, others somewhat upright and sewing, knitting, or reading. At the end of the row of beds was what looked like a thin wall, but on a track. "The last bed in each ward can be partitioned off," Doctor Murphy explained. "This enables us to keep patients with more advanced disease from those whose condition is less severe." He slid one panel of the door to the side.

In the room was a bed, a cupboard, and a single chair, all facing an open window identical to those we'd just passed. In the bed was a woman, lying flat, wrapped to her chin in a blanket, with a heavy quilted pad over her torso and legs. At first, perhaps because her eyes were closed and a knitted cap covered her hair, I didn't recognize her. But then she opened her eyes and smiled.

I started toward her, but Doctor Murphy put his hand on my arm. "Wait," he said. "Begin each visit by donning a mask. It protects you and your sister both. You'll find clean masks here." He took one from the cupboard and demonstrated how to put it on. While I did the same, he crossed to Glory. "You see I brought you a visitor today! But my turn first." He lightly touched the bedding over her chest. "How's the pain?"

"Better," she whispered.

"Than when you got here?"

She nodded.

He took his stethoscope from his pocket, folded back the pad and blanket, and listened to her chest. I couldn't read his expression. "And how did you sleep last night? Any sweats?"

She shook her head.

"Hmmm . . ." He studied her chart. "The nurse's notes say that you were feverish this morning."

She looked confused.

"Never mind." His voice was soothing—fatherly. "It's not your job to remember these things. It's your job to rest. Which reminds me." He turned to me. "Limit your visits to an hour. Glory should talk as little as possible, and no laughing. I suggest reading to her. If you think of any further questions, the nurses will know where to find me." He nodded at both of us encouragingly. "Good day."

We were alone.

"Vi," Glory whispered, "I'm so happy to see you!" And she did look happy.

I crossed to her bed and pressed my masked face to her forehead. I told myself to be strong. "I'm sorry I couldn't visit on Christmas," I said. "I was so worried they wouldn't tell you I'd called."

She answered softly, taking shallow breaths after every few words. "I saw the storm. I didn't want you to come. Except. I wanted you and Papa. To know I was here. And all right."

All right. Hospitalized with TB, but all right. I said Doctor Murphy seemed kind. She nodded, and added that the nurses were angels. "And the food. Almost as good. As yours." Talking seemed to tire her. She gazed out the window over the bare trees and the wide lawn blanketed in snow. I thought she might fall asleep, but she asked, "Do you remember? Out there. Looking up. At Mama."

"Yes," I answered. "I remember. Is it all right? I mean . . ."

"Yes. I feel. Close to her here." She might have said more, but an orderly in a mask wheeled in lunch, a fragrant stew, slices of bread and butter, milk, and a dish of chocolate pudding. He helped her sit up, and before he left, encouraged her to try to finish everything. I sat next to her while she ate. She'd finished most of the stew before a coughing spell overtook her. When it ended, she leaned back and closed her eyes.

A nurse came in and introduced herself to me as Charlotte. She lifted her mask onto her face. "Glory, would you like to rest a bit and then try to finish your lunch?"

As she rested, I told her that Jean had "contacted me" with a present for her. I unwrapped the book and turned to the first poem. It was about the poet's separation from her family. Glory's face, as I read it, saddened, and I decided not to read any others, at least for today. Charlotte returned and helped Glory sit up again to finish her lunch. Then she reminded me that visits should be brief. I put on my coat. "May I visit again tomorrow?" I asked.

She looked surprised. "Of course! Sunday visiting hours are from ten until five. But we ask that you stay no more than an hour."

When I got home, Papa was sitting by the radio listening to *La Boheme*. As I hung up my coat, he opened his eyes. "How was Glory today?" He turned off the radio.

I should have decided on the gentlest way to tell him. But I'd been so shocked, I'd driven home numb.

Panic flooded his face. "What? What's happened?"

I told him Glory has TB.

He didn't say a word, and didn't move except to close his eyes.

I sank to the floor by his chair and took his hands. I told him she's strong, that there's a new drug, that she'll make it. I have to believe this. For her sake, for Papa's, I have to.

GLORY

Papa visited me today.

I'm not a lunatic anymore. I have TB. Like Mama. Like Violetta and Mimi. He understands that. He even cried.

They came just before noon. Violet told him how to put on his mask, then said she had a quick errand to run. I wondered what she meant, because it's Sunday, but before I could ask, she was gone.

Papa took off his coat and sat in the chair by my bed. He took one of my hands and held it between his, stroking it a little with his thumb. Even though I've been gone only a few weeks, he looked older, with lines by his mouth I've never seen before, and fine strands of white in his hair. He looked tired, too, so I asked him if he was all right.

"Me?" he asked. "Who's the one in the hospital here, eh?" He shook my hand a little, up and down, then rose and went to the window. He looked out at the snow, then leaned his arm against the window frame. I couldn't see his face, so I wasn't sure what was happening at first, but then he swiped his sleeve across his eyes. I wanted to tell him not to cry, that I already felt stronger and Doctor Murphy was going to start me on a drug they didn't have when Mama was sick. But I knew I couldn't say all that. Not today.

After another minute, he sat down again. "Are they feeding you meat?"

I told him the cooking is almost as good as Vi's. I didn't tell him that I have to make myself eat.

"Are you able to sleep?"

I nodded. He didn't need to know how often I wake soaked in sweat, or that once I'm awake, the pain in my chest keeps me from sleeping again.

"Why aren't you on the ward?"

"As soon as I improve," I whispered, "they'll move me."

"Glory? I—"

I waited.

"No, you're tired. I'll read you the paper." He reached for his coat at the bottom of my bed. "I brought the front section from home."

"You didn't have to," I whispered. "The library cart. Has *The Globe*."

"But it must be hard to read, lying flat like that." He took the paper from his coat pocket. "How about if I read the front page to you?"

I asked him what he'd wanted to ask me.

He shook his head. "It wasn't important." There were voices, and the door to my room opened.

"Lunchtime!" Violet came in. "Fish chowder, carrots, and pound cake!"

An orderly set a cart loaded with food beside my bed. Violet was beaming as she took off her coat and put on a mask. "When I got home last night, I made a pound cake to bring you today. Then I woke up this morning and thought, why not bring lunch? So I phoned the nurse's station, and they said I was welcome to bring food from home. Anything to help your appetite. They even let me warm everything in the kitchen just now."

I wanted to thank her, but a cough had begun to rattle in my chest. Weeks ago, the cough felt dry and, even when it lasted, it didn't hurt. Now it feels wet and hot, as if my chest were full of lava.

When it subsided, I leaned back against the pillows. Charlotte had come in. She swabbed my face with a cool cloth. Then she lifted the head of my bed and set a tray of food over my lap. "I know you're tired," she said, "but try to eat some of the lunch your sister brought." She turned to Papa and Violet. "There are dishes and silverware for you, too. And I'll have the orderly bring another chair. If you eat, it will help Glory eat." She disappeared.

Papa was standing at the window again. Violet was staring at her hands.

I picked up my spoon. "Violet. Papa. I'm waiting."

After we ate, I think Papa felt better, because he told us a funny story about Mrs. Rasmussen misfiling Mr. Sadowski's paperwork. Then he said he really shouldn't tell us this—it was a secret—but Mr. Sadowski was planning to take Mrs. Rasmussen to the Bancroft for Valentine's Day again this year and ask her to marry him. "He's worried she won't say yes," Papa explained, "that after all these years on her own, she might be too set in her ways."

"But if she loves him," Violet said, "that won't matter."

Papa shrugged. "What do you think, Glory?"

I said of course she'd say yes, and that I'd write a poem for them. "My wedding gift."

The orderly came to clear the dishes, and Violet told him to share the leftovers with the staff. "I'll pick up the pot on my way out, and I'll be offended if it's not empty!"

After he left, Violet said she supposed it was time for them to go. She told Papa she'd retrieve her things from the kitchen and meet him downstairs. Then she stroked my hair and promised she'd visit next Saturday. "Keep eating!"

As she left, Papa gazed toward the door, then back at me again.

"Yes, Papa?" I asked.

He put his mask back on and came and sat on the edge of my bed. "Glory, I'm glad you're—well, I know you're very sick, but . . ."

At last, as if it was a terrible struggle to find the words, he asked me why, last fall, I'd gone up to the roof.

I thought back. It seemed like another life. Those nights when I couldn't stop thinking of Bobbie. Of what I'd done to him. But I couldn't tell Papa that.

"I felt better," I finally said. "Up there. I'd pretend. I was with Mama. We talked. Looked at the stars. It helped."

Behind his mask, his face relaxed. He leaned over the bed and kissed my forehead.

The door opened and Charlotte came in. She drew the curtains over the window and, gently, told Papa I needed to rest. He nodded.

I barely heard him whisper goodbye before sleep came, and a dream that I was a child again, walking between him and Mama, holding each by the hand.

When I woke, I reached for Evelina Stern's book of poems. I felt lonely, and I guess I hoped—since the poems are about her family—that reading it might help. I opened the cover. There's bold black handwriting on the title page.

To Glory—

Brilliant poet and dear friend—

From Jean

Such a lovely thing to write. And yet strange. We once considered each other dear friends. From the moment we met, there was an inexplicable bond between us. Even though we'd argue.

She was envious of me—my scholarship, my grades, Jeremy. And I suppose I was envious of her family's wealth. Still, we were drawn to each other. But more than a year has passed— nearly two—since I left. So why, after all this time, does she still care?

Everything is suddenly so strange.

I feel as if I'm trying to read a book with missing pages.

Papa and I were saying goodbye to Glory yesterday afternoon—Saturday—when Charlotte looked in and told Papa there was a phone call for him at the nurse's station. He came back to the room and said that Mrs. Rasmussen had just invited us to have supper with her and Mr. Sadowski. Three weeks have passed since Valentine's Day, and Papa said he assumed they'd invited us to announce their engagement.

"I can hardly wait until tomorrow," Glory said, "to find out." Her smile was mischievous—like her old smile. She's seemed happy these last few weeks. I think she can feel herself getting stronger. Doctor Murphy says he expects to be able to start her on the streptomycin soon.

As he drove home, Papa wondered aloud why Mrs. Rasmussen had invited us on such short notice. I said probably she's been worried about us running into Leonard. "And maybe she just found out that Leonard won't be home tonight."

Leonard has been living with Mrs. Rasmussen since just after Valentine's Day. When she told me about it, she said she never thought he would leave the Merchant Marine. And then she paused for a moment before continuing. "Until he met Jean Fields."

I was too stunned to speak.

"Leonard told me she was one of Glory's suitemates," she said. "At any rate, they spent a lot of time together at Christmas, and now he's agreed to take a job in her father's shipping business. It sounds like a good position, but . . ." Her grey eyes looked troubled. "It's all so sudden."

Since that conversation, neither Papa nor I had told Glory that Leonard was home—and dating Jean. But in the car, thinking about our abrupt supper invitation, I felt uneasy.

When we arrived at Mrs. Rasmussen's, I noticed at once that the table was set for only four. I wasn't surprised, of course, but asked Mrs. Rasmussen, softly, if Leonard was spending the evening with Jean.

"Yes." She glanced at Papa before continuing. He was talking with Mr. Sadowski. "I don't expect him back until after midnight."

"But the last train comes in at eleven."

"You haven't noticed?" She frowned. "Mr. Fields didn't want him to have to rely on the train, so he gave him a car."

"Gave him a car?" I was so shocked I spoke too loudly, and Papa and Mr. Sadowski turned to us.

"Who gave who a car?" Papa asked.

"Leonard's boss—Mr. Fields—gave Leonard a car," Mrs. Rasmussen answered. "It had belonged to Mrs. Fields, but he bought her a new one and gave the old one to Leonard."

"It's a '39 Cadillac," Mr. Sadowski added. "Not anything you or I would consider old."

Mrs. Rasmussen sighed. "At any rate, Leonard's out late most evenings now. For all I see of him, he might as well be back across the Atlantic."

At supper, as soon as she'd served everyone, Mrs. Rasmussen asked about Glory. "I'd like to send her a get-well card, if you think that would be appropriate."

"Of course," Papa answered. "I'm sure she'd be glad to receive it."

"I'd like her to know I think of her every day . . ." She glanced at Mr. Sadowski. He put down his fork and covered her hand. "And I'd like to give her our news. Stan's and mine." She blushed and lowered her eyes to her plate.

"Esther and I have decided to get married," Mr. Sadowski said. "We haven't set a date yet. But it'll be a simple ceremony. In the church, of course, but not many people. And we'd like the two of you to be there."

"And Glory if she's able," Mrs. Rasmussen added hurriedly.

"Of course," Papa nodded. "*Auguri*. Congratulations to you both."

"And one more thing," Mr. Sadowski said. "Roberto, I'd like you to be my best man."

Papa seemed to hesitate before saying—sort of mechanically, I thought—that he'd be honored.

"That's settled, then. We're meeting with Father Bouchard this week to set a date. We'll let you know as soon as we have."

Mrs. Rasmussen turned to me. "And I've asked your Aunt Blanche to be my matron of honor."

"Then why not have Eddie as best man?" There was a sharpness in Papa's voice that didn't make sense to me.

Mr. Sadowski just chuckled. "Better to rely on a man who likes baseball!"

Papa smiled back, but it seemed forced. I said congratulations, and that their wedding would give us all something to look forward to.

Now it was Mrs. Rasmussen's turn to force a smile. "Yes," she said. "I do hope so."

As we sat in the parlor after supper, Papa asked Mr. Sadowski if he had proposed on Valentine's Day, as he'd told him he would.

"Just barely," he said. "I reached into my pocket and took out the ring box, but all of a sudden my mind went blank. I couldn't think of what to say. And my hands were shaking so bad I didn't dare try to open the box. So there it sat between the two of us, until Esther rescued me!"

Mrs. Rasmussen began to laugh. "I'd wondered if Stan might have marriage in mind. But it took me by surprise even so."

I asked if I could see the ring.

"Of course!" She disappeared into her bedroom, then returned wearing a small but brilliant diamond. She held out her hand.

I couldn't help thinking of Leonard, of the ring he'd promised Glory. "It's beautiful," I said.

An awkward silence followed. Mrs. Rasmussen fingered her ring. Then Mr. Sadowski cleared his throat. "You must be wondering why it took Esther and me three weeks to tell you about our engagement. The truth is, we hadn't planned to keep it a secret. But . . . Esther, maybe you should take over."

She did, but she sounded reluctant. "Well, Leonard was arriving in a few days, and I thought he should know first. When we told him, he congratulated us, of course." She looked straight at Papa. "And then—almost as if it was an afterthought, he said it so casually—he told us that he and Jean Fields were getting married, too."

I don't know why, but her words didn't surprise me. It was like I'd already known. I looked at Papa, wondering if he felt the same thing. But he looked stunned.

Mrs. Rasmussen went on, more softly than before. "I'm sorry, Roberto. Stan and I—well, we were both upset, not only at the suddenness of it, but knowing the pain it was bound to cause you and Violet and Glory." She looked at me. "We didn't know how to tell you. Not with what you're going through. And it seemed to us that telling you about our own engagement without saying anything about Leonard's wouldn't be right. But then, Leonard called late this afternoon and told us to buy the *Evening Globe*." She looked at Mr. Sadowski.

He had already picked up the newspaper, folded into a thick slab, and was holding it out to Papa. "We didn't want you to read this without our having told you first." He stabbed his finger into the middle of the slab.

Papa took it. His read in silence, then handed the paper to me.

Engagements. Jean Victoria Fields and Leonard Peter Rasmussen. Mr. and Mrs. Arthur Fields are pleased to announce the engagement of their daughter, Jean . . .

It was a brief notice, not much more than a column inch, with no photograph and very little detail except that Jean "had attended Norcross College and was now an executive assistant at Fields Shipping," and that Leonard had had "a distinguished career in the U.S. Merchant Marine and was now a supervisor at Fields Shipping. An April wedding is planned."

But that was crazy! I turned to Mrs. Rasmussen. "It says here the wedding is in April. Is that a mistake?"

She shook her head. "The wedding is in six weeks. Leonard says it'll be a quiet affair."

"Apparently," Mr. Sadowski added, "the Fields don't like publicity."

My mind went haywire. He'd only met her in December. Just like with Glory. Only—

Papa's voice interrupted my thoughts. "Violet! What paper do they take around to the patients at the TB hospital? Isn't it the *Globe*?"

"Yes," I answered, then realized why he'd asked. "Mrs. Rasmussen, was this published in the morning edition, too? Or will it be published in the Sunday paper?"

"No," she said. "Our understanding is that the Fields preferred only a small announcement in the evening edition."

I turned to Papa. "The library cart at the hospital only has the morning paper. Glory won't see it."

"Thank heavens," Mrs. Rasmussen said.

We all sat there looking at each other, not saying anything. Then finally Mr. Sadowski picked up the paper again and said, "It's a strange coincidence. Almost like fate had a hand in it. Leonard told us he met Jean at the Twelve O'Clock Diner, of all places!"

I said it was true, that I'd introduced them.

Mrs. Rasmussen frowned. "Well, there must have been a strong attraction, because they spent the rest of his leave together. And before we knew it, Mr. Fields had offered him a job at his company. He must have pulled some strings to get him discharged so quickly."

Papa was staring out of the windows into the darkness. "She's an attractive young woman. I'm not surprised Leonard went after her."

"We wouldn't know, Roberto," Mr. Sadowski said. "Esther and I haven't met her yet."

"They're having an engagement party," Mrs. Rasmussen added. "At their home in Chestnut Hill. Two weeks from tonight. We've been invited, so we'll just have to wait until then to see what she looks like."

I thought of Glory's photograph album. "No!" I said. "You don't have to wait! I'll be right back!" I brought the album downstairs and opened it to the page showing Glory with her suitemates on the day they'd all met. I pointed to Jean.

"She's lovely," Mrs. Rasmussen said. "As is Glory, of course. They even look a little alike, don't they?" She handed the album to Mr. Sadowski.

"Yes," he said, adjusting his glasses. "I see what you mean. Though Jean . . ." His voice trailed away.

"What is it, Stan?" Mrs. Rasmussen touched his arm.

He shook his head. "I guess I'm getting sentimental again." His voice sounded gruff. "But she reminds me of Ada."

I remembered Will saying the same thing the evening he'd seen her coming out of the diner.

"Oh, darling." Mrs. Rasmussen leaned over and kissed his temple.

"Although here," he continued, looking at the photo on the facing page, "here where she's in profile, the resemblance isn't as strong."

"Jean's nose is like mine," I said, "though she carries it better than I do. She must have gotten it from her father." I looked at Papa. "Like me." He didn't seem to have heard me.

"Why not her mother?" Mr. Sadowski asked.

"Because I met her mother once, at a bridal shower for Jean's cousin. I was taking pictures. She looks nothing like Jean."

"Violet." Papa stood. "Time to go."

When we got upstairs and I headed to the bedroom to put the photograph album away, he stopped me. "I'd like to look at that," he said. "I want to see the pictures of Glory again. When she was happy." He took it into his bedroom and closed the door.

Today I visited Glory alone. When she asked me where Papa was, I said he'd come home from church with a headache. It wasn't true. He hadn't gone to church. Neither had I. He'd had only coffee for breakfast, then left dressed in everyday clothes and the jacket he wears to work. I watched him walk away, in the opposite direction of town. When he still hadn't come back by early afternoon, I left him a note and took the car.

When I returned from the hospital, he was sitting in his chair, not reading the paper or listening to the radio. Just sitting. I didn't ask him where he'd been. In my bedroom, I noticed Glory's photograph album on the night table.

Other than asking about my visit with Glory, he didn't speak all through supper. Afterward he said he was going out.

He took the car. I went to Aunt Blanche and Uncle Eddie's. Mrs. Rasmussen had told them about her engagement, and Leonard's, and we talked about it until Uncle Eddie turned on the television. I didn't feel like watching, so I came home. For a while I sat by the windows reading the Sunday paper. I checked the engagement notices. Mrs. Rasmussen was right—there was nothing about Leonard and Jean.

Strange. I would have expected the Fields to trumpet the news of their daughter's wedding. Unless . . . The thought had first come to me last night. Unless Jean is pregnant.

I sat by the windows a while longer. Will came down the street and up our steps. I heard him pass our door and continue up the stairs. I washed and went to bed.

It's almost midnight. Papa just got home. Where was he? Why did he spend the whole day alone? And why do I have this sense that something's missing, and that Papa knows what that something is?

GLORY

My third day of streptomycin is nearly over.

Everything's churning again. I've retched so many times, my body feels like an empty shell tumbling in the waves. But the room is dark now, and the ward is quiet. So if I lie perfectly still and the night nurse leaves me alone, the churning will subside . . . like the sea at low tide. I'll drift out. Carried. As if I were in Father Garcia's arms.

May I do that, Father? Imagine you holding me? You'd say I should imagine God. But it's not God I believe in. It's you.

That first Wednesday morning after I moved to the west wing—it was New Year's Eve—a nurse asked me if I'd like to see the priest. I said no. I thought, what would I say to a priest—or he to me?

I didn't know it was you.

I nearly said no the second week, too, but you'd stepped into my room beside the nurse. That's when I realized I'd met you at Saint Isabel's two summers ago. I've never forgotten your sermon, or how happy you seemed just to stand outside the church and greet us. That's why, that second Wednesday, I said yes.

She introduced me to you as Gloria, and said that everyone calls me Glory. And even though I was flat on my back and covered in blankets right up to my chin, you must have recognized me, too, because you asked if we'd met before.

I told you we had, and when and where, and even though you'd pulled up your mask, I could tell from your eyes that you smiled.

When we were alone, when you asked me if there was anything troubling me—anything I'd like to talk about—and I said no, you must have guessed there was so much I couldn't bear to say. And when you offered to bless me, and I said you could, did you guess that I don't believe in such things? And if you did guess, did it matter? Or when you offered to hear my Confession, did you mind that I said perhaps another time? Your eyes above your mask still smiled, and your voice as you said goodbye was still kind.

Since then, I've looked forward to Wednesday mornings.

You know what I like best? When you tell me about yourself. Especially about your childhood. The island off the coast of Portugal where you were born, and how you lost your father at sea and how, one morning when you and your mother had nothing to eat, you thought you heard God tell you to be patient and He'd show you a way to serve Him. And that night your father's brother told your mother that if she'd marry him he'd take her to America and raise you as his son. They settled in Fall River, and you excelled in school and went into the priesthood. And when the war broke out, you asked to serve in hospitals.

It was such a beautiful story, Father, I couldn't bear to tell you mine.

But when you came today, I was so sick with nausea I guess I couldn't fight anymore. You opened your little box with the vial of oil and I closed my eyes and heard you recite the blessing, then words I couldn't understand, flowing softly, like a song. Portuguese? It was so beautiful, I started to cry. You wiped my cheeks. And then you asked me again, like that first day, if there was anything troubling me, anything at all I'd like to share. And this time I told you everything. About Mama, and how I'd hated God, and then, as I got older, how I'd simply stopped believing. The whole time, though, you looked at me in a way that made me feel—not judged. Known. Even when I told you about Professor Turner. And the abortion. And how I lost Bobbie.

You didn't condemn me. You placed your hands on my head and prayed. "Glory, I release you from the burden of this guilt and pain. I release you not by the authority of one perfect and removed, but by the authority of my own human heart. For what we seek is to understand and to be understood, to pardon and to be pardoned, to love and to be loved."

The morning sunlight filtering through the drawn curtains made the whole room shimmer. It occurred to me that it was nearly spring. Eight months. "Father Garcia?" I whispered. "I'll never stop grieving Bobbie."

When you answered, your eyes seemed to shine with the same light that filled the room. "Of course you won't, Glory," you said. "Our grief binds us to our love."

And then I knew. Bobbie will be with me as long as I live.

Now, in the stillness, I imagine Father Garcia's words over and over again. "I release you . . . by the authority of my own human heart." And despite the nausea, I'm at peace. Someone in this world—someone good and true—knows what I've done, and has forgiven me.

VIOLET

Lately my thoughts all seem to be questions.

Why Papa's become a stranger. Why Glory should have to suffer. How it is that violets could be blooming again outside our door.

Doctor Murphy called from the sanatorium yesterday and said Glory was too sick to have visitors. She's sick from the streptomycin, and he might have to stop it. We all talked about it over supper until Uncle Eddie decided to end the subject by saying we could at least take comfort in knowing that whatever happened was God's will.

After I went to bed, I lay awake for hours thinking about God's will.

This morning, Papa said he was going to Mass. "It'll take my mind off Glory for an hour. You coming?"

I told him not today.

While he and Uncle Eddie were gone, Aunt Blanche and I cleaned up the mulch she'd put over the flower beds at the front of her building last fall. We'd nearly finished when she suddenly asked me what I'd like for my birthday. I said I'd like Glory to get well and come home.

For a while, she worked without saying anything else. But then she sat down on the steps and told me about a television program she and Uncle Eddie had watched a few nights ago. It was about a scientist named Charles Darwin. Aunt Blanche said he discovered that plants and animals didn't start out looking like they do today, that they'd evolved into different species as they'd adapted to their environments. "I didn't understand the whole program," she said, "but what I did understand explained so many things. Why your brother died, for instance, and Glory's baby, too, and why some people can't have children at all, or get terrible diseases, or drink too much or get into fights or start wars. It's because we're evolving." She looked up at me. "If there's a God, why didn't He make us all healthy and good? Surely He doesn't enjoy watching us suffer for being the way He made us."

I told Aunt Blanche about the priest who visits Glory at the sanatorium. "Father Garcia. He celebrated Mass at Saint Isabel's two summers ago. He says God is love."

She nodded slowly. "It's a beautiful thought. But in that case, why do we need the idea of a god? Isn't love enough?"

I admitted I'd sometimes wondered that, too. "Maybe he meant some sort of—I don't know—transcendent love."

"Maybe." She stood and seemed to force herself to smile. "Anyway, since I can't make Glory well for your birthday, what else would you like?"

I tried to smile, too. "Surprise me. I'm sure whatever you choose will be just what I've always wanted."

We were putting away our tools and gloves when Mr. Sadowski's and Uncle Eddie's cars pulled up to the curb. Mrs. Rasmussen was first out. "Blanche," she said, "your husband's invited us for coffee. I'd have everyone to my place, but Leonard didn't get home until the middle of the night and I'm sure he'll still be sleeping. I've got a coffee cake I'll bring over, though."

"On one condition!" Aunt Blanche said. "You have to tell us all about the engagement party last night!"

Uncle Eddie came up behind Mrs. Rasmussen. "Why do you think I suggested coffee?"

As soon as she'd served everyone a slice of cake, Mrs. Rasmussen began. "Well, I must say." She looked at each of us in turn. "It's such a pleasure sharing simple food among friends. It's quite a contrast to last night, isn't it, Stan?"

He put down his fork. "Too rich for my blood. And Esther, this cake is delicious."

"Moneybags?" Uncle Eddie asked. "Is that what you mean?"

"Let's just start with the mansion," he answered.

"Or the butler who met us at the door," Mrs. Rasmussen added.

"Or the maid who served dinner."

"Prepared by their cook!" Mrs. Rasmussen laughed and shook her head. "Three servants! I can't imagine how Mrs. Fields spends her days."

"Volunteering, I suspect," Aunt Blanche sighed. "The women's club, the garden club—"

"Oh! She does play tennis!" Mr. Sadowski said. "She introduced another woman—whose name I forget—as her doubles partner."

"She used to be a chemist!" Mrs. Rasmussen added. "She said she'd graduated top of her class at Norcross, but when she took a job in a company developing plastics, she got bored. She told me she found motherhood much more satisfying."

Until this point, Papa had been sitting away from the rest of us, in the armchair by the parlor's bay window. Now he got up and poured himself some coffee. "And what did you both think of Jean?" he asked quietly before retreating again to the window.

There was a sudden silence. Mrs. Rasmussen looked at Mr. Sadowski, but his gaze was fixed on his coffee cup. She answered, "Well, Roberto, as you know, she's a lovely young woman. And obviously quite intelligent. She's her father's assistant. And vivacious, goodness me! After dinner, we all went into the ballroom—"

"They have a ballroom?" Aunt Blanche asked.

"Oh, heavens to Betsy! A ballroom, a drawing room, a sitting room, a library! And six bedrooms upstairs, they told us, each with its own private bathroom! Not to mention a powder room downstairs with two sinks and a separate little—well, it's like a little closet with a door that locks so that someone can be using it while someone else is washing!"

"Goodness!" Aunt Blanche exclaimed. "That explains why Mrs. Fields needs a maid!"

"Yes, I suppose so. At any rate, they put on records—jazzy songs—'One O'Clock Jump' and such—and she and Leonard and Jean's cousin Pauline and her husband—what's his name?"

"Alan," Mr. Sadowski said.

"Yes, Alan—I think they said he's a doctor—well, they all danced themselves silly."

I tried to imagine Doctor Eaton dancing himself silly.

"I think Leonard must have taken pity on us older folks, just sitting there, because after a while he put on one of my favorites, 'Sentimental Reasons,' and then Stan and I danced." She squeezed his hand. "But we liked Jean very much." She darted a glance at Papa, then said quietly, "We could see why Leonard fell for her."

There was silence for a moment, then Uncle Eddie asked about Jean's father.

"He seemed friendly enough," Mr. Sadowski said, "though he didn't talk much to us. Praised Leonard, though. Said the longshoremen respect him already."

"What does he look like?" I asked. "My guess is he has a Roman nose and auburn hair."

Mrs. Rasmussen and Mr. Sadowski exchanged glances. Then Mrs. Rasmussen spoke. "No. In fact, we were talking about it on the way home last night. Mr. Fields has hair the color of dishwater, quite honestly. And his features are very ordinary. We both said it's hard to understand how he and his wife managed to have a daughter as lovely as Jean."

Aunt Blanche shrugged. "Well, she could have been adopted."

Mr. Sadowski rose and took his coffee cup into the kitchen. Mrs. Rasmussen's eyes followed him. Then she looked at the rest of us and smiled softly. "I'll leave the rest of the cake with you, Blanche. It's such a fine day—first day of spring! Stan and I have decided to take a drive along the Merrimack River. There's a place he's been wanting me to see."

After they left, Papa said he was going for a walk. The way he announced it—not looking at us and already putting on his coat—made me uneasy, and I reminded him to be back in time for Sunday dinner.

Uncle Eddie turned on the television set while Aunt Blanche and I did the dishes. In the kitchen, she asked me if I'd noticed how quiet Mr. Sadowski had become once Jean's name was mentioned. I said I had, and told her about the night we'd all looked through Glory's photo album. "When he saw Jean's photograph, he said he was probably being sentimental, but she reminded him of Ada."

"Really?" She turned to me. "Could I see that photo album? All this talk about how pretty Jean is, I'd like to see for myself."

We finished the dishes and told Uncle Eddie we were heading to my apartment to start preparing dinner. But first, we opened Glory's photo album. I showed Aunt Blanche both photographs—the one I'd taken of all Glory's suitemates, and the color photo of the Christmas party. "Glory's wearing the dress you made her," I said.

She smiled. "I thought I recognized it!" Then she peered closer. She looked from one photograph to the other, silently.

"Of course I don't remember Ada," I said. "I've only seen one photograph, and Will's painting of her."

The moment I mentioned Will's painting, I remembered the story he'd shared with me, of Magda revealing the cause of Ada's death. Did Aunt Blanche know, too? "Will told me once," I said, "that Ada died in childbirth. But the baby lived. Mrs. Sadowski told him before she died."

Now she looked up, but not at me. She was staring into the distance.

"Did you know?" I asked.

Her voice was a whisper. "I've never been sure."

"And do you think Jean resembles Ada?"

She didn't answer.

"Aunt Blanche, what is it?"

Slowly, she turned to me. "I'm sorry. What did you say?"

I asked her again if she saw a resemblance.

She seemed to hesitate. "The shape of her eyes is similar." Her fingers skimmed the photograph. "And Ada had the same widow's peak. Like Stan. And her hair has red in it. Ada had the most gorgeous auburn hair in the world. But Jean's nose—" Abruptly, she closed the album. "I can certainly understand why Stan might see his daughter in Jean. But there must be thousands of girls who share some of Ada's features. Besides, no one's ever said that Jean is adopted, have they? I mean, did Glory ever mention that?"

"Not to me, she didn't."

She handed the album back to me. "So it's likely Stan was— as he said—being sentimental."

In the kitchen, Aunt Blanche seemed to want to change the subject. As she put on her apron, she asked me how my photography project was coming along. "Don't tell me. You haven't worked on it for months. Since last October, I'd guess."

Her voice was kind, but still, I felt uneasy. "As a matter of fact, I did photograph someone in December. Someone Will recommended."

"And how did that go?"

"Fine," I said. Though I didn't really know how to answer. I'd enjoyed the session, then come home and logged and stored the film and my notes and . . . What? I hadn't really forgotten about it, but I guess I'm not sure anymore what I'd hoped to accomplish. It all seems so far away.

"Violet." Aunt Blanche sounded annoyed. "It's the first day of spring, you're almost twenty-four, and here you are, about to prepare your father's dinner then spend the rest of the afternoon visiting your sister in the hospital." She sighed. "I know Glory's terribly sick, but what about you?"

"Gosh!" I said, and reached for the phone. "You've just reminded me to call the hospital and make sure Glory's up to seeing us today." I knew Aunt Blanche meant well, but I didn't want to talk about myself anymore.

Charlotte took my call. She said Glory was too exhausted for visitors.

Aunt Blanche and I took our time cooking, then called Uncle Eddie. Papa still hadn't come home. We waited a while longer, then started dinner without him. Hours after we'd finished the dishes and they'd gone home, he returned. I warmed a plate for him, then said I was tired and went to bed.

I once read somewhere that historians think a billion people, over the centuries, have died of TB. Why would any God allow it? For that matter, why would any God allow babies to die? And Aunt Blanche is right. What's the use of saying God is love? It's just a word game. Why not accept that we don't know why bad things happen and never will? Like that German poet says. Learn to love the questions. Although the nuns would say it's a sin to even ask such questions. And the priests? They'd say Glory's suffering is a sign of God's compassion—a way of allowing her to atone for her sins here on earth and reduce her time in purgatory. She deserves her punishment. Just like Ada deserved to die in that convent.

And what about the men? The father of Ada's baby. Or of Glory's first pregnancy. Or Leonard. Why hasn't God punished them? Why are women the only ones paying for their sins with their lives?

VIOLET

Today is my twenty-fourth birthday.

It's been weeks since I last saw Glory.

Doctor Murphy phoned us Friday evening to advise against our visiting—again. Glory was feverish, he said, and couldn't keep anything—even liquids—down. So he's stopped the streptomycin.

This morning I put on the little pin with violets that Mama gave me fourteen years ago.

At work, I didn't say anything to Mr. Crane about it being my birthday. We didn't have any bookings, so I spent the day behind the counter, taking in customers' film for developing, or getting their photographs from the alphabetized bins, or selling them film or photo albums or picture frames.

When I got home, Papa wished me a happy birthday, then gestured toward the mail on the hall table. There were two items. The first was a note from Glory. Except for the signature, it wasn't her handwriting:

Dearest Violet,

Every day I wonder how I can ever thank you enough for all you've done for me. You're the sweetest, kindest sister in the world. Happy birthday!

All my love,

Glory

To keep from crying, I slipped the note into my pocket and picked up the second piece of mail. It was a creamy white envelope, already slit open, with a thick card sticking out. It was addressed to Roberto Campo, Violet Campo, and Gloria Campo, all three names on separate lines above our address. I took out the card and turned it over. The message was engraved in black.

MR. AND MRS. ARTHUR FIELDS

REQUEST THE HONOR OF YOUR PRESENCE

AT THE WEDDING OF THEIR DAUGHTER,

JEAN VICTORIA FIELDS,

TO

LEONARD PETER RASMUSSEN

ON SATURDAY, THE SEVENTEENTH OF APRIL

AT TWO O'CLOCK

CHURCH OF THE REDEEMER

379 HAMMOND STREET

CHESTNUT HILL, MASSACHUSETTS

A smaller card inside invited us to a reception at the Fields' home.

I looked up. Papa was watching me. "Why in the world have we been invited?" I asked. "Do you think Mrs. Rasmussen knows?"

"I plan to ask her tonight."

"Will we accept?"

"Of course not." He took the invitation from my hands and put it back on the hall table. Then he led me to the sofa. "I know it can't be much of a birthday for you. Still." He reached behind his chair for a large, thick envelope. "This is for you."

Inside was the current issue of *Life* magazine. There was a photo of a fashion model on the cover. She reminded me a little of Glory.

"It was your Aunt Blanche's idea," Papa said. "I've ordered a subscription for you, and until it arrives, I'll pick one up at the newsstand."

Leafing through the magazine gave me an oddly anxious feeling. But I said I was looking forward to reading it.

Papa waited to mention the wedding invitation until after I'd blown out the candles on my birthday cake and we'd all settled in the parlor with our coffee. "I don't understand why we've been invited, but to invite Glory!" He turned to Mrs. Rasmussen. "What do you think, Esther? I think it must have been Jean's idea and Leonard couldn't object without telling her what had happened."

Pain clouded Mrs. Rasmussen's soft grey eyes. "I hope you're right."

"She didn't need Leonard to tell her what happened," I said quietly. "She already knew. Some of it, anyway. When I introduced them, she asked Leonard if he was the sailor who'd broken Glory's heart."

"Oh, Violet!" Mrs. Rasmussen seemed about to burst into tears, but I went on.

"I think she found out from her cousin Pauline. As you know, she's married to Alan Eaton—Doctor Eaton, the head of psychiatry at the state hospital. I ran into them together one Saturday when we happened to be leaving the hospital at the same time. I didn't mention Glory, of course, but—"

Papa threw himself forward in his chair. "You're saying Doctor Eaton told his wife about Glory and Leonard?"

"How else could Jean have found out?"

"Listen." Mr. Sadowski reached for Mrs. Rasmussen's hand as he spoke. "We're very sorry—"

"No need for you to apologize," Papa said. "I'll send our regrets tomorrow." He picked up his coffee cup. "And now a toast to Violet. *Buon compleanno!* Happy birthday!"

Aunt Blanche gave me a book by Margaret Bourke-White called *Purple Heart Valley*, of her photographs of the war in Italy. "For inspiration," she said. Like the *Life* magazine subscription, I guess.

Of course I'm grateful, and I thanked her, but everything tonight made me feel off-kilter. I was glad to say good night and go home. It's my twenty-fourth birthday, and all I can think to do is lie here and stare at my sister's empty bed.

GLORY

Today was two entirely different days.

Two entirely different lives, really. Or two understandings of one life. One solid and familiar. The other so strange. I feel as if I've gotten off a train I'd never planned to take, and arrived in a land I never knew existed. The pitcher of water is still on my cupboard, and there's the wall calendar open to April, and I can hear the night nurse out on the ward making her rounds. Yet everything's changed. Even the stars. They're shining just as brightly tonight as they did last night, but they're not the same stars, not beacons of hope, not reminders of Bobbie and Mama, not anything but fires burning out.

The old day began as usual, with Charlotte helping me to the bathroom. Since the streptomycin, I've been so weak. Charlotte says not to worry, that once I gain weight and start walking again my strength will come back. But then I had one of those coughing spells that leave me exhausted. Charlotte said at least the timing was right and had me spit into a cup she sent to the lab for testing.

After breakfast, they wheeled me to Radiology for an X-ray. Then I slept until lunch. This afternoon I read a book of poems from the library cart—a first book, called *The Beautiful Changes*, by a poet named Richard Wilbur who's not much older than I am. The title poem is mysterious and wonderful. I kept rereading it and imagining myself walking next autumn with someone I love in a field of Queen Anne's lace. I must have fallen asleep again reading it, because when Charlotte woke me to tell me Violet was here, the book was still open to the same page.

Aunt Blanche came, too. Sometimes when she visits, she cries. She says the visits bring back memories of visiting Mama. Today she didn't cry, and said she thought I looked better.

I told her that Charlotte says TB requires patience, and that I was following Doctor Murphy's orders and hoped to be discharged in time to attend Mrs. Rasmussen and Mr. Sadowski's wedding. I said I wanted to go back to college and become a teacher and do some good in the world. I even told her I hoped to publish another book of poetry.

Now it seems so strange that I said all that. I'm not angry with myself for saying it, or ashamed. It just feels as if someone else must have said it, someone living some other life that seems now as if it could never have been mine.

Violet was quiet. I thought she was just letting Aunt Blanche do the talking, but at one point, when I asked her to remind me of the wedding date, she seemed startled.

She shook her head a little and said it was August 14th. When I said I assumed that Leonard would ask for leave from the Merchant Marine to attend, her eyes darted toward Aunt Blanche. "Leonard left the Merchant Marine earlier this year," she said. "He was discharged . . ."

Aunt Blanche jumped in. "He got a job in Boston," she said. "Something having to do with—with whatever it was he used to do in the Merchant Marine."

"Oh, I see," I said. But I didn't. I couldn't imagine Leonard anywhere but at sea, or in some exotic port with Cecilia or some other girl. I couldn't picture him in Boston.

"Does he—" I was afraid to ask it. But I had to. "Does he know I'm here? That I have TB?"

Violet and Aunt Blanche exchanged glances again. Then Violet nodded and said Mrs. Rasmussen had told him.

"I see," I said again. And now I did see. "He's been back for—what? A month? Two months? And he hasn't visited me."

Violet's hand fluttered toward me. "I'm sorry," she whispered.

Her eyes told me the rest. "Because he has someone else," I said. "In fact, that's why he left the Merchant Marine. Because he's found someone he's serious about."

She didn't answer, didn't even move.

Finally, Aunt Blanche spoke. Her voice was flat, as if she were stating Leonard's age or middle name. "He's a weasel, Glory. Esther is my dearest friend, but her son is a weasel."

I ignored her. "Violet, is it Cecilia? Has he brought Cecilia from Italy?"

"No!" She laughed a short, sharp laugh. "No, I'm sure he forgot all about Cecilia as soon as he'd broken her heart!"

"Who is it then? Have you met her?" I don't know why I was so determined to learn what could only hurt me. Perhaps I had some sort of premonition that knowing the identity of Leonard's new girl would strengthen me for what was to come.

Violet didn't answer, and her eyes seemed to plead with me to stop.

I turned to Aunt Blanche. "Have you met her? He'll have brought her to visit his mother, so one of you must have."

"No!" Violet said. "He hasn't brought her to Mrs. Rasmussen's."

"But you've met her."

Her eyes still had that pleading look. "Yes. I've met her."

"So what is she like? What did you think of her?"

Instead of answering, she bolted upright and left the room.

I looked at Aunt Blanche. Above her mask, her eyes were calm. She came and sat on the edge of the bed, and when she spoke, her voice was as soothing as Mama's when she used to wake me from a bad dream. "Glory, what does it matter who the girl is? Or what she's like? You're the most wonderful girl any man could ask for. Leonard left you because he's unworthy of you. And now he's found another heart to break. Frankly, I feel sorry for her."

"Have you met her, Aunt Blanche?"

"No. No, I haven't."

Neither of us spoke for a while after that. I lay back against my pillows and watched a pair of cardinals darting in and out of the bare branches of the trees outside my window. Then the door opened. Violet came in. Her eyes above her mask were red, but her voice was steady. "Glory." She came to the other side of my bed and took my hand. "I'd rather you hear it from me than read it in the paper." She studied my face as if seeking my permission to continue.

I nodded.

"When Jean Fields brought me the book of poems to give you for Christmas, we met at the Twelve O'Clock Diner. She told me she'd left Norcross to work for her father. We were about to leave when Leonard—he visited Mrs. Rasmussen last Christmas—when he walked in and said hello. I introduced them, then left. Several weeks later, Mrs. Rasmussen told me Leonard had left the Merchant Marine and had taken a job at Mr. Fields' shipping company. And not long after that, Jean and Leonard announced their engagement."

She'd spoken slowly, but there'd been so many words and as soon as she'd said, "Jean Fields," they'd all started churning in my mind. I closed my eyes. Saw. Heard. Leonard groaning against Jean's damp auburn curls.

And I only buried Bobbie last July.

I opened my eyes. "When is the wedding?" I whispered.

Violet looked at Aunt Blanche as if begging her to say it.

And she did. "Glory, I'm so sorry. We're all just—just mystified, really. But the wedding . . . It's today."

Today. The word dropped into the whirlpool in my mind.

She continued. "We hadn't intended to tell you yet. We thought it would be better to wait until you were stronger. But . . ."

Slowly, in the silence, it all became clear. And familiar. The churning stopped. "She's pregnant," I said. "And I am strong."

For a moment, neither spoke. Then Aunt Blanche said, "Yes, you are strong, Glory. I know you are. So I'll admit I've had the same thought. Of course no one has said so, but there's no other explanation."

"She's pregnant," I repeated, this time to Violet.

She shook her head. "I don't know, Glory. How could I?"

"For the same reason I do. Only this time he got caught."

"Or allowed himself to be caught," Aunt Blanche said quietly. When I looked at her, she shrugged. "From what I understand, they're fabulously wealthy."

"Yes," I said, "they are. And thank you."

"For what?"

"For what you said a little while ago. I feel sorry for her, too."

After that, Aunt Blanche said we should talk about something more cheerful, and she told us about a new television program she and Uncle Eddie had begun watching, a comedy about a young married couple in New York. The orderly brought milk and cookies, and then I said I was tired and wanted to rest.

After they left, I tried to sleep, but I kept thinking about Leonard and Jean. And about myself, about what I would do if I got well enough to attend Mrs. Rasmussen and Mr. Sadowski's wedding in August. I would wear a bright color, I decided. Magenta or royal blue. With creamy white pearls. And perhaps, just perhaps, I'd have someone beside me, someone learned and kind—a philosopher, perhaps, who was fond of poetry. And we would be happy.

The sky was darkening before Doctor Murphy came in. Usually his greeting is brisk and cheerful, but tonight he only nodded before pulling up his mask and sitting heavily in the chair beside my bed. He spoke softly. "I have the results of your tests, Glory."

My heart began racing. "Is something wrong?"

He hesitated.

"You don't usually sit down to talk to me."

"You're right," he said, his voice still low. "I don't. It's been a long day." He took off his glasses, wiped them with his handkerchief, and slid them back on above his mask. His warm green eyes, not for the first time, reminded me of Violet's. "I'm afraid the results aren't what we'd hoped for. The cavities haven't grown since your last X-ray, but they haven't retreated. And the bacilli—the germs—are multiplying again. Which means . . . Well. It means we still have a long way to go." He squeezed my hand. "You understand, don't you, that some of our patients are here for years?"

Tears stung my eyes—not because of his message, but because of the gentle way he'd said it. I nodded.

"So we'll continue the isolation and bed rest until we have a set of tests showing us your condition has improved." He released my hand and stood. "All right, then?"

I nodded.

He turned to go, then abruptly turned back. "Rest and eat," he said. "And don't give up."

Don't give up. I once believed Leonard and I would marry. And today he walked down the aisle with Jean, their child growing inside her, while our child, our Bobbie, is in the ground.

"Doctor Murphy?" I whispered.

He waited.

I wanted to ask him so many things. If he ever feels despair. If he's ever been in love. If I'm dying. And he knows it. And is keeping it from me.

So many things. But I couldn't ask any of them. It was Saturday evening. He was probably on his way home. And besides, I couldn't have found the words. "I'll do my best," I said. "And thank you."

He smiled. Then he slid the door closed behind him.

I picked up the volume of Wilbur's poetry, but didn't read. I couldn't even open the cover. Time passed, and the night nurse—Becky—came in. "How are you tonight, Glory?" she asked, and sat for a moment on the side of my bed.

Becky is about my age, sweet and shy. I didn't want her to feel sad for me, so I told her I felt strong. She helped me to the bathroom and settled me back in bed for the night. "Shall I leave the curtains apart again?" she asked.

I nodded.

She adjusted them and said good night. The light went off and I heard the door slide closed.

With the room dark, I can see the stars shining beyond the branches of the trees outside my window. Usually starlight comforts me. But not tonight. Tonight, the sky seems so vast and I feel so small.

I wonder . . . Will I ever walk again beneath the open sky? Will I wade in a meadow of Queen Anne's lace and feel someone beloved touch me?

VIOLET

Everything's changed.

When I woke this morning and thought about the day ahead, it all seemed predictable enough—going with Aunt Blanche to visit Glory, making supper, waiting up to hear about the wedding when Mrs. Rasmussen and Mr. Sadowski got home.

But nothing happened the way I'd expected. Every incident seemed to spiral out of control into calamity. All I could do is stand there and watch until everything recognizable was gone.

It started in the sanatorium, with Glory asking questions about Leonard—one after another, as if somehow she knew, until finally, even though Aunt Blanche and I had decided not to tell her about the wedding, we did. And then she said what we'd all suspected and hadn't said, that Jean is pregnant with Leonard's child. His acknowledged child. His now legitimate child.

She said it. When I'd wanted so much to keep it from her, at least until she leaves the sanatorium.

Or dies. Which Doctor Murphy warned us is possible. He called us into his office on our way out. He said the latest tests show the TB multiplying again. The new cells, he said, would resist the streptomycin. He used the word *implacable* and said he might collapse Glory's right lung, which has "particularly worrying lesions." But he hasn't decided yet.

I asked him if he'd told Glory.

He said he'd be stopping by her room later. "However, with patients, I try to be more circumspect. And I'd ask you to be . . . less than forthright as well."

On the way home, I kept quiet. Aunt Blanche doesn't drive, and I was afraid that if I started talking, I might not be able to get us home. When I pulled into Mill Street, I told her I'd like to wait a few days before sharing Doctor Murphy's news with Papa. "You can tell Uncle Eddie when you get home tonight. But I think Papa has enough on his mind with the wedding." She agreed.

As we were finishing supper, I told Papa and Uncle Eddie that we'd realized Glory might see the wedding announcement in the paper and had decided to tell her about Leonard and Jean. When Papa asked me how she'd taken the news, I didn't tell him she'd insisted Jean was pregnant. I just said she'd taken it reasonably well. "She even said she felt sorry for Jean."

"As do I," Aunt Blanche said.

Papa pushed back from the table. "I might feel sorry for her if I didn't suspect, every time I think of it, that she attached herself to Leonard out of spite."

"Spite?" Uncle Eddie's brows went up. "That's a pretty strong word. What makes you say that?"

"You've never met Jean," he snapped. "From the moment we walked into their suite at Norcross, she was comparing herself to Glory. And from what I could tell, she wasn't happy with the results of her comparison."

"But Papa—" I began.

"As soon as she saw Glory's suitcase, her clothes, her shoes, she must have known she'd won a scholarship."

I insisted that Jean must be very intelligent, too. "You have to be to get into Norcross."

"Not if your mother went there, and your father makes a donation!"

"That's quite a theory," Uncle Eddie said—quietly, but with a hint of mockery that seemed to make Papa's smoldering anger burst into flame.

"It's not a theory!" he shouted, and rose from his chair. "I know what I know! A girl like that—good looks, money, family—she could have any guy she wanted. So why else would she go after a lowlife like Leonard Rasmussen?"

"Roberto, please!" Aunt Blanche began gathering the dishes. I was too stunned to move. "Before Esther and Stan get here, please calm down. Or perhaps it would be better if they came to our place."

"Fine with me! You think I'm looking forward to sitting here listening to them go on and on about a wedding that should never have happened? Leonard Rasmussen had a responsibility to marry Glory! And maybe if he'd done that, she wouldn't have lost the baby, or stopped eating, or—"

"Maybe so, Roberto. But he didn't."

Mr. Sadowski. He and Mrs. Rasmussen were standing in the entryway, our front door open behind them. They must have come straight upstairs, because they were still in their coats. Mrs. Rasmussen's makeup looked smeared, as if she'd been crying.

"I need to speak with you." Mr. Sadowski's voice was flat. His eyes were fixed on Papa's face. "Not here. We can talk at my place."

I looked at Papa, but he wasn't looking at me. Or anyone. Something had come between him and all the rest of us, as if we weren't in the same room anymore. Without a word, he went to the closet, pulled on his coat, and walked out. Mr. Sadowski followed him. The door stood open. I heard their footsteps go down the stairs, the front door open and close. Mrs. Rasmussen crossed to the parlor windows. She watched for a moment, then closed her eyes.

"Esther," Aunt Blanche whispered. "What's the matter? What's happened?"

Without looking at any of us, Mrs. Rasmussen shook her head and walked out, closing the door firmly behind her.

The apartment was silent. Then Uncle Eddie threw down his napkin. "What the hell was that all about?"

Aunt Blanche was staring at the door. "Looks like the chickens have come home to roost." She resumed clearing the table. "Eddie, your program starts in a few minutes. Why don't you go ahead, and I'll keep Violet company for a while?"

"You tryin' to get rid of me?" he asked, but his voice was gentle.

"Yeah," she answered. "I am." She carried the dishes she'd gathered into the kitchen.

He drained the last of his beer and stood. "I guess I'll leave you two ladies to figure it out." Our eyes met. He looked for a moment as if he wanted to say something more, then shook his head. "See you later, my Vi." He put on his coat and left.

I brought the rest of the dishes into the kitchen. Aunt Blanche was already at the sink in her apron, scrubbing. I picked up a dishcloth. We didn't speak until after we'd finished. Then she said, "Been quite a day."

I nodded.

"You okay?"

"No." I hung the towel over the radiator to dry. "Glory's desperately ill. Leonard's married Jean. And now something else has happened. Something that started a long time ago. Involving Papa and Mr. Sadowski."

She leaned back against the counter. She looked weary.

"What is it, Aunt Blanche?"

Her eyes were fixed on my face. "Men," she said simply. "And women. Make mistakes. Blissful, dreadful mistakes. But more often than not, women pay the price."

"Like Glory?"

She nodded. But something in her face let me know she meant more.

"Like Ada," I said. "Ada Sadowski."

"You want to talk?"

"No," I said. "Thanks, but . . . I think I'd rather be alone just now."

She squeezed my hand. "I'll say good night, then. If you need anything, you know where to find me."

I heard her go out, but for a long time I just stood there in the kitchen, not moving, not even thinking, really. Then I drifted into the parlor and sat by the windows. I looked out. Up and down the street, each lamp cast a yellow spotlight on the darkness. In the distance, music was playing—a woman's voice, bluesy, but I couldn't recognize the song. Instead, I heard Mama sobbing. In her room late at night. Sobbing the name Ada.

It was simple enough. My father had taken a lover. A neighbor's daughter. A girl named Ada Sadowski. She'd become pregnant, and he'd denied the child. And Ada had gone away to give birth in shame, and had died. And the child had been raised by a wealthy couple in Chestnut Hill. They'd called her Jean. My half-sister. Jean Fields. Now, Jean Rasmussen.

The door to our building opened. Aunt Blanche went down the steps to the sidewalk. She stood for a moment looking toward Mr. Sadowski's house. Then, slowly, she crossed the street to her duplex and disappeared. The light from Mrs. Rasmussen's windows went out. And then, at the end of the street, a man entered one of the spotlights, shuffling. Will. I watched him approach. As he reached the steps, he paused and looked up at our parlor windows. He touched a finger to the brim of his hat, then slowly ascended. I heard the front door, then his steps on the stairs, on our landing, and up again. His door opened and closed.

It's past eleven. There's no sound in the street. I'll get up. I'll wash and go to bed. When I wake, Papa will be home. I'll make his breakfast, pour his coffee. We'll visit Glory. I won't speak of it. Not to him, not to Glory. She loves him so much, it would—

Oh, Glory.

GLORY

Why did you name me for the morning glory?
    Mute trumpets that will not last the day?
O, Mother Sparrow, my child is earth, my verses water.
Fly to my spent blossoms.
Carry their dust to my sister's garden.

VIOLET

Implacable.

Unable to be placated.

Like an angry god.

This morning, I woke late. The silence was eerie. The door to Papa's room was closed. I knocked. There was no answer. I went in. His closet was open and half empty. The photograph of him and Mama on their wedding day, always in the same spot on the dressing table, was gone. I looked out the parlor windows to where I'd parked the car when Aunt Blanche and I had come home from visiting Glory. The car was gone. I went into the bathroom and opened the medicine cabinet. Papa's shaving brush and soap and cup were gone.

I needed to talk to Aunt Blanche, needed someone else to know that Papa was gone. I looked at the clock. Half past nine. Soon Uncle Eddie would leave for Mass. I showered, dressed, and sat by the windows again. In a few minutes, Mr. Sadowski's car pulled up to the curb. Mrs. Rasmussen came out of our building and got in. The car pulled away. And then at the top of the steps across the street, Uncle Eddie appeared in his grey suit, descended, got into his car, and drove off. I put on my coat and crossed the street. Before I'd even rung the bell, Aunt Blanche let me in.

"I thought you might come," she said. "Coffee's ready."

I followed her into the kitchen. "I fell asleep before Papa came home," I said. "He was gone again when I got up. His clothes, his suitcase, too."

She stood still for a moment. "New York, I suppose."

"You stopped at Mrs. Rasmussen's last night."

Her brows lifted.

"I saw you leave."

"You were always such an observant child."

"Tell me what she said."

Softly, she asked if I was sure I wanted to know. When I nodded, she poured the coffee, then began.

"They were at the wedding reception. Apparently some of Jean's family members are quite fond of champagne. Anyway, after the meal, Esther went to the powder room. Do you remember her telling us how the toilet is in a separate little closet?"

I nodded.

"Well, she didn't realize she could have locked the outer door. So she was in the closet part when two women came in. One, whose voice she didn't recognize, was saying something about the wedding being so rushed and didn't Jean's parents know it was bound to give people the wrong idea. The other voice Esther recognized. Jean's grandmother, though she sounded tipsy. She said it wasn't the wrong idea at all, that Jean is pregnant. Then she said something about the apple doesn't fall far from the tree. The other said she thought no one knew anything about Jean's parents. Jean's grandmother said the nuns knew a few things. That the mother was Polish . . ."

She reached across the table and took my hand. I nodded again.

"And the father Italian. And that, when they'd asked the girl why the two hadn't married, she'd said because he was already married with a child of his own, and anyway . . ." She seemed to wince. "He denied he was the father."

I think she was expecting me to show some kind of shock. But I doubt I showed anything, because I didn't feel anything.

She went on. "When Esther went back to the ballroom, Leonard was dancing with Jean's mother. Esther cut in. She asked Leonard if it was true that the wedding was rushed because Jean is pregnant. Leonard admitted it, but said it didn't matter. That the baby would grow up respectably. A few weeks early, that's all. Well, Esther was so upset she went back to the table and told Stan she wanted to go home. And on the way, she told him what she'd overheard."

We both sat in silence for a moment. Then I told her it was all right. That I already knew.

Of course she was surprised. "What do you know? How?"

"It came to me last night," I said. And suddenly, I thought of something else. "You've known, too! This whole time. Haven't you?"

She shook her head. "It's true I'd suspected for years that Ada had gone away pregnant. But I never knew for sure until you told me what Will said—what Magda told him before she died."

"I mean about Papa," I said. "You knew about Papa and Ada."

She lowered her eyes. "Again—I'd suspected."

"How?"

"Sergeant McGowan." She grimaced. "A poker debt. Your uncle called it in. He'd thought for a while that your father was stepping out with Ada, but he didn't have proof. So he told McGowan he'd cancel the debt if he'd look into it. McGowan found the hotel. Not far. Twenty minutes by cab. A couple matching your father's and Ada's descriptions had registered there several times, early evening, always checking out before midnight. Just when your mother was worrying about your father having to work extra shifts. Second shifts. Which let out at midnight."

So he'd gone home to Mama's bed after— I couldn't let myself think about it. "Did Uncle Eddie confront Papa?"

"I begged him not to. Your mother was pregnant with Glory at the time. If she'd found out—" She stopped abruptly, looked away, then shook her head and began again. "Besides, we couldn't be sure. McGowan showed the hotel manager a photograph of Ada—her high school photo, from the newspaper. But not of your father. Lots of men might have fit his description. And anyway, by the time McGowan told us, Ada had disappeared."

"She'd gone to the convent?"

"Apparently. Stan and Magda told us she'd gotten a job in New York. I guess they were too ashamed to tell anybody the truth. And after a while, we stopped asking. But your uncle was convinced she was still in New York. Until that day—the day of your mother's funeral—when Magda told everyone Ada was dead. Long dead."

"And ever since," I murmured, "Papa has known. He must have counted back the years and realized that Ada had died bearing his child."

Aunt Blanche sighed. "Again, darling, we can't be sure the baby was his. Although . . ."

"Although what?"

"When you showed me Jean's photographs . . . Do you see it? The resemblance to your father?"

"Yes," I said. "And to Glory. And me."

"Still, it's not proof."

"But last night? How did he answer Stan last night?"

"I phoned Esther this morning and asked her. She said he didn't say a word. Didn't deny it or confirm it. Just turned his back and walked out." She waited. "Are you all right?"

"Yes," I said. But I wasn't. Because even as I sat there in Aunt Blanche's sunlit kitchen, I could hear Mama sobbing the name Ada. "Whether or not he confesses," I said, "it's true. Mama knew. Somehow, she found out."

"Yes." Aunt Blanche's voice was a whisper. "I'm so sorry. Your uncle told her."

"But you just said—"

"It was years after Ada disappeared. He'd been drinking. And I think—" She shook her head as if she didn't want to go on.

"What?" I insisted.

There were tears in her eyes. "I know your uncle loves me, darling. But he'd always been half in love—at least—with your mother as well. And one night, when we'd been arguing and he'd been drinking and your father was in New York for your Aunt Marcellina's birthday, he stormed across the street and told your mother about the affair. I ran after him, but couldn't stop him. He told her that your father and Ada were probably together that very night." She swiped at her tears. "She was pregnant with your brother at the time."

"I remember that night," I said. Even though I never had. Not until that moment. And not an image. More a sound—the anguish in Mama's voice. "She threw him out, didn't she?"

"Yes. But she believed him." She wiped her face with her handkerchief. "Oh, Violet, again and again over the years I've tried to convince myself that what he said had nothing to do with what happened to the baby. But I can't. She'd had three miscarriages after Glory. One after another. But this time, everything seemed to be going so well. Until that night. It was such a shock. She was devastated. And a few days later . . ."

She stuffed her handkerchief back into her pocket and drank the rest of her coffee. "At any rate, I learned something else last night."

"From Mrs. Rasmussen?"

"Yes. She knew about Ada's death—and the baby—almost from the start."

"How?"

"Magda told her. It was November, months after Ada had disappeared. She was dropping off some sewing. Magda seemed distracted, then collapsed at her kitchen table, sobbing. She said Ada had died just a few days before, after having a baby. But she swore Esther to secrecy. And she kept the secret until she told me last night. But she never knew who the father was. Magda and Stan didn't know. Ada had refused to say."

"She refused to betray Papa," I said. "Despite the fact that he'd betrayed her. And his wife. And his friends." Even to myself I sounded bitter. "Why else do you think he's run away to New York?"

Aunt Blanche sighed. "I suppose so. You could call your Aunt Marcellina and find out if that's where he is."

"How long would it take to drive there?"

"If he left in the middle of the night, he'd have arrived a few hours ago."

She came home with me and waited while I phoned Aunt Marcellina. When I asked her if Papa was there, she said he was, but that he was sleeping. I said I wasn't surprised, since it was a long drive. No, she said, he'd taken the train and left the car behind for me. I asked her how long he planned to stay, but she said she didn't know, that he'd been so exhausted she hadn't even asked him why he'd come at all, and did I know? I said I didn't, but to have him call me.

When Uncle Eddie got home, he drove me to the train station. We found Papa's car and I drove it home.

This afternoon, I went to see Glory alone. When she asked about Papa, I told her he'd gone to New York. She asked me why, and I told her I didn't know, that he'd decided on a whim. They brought her afternoon snack, but it seemed to exhaust her to eat it. I said she seemed tired, and she said it was nothing, that she wanted me to stay, but Charlotte came in after only half an hour and suggested I go.

I ate supper with Aunt Blanche and Uncle Eddie tonight. They invited me to stay and watch television, and I did, two programs, and when the second one ended at ten and Uncle Eddie stretched and yawned in his chair, I realized I needed to say good night.

On my way in, I noticed Mrs. Rasmussen's light was on, and heard voices. I hesitated, but made myself climb the stairs. On the landing, I listened for sounds from Will's apartment. Nothing. He probably hadn't returned from Boston yet. And even if he had, I thought, what would I say to him? *Good evening, Will, I'm sorry to disturb you, but I'm lonely.* No. And it wouldn't be true anyway. I'm not lonely. I don't know what I am.

I'll go to work tomorrow and try not to think about it all, and I'll have supper with Aunt Blanche and Uncle Eddie, and when I get back, maybe Papa will phone and say he never touched Ada Sadowski and is furious with Stan for suggesting otherwise. Then I'll tell him what Doctor Murphy said about Glory, and he'll tell me he's taking the next train home.

GLORY

What is my destiny?

Once I thought it was to be a famous poet, Leonard's wife, Bobbie's mother. Now that's all gone. And even though I still think of Jeremy's paper airplane, and my chapbook selling 78 copies, and Leonard and Jean making love, having breakfast together, choosing baby furniture together . . . the hurt is gone, too. Does that mean I've forgiven them all—Leonard, Jeremy, Professor Turner—or that I've realized there's nothing to forgive? Either way, it's as if TB is a dark angel who's erased the past and left me at peace, just to live each hour. Each moment.

The slant of sunlight on the wall.

The breeze through my open window.

Sometimes when I look out, I see people walking on the path beneath the trees—a visitor arriving, or a nurse buttoning her coat, heading home. And I wonder what their life is like. What their work is like, their neighborhood, whether they have a spouse, children—or only photographs and silence—waiting for them at home. And I think of them going to bed that night and getting up the next morning and heading out into the world again, day after day, while I stay here, in this room. I suppose it's odd to imagine such things, but it makes me feel less alone, as if I share in their life and that my life, in theirs, continues somehow.

When Father Garcia visited me last Wednesday, I told him Doctor Murphy had said the TB was growing again. He said he was sorry and that the news must be difficult to bear. And then he said something strange—that my destiny isn't in Doctor Murphy's hands, "much as I admire his work. Your destiny is the same as mine, the same as everyone's, and it's unchanged by events in the world of time."

I asked him what it was, this destiny. Instead of answering, he placed his hand on my head, as he's done before. I closed my eyes. Something moved through my body—a sensation of warmth, thick like honey.

Ever since he left, the coughing, the pain, the nightmares, none of those things seem to touch me. Instead, the people walking beneath the trees touch me. And the blossoms. They're unfurling now. Apple blossoms. I told Charlotte I remember them from when Mama was here. "They're always lovely," she said. "But they seem especially radiant this year."

Sometimes, when the fever comes, it's me who's walking beneath the apple trees, going home.

Violet visited this afternoon. I told her I'd been working on my poem for Mrs. Rasmussen and Mr. Sadowski. She asked me to read it to her, but I said I wanted to wait. "Perhaps I'll be home by August," I said, "and can read it to them at their wedding reception." I haven't told her what Doctor Murphy said. It would just make her worry.

She said Aunt Blanche would have to make me a new dress. "It could be your birthday present." Her voice got softer. "You'll be twenty-one."

After she said that, she turned her back to me.

I asked her if Papa had gotten back from New York.

"Not yet," she said, still not looking at me. "He sent me a letter with some money for the rent. Which he didn't have to do. I can pay it myself. Anyway, in his letter he said that he might stay for a while."

A while? It didn't make sense. "Last week, you said he'd left on a whim. So why would he stay?"

She turned to me. Above her mask, her eyes shone. "I'm sure he'll come back soon. Uncle Eddie says he's just cooling off, like when we were children and he and Mama would quarrel."

"But why should he need to cool off?"

"He had an argument with Mr. Sadowski. I don't know what was said. No one else was there."

I decided to change the subject. Before she'd arrived, I'd been reading—again—the volume of Evelina Stern's poems that Jean gave me. I told Violet how grateful I am to Jean for choosing it for me and asked if she'd like to borrow it.

She slid it into her purse. "Remember we talked—oh, it must have been more than a year ago now—about you sending Evelina Stern your chapbook?" She gestured toward the notebooks in my cupboard. "Or maybe you could send your new manuscript?"

I could tell she was trying to say the right things, but didn't know what the right things were. Neither did I, but I told her she could send my chapbook to Evelina Stern for me, with my gratitude for her own work. And then I asked about her photography project. "How many sessions have you done now?"

She shook her head. "To be honest, I don't even remember. I haven't photographed anyone since December."

"I'm sorry, Vi," I said. "You must not have much time, between working and visiting me."

"It's not your fault," she answered. "It's me! I seem—I don't know. I seem to have lost the thread."

Charlotte came in and suggested I rest.

As Violet put on her coat, I told her not to come tomorrow. "Spend the day on your project. Please."

"Don't be silly! Of course I'm coming tomorrow and there's nothing you can do to stop me!"

"Then I won't try." Charlotte adjusted my bed, and I lay back against the pillows. "Would you bring some stationery? I'd like to write to Papa."

"Of course. You can dictate. I'll write."

"Thanks, Vi." Already sleep was pulling me into the shallows. I felt something brush my forehead—through her mask, Violet's kiss.

"See you tomorrow," she whispered. I heard the door slide shut, and her voice and Charlotte's, fading.

When I woke, the sun was setting. These last few days, I've come to treasure this time, just a minute or two, when the apple blossoms glow as if they're on fire.

What will I say when I write to Papa? Nothing about his argument. Perhaps I'll just describe the apple blossoms and ask him to come home before they're gone.

VIOLET

Glory seems better.

When I sat with her today, although of course she's awfully ill, she seemed to want to talk about the future—even my future. So maybe Doctor Murphy is mistaken and she's beginning to get stronger, and soon—as she said, in time for the wedding—she'll be home again.

The building was quiet when I got back. Aunt Blanche had invited me to a film with her and Uncle Eddie, but I'd said no. Now I wished I'd gone. I couldn't see any lights behind the windows up and down Mill Street. I might have been the only one home.

There wasn't much food in the kitchen. I made myself some toast and an egg, washed the dishes, then went into Papa's room. I hadn't told Glory, but in the letter he'd sent with cash for May's rent, he'd asked me to mail him some clothes and papers. So he isn't planning to come home any time soon. Despite my news about what Doctor Murphy said.

I folded the clothes into neat bundles on his bed, then opened the shallow drawer at the top of his dresser. *Send me everything in that drawer,* his letter had said, *except the title to the car. Keep that for now.* How long is "for now," I wondered.

I pulled the papers from the drawer and laid them out on the bed. A bank book. A life insurance policy. A small, black journal. I opened it. The pages were yellowed, the entries in blue ink or thick pencil. The first entry:

30 June 1908

Oggi siamo arrivati a N.Y. Zio Edoardo mi ha dato questo taccuino.

Within a few pages, the entries skipped forward several months and were increasingly in English. I wondered if Papa had recorded the day his father returned to Sicily. All he'd ever told us was that he hadn't liked America, or his brother-in-law Edoardo, and had gone home, promising to send money. But no money had ever arrived, and Edoardo's inquiries had gone unanswered. Yes, there it was:

13 March 1909

Today we said goodbye to Papa. Uncle Edoardo and I went to the boat. Aunt Rosalia and Marcellina stayed home with Mamma. She was crying.

A few pages later:

1 July 1909

Today I started to work at the store. I swept and put things away. In the afternoon I went out and said Coca-Cola 5¢. I sold 34 bottles.

I never knew Papa had worked at the store where Great Uncle Edoardo had been a butcher. In fact, I'd never known about any job before he drove a taxi. Which was how he met

Mama, when she and Aunt Blanche went to New York for a weekend. Two weeks later he was at her door.

I turned the page again:

19 August 1909

Mamma's gone. Aunt Rosalia says she fell off the roof. Marcellina says she was crying and ran up the stairs. Aunt Rosalia ran after her. She made Marcellina stay in the kitchen. Marcellina heard people screaming. An ambulance took Mamma away.

The roof. My grandmother had fallen from—or thrown herself from—the roof.

I turned the page. One entry:

20 August 1909

Today Mamma died.

He wasn't even as old as I was when I lost Mama.

I turned each page to the end of the journal. There was no more writing.

I put his things in a box, then decided to bake something to bring to Glory tomorrow. I started for the kitchen, then remembered I'd had the last egg for supper. Wait. The mail. I'd forgotten to take in the mail. I went downstairs. The only item was an issue of *Life* magazine. I brought it into my bedroom and added it to the ones Papa had bought me. Then I realized: My subscription had begun. And I hadn't read a single one. I spread them all out on my bed and stared at the covers.

Footsteps—Will's—coming up the stairs. Maybe I should wish him good night. If I did that, maybe he'd ask me about

Glory, or why he hadn't seen Papa around. The footsteps passed just outside my door, then began to climb again. I heard his door open, then close.

I took out the book of poetry Glory had given me and sat by the parlor windows. I stared at the cover. *Braving the Rain.* I still hadn't opened it when I saw Uncle Eddie's car pull up to the curb across the street. Under the streetlight, he and Mr. Sadowski got out, then opened the doors for Aunt Blanche and Mrs. Rasmussen. They must all have gone to the film together. They said good night, then Aunt Blanche and Uncle Eddie disappeared into their building. Mr. Sadowski and Mrs. Rasmussen crossed the street. He kissed her, then waited while she let herself in. I heard the front door open and close, then the door to her apartment. Light from her parlor windows spilled onto the sidewalk. Mr. Sadowski headed home. I watched until he disappeared in the darkness.

Tomorrow, when I visit Glory, we'll write to Papa together. I'll put our letter inside his box. Maybe it'll convince him that his home is here with us. No. Not with me. With Glory.

GLORY

It's nearly morning.

It must be, because the moon is in the western sky, and it's full. Did its light wake me? I was dreaming that I was in labor with Bobbie and a doctor put a mask over my face and it was suffocating me. I guess that's why I woke.

If I could sit up. Just a little. And breathe. And watch the moonlight on the apple trees. It's making the blossoms glow.

I wonder if Mama ever woke and saw the apple blossoms glowing in the moonlight. If she ever beheld them the way I'm beholding them now. If she knew she was dying the way I know I'm dying, and just kept on beholding the blossoms, resting in them, as I am now.

I wonder if Father Garcia's soldier rested in the sound of that nurse's lullaby. Or Bobbie, when we drifted off to sleep that afternoon, did you rest in the beating of my heart?

Father Garcia, thank you for these days of grace.

Will, for walking me home in the rain.

Papa. Dear Papa. Thank you for bringing me daffodils.

And Violet, for holding my head in your lap and stroking my hair. In whatever time is left, Vi, I want to love you better. I want to love you from now on as I love you now.

VIOLET

A mad woman is shrieking in the east wing.

No. No. It's an ambulance.

Church bells pealing.

Church bells tolling.

The telephone.

It's barely light. Who's calling so early on a Sunday? Papa. Maybe he took the night train from New York and is calling from the station.

"Violet?" the voice says. "It's Charlotte. Glory's nurse. I'm so sorry."

Sorry?

Why sorry?

The start of her shift. Glory's room. Her body upright in bed. Ruptured bronchial artery. Sometime before dawn.

Her voice breaks.

I look out the windows. The street shines with morning. We're writing a letter today. Today we're writing a letter.

She says again, "I'm sorry."

I tell her I'll come.

I put down the phone.

I don't call Aunt Blanche. I don't call Papa. I brush my teeth. Wash. Dress. Purse. Keys. I walk out.

I drive. Along the way, I pass no one. Nothing. At the hospital, the visitors' lot is empty. I walk to the entrance. Daffodils. A poem. "To what purpose, April?"

Doctor Murphy.

"It's Sunday," I say. "You're here on a Sunday."

"Of course," he answers. "I'm sorry." He takes my gloved hand and presses it between both of his as if he's trying to warm it.

But my hand isn't cold. My hand isn't anything at all. I say, "It's only April. She isn't even twenty-one."

"Yes, I know." He pauses. Inhales. "Such a noble soul. Never a word of complaint. I certainly had hoped . . ." He drops my hand. "Your father?"

"He's in New York."

"I'm sorry he couldn't be here."

He couldn't be here.

"Violet. If you wish, you may view the body. Sometimes it helps. To say goodbye."

I think of Glory's son. "Yes."

"Follow me."

He leads me down a flight of stairs, through a hall and a door. The room is small and cold. There's no window. In the center is a gurney covered in white cloth. He walks to the gurney. He lifts the cloth slowly and folds it down. Black hair. A waxen face with closed eyes.

"I'll wait outside," he says. "Take all the time you need."

I hear the door close behind me. I step forward and look down. Glory's body. Glory's matted curls someone's neglected to comb, and for a garment, a heavy cloth.

My fingertips touch her cheek, her lips. My hand shakes. I will it to stop. Only this. I lift and cradle her head and stroke her hair.

And then I know.

She's not here. I don't know where she is, but she's not anywhere I can find her. She's gone.

I lay her body back on the gurney. I cover it with the cloth and walk out.

Doctor Murphy gestures to the stairs. I follow him back to the west wing. Charlotte has gathered Glory's things in a bag. I thank her and ask her to thank Father Garcia for me. Doctor Murphy walks me to the lobby. He takes my hand again, lets it go. He watches as I walk out.

On the way home, I pass mothers and fathers and children and lovers strolling past churches or parks or cafés. Ordinary people beginning an ordinary Sunday in late April, none of them knowing Glory is gone and that nothing can ever be the same.

I park outside our building. As I start up the steps, the front door opens. Will. As if he's been waiting for me. "Violet," he says as I reach him. "Is everything all right?"

I look into his soft eyes. "Glory died this morning," I say.

A shaft of sunlight strikes his face. It seems to release the tight stripe of his cheek. To make his mouth whole. I see him lift his face—his perfect face—to the sky. "Glory," he whispers, as if to her. "I'm so sorry." He sinks down onto the top step.

I sit beside him and put my arm around him. He puts his arm around me. We hold each other. The door behind us opens. I see Mrs. Rasmussen's slippers and the hem of her skirt. "Violet? Will? Has something happened?"

"It's Glory," I say.

She sits beside us. She says nothing, just weeps.

Will rises.

I watch him cross the street and climb the steps.

The door opens. He speaks to Aunt Blanche, then turns away and starts toward town. Aunt Blanche stands at her door, not moving.

From across the street, I reach out my arms.

Today we buried Glory's body.

I chose a plot in the town cemetery, right next to Bobbie's. Papa wired me money. Aunt Blanche and I made the arrangements for the services together, and yesterday afternoon, Uncle Eddie drove to the train station and brought Papa home.

He was carrying only a garment bag. He embraced me stiffly, then Aunt Blanche and I served supper. He said nothing at the table except to answer a question from Aunt Blanche about Uncle Giacomo and Aunt Marcellina. He said they'd wanted to come, but he'd told them no. Then he rose, excused himself, and went across the street to our apartment to dress for the wake.

At the funeral home, on a table beside the casket, Aunt Blanche and I had set out Glory's first collection of poems, from second grade, alongside her chapbook and her senior photo from Saint Isabel's. We'd decided on a closed casket, on top of which we'd placed my photograph of Glory listening to Jimmy Conlan's speech on Armistice Day two years ago. Papa knelt at the casket, then took his place at the head of our brief line and stayed there. Silently, he shook each visitor's hand—his coworkers, some friends from the Knights of Columbus, Mr. Crane, some of Glory's teachers and classmates, Jimmy and Dorothy. Only once, when Dorothy stifled a sob as she reached to take Papa's hand, did I see any movement in his face. A wince, and then it froze again. When Mrs. Rasmussen and Mr. Sadowski came in, even while they murmured their condolences, he fixed his gaze on the far wall of the room.

A few minutes before the wake ended, Will entered holding a bouquet of lilacs. He placed them on the casket beside the photograph before kneeling and bowing his head. After rising, he reached out his hand and—for a moment—touched the casket. And then the room—the walls and everything and everyone—broke apart.

Uncle Eddie eased me into a chair.

Aunt Blanche pressed a cup of water into my hand and told me to drink. The room became a room again, and I saw Will by the door, watching me. Our eyes met, and he was gone.

The visiting hours were over. After helping me with my coat, Papa picked up the lilacs Will had left on the casket. When we got home, he put them in a large vase of water. Then he said good night and went to his room.

Long after I'd gone to bed, I heard his door open again, heard him go into the bathroom and wash, then heard him cross to the chair by the windows and sit. I must have fallen asleep before he went to bed.

This morning, after breakfast, he asked me for a length of ribbon. Just before we left for the funeral, he tied the ribbon around the lilacs and wrapped the stems in damp newspaper. He placed the bundle in the back of the Buick and left it there. Inside the church were only a handful of people: Aunt Blanche and Uncle Eddie, Mr. Sadowski and Mrs. Rasmussen, Will, Dorothy, Jimmy, a few others from Saint Isabel's . . . and Father Garcia. He sat in a pew several rows back, alone. I'd told Father Bouchard we didn't want a funeral Mass, so the service was brief. As I followed the casket out, I passed Father Garcia. His eyes were closed, his face glistening with tears.

The sky over the cemetery was grey. Papa placed the lilacs on Glory's casket. After the prayers, he went back and sat in the car. I stayed until the casket was lowered into the ground.

Aunt Blanche and Uncle Eddie had invited everyone to join them for lunch after the burial. But when Papa turned into Mill Street and parked outside our building, he told me to stay in the car. He left the engine running, went inside and, within a minute, came out again with his bag. He put it in the trunk of the car and drove back into town.

As he drove, neither of us spoke. I knew he was headed to the train station.

He parked. People were hurrying in and out, shouting, waving. I watched his eyes follow a young man as he kissed his wife and daughter, then disappeared inside.

He spoke. "I never believed she'd die." His gloved hands on the steering wheel curled into fists. "She was . . . so good. So innocent." He clenched his eyes shut, but tears came anyway. "*Povera bambolina.*"

My own eyes filled with tears, watching him. I wanted to embrace him, wanted his embrace. But I didn't move.

He mopped his face with his handkerchief. Cleared his throat. "I'm not coming back," he said. "I've got a good job. Better than I had here. There's more opportunity in New York. Everything's booming." Finally he looked at me. "You could do well there. Work your way up. Maybe take photos for the *New York Post* someday."

I didn't answer.

He glanced down at his watch. "The train leaves at half past. I've got to go."

He got out. He took his bag from the trunk, then came around to the window and tapped. I rolled it down. He lifted my hand and placed the car keys in it, curling my fingers over them. "Think about it," he said, then headed toward the entrance.

I threw open the door and got out.

He swung around.

"I will," I said. "Think about it."

He nodded a little. A drop of rain fell on his cheek, his shoulder. Then he turned and disappeared.

I drove to Aunt Blanche and Uncle Eddie's. Dorothy and Jimmy had already left, Aunt Blanche told me, since they'd had to get back to work, and Will had gone home to paint. He was working on a portrait of Glory, she said.

Uncle Eddie was at the dining table having lunch with Father Bouchard. I fixed myself a sandwich, but took it to the parlor and sat with Mrs. Rasmussen and Mr. Sadowski. No one asked why Papa hadn't come.

By mid-afternoon, all the guests had gone, but I couldn't make myself go home, even to change. Aunt Blanche put out leftovers for supper, then we sat and watched television. Finally, I said good night.

I crossed the street. Light streamed from the first and third-floor windows, and when I entered the building, I heard music from Mrs. Rasmussen's parlor—Helen Morgan singing "Something to Remember You By." I went upstairs, but stopped on the landing, listening. I fingered my keys in my hand. And then I heard the door above me open. I climbed a few stairs and looked up.

"Hello, Will," I said softly. "Aunt Blanche said you're painting a picture of Glory."

"You're welcome to see it." He held the door wide, gesturing inside. I went up and followed him into his studio. The windows were open to the night air. On the walls were the same three portraits I'd seen before. On the easel was Glory.

The colors were simple, pure, the overall impression bright. She was seated on grass. Her black hair was long, loose, flowing past her shoulders, the way she'd worn it for years after Mama died. Her throat was encircled by a red ribbon. In her arms, she held a bouquet of deep purple lilacs, such a large bouquet that it completely hid her torso and most of her arms and hands. Spreading beneath the bouquet, like a cloud upon the grass, was a white skirt. Beneath it, one bare foot peeked out, its arch, its toes, delicate. I swiped the tears from my eyes and made myself look at her face—her wide, black eyes, rounded cheeks and nose, her rosebud mouth. The face of Glory at age nine or ten, sometime after Mama's death, yet gazing out at me, at the world, in serenity.

I turned to Will.

He stepped forward. "That's how I see her. How I've always seen her. Always will."

"Did you love her?" I asked.

"Of course."

"And do you love me? The same way, I mean?"

"Yes, Violet," he answered. "I do."

I lifted my arms and embraced him. He smelled of tobacco and cologne and, in the chill of the room, his chest warmed my damp cheek. His arms went around me, too, and briefly, he rested his chin on my hair. Then he turned away, took my hand, and led me into his parlor.

He made us drinks. "Concoctions," he called them, with Coca-Cola, lime juice, and rum. We sat in his rocking chairs. I told him that Papa wants me to move to New York. Take photographs for the papers.

"Is that what you want?"

"I haven't decided," I answered. "I haven't had time to think about it."

"My father wanted me to be a minister," he said.

"A minister?"

"Why not?" Half his face lifted into a smile. "He was. Had his own church. Wanted me to take over one day. And I might have, but the war . . . Well, I learned I had to think for myself, live for myself." When he said that, he fixed his eyes on mine. "Does that sound selfish?"

"I'm not sure," I admitted. "I don't think so."

"I'm glad to hear that."

"Why?"

He spoke softly. "You took my photograph nearly a year ago."

I felt myself flush. "I know."

"That wasn't an accusation. A lot of heavy things have been weighing you down." He rocked for a minute before he spoke again. "You know anything about peonies?"

"Peonies?"

"Early autumn—oh, decades ago—Magda planted peony seeds in her garden. That first spring, nothing happened. Shoots came up in time, but no flowers. She was so disappointed she told me she had a mind to dig them up. I told her I'd wait. Peonies need three years, sometimes more, I said. And now look at them. Year after year, blossoms big as dinner plates."

"So you're saying . . ."

"First time I picked up a paintbrush was after the war." He stopped rocking and turned to me. "Troubles. Loss. With time, they'll give a richness, a depth, to your art. Glory would want that for you."

"How could you know what Glory would want?" I asked. I didn't want to hurt him, but it didn't seem right to speak for her, or to suggest I might profit from her death.

He answered at once. "Because she was generous. I'll never forget her generous heart. Gave up her doll to try to save her mother's life."

Daisy. I remembered the crack from her hair to her eye. "You knew?"

"Violet, your sister lives on in the gifts she left for us—her love, and her verse. 'So long as men can breathe or eyes can see.' The full measure of her life hasn't been taken yet. Not by a long shot."

I told him I'd sent Glory's chapbook to Evelina Stern.

"The poet from Poland." He nodded. "I heard her read once on the radio. Beautiful work. Beautiful voice. I have a feeling she'll appreciate Glory's poems." He gazed at me quietly.

I took a sip of my drink. It tasted strange—and sweet.

"Do you remember the day last fall," he continued, "when you learned to swing? Remember how you felt when you soared up to the trees and swooped back down again?"

I nodded.

"Living on your own terms can feel like that."

"So you're saying I should stay here—alone?"

"I'm saying you should do whatever's in your heart to do. But whether we live alone or not, we *are* alone."

Tears pricked at my eyes. "Glory died alone," I whispered. "Her nurse told me."

"Doesn't mean she died lonely." In the lamplight, his eyes shone. "I saw plenty of men die—some in my arms, some so close, but with the shells raining down I couldn't reach them. Either way, in the end . . . Well, it's something I can't explain, except to say I like to think Glory died with you—the person she loved most—right there by her side."

I asked him if he really thought that, I guess because I wanted so much to hear him say it again.

"Violet," he answered. "You loved each other most in the world."

"Thank you, Will," I whispered. My hand was shaking, but I lifted the glass to my mouth and took another swallow.

"You don't have to finish that if it's not to your liking."

"I do like it," I said. "I just need to get used to it."

He leaned back in his rocking chair and closed his eyes. I drank slowly, until the glass was empty. Then we both rose. I gathered my purse and coat. He said he knew I had Aunt Blanche and Uncle Eddie close by, but invited me to call him if I ever needed anything: "If the sink gets clogged or the window won't close . . . or you just need somebody to talk to. And let me know when you make up your mind about New York."

I promised him I would and said good night.

Once home, I turned on the light and hung my coat in the closet. On the hall table was the photo of Glory on Armistice Day. I'd brought it home with me from the wake last night. I knew I shouldn't look at it, but I couldn't stop myself. Holding it beneath the light, I searched her upturned face, her lips full and parted in a smile almost of ecstasy, her black eyes somehow bright against the sky.

When I'd taken the photo that morning—that moment— we'd been so close I could have touched her, even pulled her into my arms. But from this moment on, through the years or decades of my life, I'll never touch her again. Never bring her tea or little gifts or read her a poem or hear her read one of her own to me.

I sank to the floor and let the pain come.

I wonder why such spasms of grief ever—always—come to an end. Maybe our eyes run out of tears. Or maybe grief is like an ocean wave, gathering and gathering until it reaches a peak, then breaks. I don't know. All I know is what's left. An entirely different life. A life in which my every thought, every act—even my breath and the beating of my heart—will bear the loss of Glory.

Mrs. Rasmussen and Mr. Sadowski married today.

And I forgave my father.

At Saint Isabel's, I ached for Glory, knowing how much she'd wanted to be at the wedding. So I imagined her there, in a brightly colored dress and pearls, sitting between Will and me—on the groom's side, as far away as possible from Leonard. Mrs. Rasmussen looked as beautiful as I've ever seen her, in a pale grey suit and a grey hat with a little veil that Mr. Sadowski lifted to kiss her. Aunt Blanche was matron of honor and Uncle Eddie best man. Even after everything that's happened, Mr. Sadowski and Mrs. Rasmussen had invited Papa. He sent his regrets.

After the ceremony, we all gathered in Mr. Sadowski's back yard. It was hot and humid, but he'd rented tables and chairs, and he and Uncle Eddie had set them up in the shade of his big old oak tree. Aunt Blanche and I had fixed cold cuts and salads and picked up the two-tiered wedding cake that Mrs. Rasmussen—Mrs. Sadowski now!—had ordered from Moreau's.

I stood to the side of the buffet table while everyone served themselves, so I could bring more from the kitchen if anything ran out. After the bridal party, Mr. and Mrs. Sadowski's friends filled their plates and drifted toward two unoccupied tables, avoiding the one where Jean was sitting fanning herself with a paper plate.

I felt sorry for her. She was wearing a short-sleeved smock dress in pink, and her face—because she was so hot—was the same color and shiny with sweat. She's not due for another month, but she's already so big and kept shifting uncomfortably in that little folding chair. Leonard got Mr. Sadowski's electric fan from the house and plugged it into an outlet in the garage and turned it so it blew toward her. Then he went over to her and leaned down. I thought he must have been asking her what she'd like to eat, but he was scowling as he walked toward the buffet. As soon as he saw me, though, his expression changed. "Hello, Violet," he said quietly. "My sincere condolences on the loss of your sister."

I thanked him.

"I'm sorry Jean and I couldn't make the funeral. We didn't even hear about it till we got back from our honeymoon."

"You weren't expected," I said, then realized I'd sounded rude. To change the subject, I asked him where they'd spent their honeymoon.

"Europe. The usual. There's still a lot of devastation, but the tourist spots are doing okay. And they need our money."

Our money. I groped for words. "Sounds like quite a trip."

"Old haunts for me, but Jean enjoyed it." His face had the same warm-and-sincere look he'd given me last December when he cornered me on the stairs. "And how are you managing? It must be lonely with Glory gone and your father in New York." He leaned in. It wasn't much, but enough to make me feel uncomfortable knowing Jean was sitting nearby.

I said I'd been very busy.

My answer seemed to take him by surprise at first, but then he snapped his fingers. "That's right! My mother told me there's an exhibit of your photographs at a gallery somewhere."

"The Foster Gallery in Brighton," I said. "Mr. Foster is a World War I vet and a good friend of my employer." Before he could say anything else, I gestured to the table. "Your turn."

"Ah!" He filled a plate with deviled eggs, potato salad, cucumber salad, bread, and a few slices of roast beef and ham. Then he looked back at me. "Eating for two, as they say."

"It's been a long afternoon," I replied. "Would you like me to bring Jean's plate to her, so you can get your own?"

He pushed it into my hands.

"I'll take it to her," Will said.

I hadn't noticed him come up beside me. I told him it was all right, that I'd like to say hello to Jean.

As I started toward her, her eyes were fixed on her husband. But when I gave her the plate, she smiled and thanked me.

"That's okay," I said. "It must be hard to get comfortable on a day like today." I was about to head back to the buffet table when she touched my hand.

She said she was sorry about Glory's death and that she'd had no idea she was that sick. "I think of her a lot. Even dream about her sometimes." Her voice got soft. "She was kind, you know? I remember—oh, never mind, you go get your food."

I told her I wasn't in any hurry.

"Well, it was the way she always helped me with my French. So generously. My final exam—that first semester—I couldn't get my conjugations straight. Of course, you two had been to Saint Isabel's, so Glory was already in French lit. Even so, she stayed up with me way past midnight, drilling them into my head, giving me all sorts of tricks for remembering them. And I got an A on that exam. The only A I ever got."

I was pleased, of course, to learn that Glory had helped Jean with her studies, but perhaps out of loyalty to Glory, I felt reluctant to show her any warmth. So I just told her I was sure Glory had been happy to help her. Then I went back to the buffet to get her some lemonade.

When I returned, Will was seated across from Leonard and Jean. I got my own plate, then scanned the lawn. The only empty seat was next to Leonard.

As I sat down, Will was asking Leonard about his work. He said he enjoyed supervising the longshoremen, but the job didn't give him much time at home.

I asked them where they were living.

"In Brookline," Jean answered. "We bought a lovely house. Daddy's helping with the mortgage."

"Just until we get on our feet," Leonard added.

"And Jean," I asked, "are you still working for your father?"

She sighed. "I was, until about a month ago. Leonard and I used to drive in together. But now I'm home, Leonard works half the night."

As if amused, Leonard swiped Jean's cheek and said, "I've discovered that my wife is prone to exaggeration."

She tossed her head. "I should think most people would describe the hours between sunset and one a.m. as half the night."

This time, he replied that she was probably right, then changed the subject, telling Jean about my photography exhibit.

I was surprised when she said right away that she'd come and see it. "Maybe next week. Pauline and I could go together."

I thanked her. "I'm still learning about these things," I said, "so do let me know what you think."

"Will, I understand you're one of Violet's subjects," Leonard said. "How does it feel to be famous?"

Slowly, Will set down his fork. "I've never thought about it," he said. "But if seeing my photograph or reading my story might somehow help somebody I won't ever know, then I'm grateful." He lifted his glass of Coca-Cola to me. "Here's to Violet." He nodded toward the head table. "Looks as if it's time for everybody to toast."

Uncle Eddie was standing with his glass raised. "I couldn't be happier for two people whose friendship means so much to Blanche and me. Here's to the bride and groom—Esther and Stan!"

We all raised our glasses. More toasts followed—Ernie and Molly Sawyer from the Twelve O'Clock Diner, and Father Bouchard, and of course Leonard. When the applause died down, Uncle Eddie got up again. "In case you hadn't noticed," he said, "there's a beautiful and I'm sure delicious wedding cake waiting to be cut, and Blanche is going to put on some coffee. But before we do all that, I'd like to invite my niece, Violet, to read a very special poem for Esther and Stan." He looked across at me. "Violet, I'll let you explain."

This was Glory's moment, and I wanted it to be perfect for her. I'd practiced and practiced with Aunt Blanche, but as I crossed the lawn, I could feel myself shaking. I was afraid I wouldn't be loud enough, or would speak too quickly, or just wouldn't say Glory's words the way she'd intended. Uncle Eddie helped me step up onto the wooden platform he'd made for me. I reached into my pocket and drew out the poem, but I fumbled unfolding it and dropped it. As I bent to pick it up, I saw Will. The good half of his mouth was smiling so wide I could see the white of however many front teeth he has left. His smile gave me courage, and I took a deep breath. I told Mr. and Mrs. Sadowski that Glory had looked forward to attending their wedding and that, as her wedding gift, she'd written them a poem. And then I read.

E*VEN NOW*

we begin again.
Perhaps dawn calls us
a breeze through an open window
fragrance of orchard and honey
the clacking of crows.
Perhaps as we rise
still webbed in dream
we dare again to anticipate
touch.

The morning understands.

Even now its ancient
worms monarchs crows press on
toward their ineluctable bliss
its gnarled apple trees quake
with heedless and holy expectancy
of light
of warmth
of bees to brush their blossoms' yearning
dust into ovaries
into fruit again
seeds again
their dark embryos dreaming
of some beloved purpose.

When I finished reading, there was silence. Then Mr. Sadowski stood and lifted his glass and everyone broke into applause. Uncle Eddie took my hand, and I jumped down from the platform and went to the head table. I thanked Aunt Blanche for helping me rehearse, and offered to go inside and make the coffee.

"Not on your life!" she said. "You sit down. I've a mind to make Leonard help me!"

We both looked at the table where he'd been sitting with Jean and Will and me. He was gone. "That's strange," she said, then shrugged. "Never mind. It hardly needs two people to fill a couple of coffee pots!"

I rejoined Jean and Will. Jean was dabbing her eyes, so I asked her if everything was all right, and if she wanted me to try to find Leonard.

Will rocked his chair onto its back legs. "He excused himself as soon as you finished reading. Said he was going for a walk."

Jean blew her nose, then apologized for "being so emotional these days." She put her handkerchief away. "But I do I wish more people could read Glory's book."

"I hope there'll be a second," I said. "Which might help sell the first."

"A second book?" her eyes widened.

The front legs of Will's chair dropped back to the ground. "You sure know how to keep a secret."

I didn't say much. Just that I'd found, in Glory's notebooks, over a hundred poems that seemed complete. I said another poet had agreed to look them over and, if she felt they were good enough, help me assemble the best ones into a second book.

"Who is this other poet?" Jean asked.

"Evelina Stern," I said.

She gasped.

I told her how much Glory had loved *Braving the Rain* and how, before she died, she'd asked me to send Stern a copy of her chapbook in gratitude. I explained that, in my letter, I'd mentioned that Glory had several notebooks of new poems. "A few days ago, I had a letter back from her praising the chapbook and offering to review Glory's notebooks."

"How marvelous!" Jean said to me. She seemed genuinely pleased.

After Aunt Blanche brought out the coffee, she joined Jean and Will and me for cake. Uncle Eddie headed indoors. He'd set up Mr. Sadowski's new record player by one of the back windows, and now an orchestra began to play Bing Crosby's "Moonlight Becomes You." Mr. Sadowski took his bride's hand. At first, they danced alone, then several other guests joined them. As the song ended, Mr. Sadowski led his bride back to the head table. Then he crossed to us. A new song began. "She Reminds Me of You." He bowed to Jean like a knight to his lady and asked, "May I have this dance?"

Her eyes widened, but she took his hand and he helped her up. They joined the others, and he led her in a slow foxtrot.

The sky began to darken. Will rose and said good night. I walked with him out to the sidewalk. "I'm heading to Gallagher's," he said. "If I see Leonard, I'll suggest he come back and dance with his wife."

When the second dance ended, Mr. Sadowski led Jean back to the table, and he and Mrs. Sadowski disappeared into the house, appearing again a few minutes later dressed in casual clothes. They were spending the night at the Bancroft, Mr. Sadowski announced, then heading to the Cape tomorrow for their honeymoon. They thanked their guests and said goodbye, but on their way to his car, Mr. Sadowski leaned over Jean and kissed her cheek.

She blushed. "What a sweet couple they are."

With the bride and groom gone, the rest of the guests slowly departed. I kept Jean company while Aunt Blanche and Uncle Eddie cleared the yard. "Why don't you come into the kitchen," I suggested, "and wait for Leonard there while I help my aunt wash up?"

She rose from the folding chair. I was helping her steady herself when Leonard appeared at the back gate. Her eyes followed him to our table, but she didn't say a word.

"Guess it's time to go home, Jeanie," he said, and took her arm. "Good night, Violet. See you around."

Jean said good night and began to walk away. But then she stopped and looked back at me. "I'll be in touch," she said.

They walked to their car—her car, the Chevy coupe. Leonard opened the passenger door for her, but she hesitated. They spoke briefly, then he got in and she went around to the driver's side. I watched until she turned at the end of Mill Street.

As Aunt Blanche and I were doing the dishes, she asked what I'd thought about Leonard and Jean. "They don't seem very happy, do they?"

"No," I said, "but once the baby is born—"

"I suspect that once the baby is born, things will get harder, not easier." She kept scrubbing. "I haven't told you this," she said casually, "but Esther found out from Jean's mother that they adopted Jean from a convent near Lowell that took in unwed mothers. The same one where Stan and Magda sent Ada. And where she died—" she looked at me "—the day after Jean was born."

As soon as she said that, it rose in me again, a bitter, wretched hatred for my father. I'd been battling it since the night he left for New York. Hatred for having done to Ada what Leonard did to Glory. And then a passage from the Old

Testament came into my mind: *Burn for burn, wound for wound . . . life for life.*

Glory's death for Ada's death.

I dropped the dishcloth onto the counter and told Aunt Blanche I needed to go home.

She followed me, wiping her hands on her apron. "What is it, darling?"

I couldn't tell her.

The back door slammed. Uncle Eddie came in. "Mind finishing up the dishes?" she asked him. "I'm taking Violet home." Sometimes Aunt Blanche's voice gets a ring in it like metal, and when you hear it, you know you can't change her mind and shouldn't even try. I guess Uncle Eddie heard it, because he picked up the dishcloth and said he'd meet her back at home.

We walked down the street together. Neither of us spoke until I'd unlocked my door. It was stifling inside. We opened all the windows as wide as they'd go.

"Let's go up to the roof," Aunt Blanche said. "Let it cool off down here. Besides, I haven't been up there in years."

We went up. Our old folding chairs were still stacked beside the door. We carried two of them out and sat looking at the twilight, all hazy with heat.

Aunt Blanche kicked off her sandals. "It was lovely to see Stan dancing with Jean."

I asked her if she thought he'd tell Jean he's her grandfather.

"Esther says not unless Jean starts looking into it. And even then, it might be tricky. He has coincidence, not proof."

"He could get proof, couldn't he?" I asked. "The convent must have records."

"It doesn't exist anymore. The property was sold before the war, and the nuns moved to Canada." She turned to me. "Violet, this afternoon, when I looked at you and Jean sitting at the table together, I—"

I interrupted her, because I didn't want to hear her say the rest. "No," I said. "I have only one sister. Glory."

Her eyes were fixed steadily on my face. "I know," she said. "And only one father. An imperfect man, but a man who—I'm convinced—dearly loved your mother, and Glory. And you."

"Are you saying I should forgive him and move to New York?"

"Yes to the forgiving. For your own sake, not just his."

I didn't answer. I knew it was crazy to blame Papa for Glory's death, but just the same it seemed true. True in a way that had nothing to do with facts, or reason. So I asked her if she'd ever thought that Glory's death could be—I struggled to find the right words—"not God's punishment. I don't believe that. But maybe—fate."

"Because of your father, you mean. And Ada."

I nodded.

She looked toward the horizon where purple clouds swelled with rain. "No. I don't believe one person's transgression could somehow . . . condemn another. That's too easy. I think it's more like what that scientist said. That we're all still evolving. Still weak. And so we fall victim . . . to fear, desire, disease. Our pride. Not to mention chance."

"What do you mean—chance?"

"Haven't you ever asked yourself how Glory got TB?"

"Sure," I said. "But—there's no way to know."

"Do you remember that Easter Sunday when we visited your mother at the sanatorium?"

"Of course."

"And that lovely young woman came to talk with us?"

"Rose."

"And there weren't enough chairs, so I pulled Glory into my lap, so when Rose coughed, we were too close, and—" She closed her eyes. "Maybe that's how she got infected."

It was preposterous. "Aunt Blanche," I protested, "you can't possibly mean you blame yourself!"

"Why not?"

"But you might as well blame Rose for hemorrhaging, or the sanatorium for allowing us to visit, or the orderlies for not putting out enough chairs! Besides, it makes more sense that Glory got TB from Mama, after she came home and got sick again." I stopped, suddenly confused. "But then—how did Mama get TB? Do you know?"

"Our parents had it. That's what they died of. We both got it from them."

"You had it, too?"

She nodded. "They tested us at school. We were both positive. Though neither of us was ever sick—back then, I mean. They say it can stay alive inside you for decades. I've always wondered. When your mother found out about your father's affair, then lost the baby . . ."

"So you're saying—aren't you?—that Papa was responsible for Mama's death, too."

"No." She took my hand. "That's not what I'm saying. Your mother, Glory, Ada—they all died of a thousand things. Disease. Random chance. And so many failures of love."

Her face softened. "As to the second half of your question—moving to New York. Your uncle and I would be sad to see you go, of course, but setting that aside, you've just opened your first show, and so I think—or perhaps I just prefer to think—that at least for now, your life is here."

I told her about Evelina Stern offering to review Glory's new poems.

"You see!" she exclaimed triumphantly. "That's wonderful news!" She stood and looked across Mill Street. "Your uncle's home," she said. "The light's on."

We went back downstairs and said good night.

As I stood at the parlor windows watching her cross the street, I thought of Papa. Of those nights when he was troubled—haunted, I realize now—how he'd walk alone for hours. I imagined him now, tonight, walking the streets of New York.

"Papa." I closed my eyes and willed my words to reach him. "I forgive you."

A breeze fluttered the curtains.

I showered and put on my nightdress. Then I settled by the parlor windows to reread Evelina Stern's letter. I haven't told anyone what else she wrote. I don't know why, but I don't want to share it.

She'd been so busy finishing her new manuscript that she'd fallen behind in her correspondence, she said. But once it had gone to her publisher, she'd discovered Glory's chapbook and my letter.

I read the book in one night, then again slowly, and again, each time something new revealing itself to me. I was about to answer your letter when I saw the notice of your exhibit in the paper. Of course I recognized your name and—as it was nearby—went to see it. Such beautiful photographs and stories. And your dedication to your sister—so moving. Although I am sad that I will never meet her, perhaps you might allow me to review her new poems. Perhaps there is a second book among them.

One thing more: I would like you to take my photograph for my new book. My publisher threatens to use my old photograph—I don't like it at all! But the academic year is about to begin. Might we meet next week?

She'd included her phone number. My heart pounding, I'd called her that evening. We're to meet next Friday.

The breeze has cooled the parlor, and I just heard a rumble of thunder. So I think I'll sit here a little while longer, and wait for the rain.

EPILOGUE

MARCH 1950

It's my twenty-sixth birthday.

I suppose some people might think me strange for visiting a cemetery on my birthday. But I'm glad I'm here. With Glory.

I worked all day—two portrait sessions—then drove to Aunt Blanche and Uncle Eddie's. When I arrived, Aunt Blanche explained that she'd invited Mr. and Mrs. Sadowski to join us for supper, but they couldn't because they were looking after little Susan. "Jean went into labor this afternoon. It looks as if the baby will have the same birthday as you."

I told them I wasn't surprised Jean was in labor. When I visited last Saturday, she looked very uncomfortable. Still, she'd served cake and tea and given me a lovely amethyst necklace for my birthday, and when I protested that it looked much too expensive, she said it was little enough to thank me for all the photographs I'd taken of Susan.

Over supper, Aunt Blanche and Uncle Eddie asked me when Glory's book is coming out. I explained that advance copies had gone to the press and Evelina Stern had written a glowing review for the *Globe*.

"And what about you?" Aunt Blanche asked. "What's your next project?"

I told her about the grant I'd received to create a collection of photographs and profiles of unwed mothers and their children. Uncle Eddie frowned and asked me why I'd chosen such a theme. "I mean, I could see including one or two unwed mothers, but why not photograph normal families, too?"

I told him I wanted to help people see unwed mothers in new ways. Aunt Blanche said she thought the project was "much needed," and winked at me.

Over cake and coffee, I opened her gift—a lovely scarf with an ivy pattern. She asked if I'd had a gift from Papa. I told her he'd sent me a birthday card with a check.

"Does he still ask you to move to New York?" she asked.

"Not since I moved to Newton," I said. "But I'm planning to visit him in June. Evelina Stern is doing some readings in New York," I explained, as casually as I could. "She's reading from Glory's book as well, and has asked me to come along and say a little about her."

"What a wonderful opportunity!" Aunt Blanche exclaimed. "Your first time in New York!"

Uncle Eddie raised an eyebrow. "In my view, it's long past time for your father to come up here and visit you."

I didn't contradict him, because I didn't want to share that Papa *has* visited me. It was last October, a few weeks after I'd moved. He took the train to South Station on a Saturday. We spent the afternoon walking the Common, then had a meal in the North End. He slept on my sofa. Early the next morning, I drove to Mill Street—he said he wanted to see our old building again—and then we visited the cemeteries. We didn't stay long or go anywhere else. He didn't say so, but I knew he didn't want to be seen. I drove him back to South Station that afternoon.

Aunt Blanche and Uncle Eddie invited me to stay and watch television for a while, but I explained that I was meeting Will before heading home.

The air in his apartment smelled of turpentine. He apologized. "I meant to stop earlier, but I lost track of time. By the way, happy birthday!" We sat at the kitchen table. I took from my purse the package I'd brought and set it down in front of him. "This is for you," I said.

He frowned. "What's this all about? It's your birthday, not mine."

"Open it and you'll see." He unwrapped it. It was an advance copy of Glory's book, with Will's portrait of her on the front cover.

For nearly a minute, he didn't touch it. He just sat there shaking his head and saying—almost reverently—"Look at that. Will you look at that."

I asked him to show me what he'd been working on, so we went into his studio. He gestured to his easel. The painting, nearly finished, showed two children—a girl and a boy—playing in the street, the girl jumping rope and the boy catching a ball in the air. "Who are they?" I asked.

"Fatima and Silvio," he answered. "They live in your place. Sweet kids, first and second grade. Stayed inside most of the winter, but now it's warmer, they've started to play outside after school. I come out to the front steps, get them to talk. At first they were afraid of me. And they're still learning English. But they're coming along. And fast as they learn, they teach their parents."

We went into the parlor and sat in his rocking chairs. I told him about my new project, and about photographing Susan Rasmussen. "She's so serene," I said. "I've never had a baby so easy to photograph. And it's helped me to get to know Jean better."

"And Leonard?" he asked.

"I never see him."

He asked me if I'm happy. I told him I am, though I still miss Glory, sometimes so much I cry.

He nodded, and rocked.

"I miss you, too," I said, then wondered if I should have, if maybe it was too forward. He didn't answer, so to fill the silence I asked him, "What about you? Are you happy?"

He smiled. "It's an early spring evening, the birthday of an old friend, and we're talking together about our work, our memories, the people we love . . ." He stopped rocking. "For me, this is happiness."

We were quiet after that, then I told him I had a long drive back and had to go. "Don't get up," I said, and even though I still wasn't sure I should have told him I missed him, I leaned down and kissed his cheek. The right side, just above the scar. I'm glad I did, because he closed his eyes and, for a moment, squeezed my hand.

His eyes were still closed when I said goodbye.

I was pulling away when I decided, on impulse, to stop at the town cemetery.

When I arrived, the main gate was locked, so I parked outside and walked in. The moon, nearly full tonight, lit the footpath to Glory's and Bobbie's graves.

For a short stretch, the path follows the river. It's swollen with melted snow and the recent rains.

The current is rushing. The sound goes up and down, like music.

The air is cold, but it smells of earth and grass and spring.

It's my twenty-sixth birthday, Glory.

And I'm happy.

Sometimes, anyway.

Now.

The moonlight is shining on your gravestone, and on the epitaph I chose:

poems unfinished—questions unanswered

journeys under invisible stars

And there, pushing through the earth at the base of the stone—clusters of bright blue violets.

AUTHOR'S NOTE

I gratefully acknowledge my use of excerpts from several poems now in the public domain. Father Garcia's prayer for Glory is loosely adapted from the prayer commonly if incorrectly attributed to Saint Francis of Assisi. My thanks also to the editors of the following publications in which two of my own poems included in the novel originally appeared:

Northern New England Review: "This Bright Limit"

Maine Sunday Telegram's Deep Water: Poems from Maine: "Even now"

photo credit: Amy Wilton

ABOUT THE AUTHOR

LAURA BONAZZOLI's short-story cycle, *Consecration Pond*, was praised by *Publishers Weekly* as "poetic and introspective . . . a solid, meditative collection of interconnected short stories that . . . leave a haunting impression." Her short fiction, poetry, and essays have been published in dozens of literary magazines and several anthologies. She works as a freelance editor and ghostwriter, and teaches creative writing with Maine Media Workshops. She holds a BA from Regis College in Weston, Massachusetts, and an MFA from the University of Minnesota, Minneapolis. She is a member of the Maine Writers & Publishers Alliance and lives in Midcoast Maine. *Our Share of Morning* is her first novel.

ACKNOWLEDGMENTS

Although I've been publishing nonfiction, poetry, and short stories for many years, *Our Share of Morning* is my first novel. What a debut novelist needs above all is a team of publishing professionals who understand, value, and support her vision. I found this with Sibylline Press. I'm grateful to Vicki DeArmon, Julia Park Tracey, and the entire Sibylline team for their thoughtful and sensitive response to the manuscript, and for sharing their talents and experience to transform it into a published book. A special shout-out to Alicia Feltman for her gorgeous cover design.

A debut novelist also needs a team of perceptive readers. To everyone who so generously read and provided feedback on *Our Share of Morning* in early drafts, thank you. My special thanks to my friend Franziska, not only for being one of those early readers, but for continuing to express, over the years of revision that followed, her confidence in the novel's worth.

My thanks also to the team at the Owl & Turtle Bookshop Café in Camden, Maine, and the staff of the Rockport Public Library in Rockport, Maine, for their unstinting support of my writing, and to Elizabeth, Cynthia, and Sarah for listening and cheering.

Finally, I offer this novel in loving memory of Andrew, Brian, and Angelica.

STUDY GUIDE QUESTIONS

1. Because of their different roles within their family, as well as their different personalities, talents, and sensibilities, Violet and Glory face different challenges as they grow from children to young adults. Which sister do you feel more drawn to? Why? Is your response due more to her characteristics, or her actions? Do you see yourself in either sister? If so, which one?

2. Haunted by his past, Roberto Campo—Papa—sometimes acts out of cowardice, despair, or rage. Occasionally, he resorts to violence. And yet clearly he loves his daughters and they return his love. Discuss the nature of their relationship. Are there relationships in your own life that help you understand this complex bond?

3. *Our Share of Morning* is the story not only of a family, but of a close-knit group of neighbors. What roles do Aunt Blanche, Uncle Eddy, Will Owen, Mrs. Rasmussen, and Mr. and Mrs. Sadowski play in the sisters' lives—and in their fate?

4. Ada Sadowski disappears from Mill Street more than six years before the novel opens, and yet her influence on the lives of its residents continues nearly until the novel ends. How?

5. As children, Violet and Glory strongly believe in God. What events in their childhood and young adulthood shift these beliefs for each sister? In what ways?

6. After asking Glory to marry him and promising to send her a ring, Leonard Rasmussen returns to the Merchant Marine and ceases communicating with her. Why? Do his actions suggest only that he was using her, or is it possible that he is—or once was—genuinely in love with her?

7. Father Garcia is a Roman Catholic priest, but his views, influenced by his war experiences, are unorthodox. What do you think of his teachings on the nature of the divine, of forgiveness, and of love? Does he remind you of anyone you've looked to for spiritual guidance in your own life?

8. Discuss the theme of free will. How do factors beyond the sisters' control, including poverty, contagion, superstition, misogyny, and family history, constrain their choices? Given these constraints, are the actions they take freely chosen? Which of their choices do you admire, and are there any you condemn?

9. By the end of the novel, both Violet and Glory have consciously acquiesced to their very different fates. For each sister, what does this act of acquiescence bring? Has there been a time in your own life when acceptance of a situation or event you couldn't change brought an unanticipated sense of healing, serenity, or grace?

Sibylline Press is proud to publish the brilliant work of women authors over 50. We are a woman-owned publishing company and, like our authors, represent women of a certain age.

www.ingramcontent.com/pod-product-compliance
Lightning Source LLC
Chambersburg PA
CBHW020327010826
48973CB00005B/1161